"My God!" Caleb said roughly. "I want to kiss you, Eliza. Really kiss you. Like a man wants to kiss a woman."

Eliza looked at him, her eyes wide. Then she felt his arms around her, holding her to him as he gently laid her back on the buffalo hide. She felt his legs, strong against hers, and a powerful surge of desire for him swept over her.

His lips brushed her forehead, then her throat. Trembling, she held his face between his hands and whispered, "Yes, Cal! Yes!" And when he kissed her, her desire for him swept through her with heat and ache, sweet and consuming. His breath was hot against her mouth, and his voice shook. "My God! I want you!"

She wanted him more than she'd ever wanted anything in her life. But where were his words of love for her? Anger suddenly raged in Eliza's soul and she heaved her body against him, thrusting him away. "No!" she cried, her green eyes blazing. "You may want me, Caleb Pride. But you're not having me! Not ever, not without love."

THE LIVES AND LOVES OF THE WEALTHY
AND BEAUTIFUL

DESIGNING WOMAN (337, $4.50)
by Allison Moser

She was an ugly duckling orphan from a dusty little town, where the kids at school laughed at her homemade dresses and whispered lies about her fortune-telling grandmother. Calico Gordon swore she would escape her lackluster life and make a name for herself.

Years later she was the celebrated darling of the fashion world, the most dazzling star the industry had seen in years. Her clothes hung in the closets of the beautiful and wealthy women in the world. She had reached the pinnacle — and now had to prevent her past from destroying her dreams. She had to risk it all — fortune, fame, friendship and love — to keep memories of her long-forgotten life from shattering the image she had created.

INTERLUDES (339, $4.95)
by L. Levine

From Monte Carlo to New York, from L.A. to Cannes, Jane Perry searches for a lost love — and discovers a seductive paradise of pleasure and satisfaction, an erotic and exotic world that is hers for the taking.

It's a sensuous, privileged world, where nights — and days — are filled with a thousand pleasures, where intrigue and romance blend with dangerous desires, where reality is *better* than fantasy. . . .

FOR WOMEN ONLY (346, $4.50)
by Trevor Meldal-Johnsen

Sean is an actor, down on his luck. Ted is the black sheep of a wealthy Boston family, looking for an easy way out. Dany is a street-smart kid determined to make it any way he can.

The one thing they all have in common is that they know how to please a woman. And that's all they need to be employed by Debonaire, Beverly Hills' most exclusive escort service — for women only. In the erotic realm of pleasure and passion, the women will pay any price for a thrill. Nothing is forbidden — except to fall in love.

Available wherever paperbacks are sold, or order direct from the Publisher. Send cover price plus 50¢ per copy for mailing and handling to Pinnacle Books, Dept. 17- 549 , 475 Park Avenue South, New York, N.Y. 10016. Residents of New York, New Jersey and Pennsylvania must include sales tax. DO NOT SEND CASH.

WINDS OF SORROW, WINDS OF JOY

DEBRA BURGESS-MOHR

PINNACLE BOOKS
WINDSOR PUBLISHING CORP.

To Fred—who believes in me; who likes a good story.

PINNACLE BOOKS

are published by

Windsor Publishing Corp.
475 Park Avenue South
New York, NY 10016

First printing: October, 1991

Printed in the United States of America

Chapter 1

July 4, 1841

Eliza Landon shaded her eyes to look across her father's roughly cleared pasture at the squawking gander hanging head down from the limb of the spreading buckeye tree. A leather thong bound the bird's pebbly, yellowed feet to a limb; its neck feathers were slick with bear grease. The bird dangled just high enough above the ground to allow a bareback rider, galloping full tilt past the bird, a chance to reach out, make a grab for the grease-slicked neck, and rip off the dirty white head.

Eliza tossed her red curls, laughed, and gleefully clapped her hands as she saw the old bird flopping and spinning on the thong. Skipping into the pasture, she stopped to look at the small knot of men and boys across the field, laughing, shouting, and churning up dust as they jostled each other while waiting their turn to ride for their grab at the gander.

Since early this morning friends and neighbors had been arriving at Thomas Landon's farm. Some had left their homes just as the sun's first rosy light struck the shadows of the Blue Ridge. Many, driving wagons or carts, riding horseback, or walking, had arrived before noon in time for the wrestling and horse racing. When the sun was high, there would be corn shucking, fiddling, turkey calling, buck dancing, and food. This was a day for games and feast—the Fourth of July in eastern Kentucky.

Now, at midday, it was time for gander pulling. Women stopped tending to deer carcasses turning on spits over open fires. Wiping their hands on their long aprons, some picking up babies from play or from sleep, they walked out to the edge of the field. Youngsters stopped their games of tag, tug-of-war, or romping in the golden piles of Thomas Landon's hay. Men and boys, gathered under a big elm tree where a barrel of rum was broached, filled their cups and laughed and joked as they walked toward the pasture, joining the women and children. Almost everybody was there, ready to watch the gander-pulling game.

Eliza watched, wide-eyed, as each of the riders reached into his pocket or pouch, drew out ten flashing copper coins, and tossed them into a shiny bucket. The bucket of coins would go to the winner today. Then, one by one, the riders kneed their horses, whooping to gallop across the grassy field and grab at the dangling gander. So far all had failed to tear the bird's head free, and as each rider rode off, he was followed by hoots of laughter and mocking jeers. Eliza's heart pounded and her green eyes danced, for the next rider would be her twelve-year-old brother, Ben. Ben would be followed by his best friend, Max Pridentz; Eliza knew that one of them would be the gander-pulling champion today.

Clenching her fist to her mouth, Eliza squeezed her eyes closed for a second, not quite ready to watch her brother take part in this bloody game. But she opened her eyes, just in time to see Ben spring up to his big chestnut mare. Reaching into the buckskin pouch tied at his waist, he pulled out his coins and tossed them into the prize bucket. *"YeeeeeAH! YeeeeAH! Hi! YoooEEE! Hi! Hi!"* he shouted, raising his whip in the air and slashing it down on the mare's rump. The big chestnut gathered under the whip and sprang forward. *"Git! Git! YeeeAH!"* Ben's long black hair streamed behind him, his cheeks puffed, and his blue eyes narrowed as he came full gallop across the field toward the spinning gander. Coming abreast of the big bird, he reached out, grabbed at the neck, and yanked hard. For a split second his horse reared back in a billow of dust as Ben cried out *"YeeeAH!"* And Eliza saw her brother lift his arm high. Holding the bloody head, he twirled it around and around, and with a broad grin on his face, he reined in his horse and yelled again. *"Whooee! Whooee!"* It was Ben's victory.

Ben dismounted as folks gathered around, laughing and slapping him on the back. Chad Green, the Landon's closest neighbor, handed Ben the bucket of copper coins. Eliza, looking back at the buckeye tree, frowned. Where was Max? It was plain he wasn't there. How strange—just yesterday he'd talked about the gander pulling. "I'll beat you, Ben," he'd said. "I'll beat you fair and square." And Max had winked at Eliza.

"Ha!" Ben said. "You'll be having a lock of my hair first." Then they had laughed while playfully punching each other's arms.

Well! Eliza thought. He missed a good show today, and he'll be sorry, too. Shrugging her shoulders, she skipped back across the pasture toward her house. It was time to help her mother.

A long, rough-hewn table covered with food stood outside the Landon's kitchen door. Eliza eyed platters of savory deer and bear meat, roasted shoats and fowl, and bowls of boiled cabbage and beans and potatoes and corn. She flicked her finger at a large gourd filled with sweet syrup, and feeling her mouth water, she licked her upper lip at the sight of puddings, pies, and bowls of summer berries.

Inside the kitchen Eliza's mother shoved hot coals off

7

the lid of her skillet that sat in the big fireplace, scooped out a stack of hot cornpones onto a heavy plate, and handed the plate to Eliza.

"Step smart, Ellie. Folks are hungry, and I don't want our guests dawdling at that rum. When the food's all set out, you'll have the afternoon free."

Eliza picked up a platter of pones and hurried outside. "Hey, Ellie!" Looking up, she saw Ben striding toward the house, his face flushed, his eyes bright. Eliza set her platter down and raced out to meet him. "You won, Ben!" she cried, throwing her arms around his neck. "You did it, you did! You got the old gander today!"

Laughing, Eliza skipped backward, ahead of Ben. "And oh, Ben! You looked so fine!"

Ben chuckled. "That'll fix old braggin' britches, it sure will! But where is he? Where's Max?"

"He's not here," Eliza answered. "He's not anywhere I could see."

"Let's go ask Ma," Ben said. "She's sure to know."

Inside the big kitchen, Martha Landon straightened from her cooking fire as Ben and Eliza came in the door. "It was a good run on that old gander," she said with a laugh. "I have no mind for the sport, but I'm pleased for you, Ben."

Ben grinned, looked around the room, and scowled. "Where's Max? I thought sure he'd be *here*. I figured he'd know he was late, and he'd heard when he got here I'd plucked the damned gander's head clean off. Why, I thought he'd come straight on here."

"Well, he's sure not here," Martha said. "I haven't seen him all day."

Frowning, Ben walked over to the stone fireplace and picked up his long rifle. "I'll go over to his place then. Don't know why he didn't show today. Seems strange to me."

"Well, go if you will, Ben, but don't stay. And if his

8

pa—if Daniel's around, and drinking again, I don't want you staying at all."

"I want to go too," Eliza said. "It won't hurt to keep Ben company, and I'll see that we get on home quick." Eliza knew Ben and her mama wouldn't argue. Ben usually liked to have her around and her mother had already told her she would be free from her chores this afternoon.

Eliza's green eyes didn't leave her mama's face as she saw her looking at her and Ben for a moment. She knew what her mother was thinking. She'd seen that look before. Her mother's blue eyes, so warm with love, taking a good look at Ben, her oldest. "A steady, easygoing lad who looks like his ma with his dark hair and blue eyes." That's what Eliza's papa often said. Followed by her mother's chuckle. "But with his easy ways he takes after you." And then there was Eliza. "Well, Martha," Thomas Landon would say. "Our red-haired, green-eyed Ellie might look a whole lot like me, but with her quick ways she takes after yourself." And then her parents would laugh. Now Martha smiled as she retied a yellow ribbon that held her long black hair in place. "Be along then, you two! But don't stay. See about Max and then come on home here, quicker'n a cat can lick its ear. Bring Max too, if it's clear he can get away."

It was hot that afternoon as Eliza and Ben walked over the hill on the way to the Pridentz place. Insects buzzed and grasshoppers clattered in the tall dry grass under the beech, oak, and buckeye trees. Big dry leaves lay in the narrow dusty road and Eliza laughed as she kicked them and stepped on them, feeling the prickly, dry crunch under her bare feet.

Ben, shouldering his rifle, turned to her, his eyes thoughtful. "Listen, Ellie," he said. "Since Max missed the gander pulling today, what if we all go fishing tomorrow! I'll catch the biggest fish but you and Max can try!" His blue eyes flashed teasingly.

Eliza whooped with delight. "Yes!" she cried. "After chores, Ben! Let's go!" Ah! she thought. Tomorrow, she and Ben would hoist their fishing poles over their shoulders and she would carry a bucket of worms while Ben carried his rifle, and they would go over the hill to Max's place. Then she, Ben, and Max would walk through big spots of sun and shade, past Biggers Bend, down to the Red River where Ben and Max kept a raft hitched to an old, silvered tree stump. After they unhitched the raft, they would pole down the river, past giant tulip poplar trees to a secret fishing hole where they would tie the raft to a tree, jump up on the bank, and drop their baited hooks into deep, black potholes where fish shadows lurked. Sometimes Eliza caught the first fish. Maybe that would happen tomorrow.

Now, reaching the top of the hill, Eliza turned to Ben. "I'll race you," she cried. "I'll race you down to Max's place, and I'll beat you, too!"

"No, you won't!" Ben whooped. *"Whoooee!* C'mon, Ellie, let's go!" And they raced, their bare feet slapping on dry dust, their laughter and Ben's shouts echoing through the piny woods. "Hurry on, Ellie! Hurry on, or I'll catch you before we even get there . . ."

The road on the other side of the hill wound down through thick underbrush to Daniel Pridentz's farm. The Pridentz cabin had no windows, and the one door sagged open unless forced shut. But the garden yielded lettuce, tomatoes, cabbage, beans, potatoes, and corn that few folks could equal.

Neighbors who lived in those hills said that Daniel and his boy planted their potatoes in the half-dark of a new moon. They said they planted their beans in the moon's full light, and years ago, on a night when there was no moon at all, it was said that's when Daniel had set the posts of his rail fence deep in the ground.

Now, coming to the far end of the cornfield, Eliza

stopped. "I got to . . . catch my breath! But just wait and I'll be—"

It was then that a piercing scream shattered the air and Eliza's words faded as she clapped her hand over her mouth and stared wide-eyed at Ben.

"Pa! Pa! Stop! Pa! No!" Again, Eliza heard the scream, and the cracked, sobbing cry. "No! Stop!"

Ben's eyes were wide and wild-looking as he stared at Eliza. "Oh, God!" he cried. "Ellie, it's Max!" He then started to run faster than Eliza had ever seen him run, and in seconds he was out of sight. Eliza, still panting from her race, felt a keen sense of dread as she hitched up her homespun skirt and followed her brother. Running as fast as she could, feeling the slaps and stings of the corn stalks and strappy leaves, she didn't stop again for breath until she came to the clearing in front of the Pridentz's cabin. "Mr. Pridentz! For God's sake!" she heard Ben's cry, hoarse and loud.

Blazing spikes of red and pink hollyhocks shot up against the blue sky. For a split second Eliza remembered a day when Max had told her how much he liked those flowers because his ma, whose name had been Lou, had planted them in front of the house before he'd been born. But Max had never known his ma.

Now Eliza's eyes grew round with horror, her throat got tight, and she felt cold then hot as she saw Ben standing in front of the hollyhocks with his rifle aimed at Daniel Pridentz. Daniel Pridentz wore no hat, and his long, blond hair was matted and dirty, as was his beard. He had on filthy buckskins, and he held a brown bottle in one hand. Eliza didn't know Mr. Pridentz. He never came down the mountain to church, or to meetings; he never came to weddings or to funerals, either. He never came to anything Eliza knew of, but Eliza knew he was a "hard-drinking man." She'd heard that and she'd heard too how, when he got to drinking, he'd talk about Lou, who

11

had died birthing Max twelve years ago. It was also said that sometimes he'd beat up on folks for no reason at all, and sometimes he'd beat Max.

Now she looked at Max, who lay at his pa's feet. His body looked crooked and his face was pushed against the ground, while a trickle of blood made a little dark path in the dust. Nellie, Max's small gray-and-black dog, stood beside Max and whimpered.

"Get away from him, Mr. Pridentz," Ben shouted out. "It's not my place to tell you this 'cause it's not my business, but you've hurt your boy again. Bad this time, and I have to say it to you. Now get on away from him or I'll—"

"Ben!" Eliza's shout was loud, her heart was walloping, and her head buzzing as she saw Daniel turn and look at her with wild, bloody red eyes.

"Get away now, Mr. Pridentz!" Ben's voice was insistent and big and loud. "Get yourself sober and then, for the love o' God, think about what you've done to your boy."

Daniel turned away from Eliza, placed his hands on both sides of his dirty bearded face, looked at Ben for a minute, and staggered across the clearing to the cabin. He stood in the dark doorway for a moment, then turned and went inside.

Eliza and Ben knelt beside Max while Nellie sniffed at him, whimpered, and lay still. Blood, making purple patterns in the dust, still flowed from Max's head and Eliza could see part of his bruised face and a puffed, closed eye. "Max!" Ben whispered sharply, leaning down close to his face. "Max!" Max moaned, but he didn't move.

Ben suddenly stood. "Ellie, you got to go!" His voice was urgent, and Eliza saw a great worry in his eyes "Go and get help. Run faster than you've ever run in your life. Get Pa! Get Ma! Max needs tending to, bad!"

Eliza stood up. "I'll run fast as the wind, Ben. But what about him?" She pointed at the Pridentze's cabin. "What about his pa? Ma said she didn't want you staying if . . . if his pa . . ."

"That don't matter, Ellie. God A'mighty, the old man's probably passed clean out. And I won't leave Max alone. You got to go now. Run!"

Eliza knew that this was the most important thing she had ever had to do in her life and she had better do it right. Hitching up her skirt, she looked once more at Ben and Max and then she turned and started to run.

Chapter 2

A ragbag of thoughts tumbled through Eliza's mind as she flew toward home. What if Max died? He looked like he might, lying there all crooked with blood coming from his head. But he couldn't die! Eliza knew that! She and Max and Ben did everything together. And Max, even though he didn't know it, was Eliza's best friend. Max was the one who had written a story for her birthday when she was six about Lame Squirrel who lived in a log because he couldn't climb a tree. And just last year, should she ever find herself in the woods and in need of food, Max had taught her how to trap and skin a squirrel and cook it on a stick. Max was also the one who would ride horseback with her and race with her, even though he knew she would win because she had the better horse. Then last week, Max had told her a fine story about Daniel Boone, the man who used to roam through these parts; the man everybody loved to talk about. Max was also best at reading and reciting his lessons out loud in the blab school down in town. Eliza remembered her teacher saying once he could outread and outspeak all the other students. No, Eliza couldn't imagine a day without Max. It won't happen, she told herself. I know it won't. He won't die. God won't let him.

14

Eliza's side hurt with a fury, and she panted for breath as she stopped at the top of the hill. Below was her own place; her ordered, safe house with big eaves covering the wide porch. There were the two maple trees that provided summer shade, and the cherry tree, loaded with bright red fruit. Beyond the house was the barn and her pa's pasture with the big buckeye tree, and beyond was the field of golden corn. Eliza grabbed her side, pinched it, and sucked her breath in as she started down the hill. No matter how she might hurt, it didn't matter. Max and Ben needed help.

Running down the hill, faster and faster now, her red hair flying, her feet slapping against the grass, she heard drifts of talk and laughter. She heard children shout and chatter, and she heard fiddling and banjos, and someone sang. *"Black Jack came a-ridin' by—to charm the heart . . ."*

"Ma! Ma! Pa! Pa!" Eliza bawled out, her voice rasping and loud. "Max's hurt! His pa beat him! He's hurt bad!" She called out again as she stumbled across the field. "He's hurt! Hurt bad! He needs help, Ben says . . ."

Things got still as the guests gathered around. Eliza had no breath left; she was hot and the pain in her side felt like needles while little black spots jumped around in front of her eyes. "He's hurt real bad . . . and his pa is drunk and in the . . . and . . . Ben said . . ."

"Sit down, Ellie," Thomas said. "And quiet down." His voice was soft, but stern. Martha brought her a glass of raspberry juice and stood beside her, one arm around her shoulders, while everybody looked at Thomas, the man who usually set things straight.

"Chad, why don't you and me go on over to Daniel's place and see what we can do." Thomas's voice was matter-of-fact. Then his tone rose so everybody could hear. "The rest of you keep on with your celebrating. No need to upset the whole day for all of you."

"I want to go back with you, Pa. I can help. Please!"

"No, Ellie. You stay here and help your ma."

Standing on the porch, Eliza watched her pa walk toward the barn to saddle up the horses he and Mr. Green would need. She sighed. When her papa used that kind of tone, there was no arguing at all.

The afternoon shadows were deep when Thomas, Ben, and Chad brought Max back in the Pridentz farm cart. All the guests had gone home except Nancy Green, Chad's wife. Seeing Max's bruised, bloody face, Martha set her mouth in a straight line, her blue eyes blazed with anger. "This boy's pa . . . a man who would do that to his boy isn't fit to walk on this earth. Take him on in, Tom. Lay him down there." She pointed to a pile of thick quilts she and Nancy and Eliza had laid out in the corner of the kitchen. "I want him close by for a day or so." Then, kneeling down beside Max, Martha took a closer look. Still kneeling, she raised her eyes to look at Thomas and Chad. "Does Daniel Pridentz have any idea as to what he's done? Was he so drunk he doesn't know what he did?"

Thomas placed one hand on Martha's shoulder and spoke quietly. "Daniel shot himself," he said. "Daniel's dead."

Chad spoke then, his words were rushed; he didn't like what he had to say. "When we got there, Ben told us Daniel had gone in the house and hadn't come back out. We tended to Max the best we could, then Ben got the cart and we put Max in and Thomas went to talk to Daniel." Chad looked at Thomas.

Thomas shook his head. "He wasn't right in his thinking, Martha. He was babbling nonsense about Lou. Still thinking she died because of Max. I told him he was talking nonsense and we were taking Max home with us. I told him when he got sober, to come on here. I don't know if he heard me right or not. But I sure wasn't

16

thinking about his rifle. Didn't give it a thought. Then when we'd started on down the road, Chad, Ben, and me, taking Max in the cart, we heard the gunshot and I knew damned well what had happened. Chad and I went back, and we found him. There was nothing to do, and when we passed by Flannery's place, I saw that Jack had come on home from here, and I asked him to get the sheriff."

Martha shook her head while fussing through an assortment of astringents and herbs. As she bent to tend to Max, Eliza saw the glint of tears in her mother's eyes, but Martha's voice was flat and firm as she washed Max's bruised face and cleaned the gash on his head.

"Ben, run down to the creek for more water, and Ellie, help neighbor Green here rip some flannel. Warm it some by the fire and hand the strips to me."

It was then that Max moaned and tried to open his bruised, swollen eyes. "Hush now, Max," Martha said. "You've got a broken rib or two and there's nothing for it but for me to bind you up some."

"Where's Pa?" His voice shook some, even in his whisper.

"We'll talk later," Martha said. "Now you rest."

That evening Eliza sat with her family at the kitchen table. Martha was busy mending a shirt of Ben's; Thomas was reading a book by James Fenimore Cooper, *The Prairie*. Eliza looked out the little paned window at the patch of black sky where stars sparkled like diamonds; she heard an owl hoot and she shivered. Not from hearing the owl, but for thinking about Max having no mother, and living with a pa who'd beat him. She'd never thought about things like that. She looked over at Max, lying so still on the bed of quilts, and she saw his face, and the terrible bruises and his puffed eyes reflected in the lantern's light, and Eliza, who had never thought about hatred one day of her life, hated Daniel Pridentz, even though he was dead. She also wondered about Max's mother. What had

17

she looked like? Except for the color of Max's hair, Max sure didn't look like his pa. But what color were Max's eyes? She frowned. For the life of her, Eliza couldn't begin to think what color his eyes were. When he woke up, she'd be sure to look.

"I reckon it's good his pa's dead," Ben whispered in the silent room.

"That's not what the good Lord would want us to think, Ben," Martha said. "Now . . ." She looked closely at Ben and Eliza. "We're thinking, your papa and me, about taking Max on with us. Having him live here with us for a while. How do you both feel about that?"

Ben leaped to his feet, forgetting to be so quiet. "Oh, Ma, I like that idea. I like it fine, Pa. I do, and I'd be glad to share my bed."

Eliza jumped up to stand beside Ben. Her grin was wide. "I like it too. I do. It would sit fine with me and we could go fishing without Ben and me having to go over the hill to get him every time."

Thomas smiled, leaned back in his chair, and took a long pull on his pipe. "We'll ask him," he said. "When we know his own thinking is straight. Now he's hurting in his own head, and we got to leave him be. But"—he paused—"tomorrow we all have to get on with our work. Ellie," he said, and laughed softly, "you can't sit beside the boy all day."

Eliza nodded. She knew what that meant. She had her chores, no matter. It was her job to carry buckets of food scraps to the barn to feed the pigs, scatter grain for the chickens, and gather up the eggs. She also had to milk the cow, and make sure the cow's bed of hay was sweet and clean. She looked solemnly at her father, and raised her chin. "But I'll be looking in on him, Pa."

"Yes," Thomas said. "As you say, Ellie, we'll be watching him. Keeping an eye on him, we will."

Late that night Eliza lay in her bed and looked out

18

at the bright moon sliding through the leafy shadowed branches of the cherry tree. She thought about Max; she wondered if, while living in the dark, one-room cabin over the hill, he'd ever seen such a beautiful sight. She thought about him being beaten by his pa, and she turned her head in her pillow to stop the sob she felt come up in her throat.

Chapter 3

Two days later, after midday dinner, Eliza stood on the porch and looked up at big, loose clouds. Her eyes were pensive as she thought about a strange new word she'd heard today at the table when her Papa had told his family about the talk he'd heard in town. Talk about folks going west to a place called the "Oregon."

"Folks are going," he'd said, shaking his head. "Out to 'the Oregon Country.' Danged fools, they are too! Uprooting their women and children, leaving good land and going out there where they'll be scalped by Injuns, or starve to death 'cause they don't have food. I don't understand their thinking. Smart men they are. But to my own way of thinking, it's too dangerous out there for men to even consider leaving their land."

Martha had agreed. "Thank the good Lord, Thomas, you have no such notion in your sound head. If you did, you'd be having trouble with me."

Ben had taken a different view. "I don't know, Pa. I'm hearing there's lots of good land out west. Max and I were talking about that just last week."

Eliza was curious. Where on earth was this place called the Oregon? She liked the sound of that word. Oregon. It sounded exciting, and glorious, and mysterious all at the same time. Oregon. Yes, where might that be? Was it far? She would ask her pa when he got back from the barn. He and Martha and Ben were all down there, admiring a new horse Thomas had bought in town yesterday. While Eliza was excited about the horse, she would rather think alone right now about where the Oregon might be. She knew Max would know, because Max knew everything, and if by chance he should wake up, she'd ask him.

"Ellie?" Startled, she turned and stepped quickly inside the house to see Max awake and watching her. His face was still swollen some, but he could open his eyes and he looked a sight better. "Ellie!" He cleared his throat and looked at her with a puzzled expression on his face. He sat up, holding the blanket up to his chin. "What day is it? Where's my pa?"

Eliza walked over and knelt beside him. "You're feeling better?"

Max nodded. "You've taken some care of me, I'm thinking. I don't want to be in the way, Ellie. And I'm sorry. What day is it? Where's Ben? How's my pa?"

"It's July sixth, Max. Ben and Ma and Pa are at the barn. Pa bought a new horse yesterday, and he's been telling us tonight about folks going west. To a place called the Oregon. Do you know where that might be?"

Max nodded. "Ummm." he said. "Way yonder. Beyond the Missouri River. Lots of Injuns out there. But Ellie, I've been here for two whole days? How's my pa? He was—well, he was . . ."

Eliza sat beside Max, ramrod straight. "Ma . . . she can tell you."

Max frowned and looked directly at Eliza. "No," he said, his voice stronger now. "*You* can tell me just as well. Where's my pa, and why am I here?"

"Your pa's dead." She blurted it out, and then she was silent. What else could she say?

21

Max stared at her, blinked his eyes, and slowly shook his head. "Dead? How can that be?"

Eliza shrugged. She couldn't just tell him he'd shot and killed himself. That didn't seem right. "Well," she said, "he just died." Then she brightened her smile and looked at him, steady in his eyes. "Let's talk, you and me, about old Boone, Max." Oh Lordy, she wanted Max to think about something good! She didn't want him thinking about his pa. "I've heard you say old Daniel Boone passed through these parts. Tell me some more about that."

Max looked at her for a long time as if he was thinking about something else. Then he spoke. "Yeah," he said softly. "Boone was right around here for a time. It's said, and I've read too, how he stood up on one of those top-knot cliffs and he looked all over this land and he saw nothin' but the Blue Ridge and cane and grass land forever and a day."

"And he dodged Shawnees and slept in caves and killed hundreds of bears," Eliza added. "I know about him too."

"Did you know he sang to his dogs?"

"His dogs?" Eliza laughed, delighted with Max's story.

"H'mm," Max said. "That's what I know. One day a couple of hunters came up on old Boone who was lying in a pretty meadow and just singing away with his dogs beside him, and . . ." He stopped talking, and looked as if he was trying to remember things.

"His little girl, Jemima, was stole by Injuns," Eliza said quickly. She had to keep this story going until her ma came back. "And then Boone, he rescued his little girl, and her friend. Isn't that right, Max?"

"You got it right." Max looked at her with his eyes keen again. "And Boone—he was taken prisoner by the Shawnees at the Blue Licks, where he fought those Injuns

22

later on. But you know, Ellie, what old Boone did makes me think about what I might do someday. Seeing new country. It's funny you said what you did about the Oregon country 'cause I've talked to Ben some, about going west. Maybe clear out there to the Oregon. I . . ."

Voices. Martha Landon's laughter, followed by Ben's and Thomas's, with quick steps across the porch and moments later the family was gathered around Max. Martha knelt, took Max's hand in hers, and smiled at him. "Ahhh," she exclaimed. "You're feeling better, and we're pleased to see it."

Max nodded. "Thanks be to you all, Mrs. Landon. But I say, as I said to Ellie here . . ." He stopped talking, he turned his head to the wall, and his shoulders shook as he started to cry. Harsh, muffled sobs. Nobody said a word. Ben bit his lips, and looked away. Martha put her hand on his shoulder; Eliza wanted to touch him and tell him it was all right to cry, but her pa said it instead.

"Times are when it's good a man cries," Thomas said. "It makes him feel better inside, and there's nothing wrong in it at all."

"But he's dead!" Max cried, his voice sounding thin and uneven. "That's what Ellie said. Oh God! He got to drinking, and he'd been gone for three days, down in town. When he came home, he was in a fit like I ain't seen before. And he beat me till I thought he was gonna kill me." Max sat up and held the quilt close to his thin chest. His blond hair was tangled and a mess; his eyes brimmed with tears. "I begged him to stop. He kept saying 'twas my fault for Ma's passing, but I told him I didn't ask to be born. That made him madder, and he kicked me until I fell. I figured I'd just stay there and maybe he'd leave me be. But he kept on kicking me, and then I don't remember anything else until today. But I got to know what happened to him." He looked up at Thomas and Ben. "You know I got to know."

23

Thomas pulled up a chair and sat down close to Max. "There's not an easy way to say it," he said, putting a hand on Max's arm. "Three days ago, on the Fourth of July, you didn't show up here for the party." Thomas stopped talking and cleared his throat.

"It was the gander pullin', Max," Ben said. "And you weren't around. But I tell you, I rode Red hard, giving her the whip, and Lordy!" Ben laughed, a short, forced laugh. "Red . . . she galloped right up to that flappin' old gander and I stuck out my hand and I grabbed that neck, and I pulled hard, and whoa, b'God, I got her, Max. And I raised my arm then, to you and to me, in a salute!" Ben nodded and looked at his pa.

"That's right," Thomas said. "But then when Ben and Ellie realized you weren't here, they went up to your place where they found you hurt and in a bad way. Ben stayed with you while Ellie ran back here to get help. Chad Green and I rode on over then. Your pa was in your house and first thing we wanted to do was to get you into your cart and bring you on here for tendin' to. I went to talk to your pa. I told him we were takin' you home with us and that he'd hurt you badly. I told him I wouldn't have him in my house, drunk as he was, but after he'd sobered up, he should come on by. But your pa, he wasn't hearing me, I didn't think. Then when Chad and Ben and I started on down the road, we heard the gunblast. He did it to himself, Max. And that was that. We have to bury him tomorrow, though, even if you're not feeling up to it."

Max nodded. "I'll be fit," he said. "And I'm sorry to have caused you this fuss. I won't be crying again."

"We'd all like you to stay on with us for a while," Thomas said. "We talked about it the other night. Mrs. Landon, and Ben, and Ellie, and we all agreed, we'd like you to live here with us."

Max looked at them, surprise stamped on his face,

24

and he smiled a thin smile. "Lordy, that's kind of you. I'll think about it, I will. And I thank you, all of you."

It was evening. The limbs of the buckeye trees looked black against the blood red sky. Inside the Landon kitchen there was the dim purple color of late day as Eliza lit the rag wick on two lamps. She placed one on the hearth of the big fireplace; the other one she put on the kitchen table where the family was seated for supper. Max was now able to join them.

"I'll be leaving here," he said. "Pa's dead, and there's no reason to stay." He looked at Ben and smiled. "You know, Ben, how I've been thinking about leaving here someday. Maybe getting myself to Oregon."

Eliza's heart jumped. There it was! That word of magic. Oregon!

"That's a mighty long way, Max," Thomas said. "Won't you consider staying on here for a little while, and then maybe, if you're set on going west, set out when you're a little ready?"

"Thanks, Mr. Landon, but I can get on. I know I can. I'll be making my own way just fine."

"Oh, Lordy!" Ben laughed, but Eliza heard the anguish in his voice. "I wish you wouldn't. Or at least wait for me, Max! Then we'll go together!"

"Maybe we'll meet up someplace, Ben. We can think about that. But I've decided now's the time for me to go. Soon, too. After we bury Pa and I get things ready."

"I'm not for you leaving, Max." Martha's voice was tight. Eliza recognized it as the way she talked to Eliza or Ben when they had to do something or were not to do something and that was that. "You can stay here for a while. No need to say how long, but I feel you shouldn't be leaving these hills for a time yet."

"I'm twelve years old, Mrs. Landon. And I probably

25

won't be going much farther than down to Lexington for a while anyway. But I feel strong about leaving here. There's not a lot of living here for me, if I speak the truth now as I think I do."

Martha's lips were firm and straight as she looked at Thomas, who sat puffing on his pipe. "It's not my business, but do you have any money, Max?"

Max nodded. "I got a little. Saved some from selling those squawking chickens down in town." He grinned. "And I'll get myself some work, I know that. It's just that I plan on going. That's all."

Thomas sighed. "There's not a whole lot more that we can say then, Max. We all wish you'd stay on here for even a little while. But I see you're mind's made up, and that's that."

Suddenly a rooster crowed and Eliza looked anxiously out the window at the sky. A rooster crowing at roosting time meant rain and Eliza's heart felt heavy and pained. She didn't want Max to leave at all. And she sure didn't want him to leave in the rain. Jumping up from the table, she ran outside. Max had never seen her cry before; he wouldn't see her cry now.

The next day a few neighbors joined together with Max to walk up the dusty wagon track leading to the hillside where tilted headstones sat among the scattered pine. Eliza kept her eyes on Max, who walked beside the old, mule-drawn Pridentz farm cart. As he walked, he kept one arm on the pine coffin Thomas and Ben had made, steadying it as the cart lurched along the rutty road. He looked much better. A clean rag was wound around his head, his face was still swollen, but the bruises had almost disappeared, and even though he walked stiff, bound as he was with flannel, he walked tall. The preacher walked behind the group, preaching. Eliza wondered if Max heard the preacher's words. "Oh Lord, take this sinner's poor soul . . . and grant him peace . . ."

Dark clouds were piled up behind a mountain ridge far away, and thunder rolled across the valley. Eliza studied the ridge and wondered if Max would cross that mountain on his way to the Oregon. Scattered raindrops dotted the dust and plopped on her face and hair as a thought suddenly came to her. If Max and Ben could dream of going to the Oregon, why couldn't they all go? Ah, that would be so fine. Her family could leave here. Just as easy as not, they could just leave. And what a glory that would be! They would see Max again, and live in a place with sparkling streams, gentle winds, and a blue sky that never stopped. It was a thought, a warm, exciting, wonderful thought. And for the first time since the Fourth of July, Eliza didn't feel quite so sad.

On reaching the gravesite, the little procession stopped, stood, and said together, "Yea, though I walk through the valley of the shadow of death, I will fear no evil . . ." Then Max picked up a shovel and there was the sound of dirt hitting the pine box. But all that time, Eliza thought of Max going to a place called the Oregon. Someday she'd go there too.

Two days later Eliza waited on the steps of her porch and watched the sun slice through the buckeye trees on top of the hill. Max would soon come by. She squeezed her hand tight around a small leather pouch that held two coins. This was all the money she had in the whole world, but that didn't matter and nobody need know that she planned to give it away. Ben leaned against a post, whittling on a piece of wood, Martha was cooking a chicken on her cooking fire, and Thomas was wrapping his own copy of Cooper's *The Last of the Mohicans* to give to Max. Nobody had much to say.

"Lord knows when he's going to find food after this is gone," Eliza heard her mother say. "But he'll have this for a while."

It was then that a shrill whistle pierced the air, along with Max's shout. "Ben! Ellie! Mr. and Mrs. Landon! I'm coming on by!" There he was, at the top of the hill, with Nellie at his heels. Eliza jumped up from the steps, Ben put down his knife, and together they raced to meet him. Max no longer had the rag around his head, and the scar on his head looked clean. He carried a long, polished Kentucky rifle and he shouldered a knapsack, while a hunting knife, sheathed in a leather case, was strung on his rope belt. Suddenly Eliza felt her eyes sting and she quickly knelt and hugged Nellie, feeling her coarse fur against her face. Then she stood and looked at Max.

"Here," she said. "This is for you." She thrust the coin pouch in his hand, grateful to Ben for not saying a word.

At the cabin they gathered around. Martha hugged Max and gave him the chicken, wrapped in thick, brown paper and tied with string; Thomas gravely handed him the book and Ben surprised him with three shiny new fishhooks. Max was quiet as he tucked his gifts in his knapsack. Then he turned to Eliza.

"I can't take this, Ellie," he said softly, putting the coin pouch in her skirt pocket. "Maybe someday we'll meet and we'll talk some more about old Boone." He smiled at her and Eliza felt her heart quicken as she saw that his eyes were as blue as the summer sky.

"Write to us, Max! Let us know where you'll be," Martha said.

"I will. I'll do that. C'mon, Nellie. We got to go." Sliding his thumbs under his rope suspenders, Max hitched up his britches, slung the rifle and knapsack over his shoulder, and started down the path toward the road. Eliza and Ben walked with him for a little way, but none

28

of them said a word. Then, after they had rounded a bend and the Landon's house was no longer in sight behind them, Max spoke.

"I best be going on alone now." Eliza heard the catch in his voice. She and Ben stopped and watched him walk on, turn, and wave. Eliza and Ben waved back.

"Someday I'm gonna find you, Max Pridentz," Eliza whispered to herself. " 'Cause someday soon we'll leave here, too, and go out to the Oregon. And I'm gonna look for you, and when I find you, we'll talk about a lot of things. And we'll sure talk some more about old Boone."

Chapter 4

The clang of a hammer striking an anvil led Max to a smith, hard at work inside a dark, smoky shed in the town of Lexington.

"I'm looking for work, sir," Max shouted.

The smith turned and moved out from behind the huge billows. "No work here. But yonder"—he waved his hammer—"there's a cattle drive. Maybe they're hiring lads the likes o' you."

Following the smith's directions, Max found the cattle drive. A narrow-faced man wearing a tattered hat, and riding a big, nickering bay laden with bedding and gear, moved back and forth among the herd. The man cursed and shouted at the drovers, four boys who looked Max's age.

"Goddamn oafs, you got rocks in your ass! Move it fast or there ain't no pay!"

"I need work, mister," Max shouted up at the man. "I work good."

The man looked down at him and grinned, showing teeth black with rot; his gray eyes looked hard as rocks. "Why do you think you can work for me? A skinny runt the likes of you, I ain't seen." The man laughed and moved his chew to one side of his mouth.

"I move fast, mister," Max cried. "I'll work for free at first, if you'll take me on."

The man's eyes rested on Nellie.

"I tell you now. Any dog except my own is a god-damn cur. Can't take you and your dog."

"She won't bother none of your cattle, mister. If she does, you can take my pay. I promise you that, mister."

The man stared at Max as if he was thinking of something else, then nodded his head. "Give it a go then, boy. But if there's any trouble with the dog . . ."

From Lexington the cattle drive moved on, across the Appalachian plateau and down the Tuscarora, Kittochtinny, and Blue Mountain ranges. All during that late summer Max worked harder than he knew he could work, moving the stubborn cattle along roads hacked through thick woods of tamarack, hickory, and walnut trees.

"Caw! Caw! Hey bawss! Hey! Caw! Caw!" Max's high-pitched voice rang out as he tended to the bawling beasts, smelling their breath and feeling their shoving bigness that was always there. *"Caw! Caw!"* Day after day Max whistled, cursed, and snaked his whip down hard on the creatures' backs, urging them on toward the east.

By early fall Max looked like the other drovers. Worn rope suspenders held up his filthy wool pants, his homespun shirt was torn; the stiff, ill-fitting boots he wore looked like piles of rusty leather, and an old plainsman hat covered his dirty, matted hair.

But Max was now used to the turmoil and the crowds. He had learned how to accommodate impatient drivers of huge Conestoga freight wagons heading east and he did his best to help move the herd through long lines of pack horses and mules. One tied to the tail of another and laden with cider and whiskey, the creatures bumped and butted their way through herds of cattle,

31

swine, geese, and pigs. Then there were the slow-moving westbound wagons loaded with mattresses, bedsteads, rocking chairs, spinning wheels, pots and pans, and heavy farming tools, harrows, and ploughs. People were moving west. Max wondered how many of them were going to Oregon.

Day after weary day, the cattle drive moved on, and the boss drover never let the other drovers alone. Day after day he cursed and screamed, flailing his long rawhide whip in the dusty air. If he struck one of the boys, he grinned, curled his tongue, and spat out a dark stream of tobacco juice. "Hey, boy. Goddamn oaf, move 'em! *Hooey! Hooey!*"

"Caw! Caw! Hey, bawss! Goddamn, hey! Caw! Caw!" Max would lick his lips, split and caked with dust and dried blood, push his hat up high on his head, and rub his stinging eyes. Lordy, it was hot! And so dusty he could hardly see.

In eastern Ohio and Pennsylvania the country surrounding the road over the Three Mountain Trail near Pittsburg was tinder dry. Rivers were low and creek beds were dried to mud where swarms of mosquitoes bred in the rank reeds. Max thought about his fishing days with Ben and Ellie on the Red River back in Kentucky, and he wondered if he would ever do that again.

The drovers and the herd moved on, passing through small settlements with a store, a grist mill, a sawmill, a blacksmith shop, and usually a tavern or inn. Late each afternoon Max welcomed the sound of the boss drover's whistle, calling the drive to a halt. The drovers then scurried to feed the cattle and bed them down for the night before making their own camp with the herd or heading for a nearby tavern. Sometimes Max preferred the taverns—close, dark places, where smoked meats, dried foods, and hanks of tobacco hung from smoke-blackened rafters, and kettles of boiling deer or bear meat swung from a spit over the open fire. Travelers of the roads and canals met here. Drovers, mule skinners, canalers, mountain men, and scouts who told tales, while they ate and drank. And after a meal of porridge, and a tankard of ale, Max listened as many of the men talked about the country west of the Missouri River; many of them talked about "the Oregon country."

"Yonder, and then yonder yet, beyond the Massoura River and St. Joe, and yonder," a scout wearing stinking buckskins said one night as he smacked his lips and tossed a bone into the fire. "Beyond them high mountains of bright stone, there's more mountains. Shining mountains so high, you can't ever see the tops, and snows so deep, you can't walk. I know. I been there.

"Yup, Pap. Yup. Ain't no lie when I say there's places where there ain't no food, and the folks yonder either died, or ate those who did and also ate their shoes. Waugh! Ain't no lie neither to say I seen fierce wolves to turn your hide! Critters with red eyes that smell you for miles, and then go git you to eat."

"Ain't nothin' on this here earth to get me to go there," a man with a stiff face and little eyes answered, putting his brown jug down on the floor. "Hell, I hear it's desert, with nothing but jagged rocks, and nothing growing there but poison berries in sand, and if a man gets there, he's likely to sink into burning sand, and right there, be buried alive. And all the water's poison, so a man has to suck bullets, and white, glassy rocks, to keep from dying from thirst. And the savage Injuns—hell! They'll scalp you alive for the fun of it, then hang your scalp from a belt, and leave the rest o' you in the desert to rot. But the coyotes and wolves—they'll clean up your bones." The man leaned back in his chair, wiped his dirty beard with the back of his hand, and laughed.

"Blatheration, you're tellin' tall tales," a mountain man, dressed in greasy buckskins, spat out. "Waugh! This coon's trapped beaver on the Missoura way up! And Yaller Stone too. And the Platte, and Columbia, and Green River. Waugh! I've raised the hair of Pawnee and Apache, takin' my share of topknots an' I seen mean Injuns so close as to see into their black eyes shinin' like coals, an' me thinkin' I was a gone possum. But I'm tellin' you now, country around the old Stonies, and on to the Oregon is a Eden, says I. And full of buffalo too!"

As Max listened to the stories, he wondered about the country on beyond the Missouri; country that went all the way west to a river called the Columbia, and then beyond to the Pacific Ocean. He listened to the stories until he fell asleep, and dreamed of jagged mountains and wild rivers where savage Indians roamed. And he dreamed of fishing in clear streams under a sky that never quit.

One night after the herd was bedded and calmed, Max and the drovers were hunkered down around a low campfire. One boy kicked his boots off, spit on a wad of his shirtsleeve, and rubbed one of his boots, trying to raise a shine. Max looked twice at the boots. God, they were nice. Strong, smooth leather and gleaming copper toes.

"Good boots," Max said.

"They do me a'right," the boy said. "Paid some for them though."

"Bought around here?"

The boy shrugged. "Yonder. At Harrisburg. We'll be passin' through in time."

Max stared into the orange coals.

"How much did you pay?"

"Two dollars."

Max whistled. He had just enough money, but he'd have to think hard on that.

The next morning, while dark still hung on the wooded hills, and before the mist was off the ground, the drovers were up and moving on, working the cattle over the rolling hills toward the Susquehanna River, and Harrisburg.

Later that day the meadow outside Harrisburg teemed with cattle and men as cattle buyers and speculators moved through the herd. Spreading his last load of hay around five big-boned, snuffling cattle and tipping his hat to the boss drover, Max, who had the afternoon off, headed for town.

Darting in and out of the crowds of people, the horses, and carriages, Max spotted Snelling's Fine Leather Goods just down the street. At the same time he heard a man call out over the crowd, "Folks! Folks! Hear me! Hear me!" The man stood on the porch of The Overland Supply House. Two Indians, wearing buckskins decorated with bright green, blue, and red beads, their long braids entwined with red and blue feathers, stood with the man. The Indians stood stiff, but quiet, and watched with glittering eyes as a crowd gathered around.

Max stared at the white man who wore a black coat and carried a Bible in one hand. He had long dark hair and his eyes seemed to turn to fire as he grabbed the hand of one of the Indians and held it high in the air.

"Hear me, folks!" the man cried. "Hear me! Take the word of the Lord west and hear this! It's easy to go west. Why, there's not a thing west for thousands of miles that anybody would be simple-minded enough to call a mountain! And safe? It sure is safe, if you use good sense, do your planning right, and believe in the Lord!" Max decided this man must be a man of the Lord, a preacher who had been many places. Maybe this preacher had been to Oregon.

The preacher put his Bible down on a chair that sat on the porch, then he placed his arms around the Indians' shoulders. "Look here, folks! Look at these two Injuns! Living proof of what God's mighty word and work can do! These two boys were once bloodthirsty savages! Hostiles! But now look at them! They've learned the ways of the Lord and now they're our friends."

The crowd grew and the preacher warmed to his audience. "I say to you again, it's easy to go west! I guarantee it! Now hear what I say! We need farmers! Like you, sir!" he cried out, pointing his finger at a man with long blond hair and a sunburned face. "We need blacksmiths, like you! And tanners! We need doctors, sir! And merchants and teachers!"

Murmurs and soft talk rippled through the crowd as the man's fingers flew through the air, singling out men, talking directly to them and at the same time talking to everybody. Then the preacher's eyes stopped and he pointed at Max. "And we sure do need trail drivers, and drovers—strong, young lads exactly like you!"

Max felt the preacher's eyes burn into him; he took a deep breath, thinking he might burst with excitement. He'd go west! He would! During these last months on the cattle drive, he'd forgotten how he'd once planned to go to Oregon. Now the preacher's words reminded him of that and his resolve grew as he listened intently.

"Folks!" the preacher called out. "Listen to me! It's a land of paradise out there! Free land for the having! And it can be yours! Beautiful, lush land carved out by the hand of the Almighty! Located in a valley called the Will—*am*—ette. So, take the word of the good Lord and go!"

"I can't afford a wagon," a man shouted. "How can I get there without a wagon?"

"Hitch up with another party," the preacher called back. "Two or three of you hitch up together. But don't forget to take the word of the Lord!"

"Is it the truth a man gets free land, just for bein' there?" The crowd was silent, waiting for an answer.

"That's right! You got to live on it. You got to farm it and fence it and plow it and plant it. But it's yours. And if you got a wife and children, you can file for more land in their names."

"What's it like for a teacher, say?" another man called out, waving a newspaper to catch attention.

"You can always start up a school. Especially schools in the name of the Lord."

"What about sickness? Like fever there? I heard there ain't none," a scrawny, pale woman holding a little boy by one hand and carrying a baby on her hip called out, her voice high and shrill.

"That's right, ma'am," the preacher answered. "There's no fevers there that gets ahold of folks like it does here. Air's good out there. Water's good out there. Out in Oregon, fever just doesn't get ahold and stay on."

"What do we take, if we decide to go?" two men asked at the same time.

"We've got plenty of lists made up, telling you what you'll need. Free for the asking right here at The Overland Supply House. But generally speaking, you got to have good supplies, and enough. More than enough for you and your family. Folks that get into trouble are those that don't take enough gear. Folks, thank you! Thank you! Now I have to be on my way." The man picked up his Bible, waved, and started down the dusty street; the two Indians followed behind.

Max stood still. He needed money to go west! He needed money to get past St. Joe and the Missouri! He needed money to get beyond the Rockies and all the way to Oregon! He sighed. He sure didn't have that kind of money, but he could begin to work and save what he earned. And he'd do that too! After he bought his boots.

Three teams of huge, restless black horses with jingling bells on harnesses hitched to heavy Conestoga wagons stood in front of the Pioneer Line Freight Station next to Snelling's. Max skirted the blowing horses that pawed at the ground. These were the Six-Horse Bell Teams, the great Pitt Freight wagons that moved thousands of pounds of freight east. Max glanced at the wagons, the wooden frames painted a bright blue, the running parts red. The long, deep wagon beds were sloped with a deliberate sag in the middle to prevent loads of heavy freight from shifting. White hempen canvas, stretched over the six to eight bows, formed the wagon top; the enormous iron wheels were a good three inches wide. These were like the wagons people took west, but they cost a lot of money. Max shrugged his shoulders as he walked on; he had boots to buy.

The boots sat in Snelling's window. Tall and shiny with gleaming copper toes. Max's heart beat fast as he opened the door and walked in. It was a big, dim room that smelled like oily leather. Saddles, harnesses, boots, and gear crowded the shelves and hung from big wall pegs. A man wearing a leather apron appeared.

"You have some boots, sir," Max said. "Boots with copper toes. Like the ones in the window. I want to buy them. I have enough money."

The man nodded, went to the back of the store, and returned with the new boots in one hand. Max paid the man, took off his old boots, wrapped them in a piece of newspaper, put on his new boots, tucked his package under his arm, and left.

Max felt ten feet tall. Lordy! He wished Mr. and Mrs. Landon and Ben and Ellie could see him now! Walking down Liberty Street, he kicked a foot out every few minutes so he could see his boots. He looked for the preacher who had talked about going west. If he found him, then b'God, he'd tell him he'd be going to Oregon. And he'd do it, too! As soon as he had a little money, and some gear. The preacher wasn't to be seen, but it didn't matter.

Putting his hands in his pockets, Max threw back his head and whistled as he walked through town and out toward the drovers' camp. B'God, those boots felt good! And he knew the copper toes flashed in the sun.

Chapter 5

Philadelphia! Buildings—lots of them. Houses and factories, and taverns and inns. And shops and stores where a boy could buy anything in the world if he had the money.

Max walked down winding cobblestone streets crowded with people, carriages, wagons, horses, dogs, cattle, and mules. Above the noisy hubbub, he looked up at a gray sky combed with trails of black smoke. Smoke spewed out of hundreds of chimneys atop row after row of houses that were connected to each other.

"Lordy, Nellie," Max said. "Don't know as we're gonna like this all that well. Lots of folks livin' on top of their neighbors here. But 'cause we're gonna' go west, I got to find work."

A man wearing thick spectacles and a wool cap told him the Morris Ironworks was hiring and Max was hired on the spot. From early morning to evening, Max shoveled coal into the jaws of a huge smelting furnace. By midmorning he was stripped naked to his waist and covered with coal dust; his eyes watered and stung, but he made fourteen cents a day and at the end of each week he collected his pay and put it in a leather pouch he wore around his neck.

He slept where he could. When winter came and it

got so cold he couldn't sleep in empty carts or wagons, he slept at a station house packed with other homeless souls. Here he huddled around a feeble fire that burned in a small stove before claiming one of the rag piles that served as a bed. Every night the big room was full of men, women, children, and babies, and all night long curses, shouts, and babbling cries filled the room. Max thought about the quiet back in Kentucky, but he dreamed now of Oregon.

One morning, before the light of dawn, Max woke up to the prick of a knife at his throat and a foul-smelling, rough hand covered his mouth.

"You best be quiet while I take your wad, lad. Else you'll be dead," the thief hissed while pushing down on Max's face. In a split second the thief cut Max's money pouch free, stood, and ran from the station house.

Max leaped to his feet. "Thief! Thief!" he shouted as he chased the man, but the thief disappeared in the cold murky dawn, and when Max returned to his ragged blanket, two rheumy-eyed men looked at him and laughed. Later that morning Max walked to the foundry, collected his wage, and left the city.

"This place isn't right for us, Nellie. I got to find us something better. But there's no point in going further east when we aim to go to Oregon. Might as well start now, 'cause we're gonna go to that valley the preacher talked about. A place where it's green and quiet and I'll bet you there aren't places there like the station house. I got to make some money, Nellie, but all the while we'll be headin' west. You and me."

The notion was now stuck hard in Max's mind. Yes, he'd get to Oregon! He'd own land in "the valley," he'd be a good farmer, he'd own a couple of cows, ride a fine horse, and he'd have Indian friends like the Indians he'd seen with the preacher in Harrisburg. But he wouldn't go begging like he'd heard some folks did. He'd start all over again saving his money and he'd go, being his own man. He had his rifle and now he had decent boots. That was a start. Next thing he needed was a warm coat and a good horse. Then he'd hire on with a wagon train trailing cattle and work his way west.

After leaving Philadelphia, Max walked back to Harrisburg, where he worked for a smithy until late summer of the following year. Then he started across the Appalachian Mountains, at times taking to the hills, where he made his way through forests and high tablelands, trapping squirrels and rabbit, catching fish and gathering huckleberries, raspberries, and blackberries, always keeping his trail west.

One fall day he found himself on the Allegheny River, east of Pittsburgh. Following the road through a dense stand of hemlock trees, he suddenly stopped, smelling the foul odor of a tannery close by.

"Lordy God, Nellie," he said, pinching his nostrils with his fingers, "that sure stinks." He walked on a ways and stopped again. A sign nailed to a shed standing at the edge of a field read MCCABE'S TANNERY. HIRING. An arrow pointed across the field to a cottage standing beside the tannery, a large, red building with two small windows.

Max whistled. "Could be, Nellie they'll hire me on. I wouldn't have to worry about you out here and I could save more money." Thinking about that, he quickly crossed the field to the cottage and knocked on the door.

A rough-clothed, gray-haired man with heavy eyebrows opened the door and peered out at Max. "I'm lookin' for work, mister. I work good."

The man looked closely at Max. "Name's McCabe," he said while scratching his large belly. "You'll work peeling hemlock. You'll pile it in the wagon, and haul it back here. Then you'll help the boys with the hides. I pay sixteen cents a day. My girl'll see you get food. You'll sleep out in the shed on the other side of the field. Keep your dog outta the way, or it'll be dead." Max went to work the next day.

In the mist of early dawn, before the long shafts of sun cut down through the forest, Max was at work. Stripping long shards of bark off the hemlock trees, he then loaded the bark into a heavy cart and hauled the cart back to the tannery. After dumping the bark into huge vats of astringents, he helped McCabe and two boys carry piles of skins to a close, humid room where they hung the skins from rafters to rot. Days later, when the skins were putrid with decay, Max and the boys used large, dull knives to scrape the loosened hair off the hides, which were then placed into soaking vats. Following the soaking, the hides were hung in drying lofts before being dipped into barrels of heavy molton grease; when removed from the grease the leather was ready for polishing. This was the girl's task, and the girl also tended a fire that burned on the hearth at one end of the room. Max felt sorry for the blond-haired girl, who was crippled but scurried about as best she could while answering to orders bellowed out by McCabe and the boys.

During the first few days Max had tried to be friendly with the boys, but they hadn't answered his questions or his greetings, and they had stared at him with hostile eyes. So Max had shrugged them off, kept to himself, and worked hard.

One afternoon, after Max had delivered his load of bark, Mr. McCabe called him into a small room at the end of the shop. A heavy table, stacked with ledger books, a desk, and a chair were in the room. This was McCabe's office.

"Do you read?" McCabe asked, looking at Max with sharp eyes under his heavy brows.

"Yes, sir."

"Do you know your numbers?"

"Yes, sir," Max answered.

43

"Good. Then you'll learn the books. My boys don't take to that kind of work. My girl has other work to do. It won't hurt you none to learn a new trade. You'll still peel the bark and bring it in. Then you'll take care of the day's books. You won't be workin' anymore with the skins. I'll help you with the books at first and I'll pay you one cent more a day."

Max nodded. "I'll do my best, sir." It was through the old man, then, that Max learned how to keep ledgers, balance long columns of numbers, and invoice sales of the hides.

One winter evening after Max had finished the books, he sat for a while, staring out the window. Snow had fallen all afternoon, but it had now stopped. A dark gray hung around the edge of the forest and a shadowed moon showed its pale face. In two days it would be Christmas and Max thought about Mr. and Mrs. Landon and Ben and Ellie. It was going on two years now since he'd left Kentucky; he'd never written to them the way he'd said he would. Maybe when he got out to Oregon, he'd have something important to write about. He also wondered if they ever thought about him; he hoped they might.

Thinking about that, Max's throat felt heavy and he blinked and shook his head, trying to shake off the sadness. That's when he saw a shadow fall across the table. Startled, he looked up to see McCabe's girl standing directly in front of him. Max had never seen her up close. He figured her to be about his own age; she was tall and she had the lightest blond hair Max had ever seen.

"Hello," Max said. He smiled at her. "My name's Max. Who are you?"

"Clara," she said. "Clara McCabe. Where'd you come from?" Her voice was small and shy-sounding.

"Yonder. From Kentucky."

"Is that far?" she asked, looking at him with wide eyes.

44

Max laughed. "A ways. But I aim to go all the way out to Oregon. *That's* far. I aim to go out there and have my own place." He lifted his head higher. "I herded cattle all the way from Kentucky to Philly, I did. I used most of my money to buy these." He pointed to his boots, feeling proud.

"Ohhhh!" the girl said with a little sigh. "I ain't seen none like that. With copper toes, too! And I know you read. Least that's what's said."

Max nodded.

"I want to learn. D'you think you might have time to show me how?"

"We can try. Sure."

"Clara! Clara, come! And be quick!" The old man's tone was sharp. "I'll be comin' back," Clara whispered, then she turned and left. As Max watched her go, he felt sad and wished she'd stayed for a little while. He saw that one of her legs was shorter than the other. As she scuttled across the big room, her shadow dipped along the wall, reflecting her uneven steps.

During that winter, Clara didn't come back and Max was disappointed. It would have been nice, he thought, to have had a new friend, especially someone who wanted to learn to read.

Late February brought the beginning of spring thaw. In the woods, water gurgled under the dirty crusted snow. The pussywillows down by the river were swollen and about to burst and Max began to think about leaving this place. Old man McCabe wasn't around much anymore. The old man had a terrible cough; he'd usually show up on payday to pay Max and go over the books and then he'd leave. Nor had Max seen Clara this past month. He'd ask the boys, but these past few days he'd come to feel especially uneasy in their presence.

It was in March, on a cold, late afternoon, when Max, walking through the shop on the way to McCabe's office, was stopped by both boys. Max nodded his head. "Afternoon."

"Afternoon, purty boy," one of the boys said. Neither boy moved.

"Yeah." The other boy laughed. "Afternoon, purty boy. Let's us tell you who we are. You asked once, but I don't recall we said. I'm Ross, and this here's Earl."

Max nodded his head and moved to pass them, but the boys moved too, blocking his way.

"Listen, bub. We know you can read and write. Old man told us. Now, don't you think you're real smart!" Earl poked Ross in the ribs and they both laughed. Peculiar laughs; hardly a sound, more of a rippling wheeze. Danger flashed through Max's mind as he eyed these two slack-jawed boys with their dirty hair and small black eyes. They looked mean as snakes.

"What's his name?" Earl asked, looking down at Nellie, who sat beside Max watching the boys with her head cocked to one side.

"Nellie. Her name's Nellie." Again Max moved as to pass by and in a split second Nellie was a piece of yelping fur, hurtling across the room, the target of Earl's boot.

"What the hell!" Max cried, tearing past Ross and Earl and reaching Nellie, who lay on her side, panting and whimpering. He picked her up and turned. "Goddamn oafs! Wasn't need to kick her," he yelled. "She's mindin' her own business and not botherin' you at all!"

"Yeah, Bub. But we don't like dogs, do we, Earl."

"Ross! Earl!" The old man's voice echoed through the big, dim room. "Git outta there. Git!" Both boys sullenly turned and left.

Max picked up Nellie, made for the door, kicked it open, and ran across the field to the shed, where he put her down on a pile of hemlock boughs he used for his bed. "You're bruised, Nellie, and you got the wind knocked outa you, but you'll be all right. We're gonna clear outa here though. Tomorrow." He rubbed Nellie's scruffy old neck. "Tomorrow's pay day, and I mean to collect my pay and then we'll head on west."

Max quickly gathered up his belongings. His old boots were still wrapped in newspaper, along with a spare shirt. He packed these things, along with his copy of *The Last of the Mohicans*, in his knapsack, picked up his rifle, and carried his goods down to the river, where he hid them in a crevice between a boulder and the trunk of a hemlock tree. Turning over a large stone, he dug out the leather pouch he'd bought back in Harrisburg with his smith's pay. After counting his money, he tied the pouch around his neck and walked back to the shed, where he slipped his hunting knife out of its sheath and tucked it in the cedar boughs of his bed, close to his side.

"Just takin' a little care, Nellie," he whispered. "I got our gear stashed and ready to go. No need leavin' it loose. Tomorrow we'll head on west, you and me." Thinking about that, Max fell asleep.

The next morning Max tied Nellie to a tree just outside the shed, hitched his sheathed knife to his belt, and headed for the woods. That afternoon he unloaded the bark then walked briskly through the big tanning room to McCabe's office. Nobody was around, but he would wait until his usual quitting time, finish off this week's books, and give McCabe a chance to show up with his pay. He had just finished his bookwork when he heard a door open and Clara came into the tanning room.

"I've been mighty sick." Her words echoed in the empty space as she scurried quickly across the room. "Now I got to fetch some goods to give to doctor whose comin' soon. You better be gone, Max. You best leave right soon, for if you don't, there'll be trouble for you."

"That's what I'm planning, but I want my pay."

Clara looked at him and shook her head. "Best forget it. He's too sick and besides . . . I got to go." She picked a new harness off a peg and left.

A sense of foreboding swept over Max. He'd pay

mind to Clara's warning. To hell with the money; he'd get Nellie and be gone. Picking up his jacket and cap, he stopped for a second to look out the window. It was getting dark, but he wouldn't wait until morning to leave. Then he stood, frozen and unable to move, as he saw, reflected in the window, a boy's naked belly. Wheeling around, Max found himself face to face with Earl, who stood shirtless, his arms dangling at his side; he held a knife in one hand and he laughed his peculiar, silent laugh.

"Hey!" Earl called out in a hoarse whisper. "Hey, Ross! Come on!" Ross appeared, rubbing his chin with one hand and grinning. "Where might you be headin', purty boy?" Ross asked.

Max felt his throat so tight he could hardly breathe, but he stood his ground and looked at the slack-jawed boy. "I've finished your pa's books, and I'm leaving."

"Huh-uh. No, you ain't. First off, bub, if you're thinkin' any about gettin' paid, you ain't. The old man, he's about gone with fever. Yeah, bub. He's about finished off. Now lemme show you somethin', bub. An' ain't it sad?"

Ross ducked behind one of the vats, and when he reappeared, he had Nellie in one hand. He held her up. A dead Nellie, covered with hardened grease.

Waves of dark and light flashed before Max's eyes as he screamed. "Goddamn you!" he screamed, lunging, trying to grab Nellie's body. Then, sensing real danger, he tried to dodge past the boys, but pinpoints of tiny lights danced in front of his eyes as he felt a heavy hand smack the back of his head. He shook his head, trying to clear his senses, but now Ross and Earl both stood in front of him, crouched low, brandishing knives.

"Get on down, bub! Get on down!" They hissed the words, their eyes glittered bright.

"No!" Max turned to run back to the office, where

he might barricade himself, but Ross grabbed him and pushed him down, flat on his back. His belt was ripped off and Max heard the soft thud of his sheathed knife bump the floor as the cold blade of a knife separated the leather thong from his neck. The thong snapped and coins clinked on the wooden floor, while at the same time his boots were wrenched off his feet.

Max fought, he kicked, he screamed as rough strong hands pulled his britches off. Then, fighting with all the strength he had, he felt a hot, stinging pain in his side and he knew he'd been stabbed. Suddenly the old man's shadow appeared on the wall above his head. The old man held a whip in one hand.

"Whoa! Whoa there!" The old man's voice sounded hollow and weak. "You two get the hell outta here. God-damned whores! Someday I'm gonna kill the both of you!"

Max saw the whip curled black against the orange firelight, and he heard it whistle as it cut and slashed through the air. But Ross lunged at the old man and forced the whip out of his hand while Earl kept his knife pointed at Max.

"Get back, old man!" Ross cried. "You're in the way! Get back!"

Ross, dancing the whip at McCabe's feet, slashed it against his legs as the old man shrieked and Earl stood steady in front of Max, silently laughing. Then Max saw it—a fire poker leaned against the chimney behind Earl. He had to reach it. He had to! He lunged, but at the same time a blinding pain pierced his groin and he heard his cry split the air; his knees buckled, and he saw the room and the fire in the firepit swirl together in a red cloud.

"Down! Down, bub! Get down, or you're gonna be killed." He heard the voices, but they sounded dim and far away as Max flailed his fists against hands that held him in a vise. Choking on blood, the room spun and looked cockeyed as he was forced down onto his knees, and bent over, bare ass up to the sky.

A ragged scream echoed through the foul air and Max felt his body released. Staggering toward the hearth, he grabbed the poker, turned, waggled it over his head, and cracked it against Ross's face. Blood spurted from Ross's nose, and one of his eyes bulged huge and red then slid down his cheek. Turning, Max saw Earl, his face twisted in agony as steaming water ran over his head and down his face and Clara, holding an empty bucket in one hand and Max's britches in the other hand, ran toward him as fast as she could. "Run, Max! Run!" she screamed. "I'll catch you later!"

Grabbing his britches, Max ran out the door and across the field, retching and choking on vomit, tripping on old corn stalks poked up out of hard-crusted snow, and when he got to the shed, he leaned against the wall and his hands shook and wouldn't stop and his teeth chattered and chattered. The thing that had happened to him filled him with shame and loathing and hatred so strong he wondered if he was crazed. Crouching low, he pulled on his britches, ran down to the river, grabbed his stash, and ran. He looked back once across the field at the tannery, looming black against a little moon.

"Pridentz! Pridentz! Goddamn your soul! Ain't done with you, boy! By God, we'll kill you, we will. Kill you, and yours to come."

He covered his ears and he clenched his teeth as he heard his name cursed in the putrid night, and rage, hatred, and despair swelled in him. "They got you, Nellie! Goddamn them! They got you!"

He ran to the outskirts of Pittsburg, where he thought he saw the shadow of the preacher he had seen a long time ago. The preacher stood on a street corner under the dim light of the moon; he waved the Bible and he looked at Max with burning eyes.

"Go West! Go where the land is a paradise!"

Max ran until he couldn't run anymore. When he stopped, he looked up at small, frosty stars and he opened his arms wide. "Oh, God! Nellie! Oh, God!" he cried. Then he lay down under a tree and sobbed.

Chapter 6

For the next two years Max worked his way west, getting as far as Illinois. He stayed by himself; he didn't make friends; he never talked to folks, and if he thought folks were becoming too friendly, he moved on. In Illinois he worked for a kind man, a farmer who told him his name was Caleb. He paid Max well for his work, and he told him if he was in want, to let him know. A short time later, Max learned that the man had drowned in a river that ran close to his place. When Max left the farm, he decided to call himself Caleb. Caleb Pride. And he vowed that from now on, nobody in the world would ever know him as Max Pridentz, Nor would they know what had happened to him. And if, by some quirk of fate, his path should ever cross that of the McCabe brothers, Caleb knew he would kill them.

After working on an Illinois dairy farm for a year, he left, bound now for Independence, Missouri. Once again he had a pouch full of money. In Independence he would buy a horse and he'd hire on as a drover, trailing a herd of livestock with a wagon train headed west to Oregon.

On a late spring afternoon east of Springfield, Caleb encountered a storm with hailstones the size of eggs hurling out of the blue-black sky. Finding refuge in a barn, he sat on a pile of hay and listened to the deafening sounds of the hail, followed by torrents of rain. But feeling dry and warm, he decided to stay the night.

Caleb hadn't thought about Eliza for a long time, but that night as he slept, he dreamed about her. Her red hair was long, and she smiled at him, and beckoned to him to come with her. It was a lovely dream, but rudely interrupted by a dog's nose sniffling against his face, startling him awake. He sat up and pushed the dog away. "Get!" he said. And then he lay back down. It was black as ink inside the barn, but the rain had stopped. Caleb, half-asleep, listened to the steady dripping from the roof, and he frowned as he heard breathing and small rustlings in the hay. Again he sat up. The pale light of a moon broke out of skudding clouds, cut down through the hay loft, and rested briefly on a small boy sleeping just inside the barn door; the dog was close by.

For the rest of the night Caleb was wakeful and aware of the boy. When morning came he stood up, shook the hay off his clothes, and made ready to move on. The boy was also awake; he sat up, then jumped to his feet, watching Caleb with a wary eye.

"Howdy," Caleb said, smiling at the boy. The boy smiled. God dang, Caleb thought. Now there's a runty, poor-lookin' young'un. The boy's brown hair was matted with filth; his clothes were torn and caked with mud. An ugly, blue-green bruise ran down the side of his face, and one eye was swollen. Caleb shivered as the memory of his own drunken, crazed father flashed through his mind.

"What happened to you, lad?" Caleb asked softly, pointing to the boy's face.

The boy ducked his head in his arm and turned away. Caleb shrugged. He needed to eat and Springfield wasn't far. He walked out of the barn, the boy and his dog following close behind. Caleb turned.

"Where do you live? Where's your kin?"

The boy smiled, but didn't answer. Caleb now wanted the boy to be gone. He didn't need a ragged boy and his dog trailing after him. But then it wouldn't hurt to buy him breakfast. "C'mon," Caleb said. "If you want food, c'mon with me. I'll buy your breakfast, but then you got to get on. I got to get on myself."

Still the boy said nothing as he followed Caleb into Springfield, where Caleb bought bread and coffee. But as Caleb left Springfield, the boy and his dog followed right behind.

That night as Caleb made his camp by a creek, he watched the boy thread a stick with a piece of string, bait it with bird gut, and then catch three fish so fast Caleb hardly had time to blink. The boy proudly offered the fish to Caleb, who cooked them, and while they ate together, he studied the boy.

He was small and skinny. His hair was a mass of dirty, brown curls that almost hid his big brown eyes. He jerked his head at the slightest sound, and he sniffed a lot as if using his nose as a flag. Caleb concluded the boy wasn't deaf, but he was dumb. He either couldn't talk, or he wouldn't. Now, ever since Caleb had found him, he'd stuck to him like a bur, not letting him out of his sight.

For the next two days, the boy worked hard. He cut wood, trapped small grouse and squirrels, and showed pleasure in what he did. Whenever Caleb talked to him, he grinned and patted his dog, but he didn't utter one word. And it was while traveling on through Illinois toward St. Louis that Caleb realized he had taken on a family. A little dumb boy and his dog. A boy he had never touched; a dog he had ignored.

Now, however, Caleb had a plan. When they got to St. Louis, Caleb would find a home for the boy. An orphanage, or maybe a vicarage would take him in. And the dog . . . Caleb would somehow leave the dog behind.

One cloudy day Caleb and the boy came to the place

north of St. Louis where the Missouri River met the Mississippi. Huge rivers, they were, where keelboats, riding low in the water, came down from the back country, bringing furs and buffalo hides; where raftsmen, poling rafts carrying lumber and hay, waved to folks on shore, and where steamboats churned upstream and back down again, loaded with cargo and passengers. Caleb smiled to himself as he, the boy, and the dog walked on.

St. Louis! Caleb walked the streets of the great Levee, piled with produce and goods. Emigrants—Irishmen, Germans, Englishmen, Negroes, Spaniards, and Indians—were all there, looking for a new home, moving through crowds of frontiersmen, guides, land speculators, traders, and drummers with their own goods to sell. And whenever the steamboats steamed in to the docks, the pitchmen were there, calling out greetings to passengers coming ashore, urging them to try the luxuries of new boardinghouses, restaurants, and fine hotels. And over all the noise and shouts, there were the clamoring steamboat bells.

But now, Caleb had a task at hand. He must find a home for the boy. He hadn't been in the city long when he found an orphanage, a grim place where a gloomy-looking man told Caleb, "One more lad won't make any difference in the eyes of the Lord. Leave the boy and pay whatever you can. But we won't take the dog."

Caleb nodded to the man. "I'll think about it, and I might be back to leave him later today," he said. Then, as Caleb and the boy walked down the street, Caleb saw tears in the boy's eyes. Tomorrow, Caleb thought. Tomorrow he would take the boy, but he couldn't do it today. Instead, he would take the boy fishing. After all, he might not have much of a chance to fish, once he lived in the orphanage.

It was a fine afternoon, and walking down a busy street, he and the boy passed a shop selling artist supplies.

R&R SMITHY, ARTIST SUPPLIES was painted on the window in curly gold letters and an assortment of paints, brushes, papers, and inks were displayed inside.

Suddenly the boy tugged hard on Caleb's shirtsleeve as he pointed to the display in the window. He then touched his own chest and made drawing motions in the palm of his hand. Caleb nodded, and they went inside where pencils, writing tablets, bundles of quill pens, and pots of inks and paints were displayed on the shelves. Again the boy pointed to the pencils and writing tablets and then to himself. Caleb laughed.

"So! You're an artist!" he said. "Well, let's see what you can do." The boy's brown eyes flashed and his grin was wide as Caleb bought a packet of cheap writing paper and four pencils. He handed the package to the boy and then he bought himself a copy of the *St. Louis Republican*. He would read that afternoon while the boy fished.

Caleb found a pretty stream, not far from town, settled back against a willow tree, and opened his newspaper. He read with interest that Lieutenant Colonel John Charles Fremont had recently been appointed governor of California. He was reading a story about Fremont's father-in-law, Senator Thomas Hart Benton, when he looked up and saw that the boy wasn't fishing at all. Instead he was drawing, his head bent over his paper, intent on his work. Caleb frowned. Tomorrow he would wash the lad's tangled hair, buy him a shirt and new pants, and then he would take him back to the orphanage. Cleaned up, he'd be a good-looking lad, and easy to take to.

But as Caleb thought about the man he'd seen at the orphanage, the plan didn't set well. That man had had mean eyes. And if he had mean eyes, he was sure to have a mean tongue. Maybe . . . maybe it wouldn't be so bad taking the boy with him to Independence. Then he'd decide what he should do. He could leave him there, or maybe . . . maybe he might even think on taking him . . . all the way to Oregon!

Caleb looked down at the dog lying beside him, his head resting on his paws. Without thinking, Caleb put his hand on the dog's head. Feeling the dog's warm, furry head, Caleb felt pleasure and he realized he hadn't felt such a touch for a long, long time and he smiled. He liked having the boy and his dog.

It was late afternoon when Caleb again looked up from his paper to see the boy's shadow in front of him. The boy held a drawing out to Caleb, and seeing a likeness of himself and the dog, Caleb laughed with delight.

"Well!" he said, tousling the boy's hair. "It looks to me as if you're anxious to stay on with me!" The boy looked at Caleb, nodded his head, and grinned. "But you got to have a name, laddie." Caleb stared at him, unable to think of a name. Then he had a notion. "I tell you what." Hunkering down, Caleb cupped the boy's chin in one hand and looked directly in his wide brown eyes. "If you ever decide to tell me your name, we'll call you that. But now, I'm going to call you Smithy, 'cause that's the name of the store back there where you first let me know a little bit about yourself. And your dog—well, we'll call him Dog. Now, we're going to stay here in St. Louis for a while, Smithy, and I'll tell you, you and I are going to work on the docks. Then, since we're kinda tired of walking, we'll go on a boat! We'll go on a steamboat, Smithy, all the way up the Missouri River to a place called Independence."

Caleb didn't know if Smithy understood or not, but he figured it was important that Smithy hear the words. And Caleb had also come to realize that, with Smithy and Dog around, he didn't think so much about the night at the tannery and the McCabes.

Chapter 7

June 1846

It was a warm morning as Caleb and Smithy, with Dog at their heels, joined a throng of folks waiting to board ship at the St. Louis docks. This is where Caleb had booked passage on *The Jennie Sue*.

The Jennie Sue was old, her timbers were rotting, and her boiler was rusty and thin, but she still plied the Mississippi between Independence, St. Joe, and Kanesville.

Caleb smiled at the turmoil around him. For the past year he'd worked as a dock hand, guiding wagons brimming with passengers and goods up the gang planks and prodding cattle, pigs, horses, oxen, and mules on board. Now he was a passenger himself and he found himself enjoying every minute.

He had also decided to keep the boy and that meant he couldn't just work as a drover and go out to Oregon. Now he needed a wagon and good, dependable gear. His decision was to get to Independence, find work there, buy his gear, and keep an eye out for a good guide. When he found the right man, he'd sign on; he and Smithy would go to Oregon.

Once on board *The Jennie Sue*, Caleb found a place by the rail close to the box-covered sidepaddle wheel where he and Smithy watched animals and passengers and bales of freight brought on board, bound for the river towns north.

When the old boat couldn't take on another soul or piece of goods, the enormous hawsers were loosed, the brass engine bell clanged, and the huge paddles began to revolve as the steamer slowly moved away from shore. Thick columns of black smoke arose from two stacks near the ship's bow, the paddlewheels slapped with a fury against the muddy water, and as the current caught *The Jennie Sue*, she started upstream.

A summer breeze brushed against Caleb's face as he looked back over the swollen, muddy river toward St. Louis. Long lines of waterfront buildings and limestone warehouses began to look small; the upper arches of the great City Market were silhouetted against the summer sky and Caleb silently said good-bye to this country east of the Missouri, knowing he was leaving the roots of his early life behind forever.

He thought about the Landons. He hadn't yet written to them because there hadn't been anything to write about. Well, once he got to Independence, he would write them that letter he'd said he would write—how long ago? Five years. Yes. It was five years now since he'd left Kentucky. Sometimes he thought back to that time. Sometimes in the early evening a blue in the sky would bring to his mind the shadow of the Blue Ridge, and a smell of pine might remind him of the piny woods. Once, not too long ago, he had seen a young man about his own age with black hair and blue eyes and Caleb had thought the young man looked like Ben might look now. And just today, while standing in line to board *The Jennie Sue*, a young girl with red hair had stood with an older woman in front of him. The girl had turned to comment on the pretty day, and Caleb saw that she had a fair sprinkling of freckles, and blue eyes. She was maybe fifteen or sixteen years old, and he'd thought about Eliza, who was probably married now and had a couple of children of her own. He hoped she was happy. If he wrote that letter, one of them might write back and then he'd know those things.

The next few days on *The Jennie Sue* passed quickly by. Many of the passengers, including Caleb and Smithy, gathered around the pilot house and listened to the river pilot tell tales about the great rivers he had sailed, especially the Missouri River "cut deep into its own sides, and so danged crooked a flock of geese have trouble flyin' across."

Every now and then the trip was interrupted as deck hands shouted out "Woodpile! Woodpile!" The steamer would then head toward the riverbank and nose into shore, and Caleb and Smithy, joining other men and older boys, would laugh and jostle each other as they leaped onto land and heaved chunks of wood back on board. That done, the steamer would back up, turn, and continue on her way.

When *The Jennie Sue* met a boat heading downstream, both boats paused in passing while the pilots swapped information about the old river. Unpredictable "crossings" occurred when the river's current changed and the presence of "sawyers," or uprooted trees, and snags caused problems for river craft bound both ways. But things had gone well on this trip, and tomorrow the steamboat would land at Independence.

One night the light of a half-moon slid out from behind a long stringy cloud and settled on *The Jennie Sue*, anchored off a desolate stretch of shore. Caleb, who was sleeping in a corner of the bottom deck with Smithy and Dog by his side, suddenly awoke. There was no *chuk-chuk-chuk* of the boat's engine, only hissing steam. Caleb knew the boat was stopped, dead in the water.

What the hell's going on now, he thought, unwinding his long legs and standing up. Curious, but also feeling a sense of dread, Caleb climbed the steep steps to the top deck, Smithy and Dog behind him.

Cholera had struck three passengers the day before, and Caleb had seen two of the crew hastily making three crude wooden coffins. Caleb had talked to those folks; they had all boarded ship together, and he'd gotten to know them a little bit. There was a soldier who said he'd fought Pawnee and Sioux Indians close to the Missouri River frontier. The soldier was now going out to Fort Hall. There was the little girl who held on to a rag doll. The little girl had told Caleb she was anxious to see her papa, who was waiting for her in Independence; then they were going west, out to Oregon. And there was the grizzled fellow who had told Caleb that years back he'd trapped bear and beaver out in Oregon for the Hudson's Bay Company and a man named John McLoughlin. The old trapper was on his way to Green River to rendezvous with old friends. Those three were now dead.

Standing close to the rail along with other curious passengers, Caleb and Smithy watched two dinghies, rowed by black men, heading toward shore. Once there, the men hoisted the coffins out of the dinghies, and while two men held lanterns, the others dug a large pit. Sadness swept over Caleb. He especially wished that the little girl had lived to go to Oregon with her pa.

"God A'mighty, Smithy," Caleb whispered. "They're burying those folks there. I feel bad about them. Especially the little girl." Smithy looked at Caleb with somber eyes and nodded.

The next day there were further delays. "Passengers to shore! Passengers to shore! Men all stay! Men all stay!" the deck hands bellowed out over the humid air. "Ship's aground! She's aground! Passengers to shore! Men all stay!"

Then the women and children and the older passengers went ashore and walked along the riverbank while the ship's crew and all the men on board helped lower the heavy booms on both sides of the boat. The booms were then driven solidly into the riverbed, pointing upstream. Ropes were attached to the booms and wound around the capstans as all the men worked at the capstan bars until the huge paddle wheels began to work in reverse, backing up the water under the boat and lifting the vessel over the shallow waters to deeper waters where she could make her own way. The passengers on land were then rowed by dinghy back out to *The Jennie Sue*.

It was late afternoon when *The Jennie Sue* made the last sweep around the bend, and chugged toward Independence. The docks there were small, but teeming with activity, and it smelled like St. Louis, hot with heavy odors of rank water, oil, tar, and animals. Black men, white men, and Mexicans, stripped to their waists, their skin glistening with sweat, hoisted bales of heavy freight, and pushed and prodded pigs, mules, and cattle along the wooden planks. Caleb and Smithy, with Dog following, made their way through the crowd, and up the steep bluff toward town.

Independence, Missouri! The great "jumping-off place" for folks heading west. A place exploding day and night with folks outfitting themselves before starting the two-thousand-mile trek. Pushing his hat back on his head, Caleb looked at Smithy and grinned. "We're gonna like it here, Smithy. It's not like Philly, or Pittsburgh, and that's fine with me! Yeah! We're gonna like this place fine for a while."

Walking along the noisy, dusty streets, they passed saloons and bawdy houses and log huts where wild-looking men stood in dark doorways and held jugs of "skull varnish" in their hands. Caleb laughed. "Don't try that stuff, Smithy," he said, pointing to a milky-looking bottle. "It's raw whiskey and molasses, and it'll eat your guts clean out!" They passed by livery stables, banks, stores, and the state capitol, a pretty white building with a spire that stood behind a white picket fence. "Yeah!" Caleb said softly to himself. "This is where we'll stay for a while. Until we're ready to roll out to Oregon. This will do us just fine."

Moody's Merchantile was a large outfitting store that smelled of leather goods, grains, and tobacco. Long shafts of dusty sunshine fell on shelves stacked with tin plates, and cups, lanterns, buckets, shovels, clothing, blankets, tobacco, jerked meat, and staples. Barrels of oats, grains, rice, and wheat stood against the walls and in the aisles; boots, baskets, and tools hung from the heavy rafters. This was where Caleb worked.

Moody's was a hub of activity year around. In winter, men gathered around the big pot-bellied wood stove and swapped stories about going west, or told tales about where they'd come from "back home." Moody's was where women shopped and gossiped and worried about the long trek west they'd be taking, come spring.

From early April to late June, sales at Moody's boomed with a din of noise as men, women, and children milled about, crowding the narrow aisles and jostling each other in their clamor for goods. Huge wooden boxes and barrels were then hoisted up into waiting wagons, scraping and squeaking against the heavy wooden floors and shoved into place. The emigrants were preparing to go.

Day after day Caleb ordered and sold supplies, kept inventory, and helped load gear. Smithy's job was to sweep the store twice a day, but Smithy always found time to draw, and emigrants and townspeople got used to seeing the boy with the curly brown hair sitting on the big porch in front of Moody's, sketching scenes of the frenzied activities. He drew pictures of "greenhorns" learning how to ford the river and yoke up teams of balking oxen. He sketched the huge prairie schooners, some of them emblazoned with slogans: OREGON OR DIE. ON TO OREGON. IT'S CALIFORNIA OR BUST!

One day Caleb talked to a Pawnee horse trader and bought a sorrel for himself and a smaller bay for Smithy. He named his horse Sweetface, and he called Smithy's horse Dolly.

Then, in January 1848 a tall, lean man with reddish-brown hair and a full beard walked into Moody's. He had a keen eye, and he poked with care through the shelves and racks, while puffing quietly on a pipe. Caleb had never seen the man before.

"Can I help you, sir?" Caleb asked.

"Looking for now. You got good stuff here. Good gear for folks that'll be gathering here come spring, looking to head out west." The man walked over to where Caleb stood, leaned on the heavy, scarred counter, and studied Caleb's face.

"Been working here long?"

"Some, yeah."

"You from around here?"

Caleb shrugged. He didn't like the man's question. He felt the old knot of fear in his gut, and he moved away and fiddled with setting some knives straight in a display case. The man didn't move to where Caleb had moved, but the man pressed him.

"Reason I ask," he said, "and I respect your want for not talking, but the reason I ask is some years back I came out from Philly. Brought out some folks heading for Oregon, and they hired me on as guide. There was a girl traveling with them. A crippled girl with the whitest hair I ever saw. She was asking me and other folks, like a lot of folks do while they're traveling out, if I knew of a young fella about your age. Said he had blond hair and blue eyes, and a dent like you got in your chin. Goes by the name of Pridentz, she said. Max Pridentz."

Caleb's knees felt like water, his stomach turned, and he felt sick as an old dog, but he kept his voice easy as he rearranged the knives.

"Never heard of him, mister."

"Hm. Well, the girl, she left the train at Fort Hall and took up with an Indian there, and as I say, that's been some time. But the reason all this sticks in my mind is that I've just come back from Oregon, and when I was passing through Hall, I seen the girl again. She hasn't forgot the lad and she asked me again to keep an eye out. So I'm telling you the same thing. Lots of times folks get separated, and word of mouth works best."

Caleb shrugged. "I suppose so."

The man walked over to a shelf stacked with tin goods. "Come spring, probably April, I'll be starting to load up for a roll west. By the way, name's O'Shea. Padraic O'Shea. Known as Paddy, or just O'Shea. I aim to take a bunch of folks on out to Oregon and the Willamette Valley."

O'Shea put his hand out, Caleb shook it, and as O'Shea looked at him with steady, brown eyes, Caleb had the distinct feeling that O'Shea knew damned well he was talking to Max Pridentz. Then O'Shea left.

Padraic O'Shea! Caleb walked over to the window and watched him mount a black horse. So that's Paddy O'Shea! That clinched it. Even if this man did have a notion he was Max Pridentz, it didn't matter. This was the man he would go with. This was the man he'd been waiting for. And in spite of the man's questions, Caleb liked him a whole lot.

Later that evening as Caleb walked down the street toward the Silver Moon Hotel, he whistled softly. From what he'd heard, they didn't come any better than Paddy O'Shea! Fur trader! Trapper! And a Rocky Mountain man! A man who had lived on the edge of civilization all his life! Lived with Indians too! Now, Caleb thought, O'Shea says in April he plans on making another roll west. In three months, Smithy and I'll be going to Oregon with Mr. Paddy O'Shea!

The lights of the Silver Moon Hotel glowed up ahead; the tinkle of piano keys and laughter spilled out into the cold winter night. Caleb smiled, and picked up his stride. He'd sure have something important to tell Janie Marie tonight. He wondered what she'd say when he told her he'd be leaving here, come spring.

Chapter 8

April 14, 1848

The April night held the promise of spring; the windows of the Silver Moon were open wide. Inside the hotel men paid high prices for the pretty whores and sometimes higher prices at the gambling tables.

Caleb sat at one of the tables playing five-card stud with four men—Stilly Peterson, George McVey, Clancy Evans, and Leonard Hagen. Caleb knew Peterson, McVey, and Evans. They'd all signed up in March to roll west with O'Shea.

Peterson, a tall, sandy-haired man with an easy smile, was married to a pretty, dark-haired woman named Lucy Ann. They had two children, and it was obvious another baby was on the way. They came from Pennsylvania and planned to start a new life farming in the Willamette Valley.

McVey was an older fellow. His wife, Margaret, a large, big-boned woman, had a lot to say, but she also had a twinkle in her eye and a hearty laugh. The McVeys came from Illinois, and had fifteen-year-old twin boys, Danny and Dooley.

Evans and his wife, Lorene, had left a cotton plantation and Lorene's wealthy family back in Virginia. Lorene was shy, and hardly said a word, but Caleb bet she was tough.

Caleb didn't know Hagen, a short, stocky man with a red face and dark beard. Hagen had come to town only two days ago and he'd come into Moody's and told Caleb he was a farmer from Ohio. He'd said he wanted to sign on with O'Shea's wagon train for the trek west, and he'd wanted to know what gear he'd need to buy. Caleb had told him where he could find O'Shea and he'd advised him on what he'd need.

The next day Hagen had returned, this time with his wife and three children. His wife looked like a child herself, and all she did while they were in the store was yell at her brood and twist at a piece of her hair.

Hagen was also a man full of opinions and complaints. He'd complained about the cost of flour, salt, and coffee. Then he'd raised a fuss when he'd found out how much the trek west was costing him, and he'd said maybe he shouldn't have uprooted his family, but stayed put. Caleb had shrugged and told himself they were probably poor folks who deserved a better shake out of life. Maybe going west would help.

Tonight Hagen had come into The Silver Moon, and he'd asked if he could join the poker game. It was a good game; the cards were running in Caleb's favor. There were the usual onlookers. A couple of scouts, wearing fringed buckskins stained black from grease and old blood and smelling strong of smoke, the woods, and liquor, stood quietly while moving their chew. There were three other men with wild hair wearing miners' high black boots, and there were two "greasers"—Mexicans with dark skin and glittering eyes who had come in today from Taos on the Santa Fe trail. And then there was Janie Marie.

68

Dazzling thoughts of Janie Marie had wrapped Caleb's mind in a web of lust for over a year when he'd first started coming to The Silver Moon Hotel. She'd worn a green velvet dress then and long diamond earrings had dangled from her ears. Her blond curls had been piled up high on her head, and her blue eyes had teased Caleb as she called to him.

"Hey! Hey now! Caleb Pride!"

Beautiful Janie Marie. The most sought-after whore in town. Caleb's passion for her had consumed him; he'd thought of her day and night. The way her tongue played in his mouth and in his ear; the feel of her hands running over his back, and her fingers caressing his buttocks then trailing around to his belly, and down his belly, teasing him, caressing him.

"Darlin'—Cal! No! Not now, darlin'! Hold on now!" and her hand had held him just right. "Darlin'," she'd said to him once. "You're sure one of the best I've ever known." And she'd put her tongue on his belly, and she'd laughed, delighted with his hot aroused maleness. And she'd taught him, she'd mounted him, and she'd let him do things with her she hadn't let other men do because she felt for Caleb feelings she'd not ever felt for another man.

All this time Caleb had come to the Silver Moon, night after night, and he had watched Janie Marie as she'd moved among the tables and the men. In winter, she'd worn gowns of dark green, red, and white velvets; in summer her dresses were pink and yellow and lime green and lavender. Caleb would wait for her playful glance and her dazzling smile. And his heart would pound as she fingered a glittering brooch that lay at her beautiful throat, just above the delicious crease at the top of her snowy white breasts.

Later as they had lain together, he'd feel his hardness and his loins had burned, wanting her. And when she had let him enter her, he'd explored the warm, soft, mysterious place that held for him a wild joy and heights of ecstasy. More that he'd ever imagined.

But later that same night, he'd watch Janie Marie as she would banter and laugh and tease other men. And when she cursed and gambled and drank, Caleb's heart turned to ice.

One night he had told her he loved her, and he'd asked her to marry him and go with him out to Oregon. Janie Marie had laughed. "Darlin'," she'd said, trailing her fingers through the warm, curly hairs of his chest and on down his belly, "I ain't one of your kind, Cal. And never could be. But that ain't stoppin' me from lovin' you, and enjoyin' you a whole lot."

When Caleb had told Janie Marie in January that he planned on going out to Oregon, come spring, and he'd be going with the great guide, Paddy O'Shea, she hadn't had a lot to say. But a couple of weeks later she'd told Caleb she might go too.

"I've given thought to going west to Oregon myself, Cal. Or maybe to California. I sure ain't left nothin' here and it might be a real lark to find me a little wagon and hitch up and go."

"Janie!" He'd laughed. "You have to have money, and gear. You can't just pick up and go. And who are you going to travel with? A woman traveling alone? I . . ."

Janie Marie, sitting in front of her dressing table, had looked at Caleb through the mirror; her eyes narrowed as she'd tied a blue ribbon in her hair. "I'll tell you what, Cal," she'd said softly. "If I decide to go, I'll go. I know where I can get the money and all the gear I'll need. So don't you bother your handsome head about that. Besides, if I go, I promise you, Caleb Pride, you won't be sorry. I sure do promise you that."

* * *

Janie Marie now watched the poker game, her blue eyes cool, her face expressionless while Caleb detected changes in the play that meant the game would soon end. He knew his cards, and all evening he'd watched the growing stack of coins in front of him. He'd played carefully. If he won tonight, it meant that tomorrow he would buy an extra yoke of oxen. It wouldn't hurt to have that along for the roll west.

He knew Peterson, McVey, and Evans were good players, but they weren't as cautious as he was. Caleb now had their money and his silent estimate of the stacks in front of him was thirty-eight dollars.

But Hagen's play was different. Caleb knew he'd won all of Hagen's stake and Hagen had barely spoken during the play of the last hands. Hagen had also bought himself a half-bottle of whiskey and had drunk nearly all of it himself, not offering to pass it around the table as was the custom of most gambling men.

Caleb won the next hand with a pair of kings. The four other men stayed because each had a pair showing on the first three up cards. But Caleb had a king in the hole and caught the other on the last up card. There was now eight dollars in the pot.

Stilly Peterson pushed his chair back from the table. "That's all for me, boys. Cal, you got all my cards." He looked at Caleb with a twinkle in his eyes. "Lucy Ann's expecting me. Best be leaving."

Caleb nodded and smiled at Stilly. "See you at the auction yard tomorrow."

Stilly laughed. "No, Cal. I've spent my coins. But I'll see you at camp tomorrow afternoon. We've got business to tend to." Then Stilly tipped his hat toward the ladies in the room and left.

"Deal 'em," Hagen said, taking another pull from the whiskey bottle. It was Caleb's deal.

Caleb dealt the four down cards and slowly snapped

71

the up cards around the table. To McVey, a two of spades; to Hagen a queen of diamonds; to Evans, a seven of clubs; and to himself, the six of diamonds.

"Queen bets," Caleb said.

"A big dollar for this queen," Hagen replied.

Caleb looked at his hole card, the jack of diamonds. Two diamonds now in his hand. "Call," he said, shoving a dollar into the pot.

"I'll call you." It was McVey this time who flipped his dollar into the pot.

"I'm through." Evans folded his hand and leaned back in his chair, but he didn't move from the table.

"Pot's right," Caleb said as he started to deal the second round. McVey caught another two for a pair, Hagen got a ten of spades, Caleb turned himself the nine of diamonds. He now held three diamonds in his hand.

"Pair of deuces bets," Caleb said.

"Hell." McVey smiled a wry smile. "This game's changed its course. Try it for another dollar."

"You're called, McVey, and I'll raise you fifty cents," Hagen said.

"I'll see that raise," Caleb answered, slowly pushing six quarters into the growing spread of coins on the green baize. McVey called the raise, hoping to make his small pair last.

"Pot's right," Caleb said, and he snapped over the next card. "Here's what you're looking for." It was a nine of hearts. "No help, friend." He then snapped the next card across to Hagen. Queen of Diamonds. Hagen now had a pair of queens showing. Caleb turned the three of diamonds on his three other diamonds showing. He now had four diamonds.

Digging into his pants pocket, his eyes rubbering around the room, Hagen pulled out a handful of silver dollars, which he held in his fist over the spread of bets in the center of the table. He pushed out two of the dollars

72

from his fist with his thumb and they clinked on the pile of coins.

"Two dollars just to look at them queens, and a lot more to look at this hole card," Hagen said, tapping his finger on the down card and glaring at Caleb.

Caleb calculated with care. There were nearly nine dollars in the pot. Almost four times what he'd brought into the game. He'd have about sixteen-to-one odds now to draw another diamond for the flush he needed to beat Hagen. McVey was only holding the deuces and would fold under the attack of Hagen's two-dollar bet. Caleb had to stay or let Hagen bully him out of the hand.

"I'll call you, Hagen," Caleb said.

"I'm done." McVey flipped his cards over with the edge of his hole card.

"Deal 'em." Hagen spat out the words.

Caleb turned a six of clubs into Hagen's spread. "No help for the queens." He paused for a moment before snapping over his last card. It was an eight of diamonds. A diamond flush. He laughed. "Well, well. Look at all those red cards. Your bet, queens."

Hagen didn't pause. "Three dollars for you to stay in this game, Pride." Hagen was angry, his face flushed.

Caleb looked at Hagen's card, then he placed his left hand in front of his hole card to shield it from Hagen and he slowly picked up one corner. He knew it was the jack of diamonds, but he played it slow to wear Hagen down.

"That little look made it worth calling you and raising you back three dollars, Hagen."

"Damn!" Hagen took the last drink from his bottle and wiped his mouth with the back of his hand. "I'll see that." He dropped three dollars on the pile. "And raise you back." He dug deep into his pockets. "Seventy-five cents!"

"Call you, Hagen. Just call."

"What you got, Pride?" Hagen rose from his chair

73

before turning his hole card and looked down on Caleb's cards while Caleb slowly turned up the jack of diamonds and placed it neatly in a row with the other four up diamonds.

"Sonuvabitch!" Hagen stood up and smacked his fist against the table. Leaning across, his bleary eyes sought Caleb's face. "I aim to play with you again, Pride. And I aim to win."

"Sure. I'll be playin' again. But not till we get to Oregon. From what I hear, we won't be gambling on the trail. As soon as we get to where we're going, though, we'll deal 'em out."

Caleb then quietly raked in the quarters and silver dollars from the pot and sacked them in his leather money pouch.

"I tell you one thing, Hagen," McVey said. "If you're going to play with the likes of us, it's better to figure from the start you've got it to lose. Then when you do, it don't hurt so much."

"That's my business, McVey. No need to be telling me when to play." Hagen turned from the table and left.

Caleb watched him for a moment and found himself wishing Hagen wasn't among those going with O'Shea's train. He was the kind of a man who could cause a whole lot of trouble for himself and for other folks too. But then he picked up his sack of coins, and grinned at Janie Marie. He now had other things on his mind, and as he and Janie Marie walked upstairs together, Caleb decided it was a damned good night.

Chapter 9

"Eighteen dollars! Eighteen! Eighteen! Do I hear twenty! Twenty? Twenty?"

The cadence of the auctioneer's words spun out over the crowd standing in front of the auction barn. Caleb squinted in the bright sunshine and pushed his straw hat up high on his forehead. His mouth tasted bad and was dry as cotton. Too much whiskey last night. But he'd won enough gambling money to let him bid on this team of oxen. He'd bid that eighteen dollars, and was prepared to go to twenty-five, but no higher.

Putting an arm around Smithy's shoulders, he took a deep breath and waited. This team would be his bonus. If he got it, he'd name it the Five-Stud High. He grinned. Stilly, George, and Clancy would get a laugh out of that.

Aside from the feeling of too much whiskey last night, Caleb felt good. He had his yoke of strong, healthy oxen to pull his sturdy wagon made of well-seasoned hardwood. The inside of the wagon's sparkling white cotton cover was sprinkled with pockets of various sizes where Caleb had carefully stashed soaps, buttons, beads, needles and thread, tobacco, fish hooks, knives, mirrors, and medicines. Some of these articles would be used in bargaining with Indians; all the articles would come in handy.

Extra clothing, ammunition, blankets, and lanterns were stored toward the back of the wagon, along with tools and coils of rope. Barrels of foodstuffs—coffee, flour, bacon, grain, sugar, salt, rice, dried meats, and fruits—were packed in tight, along with his new Dutch oven, a sheet iron stove with a boiler, two iron skillets, tin plates, cups, and silverware. Two heavy guns, including his Kentucky rifle, hung suspended from the wagon's hickory bows.

Now Caleb paid careful attention to the auction. He didn't want somebody outbidding him without him knowing. "I'm going to twenty-five, Smithy. That's it. We've got a good roll of cash to take with us and I aim to keep that, but we can spare the twenty-five."

"C'mon, folks!" the auctioneer called. "Lemme hear twenty! Twenty dollars for this fine three-yoke team! These here critters are among the best I ever saw. Count on 'em! Count on 'em, I say! They're sure to get you to Or—ee—gon! All the way, I say, to Or—ee—gon! Or maybe a trade? A trade? Do I hear a fair trade?"

"Twenty! Twenty dollars here! I say twenty!" someone in the crowd called out.

"Hell!" Caleb pushed his hat up higher on his head and squinted out at the crowd. "Here we go, Smithy! I'm giving it one more go. If we don't get 'em, we'll forget it, but I got to give it another try."

"Twenty-five! Twenty-five!" Caleb yelled, waving his hat in the air.

"Twenty-five! I now got twenty-five! Do I hear twenty-eight? Twenty-eight, folks? I'm still at twenty-five! Going now for twenty-five! This fine team of critters! Going for twenty-five once! Twenty-five twice! Twenty-five dollars three times, and *sold!*"

The auctioneer's gavel banged down on the heavy table as he pointed his finger at Caleb.

"Sold! To you! You, in the straw hat! They're yours! Come on and get 'em. Clear 'em on out."

"C'mon, Smithy. Let's go." Caleb moved quickly through the crowd, paid the auctioneer, and with his drover's whip in hand, he moved the team out of the yard and down the road as the auctioneer's cries echoed in his ears: ". . . and a good brown mare, folks! You'll never see the likes . . . Going! Going! Gone, and *sold!* . . . And now, folks! This pretty steamer trunk. Look at it! Banded with solid copper . . . a real steal for five . . ."

Driving his new team of oxen through town, Caleb passed the bank where last week four masked men had stirred up the dust and brandished rifles before making off with five hundred dollars in gold. He passed wheelright and blacksmith shops where fiery forges were tended day and night as smiths repaired wagon wheels and set wagon tires. He passed saloons where he'd drunk many a night. And he passed whorehouses, including the Silver Moon, where the roll of dice, snap of playing cards, clinking of glasses, tinkling of piano keys, and sounds of men and women bantering and laughing were sometimes jarred by sounds of curses, screams, and gun shots. Tempers rode the wild wind here then the acrid smell of gunpowder hung thick in the air.

He thought about Janie Marie and he shrugged. She'd signed on as she'd said she might. And she'd told Caleb last night she was ready to go. Caleb had laughed, kissed her, and told her the trip was going to be a helluva lot of fun. Especially with her along, and now, with his own spirits high, he believed it too.

It was midafternoon when Caleb and Smithy joined O'Shea's train camped several miles out of town. At last count there were twenty-three wagons, eighty-four people, and fifteen herds of livestock—horses, mules, cattle, and milch cows—livestock the emigrants were taking along.

O'Shea had set the limit of wagons at twenty-four;

77

another party from St. Louis was expected sometime today. Then the train would be complete. As Caleb drove his oxen toward his wagon, O'Shea called out to him.

"Pride! Hey, there! We've been waiting for you. Meeting time. Time to elect officers. We need you. Hurry on with your cattle, then come on."

"Yes, sir." Caleb and Smithy worked fast, bedding down their oxen and making sure their camp was neat and well tended. Then they hurried toward the meadow, where a sizable crowd had gathered.

Last week most of the men who'd signed on with O'Shea had met and had elected a rules committee who had been asked to prepare a committee report with a set of rules. Stilly Peterson had been elected chairman; Stilly had appointed George McVey to draw up the report. Now Peterson stood on a stump and beat on a tin plate with a spoon, while calling out to the crowd. "Come around! Come on around, folks. Time we elected officers. And we got to adopt rules."

"O'Shea! O'Shea! He's gotta be pilot!" several men called. "Yeah, Yeah! Paddy O'Shea! He's our man."

Stilly raised his hand to silence the crowd. "Now we're going to do this the democratic way. I'm going to ask for the committee report, and you folks will be so kind as to listen. Mr. McVey has drawn up the rules. Are you ready, sir?"

"The committee is, sir," George called out, waving some papers while approaching the stump. Then, standing beside Peterson, McVey looked out at the crowd. "We recommend that Mr. Padraic O'Shea be officially elected as our pilot, and that you, Mr. Peterson, be elected captain. That Clancy Evans be treasurer, and Caleb Pride captain of the livestock guard."

"I'd be pleased to accept a second," Peterson called.

"Wait just a minute now! Just a minute, folks," Hagen's voice bawled out over the crowd. "I got to say I question the nomination of Pride. All's I know about him is that he's got a certain responsibility none of the rest of us has. That boy of his might be a whole peck of trouble and one that needs special watching."

Caleb's face felt hotter than a red ant! Hell to damnation on that man! Everybody in town, and those going west that knew Smithy, knew he could take damned good care of himself. Just because Smithy couldn't talk . . . Caleb started to shoulder his way through the crowd toward the stump, but O'Shea got there first.

" 'Scuse me," O'Shea called out. " 'Scuse me." O'-Shea's voice rose. "Now you folks are gonna vote the way you want, but before you do, I got to tell you this. You won't be making a mistake by allowing Pride this responsibility. Take my word. He's got more experience working with cattle than any of us. Worked 'em as a young lad, all the way from Kentucky to Philly."

Caleb stared at O'Shea. How in the living hell did Mr. O'Shea know that? Caleb had never told anyone anything about himself. Then he remembered O'Shea's questions last winter, and the story about Clara McCabe. Clara must have told him! The thought of Clara brought back the rush of memory of that terrible night, and he felt his stomach knot up. He sure wished that O'Shea had never met the girl.

"And as for young Smithy," O'Shea continued, "I reckon he'll get along just fine. Now that's all I'm gonna say."

Loud calls arose from the men. "We want Pride! We want Pride!"

"Quiet! Order!" Peterson cried. "You've made it plain what you want. Mr. Hagen, your objection is clearly overruled."

"Yeah! Yeah! Hear us, Peterson! We want McVey's recommendations. All of 'em. All of 'em."

"Do I hear it unanimous then?" Peterson asked.

The yeas came through, loud and clear.

"Opposed? Anyone opposed?" It was silent, except for the shouts and laughter of youngsters playing in the big camp.

"So be it!" Peterson proclaimed. "Now gentlemen, we get to the rules. I'll call for voice votes, and if I don't hear a majority the question goes to the Executive Committee—O'Shea here, and McVey, Evans, Pride, and myself. Let's hope we don't have to do that. Now, ready? Mr. McVey?"

"The committee recommends we call this train of twenty-four wagons, counting the folks from St. Louis who are supposed to come in yet today, *The Oregon Roll*," McVey shouted.

"Agreed?" Peterson called out.

"Agreed!" The shouts were of one, with whistles and shouts. *"The Oregon Roll! The Oregon Roll!"*

"Now, down to some serious business. First, I got to remind you folks, even though it's probably not necessary, that once we get across the Kansas River, we're out of the states and in Indian country. Country where laws of the United States don't mean a thing." McVey stopped talking for a minute as if wanting that to sink in. "In other words," he continued, "we're gonna be outside the laws of American government. Now that means we got to make some pretty firm rules. And this is what we've written up. I'm gonna read parts of it. Then Mr. Peterson will nail this paper on this tree here, and you can all have a chance to read it. We"ll take a formal vote on all the rules and bylaws two days out on the trail. That'll give everybody a chance to think about them and everybody has a chance to speak his own mind. But now I'm gonna give you a short summary."

McVey then read the introduction to the Constitution and Bylaws of the wagon train, noting the promises to help fellow members of the company with loss of livestock, Indian trouble, breaking wagons, and sickness.

He then explained the organization of the trek, emphasizing that each wagon would take its turn moving from the front of the train to the rear. That way the burden of trail breaking and eating dust would be fair to all. The folks nodded their heads and agreed.

"Any man who threatens the life of another will be expelled from our train," McVey shouted out. "He'll be given his gear and ordered to leave within two hours. If he doesn't leave, he'll be shot on sight. Agreed?"

A silence fell over the crowd, but when some folks called out "agreed," the rest joined in.

"There won't be any gambling while on the trail, men. What you choose to do while we're stopped over at Laramie, or Fort Hall, is up to you. But no gambling on the trail. Agreed?"

The yeas held a weak edge here, but they held.

"Sunday is the day of rest, and recognizing the Sabbath. We plan to do this whenever possible, proclaiming the same as a layover day. We'll be doing this unless the safety of our train says we can't. But we sure don't expect that to happen. Agreed?"

The crowd called its approval, and this time the women's voices were heard, even though their votes didn't mean a thing.

"Now, nobody can carry a loaded gun or pistol in his wagon. It's dangerous, and we're not gonna allow it. Too many accidents happen that way. Agreed?"

"Agreed! Agreed!"

"The Executive Committee will take care of necessary business along the way and we're pledged to mind the desires of the majority. Agreed?"

"Agreed."

Caleb smiled. This was going well. Sometimes these meetings got bogged down with bickering that could end in split trains and delays. Caleb was also pleased. He'd never thought of himself as an officer on this trek. It would be a big responsibility, being captain of the livestock, because he'd have to make sure each man took his turn of guard duty and that all day and all night, every day and night, there were enough men to hold all the animals safe, and guard them well.

"There'll be no drinking of spirits," McVey continued. "Except for medicinal reasons, and maybe a party or a wedding along the way."

Laughter rippled through the crowd, accompanied by a few hoots, but when Peterson called "Agreed?," he got the unanimous response.

"Punishment! Our committee recommends fifty lashes for three days for rape; forty for adultry. Death by hanging for murder. And indecent language will not be tolerated."

A brief silence hung over the crowd before Peterson called out once again, "Agreed?"

"Agreed!" It was a resounding response.

"One last rule, folks. The day will begin at four o'clock, when the guards fire their rifles. We'll start up then, eat, and strike camp. The herders will tend to the herds, the rest of us to our own business, while helping our neighbors, if need be. We'll begin our march each day at daybreak, starting tomorrow. Those not ready to take their proper places will fall to the rear. We expect to travel from twelve to fifteen miles every day, and that's on the conservative side. Traveling like this, under this set of rules, we figure we're gonna get to Oregon and to the Willamette Valley in good time. We figure early September, folks! And that isn't long!" McVey's voice rose with excitement and the folks caught hold of his tone so that when Peterson called out "Agreed?," he was hardly heard.

"Agreed! Agreed! On to Oregon! We're on our way with *The Oregon Roll!*"

The meeting broke up, and shouts and laughter rang out. Men clapped each other on their backs, women hugged one another, children jumped up and down as everyone felt the surge of excitement. Janie Marie, wearing a blue and white gingham dress and a red rose in her blond hair, ran up to Caleb. "I can't believe it's happening and tomorrow we go! Oh, Cal! I'm so glad I decided to go! Come and see my wagon! I've fixed it up and you'll like what you see!"

Reaching Janie Marie's wagon, Caleb pulled aside the flap, looked in, and whistled. A blue flowered carpet covered the wagon floor. Two small rocking chairs with green velvet cushioned seats stood beside a feather bed covered with a blue, green, and red satin patchwork quilt and a creamy, heavy lace coverlet. A long mirror in a gilded frame stood behind the bed, and a silver vase with red roses sat on a small dressing table.

"Lady!" Caleb said, grabbing Janie Marie and kissing her. "You sure know how to travel in style!"

Who in tarnation had bought all of her fancy gear, he wondered, and he chuckled to himself. Hell, he'd better not ask. He still liked Janie Marie. Liked her a lot. But he knew he sure wasn't in love with her, and he was glad she understood the difference.

He whistled again. "You'll be real comfortable, Janie. No need of worrying about that. Now, let me ask you this. When we get to where we're having the first dancing, I'd sure like a couple of whirls."

Janie Marie hugged Caleb's arm, looked up at him, and laughed. "We'll just see, Cal. But you sure can have the first and last dance."

"G'night then, Janie. I don't want to go, but I got to. Got to get on my way."

"Night, Cal." She watched him as he walked across the meadow. As handsome a man she'd never seen—tall and slender with blond hair and the bluest eyes, and that delicious dimple on his chin. But Cal could be strange too. Once when she'd teased him and suggested that he tie her to her bed and give her all he wanted to give her, any way he wanted, he'd refused. No man Janie Marie had ever known had refused that, and she remembered what he'd said.

"I've no heart for that, Janie. Even if it seems like fun, you're like . . . like forcing something." After that time, Janie hadn't seen him for a while.

Then there was the night she'd asked him where he'd come from and what he'd done before coming to Independence. He'd told her he'd lived in Kentucky as a boy and he'd done a lot of things, but that's all he'd said. Most men she knew liked to tell her about where they'd been, and what they'd done, even if what they told her were lies. But not Cal. He'd never said anything about himself and it seemed to Janie Marie that life had begun for Cal in Independence. As far as Smithy was concerned, all he'd ever said was that Smithy was his own boy.

Caleb's spirits were high as he made his way toward his own wagon. He'd met and talked to some of these folks, and he enjoyed greeting them this late afternoon.

"Afternoon, Mrs. Peterson," he called out to Lucy Ann, who sat under a yellow parasol on a bench beside the Petersons' wagon. A little girl sat beside her, helping her pick through a bucket of dried beans.

"Afternoon, Mr. Pride." Lucy Ann stood up, her belly poking out some against her long yellow cotton dress. Her face glowed with excitement. "I'm thinking on how grand this trek is going to be. We've been making plans on going west for the past two years. Me and Mr. Peterson, and Betsy here, and Jeremy too. And now we're about to be on our way."

"Looks like you've got good help there," Caleb said, looking at Betsy with a smile.

"Oh, my yes. Betsy's a big help, and Jeremy is good at helping his papa. Especially at cleaning fish." She laughed. "I tell you, we're pretty excited. It's going to be hard to sleep tonight."

Caleb smiled. "I sure do agree." He tipped his hat and walked on.

"Afternoon, Mrs. McVey. How are you doing this afternoon?"

The large wagon with OREGON HERE WE COME painted across the white hempen cover provided ample late-afternoon shade for Maggie McVey, who sat in a rocking chair mending a pair of boy's britches. Her thimble and needle flashed in the sun as she worked, and when she looked up at Caleb, she laughed her big laugh.

"I'm just fine, Mr. Pride. And we're all set to go." Then she frowned, put her mending down, and got up. "It's none of my business," she said while walking toward him, "but I don't know who to talk to. George and I are both worried about those Hagen children. They're hanging around, looking hungry, and I gave them some biscuits and jelly this morning. But then they came back twice, and I had to tell them I didn't have any more. It wasn't the truth, but George said we'd have to do that or we'd be feeding them every day, on top of our own boys. But it worries me 'cause if they're looking for food now, well—it's a mighty long way out to Oregon."

Caleb nodded, thinking of the money Hagen had gambled away last night. "There's not a whole lot we can do," he said. "But between and amongst all of us on the trail, I'm sure those children won't go hungry. Don't let it worry you, Mrs. McVey."

"Well, I hope to goodness you're right." Maggie smiled. "Just let me say this too. If you need help herding, both Danny and Dooley are hoping you'll ask them. They're both ready to go."

"I'll sure remember that, Mrs. McVey. Good afternoon now."

"Good afternoon, Mr. Pride."

When Caleb passed by Clancy and Lorene Evans's wagon, he saw that they were both busy packing cooking gear into two long wooden boxes that would also serve as a bed. "Good afternoon, folks," Caleb said, tipping his hat.

"Afternoon, Caleb," Clancy answered, hoisting one of the boxes into place, turning, and walking toward him. "Good meeting and I'm real pleased you're to be our livestock captain. From what I hear, you'll do a good job."

Lorene, a small woman with brown hair, blue eyes, and a big, wide smile, joined them. Caleb had a hard time thinking about Lorene Evans as a rich man's daughter, but then he remembered last week when Clancy was in Moody's one day and how he'd talked about her.

"Hell, she's doin' fine! Never did a speck of work in all her high-born days! Always having had darkies around to wait on her, and do everything from tying her pretty little shoes, to drawing her bath, and laying out her clothes. But Lorene—she's caught on quick. She can bake a batch of biscuits that'll make your mouth water for more. And you won't find slam johns better'n hers. Then last night she took it to mind to chop the wood for the fire, and nothing was getting in her way. Did a fine job, too." Caleb remembered the pride he'd seen in Clancy's eyes.

"Well, Mr. Pride, the tomorrow we've been thinking about and talking about is almost here." Lorene's face was flushed with excitement. "And I'm pleased to tell you that Clancy and I are all ready. I'm thinking it's going to be a grand time too."

Caleb smiled. "And I'm inclined to agree. See you tomorrow." He tipped his hat and walked on, hearing the good sounds. Campfires, readied for cooking the evening meal, sputtered and popped. Men and women called out to each other, offering advice.

"Eggs travel well and will hold for a while if you bury them in cornmeal . . ."

86

"When we get on the trail, hitch your bucket of milk each mornin' to the end of the wagon. At the end of the day you'll get some good cream or decent butter-milk . . ."

"And as for tarring up the wheels, let me tell you . . ."

The children played. Some were building forts with twigs and pieces of wood, some were playing tag, and hide-and-seek, and some were playing whipcracker. Others whooped and hollered while playing Indian war, and some were coming back from the river, looking proud and carrying strings of fish.

It was then that the shouts of "Gee! Gee!" rang out as a new wagon approached camp. Caleb was pleased. These people were bound to be the folks from St. Louis and now the wagon train was complete. He stood and watched the driver coax his team of oxen slowly into camp. Then, dumbfounded and unable to move or speak, Caleb's eyes followed the group. A tall man wearing eye-glasses and sporting a red-brown beard brought his team to a halt next to the Petersons' wagon and handed his whip to a young man with black hair. A red-haired girl and a dark-haired woman jumped down from the wagon as the bearded man approached Stilly and talked for a moment. Stilly pointed toward O'Shea's big tent.

Caleb felt as if he were in a dream. His feet wouldn't move, his voice wouldn't come. His heart pounded. He couldn't believe his eyes, and then he started to run. Faster, and faster, as he yelled and cried out.

"Mr. Landon! Mrs. Landon! Ben! Ben! Ellie! It's me! It's . . . it's me!" He saw them turn and stare as he raced across the meadow toward them. "Ellie! Ben! It's me!"

"Max! Max!" he heard them shout. And then Eliza's voice rose above the others. "Max Pridentz! It's you! It's you! I can't believe this! Oh, Max!"

Half-finished sentences, whooping shouts, and laughter cracked the air. Ben and Caleb whopped each other's back again and again, disbelief and joy stamped on their faces.

"Max!" Martha said, after the shouting had ebbed some. "Max Pridentz! I can't believe my own eyes!" She hugged him and kissed his cheeks, then she stood back, arms akimbo, and looked at him. "I can't believe it's so! If you aren't a handsome young man, Max! Handsome, indeed! Well, I always knew you would be!"

They all laughed and looked at each other; Caleb felt his face hot and flushed. He'd have to tell them about his name, and right away. He didn't want folks hearing his old name. Then he hit out at Ben again, and Ben grabbed his arm and slapped his arm around him.

"Well, Max, we were all talking about you just yesterday," Ben said, his blue eyes flashed with laughter. "Yes!" Eliza chimed in. "As we came up river, Mama and Papa, and Ben and me were all saying how much you'd love doing what we were doing, coming up that big river, and we wondered whether you might have already done that, and Ben and I were laughing about our old raft, and..."

Thomas held up his hand. "I'll tell you what," he said. "Let's save our funning for later this evening. Right now we've got to see Mr. O'Shea, Max. Right away."

"Max, you'll be coming by and having supper with us," Martha said. "There's no arguing with me."

Caleb nodded and grinned. "That sounds pretty good. On one condition though. And that is that I bring my boy. My boy's name's Smithy. He doesn't talk, but he's a smart one and I'll tell you about him too, along with some other things I want to say."

"Of course you bring your boy," Martha said. Eliza, who hadn't taken her eyes off Caleb for one second, felt a thud of keen disappointment. If Max had a boy, he must be married! She wanted to ask him if his wife was with him, but that would be forward and rude. Eliza knew that sometimes wives refused to make the trek west, while their husbands, and she supposed their sons, went out alone.

She felt, however, that her smile was stiff, and she was quiet, trying to cover her let-down feeling. Then, watching him cavort with Ben, she told herself that she couldn't possibly be surprised. After all, he was some older than she; and as her mama had said, he was terribly handsome. What girl wouldn't want such a fine man? A girl would be crazy *not* to, she thought. So, she told herself firmly . . . let it be, and enjoy getting to know him again.

Once more, Caleb and Ben hooted and yelled as Caleb, feeling a great warmth of pleasure, and the smart of tears in his eyes, blinked, clapped his hands on Ben's shoulder, tossed his straw hat in the air, and sprinted across the meadow to his own wagon across the way.

The big camp was quiet after supper. Fires were low and banked for the night, but an occasional snap and a lick of flame reflected in the eyes of some who were still up and hunkered close to the coals.

"Two things I'd like to say," Caleb said in a soft voice. "One's hard; the other's easy."

Nobody said a word and he looked at this family he had known so well when he was a youngster. Mr. Landon looked about the same with his red hair grayed out a little, and he wore eyeglasses now. Mrs. Landon, whose thick black hair used to hang long, was now knotted back in a no-nonsense roll, but her blue eyes still sparkled with fun. Ben, with his wavy black hair and gentle nature, seemed to take after his pa. And then there was Ellie. Grown up now, and she must *not* have married. Caleb was pleasantly surprised. It would seem as if all the young men in the hills of Kentucky would pursue such a pretty young girl. Tall and slender, with red curls framing her face, pretty green eyes, and small, round breasts poking against her dress. Ellie's turning out to be a real woman, Caleb thought. Then he turned his attention to what he must say.

"I'm going to talk about the hard part first," he said

as he paused for a moment. "That is that I've changed my name. Folks don't call me Max Pridentz anymore. No one but you people know that was once my name."

"Why would you want to do that?" Ben asked. "Max Pridentz is a good enough name."

"No!" Caleb's tone was sharp. Eliza raised her eyebrows, wondering what had happened to cause him to do that. Caleb again fell silent for a minute before he continued. "Caleb Pride's better," he said. "I have my reasons, so please! My name is Caleb. Caleb Pride."

Ben shrugged. "Well, so be it. Do you mind, though, if I call you Cal? Cal's a bit easier to say." Caleb laughed. "That's fine, Ben. Cal is fine. Lots of folks call me that."

Thomas, who had lighted his pipe, spoke up. "All I'm going to say is that I'm mighty glad you're with us, Caleb Pride."

"Thanks, Mr. Landon." Caleb then reached over and touseled Smithy's hair while looking closely at the boy. "Now I'm going to tell you all a little bit about this boy of mine. I found him in a barn in Illinois."

"Found him?" It was Eliza now who spoke up. Eliza was delighted! This meant Max . . . or Caleb *wasn't* married! Suddenly this whole trip west took on a new meaning. She would be traveling, day after day, for at least four months, with Max . . . Caleb Pride! She would get to know him again! They would have long talks as they rode west! They would find time to go fishing together, and they would find pleasant meadows and streams where they would read together, and watch the birds and butterflies. They would sing songs around the campfire at night, and when there were prairie dances, as Eliza had heard there were almost every night, she would dance in Caleb Pride's arms. Eliza was ecstatic!

". . . in the barn," Caleb was saying, as Eliza made herself stop thinking such romantic thoughts and listen to what Caleb had to say.

". . . and I saw he'd been beat, and I figured he'd

run. Maybe from his pa. But I tell you!" Caleb paused and chuckled. "He stuck to me like a bur! He and his dog. Now like I said earlier, Smithy doesn't talk, but he's smart, and even though he's a little one for his age, he's plenty able to handle our oxen, and take on responsibilities. He's a good boy, and I'll tell you this—he sure can draw."

Now it was Martha who laughed. "He's a wise boy, Max . . . I mean Caleb. I'd say he knew he'd found a good man."

Caleb's eyes glowed warm in the firelight. "He's like my own, you know. I tell you, though, I don't know his real name. He's never said. So, when I decided to take him on, I named him Smithy." Caleb then told the Landons why he'd named him that. "And his dog here . . . I named him Dog."

"What happened to Nellie, Max? . . . I'm sorry!" Eliza laughed. "That's *hard,* calling you by a different name, but I'll be not forgetting again." Her green eyes sparkled as she thought about the wonderful times she and Caleb would have. "Did Nellie grow old and die? Or do you still have her?"

"No!" Again, Eliza was startled at Caleb's sharp response. "She was killed." His voice cracked as he said it, and it was quiet around the fire for a moment before Caleb turned to Ben. "You still ride as good as you used to, Ben? You still good at gander pulling?"

Ben laughed. "Sure," he said. "But I got to say Ellie's a better rider than me. Least she likes it better. But sure, I still ride. We left old Red behind. She was too old to come, but I have a danged good horse named Babe. Bought her in St. Louis."

"I tell you, I could use your help, Ben. Every day, working with me. I've been elected captain of the livestock, and I need a man I can depend on. It's hard work, but I sure could use you if your folks don't need you to be with them."

Ben looked at Thomas, who puffed silently on his

pipe for a moment, then he nodded. "You go ahead, Ben. We can manage just fine."

"Sure!" Ben's voice was high with excitement. "I'll ride with you then! And I'm real pleased you asked me."

"I'll be coming on by tomorrow, early morning, and I'll start showing you what to do." Caleb stood up and rapped his knuckles against one of the wagon wheels.

"Mr. Landon, can I offer you some advice, sir?"

"Of course you can, Max—or Caleb. Sorry. As Ellie said, that's going to take a little getting used to, but of course. I welcome advice anytime."

"Well, sir, if you grease up and tar your wagon wheels every night or so, they won't get dried out and splintered. When folks don't take proper care, they'll lose the blamed things 'cause they fall apart. And you sure can't go far out here without wheels. I've got plenty of grease and tar, so I'll give you some of mine. Mr. O'Shea told us about that a couple of nights ago in a meeting, and . . ."

It was then that a shadow fell across the fire. "Excuse me, folks. Excuse me." It was Mr. O'Shea. "Awfully glad to have you people with us, Mr. Landon," O'Shea said, nodding his head toward Thomas, Martha, Eliza, and Ben. "And I hate to interrupt your evening, but I need Cal."

Caleb turned to Mrs. Landon. "Thanks for the supper," he said. "See you tomorrow, Ben. Good night, Mr. Landon and Ellie. Come on, Smithy, let's go."

Walking toward O'Shea's big tent, Caleb felt an elation he'd never felt in his life. He was going to Oregon with people who had loved him when he was a boy. That must be the feeling one had when one had real kin! But he also had fierce feelings about ever having any of them learn about what had happened to him, a long time ago. They must never, never know.

"Cal," O'Shea said, breaking into his thoughts. "Before you turn in, you best check the roster of men.

You can then start dividing up the guards, and you need to add Mr. Landon and his boy."

"Yes, sir. They'll be a help to us, sir, and Ben plans on riding the herds with me."

"I take it you knew them before."

"Yes, sir. Back in Kentucky."

When they reached O'Shea's big tent, O'Shea picked up the roster from the table and handed it to Caleb, who scanned the sheet, quickly counting all males over fourteen years. Suddenly Caleb's eyes stopped at two names and he felt his heart slide to his stomach. *Earl and Ross McCabe.* Scratched out, but there.

"Look all right?" O'Shea asked.

"Yes, sir." Caleb's voice shook as he put his index finger below the scratched-out names. "But I got to ask you, sir, what does this mean?"

"Those fellas came in early this morning," O'Shea said. "I wasn't around so Stilly Peterson talked to them. Said one fella had only one eye, and didn't have the dignity to wear a patch. Said the other fella's got a head that looked like a prune. Stilly said they asked to sign on as far as Hall, and not quite knowing how I felt about taggers-on and since they had all their own gear, he said fine. Well, this afternoon they came on back, shortly before you came in with your new stock. Took themselves off the list. Said they'd been hired on as freight drivers and heading out tomorrow to Taos. It was then they told me they're looking for a young fella named Pridentz. Same name as the little white-haired gal asked me about last year. I told them I'd heard some time ago that a fella by that name had gone on to California. Seems odd, don't it." O'Shea looked at Caleb, his brown eyes steady and calm. "Let me know, Cal, if you run across a fellow by that name. Three folks have now asked me about him in the last year. I guess I have to wonder why."

Caleb nodded, while looking at O'Shea straight in

the eye. "I will, sir. I sure will." Carefully putting the roster away, Caleb tipped his hat to Mr. O'Shea. Then he and Smithy walked back across the meadow, past the dying fires, and disappeared into the night.

Chapter 10

"I can't believe it. I can't!" Eliza whispered softly to herself as she pulled her shawl close around her shoulders. It was early morning with the gleam of a moon and a few scattered stars still in the sky. Unable to sleep, Eliza stood beside her family's wagon and looked out over the camp. A few people were up and moving about—here and there a campfire popped and came to life. A baby cried, a dog barked. Sounds of low voices, quick sounding, caught with excitement, drifted over the dewy meadow. Ah, this was the grand day everybody had been waiting for.

Eliza leaned her head back against the wagon and hugged herself. She would be treking out to Oregon with Caleb Pride! She smiled as she remembered the time when she'd asked him about the country called the Oregon. She remembered how that name had fascinated her and it still did. "Oregon" still brought to her mind the notion of gentle winds and clear streams; a place of glory where beautiful flowers grew; a place where she would live for the rest of her life and be utterly happy.

Thoughts of Caleb also crowded her mind. Oh, so many questions to ask him! Where had he gone after leaving Kentucky all those years ago? And why had he changed his name? Surely he would tell her when they had time to talk. And why had he decided to trek out to Oregon now? Why hadn't he gone some time ago? Surely he would explain all those things when there was time.

She thought about how he'd looked last night as she had watched him walk across the meadow to join them for supper. His blond hair was darker now than it used to be, and long, almost to his shoulders. He'd had on a gray, broad-brimmed felt hat, light brown buckskin pants, and a jacket with fringes and thrums. She and Ben had walked out to meet him, and when Caleb had smiled at her, she'd seen that his eyes were as blue as the summer skies. Just as she had remembered.

Now she reached out and touched the sparkling white hempen cover of her family's wagon. It was brand new, bought in St. Louis only ten days ago, and it was beautiful! She ran her hand down the blue wooden side, feeling the cold metal of the huge steel-banded hickory wheels. She thought about the miles and miles—two thousand miles, her papa had said—those wheels would take her and her family before finally coming to the Willamette Valley of Oregon. She took a deep breath. Yes! she thought. Yes! It's all true!

Then she remembered the time three years ago when the notion of going out to Oregon had first come to light. Will Green, Chad and Nancy's son, had been home from St. Louis, where he worked for Chouteau's American Fur Company. Will had talked a lot about going west. He'd told them about the good land that was free—good farming land. He'd said the climate was warm and mild, and there wasn't fever there as there was in so many places east of the Missouri. Will also had his keen eyes on Eliza.

One bright Sunday afternoon he'd come to call, bringing Eliza a bouquet of flowers and a box of delicious chocolates he'd bought in St. Louis. Another Sunday when Will was home, Martha invited him for dinner and he brought Eliza a beautiful lace shawl. Later he asked to speak to Thomas alone, and the two men went for a stroll. When they returned, Will asked Eliza if she would walk with him. Eliza smiled and said yes as she draped her new shawl over her shoulders, noting how perfectly it matched her pretty Sunday best dress. Together, she and Will walked out to the buckeye tree.

"Miss Eliza Landon." Will's face was solomn. "You wouldn't know it to look at me, but . . . I have a certain amount of money, and I'm thinking seriously about going west. Either to California or Oregon."

Eliza's eyebrows shot up. She was surprised to hear, again, the magic word that she hadn't heard for a time. Oregon. "And I'd be the happiest man in the world, Eliza Landon, if you'd . . . if you'd consider marrying me. I'd provide you with the best; there's not a thing in this world that I feel I can't do. And it's my plan to have plenty of money. I . . . you mean so much . . ."

Eliza touched him lightly on his arm. "Oh, Will," she said, "I'm mighty flattered. But I'm not thinking of marriage. Maybe in a year or two . . . maybe . . . and I wish you all the luck, Will, and I sure think kindly of you . . ."

Later she'd told her parents that, while Will Green was a very nice man, she wasn't interested in marrying him, even with the tantalizing notion of going to Oregon. "But," she'd said, "why can't we think on going! What's keeping us here? Our land? We can get better land, for free, in Oregon! Money? We have some, and I know that. And if we sold our place, well, we'd get plenty more! What's keeping us here?"

Martha sighed. "It's far, Ellie! It's real far, and I'd probably not see my people in St. Louis, ever again."

"Mama! Aunt Em and Uncle George have been to see us *once* in all these years. And you never get to St. Louis to see them! So what . . ."

"I'm not inclined to go, Ellie. And that's that."

Eliza knew by her mother's tone of voice there was no use in arguing further, but the notion of going was now firmly in Eliza's own mind. Why not go? Why wait for her parents? If she could get to St. Louis, she could stay with Aunt Em, and then she'd find work. If she worked, say as a maid in a grand house, she would make some money, and with the money, she'd get herself to Oregon. And that notion didn't leave Eliza's mind.

The following winter, Ben was ill with fever. And even though her mother never said, Eliza knew that he'd almost died. Once again Eliza argued for going out to Oregon, using Ben's illness this time, as the reason to go. Her mother still quietly stated her intention to stay, and Eliza knew that her father wouldn't argue otherwise on such an important issue.

But one night that early spring, the Landons were having Sunday dinner with the Greens and a most surprising turn of events occurred. Eliza noticed that Chad had been fidgety all evening, and after dinner when he and Thomas lighted their pipes, Chad took a deep breath.

"Thomas," he said, "I have to tell you my mind's made up! You know how we've been hearing more and more talk about going west, out to the Oregon states. Well, we're going. Nancy and me, to join up with Will, in California. We're packing up to go soon, and I'm telling you first, 'cause I'm going to sell my place. If you want to buy me out and can offer me a fair price, so be it. I want you to have first chance. You might want to think on it, but I'll need to know by next Wednesday when I go down to town."

A great wave of envy swept over Eliza. But then she was astounded to see that her papa didn't quietly nod his head in agreement to Chad's offer. Instead he leaned forward and knocked the bowl of his pipe against the inside of the chimney and everybody knew he was getting ready to talk.

"I've been hearing the talk," he said. "And I've been paying some attention to it. I've been talking to Martha, and while we still don't quite agree, we're thinking more and more we just might make that move west ourselves."

Eliza looked at her father with unbelieving eyes. What was this? She looked at her mother, whose expression revealed nothing, and when she looked at Ben, he grinned at her and winked.

All that next week Eliza waited for something to happen, some word that they might go. But nothing happened, except Thomas Landon didn't buy Chad Green's place.

That winter both Ben and Martha were sick with fever, suffering with chills, weakness, and aching limbs all through the long, dark months. On a day in February, Eliza made her stand. It was a late afternoon, and she had just come up the hill from school. After taking care of her afternoon chores, and preparing the lantern for lighting, she turned to her mother.

"I'm going on out to Oregon, Mama. If you and Papa won't go, I will. I'm going to St. Louis and I'll stay on with Aunt Em while I work. I know I can work as a maid in a rich house, or teach young'uns to read and write. As Max said, a long time ago, there's not much livin' here for me in these hills, Mama. And I'm planning to leave."

"Hush!" Martha's face was white as chalk. "I'll not be hearing you talk like that. You'll not be working for folks as their maid, Ellie. Now that's all!"

Eliza nodded. "That's all I'll be saying then, but I'm going."

The next evening after supper, Martha asked the family to sit at the table for awhile. She looked at her two young'uns, her eyes lingering on Ben's pale face. She then turned to Thomas, her voice firm and clear.

"I'm for going," she said. "I'm not going to stay here another winter and see Ben so sick. I'm not going to hear our Ellie say she'll be leaving us. I'm not happy, knowing as I know, Tom, how much you're yearnin' to go." She then took a sip of tea while her family sat very still. "It's February," she said. "I think we'd best prepare ourselves to go, come spring."

Thomas stood up, walked over behind Martha's chair and put his hands on her shoulders. He then bowed his head and kissed her hair. "You won't regret it, Martha," he said. "I promise you that."

Crackling fires, clattering cookpots, laughter and talk drifted over the big camp. Picking up a water bucket, Eliza started down to the creek, stopping now and then to look at clusters of tiny white flowers growing under the trees. Maybe today, as they traveled along the trail, she would find some. If so, she'd pick them, and after they made camp this afternoon, she'd put them in a jar of water and set the jar on the boxlike steps leading up to her wagon. She'd seen flowers on the steps of the Peterson's wagon last night when she had talked to Mrs. Peterson. Lucy Ann Peterson. That was her name. Eliza liked her; she had liked the look of pride in Lucy Ann's eyes when she'd told Eliza that her husband, Stilly, had been elected captain of the wagon train.

Reaching the creek, Eliza quickly dipped her pail in the rushing water and scooped it up, brimming full. As she turned to leave, she saw a girl come out of the shadowed path and walk toward her. The girl was beautiful. She had clear white skin, blond hair, and large blue eyes. She had on a blue cotton dress with a white lace collar. Eliza, aware of her plain brown cotton dress, suddenly felt plain. A feeling she'd never experienced before, but then she realized she'd never met such a pretty girl.

"Mornin'," the girl said, tossing her head. "You're Ellie, aren't you? You got to be." Eliza nodded. The girl looked around. "It's been a long time since I've been up this early. It's sorta nice, ain't it?" Then she turned and looked at Eliza closely.

"It's real nice," Eliza said. "You are . . . ?"

"Janie. I'm Janie Marie." Janie Marie laughed a low, throaty laugh. "I'm Caleb's friend. Only I call him Cal. Matter of fact, the reason I'm on this trek is 'cause of him. He told me about you last night. After he'd had dinner with you, and your mama, and papa, and your brother . . . Ben?" Eliza nodded.

"Well," Janie Marie said, "Cal *said* you were a pert, spunky girl when he saw you last." Her blue eyes swept over Eliza and she laughed again. "I believe him too."

Eliza felt her face turn red. She hated being called "pert" and "spunky." But she laughed too because right now there wasn't anything else she could do. "Yes," she said. "I'm Ellie. And I knew Max—or Caleb—years ago. So, you're a friend of his too. Well, it looks to me like we'll all be traveling out to Oregon together. I'm glad to know you, Janie Marie."

Janie Marie didn't answer. Instead she turned, lifted her skirt, and with her head held high, started back down the path toward camp. Eliza watched her while fighting a sinking feeling in the pit of her stomach. All thoughts of spending glorious moments with Caleb vanished. His heart belonged to this beautiful but rude and unfriendly girl! This . . . Janie Marie! But then, Eliza told herself, as she had early last evening, of course Caleb would have a girl. It was a miracle in itself that he wasn't married.

Suddenly she straightened her back and tossed her head. Her eyes blazed. Why should she get caught up like this with him? She had lots of other things to think about. A whole lot of things that were far more important to her than being lovesick over a *man*. After all, she'd never in a million years thought she'd be meeting up with him on this trek, and Eliza Landon was on her own way to Oregon.

* * *

The big camp teemed with activity. Smells of fresh
boiled coffee, hot bread, and bacon drifted through the
air and there was a sense of hurry as Eliza, Martha, and
Thomas stood around their campfire, ate their breakfast,
and packed away their things.

"Ben went with Max—I mean Caleb, Mama?" Eliza
asked casually as she tucked the dishpan, tin cups, and
plates into their nitch inside the wagon.

"Oh my, yes," Martha said. "Caleb came by while
you were out getting water. He had a pretty girl with him
too. The girl went on down toward the creek. Didn't you
meet her? Her name is Janie Marie. But Ben and Caleb
left together, and I have to say I can't remember when
I've seen such a smile on Ben's face. Now Caleb says we
may not see too much of either of them because they'll
both be riding with the livestock at the rear of the train.
Every day. And I guess that means Ben will sleep out
there with Caleb and the herds." Eliza smiled. She
couldn't remember when she had seen her mother so
excited or happy.

Four shots rang out over the camp. "That's the signal we've all been waiting for." Thomas cried out. "Ha!"
Eliza heard the tremor of excitement in his voice. "We're
sure ready to go!"

A flurry of activity rippled among the emigrants as
the great camp was struck. People hurried and milled
about. Oxen, cattle, and milch cows bawled. Horses nickered and blew. Laughter and talk carried over the light
gray haze of the early morning while some babies wailed.
Thomas grabbed Martha and gave her a kiss. "We're
going, Martha," he said softly. "And it's good."

He turned to Eliza, and for a moment she felt the big
warmth of her papa's arms. Then she watched with pride
as he picked up his long bullwhip. "Gee! Gee!" he called

102

out, slowly working the oxen team that pulled the Landon's wagon into position at the rear of the line.

The sun was just rising, splashing a pink and gold light across the meadow where the wagons had formed a big circle. O'Shea, astride his black horse, turned.

"Folks ready? All ready? Then let's roll!" His voice boomed. "*The Oregon Roll* is on the way to O—re—gon! C'mon, folks! Let's go!" Then, raising his right hand, he whistled three times and took the lead as the big wagon train circled out of the meadow and headed west.

Chapter 11

"We're in Pawnee country, folks!" It was the first night on the trail, and after setting up camp, Stilly called a meeting. "We're in Pawnee country, and Mr. O'Shea's going to tell us more about that. "It's important that we hear his words."

O'Shea climbed up on the big, square box that served as a speaking stump. "Mr. Peterson's right," he said. "We're in Pawnee country, and we're gonna be in Pawnee and Sioux country for the next forty miles. After that we're gonna be in Cheyenne and Arapaho country. And then it's the Shoshone, the Nez Perce, and the Paiute and Cayuse." He paused and his voice rose some.

"That's right," he continued. "We're in Indian country for the rest of the trip. Crossing over country that belongs to them, and they know it. And it's gonna be that way for the whole way and after we get there. Two thousand miles from here." He stopped, as if wanting that to sink in.

Shivers ran up Eliza's spine as low talk rippled through the crowd. "Now," O'Shea continued, and his words were measured. "Indians don't have the same ideas we have, and you folks got to remember that. For one thing, they think a man's possessions belong to everyone. And that's how they're gonna behave. What we call begging and thieving, they don't. But all of you got to treat these people with respect." Dropping his voice, he spoke slowly; it was crucial that everybody understood. "Listen to me carefully now, please. Like as not, Indians won't take your stuff if you offer them a handout or two. Eats, and little presents like most of you brought. Buckles, beads, mirrors, fishhooks . . . all that. And let me deal with them if there's call. I know them. I lived with them. And I'll say it again. There's no need for trouble, so don't look for it. Trouble this early could mean trouble later on, 'cause in spite of their own bickering among themselves, they got a good link of say-so with each other. Any questions?"

There were none.

Two days later Eliza walked beside her wagon with her mother, Lucy Ann, and nine-year-old Betsy. The Landons' wagon was second in line today, behind the Petersons'; twelve-year-old Jeremy Peterson proudly drove the Petersons' team.

"Stilly and I are depending a lot on Jeremy to do the driving," Lucy Ann said. "Especially with Stilly riding up front with Mr. O'Shea every day and having the responsibility of seeing that everything goes right. And I don't plan on doing much riding in the wagon. That kind of shaking will shake this baby so it'll come before it's ready. Better for me and it that I walk." She laughed. "But I sure do feel good, and isn't this country something though. All the wildflowers growing out there under that big blue sky."

Martha nodded while pointing out ahead where the air looked like an enormous blue bowl placed over the land. "Seems funny," she said. "There's no trees, and it's all so big and bare. It feels different." She shrugged. "We'll get used to it though 'cause Oregon's a mighty long ways."

Lucy Ann nodded. "Mm-hm. That's right, Mrs.

Landon. But Stilly told me last night Mr. O'Shea is sure pleased with all of us on this train. The one family that's cause for worry is the Hagens, and I know for fact that Mrs. Hagen doesn't pay enough mind to her own children. Two of them ran rough-shod through camp last evening and Mrs. McVey had to collar them and take them home."

Eliza laughed and rolled her eyes. "I don't think I'd want to be 'collared' by Mrs. McVey, Lucy Ann. I'll bet she's had good practice too. Raising up her twin boys. Mama, what's her boys' names?"

Martha and Maggie had spent last evening together, sitting in two of Maggie's rocking chairs where they had chatted and knitted in front of the fire until the fire had died and there was a chill in the air.

"Danny and Dooley," Martha replied. "They're Ben's and Caleb's age. Nice boys, too. They're riding back with Caleb and Ben, and from what Mrs. McVey says, they're just as tickled as Ben is to be herding with Caleb."

"Shoot!" Eliza kicked her boot in the dust and pushed her blue poke bonnet back on her head, exposing her freckled nose. "Back at Independence Camp, Lucy Ann, that very first night when Mama asked Caleb to stay for supper, well . . . the first thing Caleb did was ask Ben to ride with him." Eliza's green eyes flashed, and she set her chin. "Ever since then I've hardly set eyes on Ben. Or Caleb either. And Caleb wouldn't think of asking a *girl* to ride with him and I'm a sight better rider than Ben! I always have been."

"Don't toot your horn, Ellie," Martha said. "It's not becoming to you. You might be a better rider, but you don't know a thing about herding livestock. And besides, that's not the point. All of us women have plenty to do to keep things going right along. You'd best be paying mind to that. And I imagine, if the truth were out, there are

106

times when Ben would like to trade places with you. Riding at the rear of the train all day, eating and breathing dust, and working the livestock can't always be fun. It's also good for Ben to work with Caleb, and learn about herding. Caleb seems to know what he's doing all right."

Martha then turned to Lucy Ann. "We all knew Caleb back home, years ago. He left when he was just a lad and none of us dreamed we'd see him again."

Suddenly the wagon train came to an abrupt halt. Looking on ahead, beyond the Petersons' wagon and O'Shea and Stilly at the lead, Eliza saw a long line of tattered wagons with dirty, gray tops moving along the trail.

"It's the train going south to Taos," O'Shea called back to those who could hear him. "We've caught up with them and they're now making the swing off the trail here. We got to wait for them to get out of the way."

Eliza and Lucy Ann walked ahead to stand with Stilly and O'Shea. The afternoon wind was up, and Eliza tied the strings of her poke bonnet firm as she watched the slow-moving freight train ahead. There were no women or children on that train. Only men. Tough-looking men who yelled and cursed while snaking their whips over the long lines of mule teams. Eliza stared at the last wagon making the slow swing off the main trail. A piece of gray cloth, stretched over two of the wagon's bows, served as a ragged cover. The two drivers turned for a moment and looked back. One man had only one eye; the other man's face was a red purple color, wrinkled and shriveled; he had no hair, and one ear was only a small knob. Eliza shivered and nudged Lucy Ann.

"That man's been burnt," she said. "Bad. But from the looks of him, I bet he deserved it."

"They sure don't seem to be having a good time, Eliza. Only thing you hear is the creaky old wagons, and the clattering gear. And those men—whoa! Swearing, and spitting their tobacco juice!"

"Well, all sort of folks go south to Mexico. Isn't that right, Mr. O'Shea?" Stilly asked.

"Yeah," O'Shea said. "They sure do."

"I'm mighty glad those sorts aren't traveling with us, Mr. O'Shea," Eliza said.

O'Shea nodded and then turned to Stilly. "Cal's riding the drags today, isn't he?"

"Yeah. Cal, and the McVey boys and Ben Landon. They're all bringing up the rear. Why do you ask?"

"Um—just thinking ahead some. Well—they won't be coming by this junction for a while yet." O'Shea then raised his hand, whistled, and cried out. "Let's roll, folks! Let's roll!"

A while later Eliza saw a sign beside the trail. The sign was written in black letters on a large board nailed to a tall pole. It read THE ROAD TO OREGON, and an arrow pointed northwest. Behind her she saw the long line of bright new wagons with their sparkling white hempen tops weaving their way through the swells of green grass, making the slow turn north. Looking south, she saw the train headed for Taos, dirty specs against the blue sky. Eliza figured that by the time Caleb and the drovers got to the junction, the southbound train would be long gone. She then turned her mind to tonight. She'd heard there might be some dancing. Lordy, she thought, I do hope so. If there is, I'll wear my best dress and put a ribbon in my hair, and I'll dance with Dan and Dooley, and . . . fie on Caleb and Janie Marie!

Chapter 12

Long scissors of sunlight cut through strings of early morning clouds; sounds of distant thunder boomed across the high plains.

"Eight hundred miles to Laramie, Miss Landon, and twelve hundred miles yet to Oregon. But right now, it looks to me like there's a storm coming our way."

Eliza, who was driving the Landons' wagon, turned, smiled, and waved at Sam McIntyre, astride his big bay. Sam, a tall, thin fellow with pale blue eyes, wavy brown hair, and a small clipped mustache, had spent the past four evenings visiting the Landons, while his eyes had followed Eliza.

"Storm may be coming, Mr. McIntyre, and I'll grant you that's what it looks like from here, but let's hope we get to Alcove Spring first. That's where Mr. O'Shea wants to take us today."

Sam nodded. "That's right. With hopes for crossing the Big Blue tomorrow. But I'll bet you my shoe there'll be dancing tonight."

Eliza laughed. "There won't be any excuses like there's been the last couple of nights. We're all feeling right at home with treking; Lucy Ann found Stilly's fiddle, and Mrs. McVey told me and Mama that Danny is itching to play his accordion."

Sam pushed his straw hat back on his forehead and chuckled. "That'd sure suit all of us dancers just fine. We've been waiting now for a time when everybody's ready, and I'm thinking that time's now. Let me ask you, if we dance tonight, I'd be delighted if you'd consider saving a couple of dances for me."

"If the dancing comes on, I'd be pleased."

Sam grinned and tipped his hat. "See you then, this evening for sure."

Eliza watched him ride to the front of the train, where beyond the swaying wagon tops, the rutty, dusty trail cut a wide swath through the gentle, green swells of prairie. Lordy, Eliza thought, this country, as her mama had said, is big. Big and flat, with few trees, and it felt so different Eliza couldn't put a name to it. Even the wind felt different. Back home the wind could be sassy, and a bother, but here, what looked to be a slight breeze coming off the land would billow and flap the heavy wagon tops, and lift untied poke bonnets off the women's heads quicker than a wink of the eye.

But there was no wind today. Today the air was heavy and insects buzzed, and by midmorning the thunder had faded to a far-off rumble. The wind would come though, soon enough. And Eliza, who had heard plenty of stories about prairie storms, knew she wouldn't have long to wait before she'd have her own story to tell.

Alcove Spring on the Big Blue. It was afternoon when The Oregon Roll set camp, and still the storm held back. As Eliza walked down to the river to fill her water buckets, she looked anxiously at the dark clouds against the horizon. After filling her buckets, she stood and watched O'Shea set his tent farther down the river. O'-Shea had no wagon, but his tent was large, and as was his custom, he always camped apart from the others. Eliza

110

watched him quickly set the heavy pegs and tie the canvas down tight. Then, mounting his horse, he galloped away on one of his scouting expeditions. Eliza smiled, thinking what a strange man Mr. O'Shea was. A man who liked roaming desolate country alone, a man who had lived with Indians, and a good man who knew a lot. Eliza held him in high regard, knowing he had been out to the Oregon country many times.

It was a busy camp that late afternoon. Axes rang as the men and older boys chopped wood from stands of ash, sycamore, and elm trees. Eliza helped Thomas lash three slender tree trunks under their wagon, heeding Mr. O'-Shea's warning that during the days ahead wood would be hard to come by.

Thomas then helped Clancy fix a wobbling wagon wheel; Martha took a large ball of bread dough out of a pan, and slapped it and kneeded it on the small, squat bread table Thomas had made for her, while Eliza set the cooking fire. Eliza liked this time of day. She liked the sounds—pans thunking on top of ovens; people visiting each other, laughing and sharing stories and advice. She liked the smells—of fresh-baked breads, coffee, beans, salt pork and bacon mingled with the pleasant smell of the wood smoke and campfires.

Pulling turnips and potatoes out of a sack, she started cutting them up for the stew left over from the nooning today. Supper tonight would be earlier than usual because everybody was set on the dancing. Eliza could hardly wait.

"Ellie! Mrs. Landon!" Eliza's heart quickened as she looked up from her work to see Caleb striding toward her camp. He had on the same good pants and shirt he'd worn back at Independence when he'd come for dinner, and as he held up his hand in greeting, she heard him shout with a tease in his voice, "I'm coming on by."

Eliza felt pleasure and delight wash over her as she

111

waved back. "We're real pleased to see you coming on by too," she called. But as she ran her fingers through her tangled hair, she was aware of her plain dress, and she felt that she looked a mess.

Shoot, she told herself. I can't be looking nice, expecting Caleb to call every night, or I'd be going crazy. Putting her knife down, she started out to meet him, smiling, so pleased he was coming to call.

But her smile quickly faded when she saw Janie Marie run across the meadow toward Caleb. She and Caleb then talked for a moment, Caleb took Janie Marie's arm, and they walked away.

Eliza was furious. How dare this man start to come to her camp, as if to pay a call, and then become distracted like that. Who did this—this oaf think she was? Eliza turned on her heel, knowing very well that she'd looked like a fool. Holding her head high, her face flushed with embarrassment, she bit her lips and vowed that nothing like that would happen to her again, and she had best forget the ill-mannered Caleb Pride.

It was with anger that she heaped the vegetables in the stew pot. She then picked up the milk bucket. She would walk out to where the livestock were grazing on the green, rich prairie grass. She wouldn't be around in case Caleb later decided to call.

Making her way through camp, she passed Smithy, sitting beside the McVeys' wagon, his head bent over a large drawing pad.

"Smithy!" Eliza called out. "Come and have supper with us tonight." Smithy jumped up and grinned, while holding his drawing out toward her. Eliza looked at it and laughed with delight. "It's beautiful. What a beautiful wagon! With an eagle painted on it! And I like the name. *The Lone Eagle*. And there's Dog sitting beside the wagon, with Papa and Mama. It's grand."

Smithy thrust the drawing toward her and Eliza

realized he wanted her to keep it. She nodded, then he gestured toward the Landon's wagon and back to his drawing of the big bird.

"Ah, you want to paint a picture of this bird on our wagon?" Smithy smiled and nodded.

"That's a splendid idea," Eliza said. "We'll ask Mama and Papa tonight. I know they'll like it fine. But now come with me. I have something to show you."

Putting his drawing pad and pencils inside a bag, Smithy joined her. As they walked out toward the pasture, Eliza watched the boy, wondering if Caleb had ever tried to get him to talk. Had he really tried, or was he so taken with that silly blond goose of a girl named Janie Marie that he couldn't think beyond his own rude nose?

Once the milking was done, Eliza clamped the heavy wooden lid down on the bucket and rubbed the cow's nose. "You're an old princess, you are," she said. "Nothing riles you. Here we are, hundreds of miles from home, and you're still giving us milk like you were back in your own barn in Kentucky."

Then, putting an arm around Smithy's shoulders, she pointed out at drifts of sparkling blue and yellow flowers. "Look," she said. "This is why I asked you to come with me. Look at the buttercups and bluebells. Those are flowers you might want to draw. Let's go pick some and . . ."

A cloud of dust moving in the direction of the camp caught her eye. She watched the dust closely. It could be Robidoux trappers coming in from Fort Laramie. Just this morning Eliza had stared, wide-eyed, as the wagon train had passed five grizzled men who looked like they'd never spent a day of their lives in a civilized place. They'd been riding mules as they led a string of bulls laden with mounds of stinking buffalo hides, surrounded by swarms of flies.

"We come out of Laramie," one of them had called

out. "Heading for St. Joe. Pawnee and Sioux are still fighting on ahead. Not paying much mind to white folks."

Eliza had learned from Sam who they were. "Buffalo hunters, or trappers. Probably working out of St. Louis. They also work the buffalo and they know country west of the Mississippi like the palms of their hands. Every bush and tree—they know. I've heard O'Shea used to do that kind of work. That's a reason why he knows the country so well."

Eliza had been repulsed by the men, but also awed. Again she knew she was looking at a strange breed of men. But now she knew she wasn't watching trappers, or white men. She was looking at Indians. She could see their nakedness and their long feathered lances.

"Come, Smithy, it's best we get on back to camp." Eliza tried to make her voice light as she picked up her milk bucket. Smithy stared out at the dust for a moment, looked at Eliza, and nodded.

"Ellie! Smithy! Company's coming, and it's best you be here when they arrive." Martha Landon's quick stride matched the tempo of her words as she approached Eliza and Smithy, and they all walked rapidly back to camp.

Six loaves of fresh bread sat on top of Martha's Dutch oven. Eliza laughed. "I'll bet those Indians are going to want some of your bread, Mama. Remember, Mr. O'Shea said we should offer them food. That seems reasonable, seeing as how we're crossing their land." Eliza felt giddy with excitement, but uneasy. She hoped Mr. O'Shea had returned, but if he hadn't, Stilly would do his job just fine.

Fifteen Pawnees, eight men and seven women, rode into camp. The men held lances, decorated with blue, black, and red feathers and clusters of brass bells. As they rode, the only sounds to be heard were the soft thudding horses' hooves and the tinkling bells.

Eliza had seen Indians back in Kentucky and she'd

seen them hanging around St. Louis and Independence, but she'd never seen Indians on their own land and removed from white men. She felt her mouth go dry as sand, her eyes felt stretched out of their sockets, and her skin prickled from her scalp to her toes. She was fascinated, awed, and afraid as she stared at the warriors. Their heads were clean-shaved, except for one long tuft of hair drawn up into stiff plumes, roached, and decorated with brilliant blue and red feathers. Their high cheekbones blazed with slashes of red paint. They were naked down to their waists, and their mahogany-colored skin glistened in the sun. They wore fringed buckskin pants, decorated with bright beads, and they rode bareback on horses bearing black and red handmarks and hoof marks. The lead warrior's horse had a rectangle painted on its neck.

Eliza stared at this warrior. A heavy gold chain gleamed against his naked chest and loops of bright quills decorated his ears. His glittering eyes swept the crowd, and when he looked at Eliza, she met his gaze while her heart pounded so hard she was sure he could see it beating under her dress. She felt her hair all prickly on her head as she was sure that his eyes burned into her soul. Lowering her eyes from his, she saw the long flowing tresses of scalps dangling from his jeweled warrior's belt; one of the tresses was the color of light cream.

Eliza's knees were as water as she turned her eyes to the women. Seated in heavy wooden saddles decorated with brilliant beads, they rode tall. Blue and white feathers and brilliant red painted porcupine quills were woven throughout their long braids. Bright quills and sparkling glass beads decorated their white buckskin dresses. They were the most beautiful dresses Eliza had ever seen.

Nobody spoke as one warrior, carrying a rawhide pouch in his left hand, joined the lead warrior. Surely, Eliza thought, these two men are chiefs. As Stilly approached them, Eliza sensed his uneasiness, noting little twitches working along the side of his set jaw. But Stilly smiled a tight smile and held out a knife with a packet of tobacco. The sun reflected on the gleaming knife blade as the chief accepted the presents, turned, and said something to his people, who had gathered behind him. Stilly stood aside, and the Indians proceeded to ride through the camp.

Then some of the Indians dismounted, and as they strolled from one camp to another, they picked up whatever caught their fancy, while looking at everything and everybody with curious eyes. One Indian woman, holding a washboard in her hands, laughed while running her fingers over its grooves; another woman picked up Stilly's fiddle and examined very carefully. Lucy Ann quickly offered the women two small mirrors and some brass earrings. The women smiled, put down the washboard and fiddle, took Lucy Ann's gifts, and walked away, laughing softly and chatting between themselves.

Martha's bread caught the attention of two of the warriors. Martha smiled bravely as she broke a loaf in two and offered half to each. Eliza started to climb up into her wagon to get mirrors, buttons, and fish hooks, but the men somberly walked away.

Eliza turned her attention to the chief, who was holding the pouch and appeared to be studying the crowd. Holding the pouch out to Stilly, he ran his fingers down both sides of his face, and pointed to Stilly then to himself. Stilly, looking utterly confused, shook his head.

Suddenly Smithy broke out from the crowd and walked out to the chief. Running his fingers down the sides of his face, just as the Indian had, Smithy then pointed to him, then to one of the warriors' black horses, then he pointed south. The warrior smiled, turned, and said something to the warrior with the gold chain, who in turn said a few words to the rest of the party. Then,

116

without further hesitation, the entire party sat down and made themselves comfortable. It was obvious they planned to stay.

A few moments passed; the emigrants were tense and uneasy. This feeling wasn't helped at all when the warrior with the gold chain got up, looked around, and started to walk slowly around the camp, studying some of the women. He didn't linger long as he walked, until he saw Eliza again. He stopped and looked closely at her face and her hair. Eliza, stiff with fright, felt beads of sweat on her forehead and her heart pounded so hard she could feel it in her head. But she saw, out of the corner of her eye, her papa beside her, a cool smile on his face, and she willed herself to hold this warrior's gaze. It was then that she realized that she was looking at a remarkable face; a handsome face with a glint of humor in the bold, black eyes. Abruptly turning from her, he cast his eyes on Janie Marie, who stood beside her small wagon, not far from Eliza.

Janie Marie, her hair gleaming in the sunlight, smiled easily at the warrior as he walked slowly toward her. Then she said something that caused the warrior's eyebrows to raise. And taking his hand, they both climbed up inside Janie Marie's wagon. Within moments they reappeared, the warrior wearing a beautiful satin patchwork quilt wrapped around his shoulders, affecting a shawl. He then sauntered back to his people, some of whom made a fuss over the pretty quilt.

The tension in the camp had eased, and some of the Indians were involved in playing a game, rolling small carved bones like dice. Others seemed content to sit quietly and watch the emigrants as they tried to resume their evening chores.

In a flash the peaceful scene changed. Jeers and angry words cut through the air as Hagen ran up to the warrior wearing the quilt and tugged at it.

117

"Take her quilt off your stinking body. Take it off!" Hagen cried, clawing at the quilt. The Indian appeared unruffled as he stood, ramrod stiff, holding on to the quilt. But the warrior carrying the pouch stood and started to speak. At the same time Stilly approached Hagen. "Stop it, you fool! Hagen! Stop it!"

Hagen turned, his eyes wild with rage. Stilly grabbed Hagen, but Hagen swung at him, and knocked him to the ground. Hagen then kicked at the pouch-carrying Indian. His boot hit the man's hand and sent the pouch flying, spilling and scattering its contents on the ground.

"God damned savages!" Hagen cried.

Eliza stared, dumbfounded, at the things on the ground. There was a small pipe carved out of stone, a few dried corn kernels, dried beans, a small bunch of blue feathers, and a dried, withered thing Eliza couldn't identify. Nothing looked as if it had any value at all.

"God damned savages!" Hagen screamed as he started toward the quilt wearer. "Don't have any right taking our stuff. Not even from a god damned whore! Git on out of here! Git!"

"You bastard!" Janie Marie's cry was shattering. "Bastard!" Holding her long skirt just above her boots, she raced across the meadow, stopped in front of Hagen, and spat in his face. "Bastard!" she cried out again, her mouth curled in contempt, her eyes blazing. At the same time Stilly and George grabbed Hagen and were leading him away just as O'Shea galloped into camp.

O'Shea quickly scanned the scene, dismounted, carefully picked up the scattered objects, and walked up to the Indian who had been carrying the pouch. The two men conversed in quiet tones, and the quilt wearer said something in a tone that caused fingers of ice to crawl down Eliza's spine. All the Indians then mounted their horses, and in moments were gone.

O'Shea's eyes rested on Hagen, who stood glaring at

118

the emigrants. O'Shea was silent; nobody moved. The expression on O'Shea's face was cool. It was also the expression of a man wanting to kill. His voice was soft.

"You must be mad, Hagen," he said. "Now, I'm going to say one thing to you, and you listen well. If you ever take it to mind to do something like that again, I'll ask the executive committee to see that you leave this train, and that you never come back."

O'Shea then mounted his horse and rode out of camp, not far behind the trail of the Pawnees.

The Big Blue glistened in the glow of evening, and the camp smelled of pungent wood smoke and cooking. Stars glittered in the prairie sky and a new moon showed its face. It was a glorious night on the great plains.

But there wasn't any dancing that night. Nobody moved to start it up, and after supper, O'Shea rode back into camp. For the first time on this trek O'Shea directed that the wagons form a circle, each wagon connected to another by the wagon tongue and heavy chain. Everybody knew this was a precaution against a possible Indian attack.

It was dusk when Thomas and some of the other men walked over to talk with O'Shea. Later, many of the emigrants gathered at his camp, where they sat around a large fire, their somber faces reflecting concern. Eliza, Ben, Martha, and Thomas sat close together, Thomas with his arm around Martha's shoulders. The Petersons were there, and so were the McVeys and Sam and Clancy and Lorene. Smithy was sitting close to Caleb, who sat beside Janie Marie. Eliza turned her full attention to O'Shea.

"We were honored today to be visited by worthy people," O'Shea said. "A great Pawnee chief named Thunder Eyes, an old friend of mine, sent two of his sons,

119

Chief Two Bears and Chief Red Cloud, to give to us words of welcome and advice. Accompanying these chiefs were members of Two Bears' and Thunder Eyes' family. I know them all because I lived with them one winter."

O'Shea paused, his eyes reflecting sadness. "It's the case," he continued, "that Thunder Eyes is cousin to a Mandan named Tomschini, a troublesome fellow at best. And one of the reasons these people came to visit us today was to tell me news about Tomschini. To warn me, and you folks too, about possible trouble ahead. Thunder Eyes himself would have come, but he is an old man and no longer rides well. So he sent his family."

Again, O'Shea was silent. The fire popped, a man in the crowd coughed, and then it was quiet again as the people waited for their guide to speak.

"You did a fine job, Stilly," O'Shea said. "You did just fine. And Smithy, you did fine too by letting Two Bears and Red Cloud know that I was out, but would be coming back. That was important. As it turned out, very important."

Caleb put an arm around Smithy and tousled his hair, but Smithy watched the fire and frowned.

"Now, I'm going to tell you folks something about that pouch that spilled," O'Shea said. "That pouch's called a parflech. It's made of rawhide, and most Indians decorate them with beads, and lots of color. They pack them with stuff called pemmican, slices of buffalo meat that's been dried, smoked, pounded thin, and mixed up with fat and berries. It's been used by Indians for hundreds of years, and those pouches have saved many lives, including mountain men and trappers."

Again he paused, and when he spoke, his voice was rough. "The pouch that Two Bears was carrying was given to him by his father to give to me. The things that got spilled might not look like much to you, but they mean a whole lot to Pawnees. The dried corn and beans—the

120

tobacco, the little bundle of feathers, the pipe and the dried bird skin are all part of the picture of the world to them. And if Two Bears knew you and trusted you, he might tell you that his pouch carried a song given to him by his father. That pouch and its goods are magic to Pawnees 'cause those goods are considered as coming from things not of this earth. The pouch is supposed to bring the owner power and luck. Two Bears had brought his father's own pouch to give to me. That is the highest honor a Pawnee can give to a man."

Thomas broke the silence that followed. "What can we do? What can we do to let them know we're sorry, and we welcome their friendship?"

"Nothing," O'Shea said. "They know it wasn't bad feeling all around. But they know who did what, and they won't forget."

He then stood up. "Tomorrow we'll be getting along real early. Cal here went scouting on ahead for me late this afternoon, and when we met on up ahead, we saw country we're going to want to get through as early in the day as we can. We'll cross the Big Blue, and then we'll be headin' for the Platte. You all know wood's going to be scarce. So is good water. Remember what I said. Store and save as much water as you can. Remember, too, lack of wood won't be such a trouble. You'll all get used to gathering up dried buffalo chips, and be mighty thankful for them too. Good night, now."

Folks murmured good night, and as Eliza watched Caleb drift off into the shadows with Janie Marie, she tried to resist her desire to be with him. She also fought her jealousy as she recalled how Janie Marie had faced the handsome warrior, Red Cloud. It was, Eliza thought, almost like an invitation to him. But for what? The image of an Indian bedding a white woman flashed through her mind, and she felt her face grow warm with embarrassment. But when the image returned, she played with it for a moment or two. Then the image turned to Caleb and herself and she savored it, letting herself think of Caleb's arms around her, caressing her, kissing her and declaring his love for her.

That night she dreamed about Caleb. He was standing beside a sparkling lake where a gentle wind blew softly through his hair. It was a fine dream of Caleb and a glorious dream of Oregon.

Chapter 13

Dawn had just broken when the emigrants gathered by the Big Blue, preparing to cross. "George," Stilly called out, "You and Sam snake up some logs. Then I want you to lash Hagen's wagon on top. He's not gonna make it across otherwise. Wagon's too dry and loose."

Resentment toward Hagen was keen. George started to say something to Stilly, but stopped himself as he handed his whip to Maggie and walked over to help Sam, who was already whipping logs in place, following Stilly's request.

A cool mist drifted over the river and clung to the shore where the Landons' wagon was second in line behind the Petersons'. Janie Marie was behind the Landons, and as they waited, Eliza heard Caleb's voice as he turned and called to Janie Marie from the front of the line.

"You're a stubborn one, Janie." He turned his horse and rode back to where she stood. Passing Eliza, he started to say something, but Eliza turned away. Then she heard him talking to Janie Marie. "I know you can do it, but you might consider letting me ride with you."

"Cal, you've got know-how about crossing that lots of folks don't have, but so do I. Most of these people don't even know how to ford a little stream. So you worry about them, and let me be. I'll do just fine."

"You've got the say-so," Caleb answered as he laughed and started to ride away. "But Janie, if there's dancing tonight, like I hear there's going to be, then . . ."

Janie Marie laughed. "Yes, Cal, I know. You've got the first dance."

Eliza stared straight ahead. Her face felt hot with anger. She knew Janie and Caleb had been talking about folks like her family, who really didn't know a lot about crossing rivers and streams. Where had Janie Marie learned how? And if she could do it, then why couldn't Eliza learn how? She would watch carefully today and learn what to do.

O'Shea's shrill whistle cut through the air, just as Ben rode up on Babe. "It's time to go," Ben said, grinning. "Hey, Ellie, I'm getting to be a pretty fair drover. Just ask Cal."

"You ask him, Ben. You can bet it won't be me." Ben looked at her with surprise, shrugged, and rode off to join the front of the train.

Eliza watched Ben, O'Shea, Caleb, and Stilly take their horses and lead the Petersons' oxen through the shallows and into the cold, surging waters. "Git on! Git on!" the men shouted then whistled, keeping their horses close to the snorting, frightened animals, forcing them on through the water to the other side. Then, with bellows of protest, the straining creatures pulled the dripping wagon up onto land while Ben, Caleb, and O'Shea plunged back across the river to help the others across.

"Come on, Martha, and Ellie. It's time for us to go," Thomas called out. Eliza and Martha climbed up into the wagon; Thomas and Ben urged their oxen into the water, and in moments the wagon swooshed against the current and bobbed like a boat, the river slapping against the wooden sides with smart slaps.

"Well, Mama. Now this isn't so bad, is it, now."

Eliza laughed. "But I have to say I want to learn how to take our wagon myself. It would be more fun than riding here, inside."

"Let Ben and Caleb teach you then, Ellie. And teach you well. But I have to say it's not as bad as I thought, sitting here, and bobbing along, just as sweet as you please, and feeling the water under us, rushing by. Your papa made sure he was buying a good wagon and a fine team of oxen. The best. And for that I'm glad."

The wagon suddenly lurched as the oxen, with quick tugging pulls, hauled it up on the shore. Eliza quickly jumped down and turned to watch Janie Marie, astride a beautiful Appaloosa, take her wagon across. Eliza saw that Janie Marie had perfect control of her team and kept her horse abreast of them, coaxing the wild-eyed animals through the water and on to the shore.

The Hagens were next. The wagon, lashed to the log raft Sam and George had built, looked flimzy and worn. Once in the river, Hagen flailed at his horse with his whip, the creature balked, and would have thrown Hagen in for a cold swim at best, but Sam was there. Sam quickly grabbed the horse's harness, but the raft spun around crazily, and the shoddy, ill-made wagon tipped, dumping Mrs. Hagen and the baby into the water while the two older children clung to the raft and screamed with terror.

A swarm of men came to their aid. Sam scooped up the baby, Caleb plucked one of the children off the raft, and Ben was able to reach the other. In a flash, Janie Marie, using strong, powerful strokes, swam out to Mrs. Hagen, who was beating against the water, her thin white arms as useless as straws, her eyes wide with fright. Grabbing the woman by her hair, Janie Marie jerked her head up out of the water just as Dooley reached them. Dooley reached down and, with Janie Marie's help, got Mrs. Hagen up on his horse and brought her to shore.

The women had wrapped the children and the baby

in blankets and a short time later Eliza found herself on her knees beside Janie Marie, wrapping up Mrs. Hagen in a warm blue wool blanket that Eliza recognized as her mother's. Mrs. Hagen's face was chalk white tinged with blue, and her teeth chattered as she babbled. "He's goin' t' take 't me for causing' trouble. Oh, God A'mighty, he is . . . he's goin' t' . . ." Hagen then ambled up to her. "Git up!" His voice was harsh. "You had yourself a goddamn cold bath. Now git on with the young 'uns." Then he turned on his heel and walked away.

Janie Marie and Eliza helped the woman walk to her wagon, which was now standing upright. Leaving her there, they walked together silently for a few moments. Then Janie Marie looked at Eliza and laughed. "Well, I guess I look a sight." She ran her fingers through her long wet hair. "I sure wasn't expecting that!" Then, hitching up her drenched skirt, her back ram-rod straight, her head held high, she started for her wagon, meeting Caleb on the way. Caleb grinned at her, his expression one of admiration. "I'll say, Janie. I'll say you've done enough for today."

Janie Marie shrugged. "The woman needed help, Cal, and I don't know how many folks know how to swim, so . . . But I sure do look a sight." With that she climbed up into her wagon and dropped the flat shut.

Eliza felt reluctant but strong admiration for this girl, who not only took her own wagon across the Big Blue alone, but also saved a woman's life. Where had she learned to do those things? Most women couldn't do them. And there were other things about Janie Marie that puzzled Eliza. Why was she traveling alone? Where had the money come from for such a fine wagon, the wagon team, and the very fine horse? And most important— where had she met Caleb?

Now Eliza had to admit that she'd come to like Janie's fiery spirit and she admired the things she knew

126

how to do. She also especially liked her for turning her anger on Hagen as she'd done. Maybe tomorrow she'd try to get to know her a little. It sure couldn't hurt as long as Eliza understood very well that Janie Marie was Caleb's girl.

"It's dancing tonight. It's dancing tonight or my name isn't Sam McIntyre," Sam shouted as he stood on a large rock. "Pass on the word. See if Stilly and Paddy O'Shea don't agree."

"Hell, Paddy doesn't have a say in the matter," Dooley called back, laughing and pushing his hat back on his head. "He's our guide, but he sure ain't the social chairman. Ask Stilly. He's trail boss."

Stilly jumped up on the rock beside Sam. A broad smile played on his face as he shouted out, "It sure is dancing tonight, folks! It's time for a little party, and tomorrow, according to Mr. O'Shea, we're heading on to the Platte!"

Chapter 14

A fiddle twanged, a harmonica whined, a banjo was strummed and an accordion pumped as the sounds of good times rang out across the prairie with a brand new song everybody loved. *Oh, Susanna! Oh, don't you cry for me!* And the people danced around and around the campfires, their shadows playing on the wagon humps inside the large circle.

It was a time for dancing; it was a time of joy. Nobody was sick, the crossing of the Big Blue had gone well, and the trek was moving right along.

Eliza, wearing a flower in her hair, danced with Sam, George, Stilly, Dooley, and other young men, whirling through reels, and waltzes. She saw Caleb, dressed in light brown buckskins and a white shirt with full sleeves, dance time after time with Janie Marie. Eliza found Danny McVey to be an excellent dancer, and while doing a schottische, she realized the two of them were the focus of attention as they danced their way through the various steps. Eliza looked beautiful. Her red hair, cascading down her back, was held off her face with a yellow ribbon, her color was high, and her green eyes flashed with the excitement of the dance. And it was during the next set, when she was dancing with Sam, that Caleb cut in and asked her for the dance.

"Seeing you all dressed up, I hadn't realized how grown up you are, Ellie," he said, looking down at her with a smile crinkling his blue eyes.

Eliza looked at him and held his gaze. But she didn't smile, and she kept her tone cool. "I'm as grown up to you as you are to me, Cal. You just haven't noticed."

"That's not quite fair," Caleb replied. "I've been busy, but that's not fair either. We've all been busy. It's not to say I haven't given you thought, though. I found out from Ben that you came close to marryin' Will Green, back in Kentucky. I remember Will. A nice-enough fellow. But then Ben said you had it fixed in your mind to trek west, and Will didn't mean a whole lot to you after all. I got to say I'm glad, Ellie. Glad you all came."

Keenly aware of Caleb's hand holding hers, and of the brush of his body against hers, Eliza kept her tone light. "We all decided to come," she said. "As Papa said, that night you had supper with us back at Independence, it was mainly on account of fever that we left. But I'd wanted to leave there for a long time, and as I got older, I knew, as you said once, there wasn't a lot of living there for me."

Then, not wanting this dance to end, and wanting to forget her anger with him, she laughed. "Oh Cal, remember when you left, you told me someday we might meet again, and we'd talk, for sure, about old Boone?"

Caleb nodded, his eyes never leaving Eliza's face. "I do, Ellie. I remember all of that. I remember how we talked in your house when I was hurt. I thought about that a lot, after I left Kentucky."

"Ten-minute break, folks," Stilly called out. "Ten minutes, and we'll tune up again."

"Please, Ellie—walk with me?" Caleb asked. "There's a whole lot to talk about."

Ducking out of the big circle of wagons, they walked into the dark, away from the campfires. Caleb took a deep breath. "I never did stop thinking about you," he said.

"Seems funny, but I remember a Christmas in Pennsylvania, and I wanted to be with all of you so bad. I . . . I remember seeing a pretty girl back in St. Louis one day, and I thought about you. Thinking you were married, of course. I . . ." He drew her to him, cupping her chin in his hand. "You're sure pretty, Ellie!" Eliza felt his heart beating as hard as her own, and she trembled a little, feeling the sudden heat course through her body. Then she stepped back and looked at him.

"You've not been all that friendly, Cal. In fact you were downright rude one evening when it looked to me that, for all intents and purposes, you were coming to pay a call. Dressed up and walking my way. But then Janie Marie—by the way, what is her last name? She's not allowed us to be so friendly that I feel I can call her by her first name." Eliza's tone held the edge of anger.

"I don't know her last name," Caleb replied. "But more important, let me explain. Yes, I was coming to call, but Janie told me about a problem she was having . . . a personal problem. I felt obliged to help her, and by the time I'd taken care of that, I had to peel off my good clothes and go out and meet Mr. O'Shea. And then the Pawnees came, and that day was over before it'd begun." He laughed a little nervous laugh. "Lordy, Ellie, I haven't intended on being rude. I hope you believe me. It's just that we've all got lots of work to do and lots on our minds, and I haven't had a whole lot of time to—"

"That's fine. No need to explain, Cal. But we'd best get back to the dancing."

Caleb held her gaze. "We might be getting on back to the dancing and that's fine, but Ellie—I want to dance with you again tonight."

Eliza looked at him and smiled a sweet smile. "I can't do that, Cal. I've probably promised more dances than the dancing will last and I won't go back on my word."

"Then walk with me again for a while? After the dancing?"

Eliza hesitated. "Why . . . why don't you and Janie Marie, and Sam and I walk together? That's sure to please Janie Marie. And maybe I could at least ask her her last name. That's the civil thing to do." She heard the cool tease in her words.

"Ellie . . . Ellie, let me tell you a little bit about her. She . . . you see, she . . ."

"So! There you are!" Sam's voice boomed out as Caleb and Eliza approached the circle of firelight. "Come on, Miss Landon! Let's dance!"

Again, Eliza spun around while the good times music hammered out "Old Dan Tucker." And as she danced, Caleb's words echoed in her mind. "I never did stop thinking about you . . . I want to dance with you again tonight . . ."

Eliza felt giddy and she thought her heart would burst with joy as she sashayed under the prairie moon. Then, while dancing with Dooley, she saw her parents, looking younger than Eliza could remember, dancing and laughing. And it seemed that everybody traveling with *The Oregon Roll* was dancing and twirling to the good times sound. Every time she happened to glance at Caleb, his eyes met hers, even as he danced with Janie Marie, and she wondered if there had ever been a time in her life when she'd been so happy.

"Last dance! Last dance, folks!" Stilly called out. Eliza had promised Sam the last dance, and as the music changed its tempo to "Home Sweet Home," she felt Sam's warm hands around her waist, trying to draw her a little closer.

"Finally, Sam McIntyre, we got ourselves a dance," Eliza said. "Now you won't have to go around betting your shoe anymore about that."

Sam laughed. "And what dancing we've had. Everybody's had a fine time. How about walking with me, Eliza? I'll bet you my shoe that Cal and Janie Marie are going to go. We could all four go together."

131

"That's a perfect idea. Sam. Yes, I'll go."

The music stopped and the folks milled around some before heading back to their own camps—their tents, wagons, and beds. Some of the young folks walked off together, away from the camp. It was a time to be alone for a while; a time to talk, make plans, get better acquainted, and for some, a chance for courting.

Sam, Eliza, Caleb, and Janie Marie walked out toward the herders' campfire. Janie Marie had her arm linked with Caleb's. The night air was cool and Eliza pulled a shawl around her shoulders.

"How'd you and Ben manage to get off watch tonight?" she asked Caleb.

"Four of the boys don't care about dancing. We told them we'd take extra duty for them when they want a night off. It works out that way."

"I sure do smell rain," Sam said, looking up at the sky where scattered clouds moved across the face of the moon.

"So do I." Caleb took a deep breath. "And I'll bet we get a real storm soon."

"If it storms, we'd have a layover," Sam said. "That should give Hagen time to fix up his gear. Folks aren't feeling keen on giving him a hand, but he's got to tar and grease up before we ford any more rivers. That's a fact, Cal. His gear is loose, and in bad shape. Won't hold the way it is, and could cost us all time. I told him today I'd give him a hand. I'm in good shape, and don't have family to account for."

"Hagen's a ignorant sonuvabitch!" Janie Marie's voice was hard and flat. "Ain't many men I detest, but he's one. Cal here knows. Sam and Ellie . . ." She hesitated for a moment. "You might as well know that I'm hoping to put my past behind me. I can do it too, but not with old snakes like him around." Janie Marie tossed her head. "That old buzzard came around my wagon some

132

evenings ago. Didn't say a word, just hung around, watching me and making me nervous as an old cat. I knew he was thinking about what I did to him the night the Pawnees came to visit. I ignored him best I could, and kept on minding my own business. Half expecting Cal here for supper, but nothing was fixed for sure. Then I told the old fool Hagen to get away from my camp, and if he didn't and if he tried any funny business, I was gonna call out 'rape'! He laughed at me and said nobody'd believe me cause it was *me*. I don't hold with that, and I told him so. Then I saw Cal, heading across camp toward your wagon, Ellie. So I just walked out and stopped him and told him the old cuss was giving me a rough time."

"You did right, Janie," Caleb said, nodding his head. "He's been reminded again, and in plain words, about the laws we all voted on. He'll let you alone now. I'm certain of that."

Janie Marie laughed. "Oh, Cal! You're still carrying some of the innocence you've always had. Hagen ain't about to let me be, 'cause in his old buzzard eyes I'm nothing but a whore and won't ever amount to anything else. But I will, and I'll show him and a lot of folks! I broke loose from Independence. I got my own gear, and I'm planning on a new life."

Eliza frowned. She was confused. This was the second time she'd heard the word "whore" used in connection with Janie Marie. But why? Janie Marie a whore? That couldn't be! Whores were old, coarse, rough women who wore gaudy jewels and fancy clothes, and lived in dreadful places. Women of no account at all. Cal wouldn't know any such women.

Sam spoke then, smooth as could be. "No need to put up with that, Janie. You've got friends all around. Cal, and me, and O'Shea, and . . ."

"And me," Eliza said firmly. "I'm your friend, too." There, it was said. She did want to be Janie Marie's friend. What did it matter about Janie Marie's past? It was what it was.

"So, you see," Sam continued. "I agree with Cal, and I'll bet you my shoe he doesn't come around you again."

Caleb laughed, his eyes on Eliza. "I'll bet you my other shoe the man doesn't make it to Oregon. He sure doesn't have a lick of good sense."

The image of Hagen kicking at the Indian flashed through Eliza's mind. "I detest him," she said quietly. "I think he's going to cause us more trouble, and trouble he'll find. If I were you, Janie, I'd keep my whip handy, just in case."

Janie Marie looked at Eliza with surprise. "I'm glad you agree with me, but I don't want this talked about. No point in riling up folks. I tell you, though, it's good being able to talk about that snake. Especially to another woman. Thanks, Ellie. I appreciate it."

Chapter 15

The eagle appeared to soar in flight. Flecks of yellow-gold gleamed through its dark brown feathers, the beak looked cruel; the yellow-green eyes in deep sockets appeared wild, but wise. Smithy had painted the great bird boldly across the length of the graying hempen cover of the Landons' wagon. Eliza and Lucy Ann had painted fancy letters below: *The Lone Eagle*.

The Oregon Roll moved on. Day after day the big wagons tilted and swayed as the train moved along the river lands of the Little Blue. Spring sunshine brought clear skies, and the emigrants marveled at the wild roses and drifts of wildflowers nodding their heads in the tall, green grass. But other days brought sudden squalls from the north with cold, slanty rains, chilly wind, and mud. Mud that sucked at wagon wheels and at feet and hooves alike, trapping the wagons and burying them to the hubs. Huge sticky gobs stuck to the emigrants' boots and shoes as they worked with the straining oxen, moving them through the squishy morass, sometimes gaining only a mile or two a day.

One day the train passed an Indian village with lodges made of logs and covered with large, flat, root-tangled slabs of dirt. Five raised platforms were silhouetted against the sky. Dead Pawnee braves, wrapped in buffalo skins, lay on top. Horse skeletons lay below. A woman sat beside one platform, silent, not moving as the train passed by. Eliza stared at the woman. Maybe she didn't want to hear the creaking wagons, the clopping hooves, the cracking whips, and the drivers' shouts. Maybe the high, scattered shouts and laughter of the children, their chatter and the women's chatter too, signaled change to the woman, a change she didn't want to think about.

On a day when billowy clouds drifted across the sky, *The Oregon Roll* came to the top of a knoll and stopped. It was then that the emigrants saw before them an enormous land with huge bluffs and strange towers of rock. They also saw a flat, wide, gray river. A river they'd heard was shallow, but treacherous with quicksand and silt. A river that meandered through a barren land, treeless except for clumps of cottonwood and ash rising from the many river islands. A brooding, mysterious land, it was the beginning of the great plains.

"It's the Platte, folks!" O'Shea turned in his saddle and called out. "That's Fort Child there where we can see some sign of living. That's where we'll stay the night and tomorrow, since Sunday is a layover day."

Tents and wagons surrounded Fort Child's adobe walls, while inside the fort there were a few sod huts, two stores, a tavern, and a smithy. Ragged United States soldiers mingled with emigrants, a few Indians, and trappers with their Red River carts. A bleak place, Eliza thought. Not a place to stay for long.

The next morning many of the emigrants met for a church meeting inside a small, mud-walled meeting house. Sitting in the shadowy windowless room, Eliza listened to the preacher. It occurred to her then that all the sermons, including the one today, dwelt on one thing: sin. The dark world of sin. Sin of the flesh and of men and women. Sinners all, mired in sin, condemned forever to a life of burning hell. While the preacher today worked himself up about these sinners, Eliza let her thoughts drift off to Janie Marie and Caleb. If they were sinners, were they living in hell? Eliza didn't think so. Not at all.

After the meeting, as Eliza walked with her mother out beyond Fort Child to the camp, she thought about the preaching. It continued to bother her; she might talk to her mother about it when there was time.

Most of the emigrants were busy that Sunday. It was not a day of rest as it was intended to be. Women washed and mended clothes and helped each other roll back the heavy wagon covers to air out the wagons. Barrels and boxes were repacked, some things discarded, and others reorganized. Some women then took time to read, or write in journals, or write letters that would be given to mountain men, trappers, or sometimes Indians, riding east.

Ailing animals, wagons, and weapons were tended to by some of the men, while others, along with the older boys, set out on hunting forays.

It was shortly before the nooning when Ben and Caleb joined the Landons. They both immediately set out to help Thomas mend a split wagon seam. Eliza looked closely at her brother, whom she hadn't seen for several days. He's a good-looking boy, she thought. Lordy, he's almost a man. Of course, she thought. Ben's as old as Cal. Suddenly they both look so tall against the big sky. Eliza frowned, remembering the sermon this morning. Had Ben ever had a woman as Eliza was sure Caleb had had Janie Marie? If so, did that make Ben a sinner too? That was impossible for her to believe.

"Cal and I plan on spending the rest of the day in camp, Ma," Ben called out as he grinned. "Staying on for supper, too. If that's all right."

Martha smiled. "That pleases me. It pleases me indeed."

"Ellie," Caleb called while lifting the heavy tar

137

bucket from the fire and carrying it over to Thomas to use for the seam patch. "Let's pack up a picnic and go riding. This is buffalo country, you know. Maybe we can see some before we start on tomorrow and have to put up with the danged dust again. How about it?"

"Yes, let's!" Eliza was delighted. What a perfect day this would be. She'd ride with Caleb, and as they talked, she'd learn what he'd done since leaving Kentucky. She'd learn about what he intended to do out in Oregon, and she'd probably hear about Janie Marie. Eliza smiled. She had news of her own to tell Caleb about Janie Marie.

During the past week, Janie Marie and Eliza had become friends. Eliza had been awed to learn how much Janie Marie knew about this country. It had been Janie Marie who had taught Smithy how to make powders from plants and then mix them for the paint he'd used to paint the eagle on the Landons' wagon. Dried duck dung made a rich blue, yellow came from bullberries, black from charred wood, and a brilliant green from prairie plants. And Janie Marie's own wagon cover now sported a butterfly with blue and green markings on its golden wings.

Yesterday afternoon, after *The Oregon Roll* had made camp for the day, Janie Marie, Eliza, and Smithy had walked out to a meadow where clumps of wildflowers grew. Suddenly Janie-Marie had gestured to Smithy to follow her as she'd chased a butterfly and caught it too. "Now watch, Eliza," she called out. "I'll give Smithy swift running feet. Take off your shirt, Smithy." Smithy had looked at her wide-eyed; he'd then looked at Eliza, who had laughed. "Go ahead, Smithy. Janie Marie has magic in her hands."

Smithy had pulled off his rough linen shirt and Janie Marie had gently rubbed the wilted butterfly against his chest. "Now run! You got beauty in your soul, Smithy! And your feet are fast!" Smithy had looked down at his feet and then he'd leaped away, running out to a small hill and back again. When he returned, his eyes were bright and his smile wide. Janie Marie had laughed as she'd put her arm around his shoulder. "It sure does beat all, don't it," she'd said.

"How do you know all this?" Eliza asked as they'd walked back to camp.

Janie Marie stopped and stood silent for a minute, looking out over the land. "Not many folks know this, but I'll tell you, Ellie. Because you're my friend. See, my own people crossed here back in '38. I was only seven. They were following folks by the name of Whitman and Spaulding who were the church folks killed last winter by Cayuse. You know about that?"

Eliza nodded, her face somber. "When we heard in the spring, I was afraid Mama would change her mind about coming out. But it didn't. Please now, tell me more. I never dreamed. I . . ."

Janie Marie laughed. "Well, you'll be surprised out of your skin then when I tell you the rest. See, I was kidnapped by Sioux. Maybe because of my light hair. I never . . ."

Eliza gasped. "Oh, Janie! How . . . ?"

Janie Marie shook her head. "No," she said. "If you're thinking it was dreadful, it wasn't. Not at all. Looking back, I guess I yearned some for my mama. But there was a passel of us and, well, the Sioux took mighty good care of me. So, I just grew up with them, and took to their ways. I liked living with them. I felt like one of them. But when I was twelve, a trapper came through who took a fancy to me. He gave the Sioux a couple of Appaloosa roans, some whiskey, and tobacco for me. Then, he and I went to St. Louis. He was an all right sort—never beat me or nothing—but he went away in the spring one year and never came back. I was fifteen then, and never liking the city all that well, I left and got myself to Independence. Then a couple of years ago I decided I'd go west with a train led by a man I trusted a lot, Mr. O'Shea. And when Cal told me he was going out with Paddy this spring, I took it to be my chance."

"So that's why you ride so well. That's why you could drive your own wagon across the Big Blue without batting an eye. And you . . . you know all about this land, and the plants, and you even know how to swim."

"Sure. It comes easy. You ride as good as me. And taking animals through water—well, you just have to be gentle and tough, and let them know you know a lot more than they do. And I can sure teach you about growing things out here. And I can even teach you how to swim!"

They both laughed. "What will you do, Janie, when we get to Oregon?"

Janie Marie shrugged. "It doesn't matter a whole lot. I just don't intend to get back into whoring. I'd like to claim a little land and run a farm. But it doesn't really matter. When I find a place with a good feeling, I'll settle in."

"When we get to Sioux country, might you see some of the people you lived with, and if you do, won't that be something?"

"It's not likely. That was a while back. I'll tell you, though, and it's between us. Remember the Pawnee back there at the Blue? Red Cloud? The one that took a liking to me and my quilt?"

Eliza nodded, remembering very well the image of the handsome Red Cloud.

Janie Marie looked closely at Eliza. "What I'm telling you has to be between you and me."

Eliza nodded again solemnly. "Of course."

"Well, now Red Cloud made it clear that day he wants me for his wife. He told me I'd see him again, and I'm expecting to, and I know when and where. Please, don't go saying anything to anyone because I don't want trouble. And old Hagen still worries me."

"Has he been bothering you again?"

"He's come by a couple of times. Says he's wanting to talk, but I don't say a word, and then he just hangs around and watches me until I have to leave what I'm doing. Lord God, I hate that man. He's a slime worm I can't put a name to."

"I agree, Janie. I sure agree." But now a question blocked Eliza's mind like a cloud. If Janie was the friend Eliza thought she was, she wouldn't mind Eliza asking. If not, well . . . Eliza would know. "I have to ask you something, Janie. I hope it won't offend you seeing it to be none of my business."

Janie Marie reached out and took Eliza's hand. "Oh no, Eliza. You can ask me any old thing. Now that you know about me. After all, you're my best friend."

"Well, you told me back in Independence that the reason you had signed on with this train was because of Cal. And now you're thinking about Red Cloud. You're thinking differently?"

Janie Marie hesitated for a moment before answering. "Things change," she said. "I might have told you that about Cal but, well, there comes times you got to face reality, and . . ." Her voice trailed off, and she was silent.

Yes, Eliza now thought, as she packed up a lunch of dried fruit, salted meat, biscuits, butter, and blackberry jam. She had news to tell Caleb herself. As well as some questions, and now the subject was sure to come up.

The sun was high when Eliza and Caleb mounted their horses and rode out from Fort Child. "Still Pawnee country, Cal," Eliza said. "That's what Janie Marie says. Pawnees have lived here for hundreds of years. And look at the lizards." The sun had warmed the land, and dozing lizards sprawled on many of the rocks. "Sunning themselves, lazy as can be. Aren't they curious?"

141

"We'll see more curious things before we get to the Oregon country," Caleb said.

They rode on, laughing at the prairie dogs—small, striped, yellow-furred pups that stood on their hind legs and stared intently at the intruders for a moment before diving back into their holes. And once Eliza clapped her hand over her mouth in delight as she watched rabbits with long, black-tipped ears leaping high in the air. "Those are jackrabbits, Cal! Janie Marie says they can jump higher than our wagons!" Caleb laughed. "From watching them, she's right." He then pointed to big circles of dimpled, cracked mud surrounded by clumps of grass and white-domed mushrooms. "And do you know what those might be?"

"Yes, I do! Buffalo wallows. That's what they are. And when it rains, water collects here. Janie Marie told me about them." Eliza caught her breath. "Lordy, though, they sure smell bad. But Janie Marie says the buffalo will stand and lollygag and roll around in these wallows for hours on end under the blazing sun."

Reining their horses in at the top of a hill, they suddenly hushed their talk as the echo of a strange hum rolled over the land below. Then Caleb leaned forward in his saddle and pointed out toward the sound.

"There they are! Look, Ellie! Buffalo!" His voice was low as they both saw a brown mass moving slowly away from the river. "They're feeding, Ellie. Just look at them! There's got to be thousands, and we're downwind from 'em so they can't know we're here."

They watched for some time in awed silence, their eyes wide with amazement as the slow-moving herd lumbered along the plain, grazing as they moved. Some of the shaggy bulls stopped, rolled in the grass, then stood and shook out their manes. And every few minutes, plumes of dust rose in the warm air as pairs of bulls, bellowing with rage, pawed the ground and charged one another.

"I tell you, Cal, I never thought I'd see anything like this," Eliza whispered. "That's something, indeed." As they turned their horses to ride away, Eliza reached over and she smiled as she touched Caleb's arm. "I'll not ever forget that sight," she said. He looked at her and grinned. "Nor will I."

Turning south, they rode toward a shallow canyon where cedar trees and a few patches of green grass grew along the bed of a small creek. Picketing their horses, Caleb spread out a buffalo hide while Eliza unpacked her picnic basket and arranged the food on the wicker lid. Then, as she offered Caleb a slice of bread, spread with butter and jam, he held up his hand. "Just a minute," he said. "Before we eat, I want to tell you about Janie Marie."

Eliza nodded. "She's my friend, Cal, and I like her. She knows a whole lot about this country."

"She's proud to know you, Ellie. She's never had a friend like you. You know she grew up with Sioux?"

"She's told me about that. I can't imagine it, Cal. And she took to them, too. But . . ." The notion so much on her mind wouldn't be stopped. "Back at Independence, on the first day of trekin', she said she was on this train because of you, and . . ." There it was! She'd blurted it out, and she hadn't meant to. It sounded small and mean.

Caleb looked at her with surprise. "That might be part of it, Ellie. I told her last winter when I first met Paddy O'Shea that I'd be trekin' west in the spring. Janie Marie told me she thought she'd be coming along too. Said she wasn't leaving anything in Independence and she could get the gear. She did too. You know she's set on making a new life for herself. You heard her say. But Ellie, you've got to know there's nothing between Janie Marie and me. What I might be feeling for you doesn't have a thing to do with her."

143

"Maybe she doesn't want to see it that way."

"Maybe not. And maybe once, for a little while, I thought I loved her. But that was then, and now is now."

Eliza sighed and frowned as she watched summer clouds hurrying across the sky. Did Cal know about Red Cloud? If he did, was he upset? Would he be upset if Janie Marie left the train and went off with Red Cloud? If he thought so much about her once, why wouldn't he now? She had to know. She looked at him, and he met her gaze as she spoke slowly.

"If you told her you loved her once, maybe she still thinks you do. You can't just go turning hearts on and off at your own whim."

Caleb sighed. "I'm not that way, Ellie. I told her once I loved her because I thought I did. And once I asked her to marry me and come west with me. But she laughed at me, and she said she wasn't my kind, and she was right. We still liked each other though. And we still do. But that doesn't mean . . ."

A flood of uncertainty and jealousy swept over Eliza. So! Caleb had even proposed to Janie Marie. And he'd also . . . he'd most certainly taken her. "And you . . . you . . . ?" She felt confused and her face got hot with flush. She didn't know how to ask him what she had to know, but she remembered what the preacher had said this morning. And now she was feeling doubt about Caleb, a decent man if there ever was one. But he'd also loved a whore well enough to ask her to be his wife. Eliza couldn't accept that.

Suddenly Caleb stood up and looked down at her. "What you're wanting to ask doesn't have a thing to do with me and you. Ellie, this talk isn't going right. I'm not going to talk anymore about Janie Marie. What I've said is truth, and I'm not denying a thing. But it's best we don't talk about her again. Not like this."

He sat down again beside her. "Besides, there's lots

of other things to say to each other, Ellie. Let's leave that subject be. Agreed?"

Eliza picked up a twig and traced a square in the dust. He was right and she knew it. There was no point in disagreeing because that would only bring unnecessary grief. "Yes," she said softly. "Agreed. Let's talk instead about old Boone."

Caleb threw back his head and laughed. "All right," he said, but then suddenly he got quiet. "We'll talk about old Boone after you let me tell you how much I like you, Eliza Landon." Taking her chin in his hand, he turned her face to his. "And could you consider giving me a kiss?"

She looked at him, still wondering about all of her strange, mixed-up feelings. She liked him so much . . . no . . . she loved him. That was it! She loved him and she was afraid. She nodded and Caleb kissed her gently. "Now what do you want to know about old Boone?" he whispered, his blue eyes crinkling with a smile.

Eliza touched his face and ran her finger down his cheek. "Well . . . you could tell me what happened to his wife."

Again Caleb laughed. "Danged if I know, Ellie. I got to think about that."

"Well, then, we don't have to talk about Boone, Cal. Tell me about you. Where did you go after you left Kentucky? What happened to Nellie? Why did you change your name? I want to know those things."

Caleb looked away and was quiet for a moment. "That was a while ago," he said. "But I'll tell you this, I'm glad I left Kentucky, and I'm glad we met up again." He drew a pipe out of his shirt pocket and lighted it. When he spoke, his tone was matter-of-fact.

"The trip's going well, Ellie. O'Shea says we're about to leave Pawnee country, and then we'll be in the land of the Cheyenne and Arapaho. He says we'll pass by

Thunder Eyes' village, and O'Shea won't be surprised to see Two Bears and Red Cloud there."

Eliza couldn't suppress a shiver of excitement. So, this might be where Janie Marie would see Red Cloud again!

"When?" she asked.

"In a couple of days."

Again they sat in silence, but Eliza felt the closeness of him, the warmth of his body. How would it be, she thought, to have him kiss me. Really kiss me. How fine that . . .

"My God, Ellie." Caleb's voice sounded uneven. "I want to kiss you. Kiss you like a man wants to kiss a woman he likes a lot."

Eliza looked at him, her eyes wide as he drew her to him; she held him close as he gently laid her back on the buffalo hide. She felt his legs, strong against hers, and his aroused maleness, pressing into her. A powerful surge of want for him swept over her as she arched her body to him, hungry for him. He touched one of her breasts, and she trembled. "My Ellie! My little Ellie!" he whispered as his lips brushed her forehead then her throat. She held his face between her hands. "Yes, Cal! Yes!" When he kissed her, she felt a wild, unexpected exhilaration, and when she felt his tongue, insisting inside her mouth, desire swept through her, hot, sweet, and consuming. He lay, holding her to him, so close, and his voice shook. "Oh, Ellie, I want you, I do!"

Images came to her. Dreadful images of indecent women, wanton women, and whores—women who had sinned; women with serpents circling their breasts, women with dismembered heads and hands; women who were stained forever because they'd offended a vengeful God who struck them down with his anger. Nice girls didn't ever give themselves to a man before marriage. No matter how great the want. And where were Caleb's

146

words of love for her? She knew without doubt that she loved him. She adored him; she would marry him tomorrow if he asked her to. And she wanted him with a want stronger than anything she had known in her life. But for him to presume she would allow him to take her because he felt passion for her at this particular time—that enraged her.

She heaved her body against him, thrusting him away. "No!" she cried as she sat up. Her green eyes blazed. "You may want me, Caleb Pride. But you're not having me! Not ever, without love. If you want a woman, you go to Janie Marie!"

Caleb looked at her, stunned. He quickly stood, his face pale. "My feelings for you don't have a damned thing to do with Janie Marie, Eliza Landon. If you're twisting all of that up, you'd best learn how to untwist it. You must know I care about you. A whole lot. But I'm not near ready to talk about love and all. We all have to get out to Oregon, and I have Smithy to think about. And know this. Until we both get some things set straight in our minds, I won't be bothering you again. Come on now, we best be getting back."

They rode back in silence, a silence as thick as a wall; they shared nothing, their eyes never met. Eliza felt sick inside. She longed to talk, and yet she wished today had never happened. The colors of the late afternoon were glorious and she wanted to point out flocks of whooping cranes, silhouetted black against the orange sky. But setting her lips in a tight line, she stared straight ahead. She'd best forget this man, she told herself. She and Cal didn't see things the same way.

That night as Eliza lay in her bed inside the inky darkness of *The Lone Eagle,* she turned her face into her pillow, and for the first time since that night in Kentucky when she had worried about Max being beat by his pa, she cried.

Chapter 16

True to his word, Caleb didn't come around. And as one day followed another, Eliza tried not to think about him. Once, in the midafternoon after setting camp, he and Janie Marie came riding by. "Ellie!" Janie Marie called out. "Come ride with us. We won't be gone long." Eliza walked up to Janie's horse and patted its nose while looking up at Caleb.

"Well," she said, "I just might." But Caleb, sitting stiff as a stick and looking straight ahead, treated her like air. Eliza shook her head. "Thanks, Janie. On second thought, I guess not." Once again, Eliza vowed to put Caleb out of her mind.

On the following afternoon, the sun looked like a red ball in a sky full of dust. Eliza, walking beside *The Lone Eagle*, couldn't see her own lead ox because of dust. Carrying a big cotton sack, she'd spent the morning leaving the trail to gather big flat cakes of dried buffalo dung that she had then slipped into her bag. It was as O'Shea had said—not much wood out here in the Platte Valley and buffalo chips were used for the cook fires at night. That was fine. They made a good fire, hot and bright; better than some of the wood fires they'd had.

Now the air was so dust-laden that even the kerchief Eliza had tied over her face didn't help. The wind was up and an occasional raindrop plopped on Eliza's poke bonnet and made puffs of tiny swirls on the dusty trail.

"Signal is to strike camp." Martha, riding inside the wagon, leaned out and called to Thomas and Eliza. "Storm's on us any minute now."

As the train slowly formed its circle, Martha jumped down from the wagon and she and Eliza worked quickly with Thomas as they pulled their wagon in place. Moments later the storm closed in. Sheets of rain, whipped by howling winds, battered the circle of wagons as thunder crashed and forked lightning danced across the sky.

"I hope Ben's all right," Martha shouted to Eliza and Thomas as they crouched together inside their wagon.

"He's fine," Thomas shouted back. "He's doing—"

They all heard it. The sound of a distant rumble, unlike thunder; unlike anything they had heard in their lives. Eliza watched lanterns, pots, and pans jingle and tremble and the wagon began shake. Puzzled, she grabbed the wagon flap and pulled it aside. The roar got louder, and wide-eyed, she turned to stare at her parents. "Stampede!" she screamed. "My God, it's a stampede!"

She felt cold; she started to shiver and was unable to stop. "Stop it, Ellie!" Thomas Landon's voice cracked with his sharp command. "Stop! We're going to need all the level thinking we can get," he shouted, his own eyes wide with fright.

Eliza stared at her father and shook her head, trying to clear her senses as she looked out at a black wall that moved in waves as far as she could see. She heard pounding hooves and clattering horns and she smelled a heavy, wet wool stench and she saw the creatures' big shaggy heads and their yellow and red crazed eyes as they ripped through the land, bellowing with rage.

"There's nothing we can do!" Thomas cried. "Not a goddamn thing!" But suddenly the black violence veered away from the train, and Eliza stared in disbelief as she saw riders galloping with the beasts.

"My God! My God!" Thomas cried over and over. "My God, it's Indians!"

"Hiyee! Hiyee!" The warriors, their long hair streaming, and holding enormous bows and arrows, raced alongside the animals, forming a nearly solid line between the emigrants' wagons and the beasts. *"Hiyee! Hiyee!"* the warriors' cries echoed, high and keen until there were no more animals in sight. The warriors disappeared with the beasts, the sounds of the Indians' cries and the thundering hooves growing dim as a strange silence fell over the watery land.

The rains stopped; dark, ragged clouds scurried across the sky. Eliza jumped down from her wagon, her knees feeling like rubber, and she looked out to where the herders should be camped. "Thank God," she whispered to herself as she saw the drovers astride their horses, slowly circling the herds.

She stood for a moment, pondering the stampede. She wondered if the warriors who had surely saved their lives had anything to do with Red Cloud's feelings for Janie Marie. If so, Red Cloud had saved a group of people, including a man who had shown a hatred for Red Cloud's people. But the group also included Red Cloud's love. That act then was a superb act of something Eliza couldn't put a name to. She must ask Janie Marie.

"Set camp, folks!" Stilly's words rang out as he and O'Shea rode among the camp of dripping wagons and frightened emigrants. Thomas put his arms around Martha and Eliza and held them close. "You have to know, Ellie," he said. "When there's real trouble, you got to

150

grab ahold of yourself. You can't let go. Not then. Maybe later, but not then."

Eliza smiled, but her voice sounded thin and she still felt as if she had water in her veins. "Yes, Papa. You shook me out of a fright. Lordy, what a time! Now that's something we won't forget."

Martha nodded and her voice shook a little as she asked the question on everybody's mind. "Where do you suppose the Indians came from, Tom? They saved our lives, you know."

"I don't know," Thomas answered. "Perhaps Mr. O'Shea knows. But it sure was a damned scare, I'll agree. Now, how about getting ready for that buffalo feast tonight."

Buffalo country might mean stampedes and using buffalo dung for cook fires, but it also meant fresh buffalo meat. The day before, a large hunting party had gone out and brought back meat for the entire camp. According to O'Shea, there wasn't a thing in this world better to eat than fresh buffalo. He had carefully described the best edible parts and had told the folks how to prepare them. Everybody was anticipating this event.

Eliza nodded. "Let's do that."

Inside the wagon, Eliza carefully pulled big knots of dry grass out of a dish barrel, then repacked the dishes. She'd stashed the grass there last week, in preparation for a time like this. Once the cook fire was right, Thomas skewered whole buffalo hump ribs on sharp sticks to be seared and eaten when just done—rib after rib of dark red meat. Martha cut a large chunk of tongue into strips and poked them on small sticks. They would be roasted quickly and eaten right off the sticks while marrowbones, placed directly on the hot coals would yield a rich pudding of blood and fat. "Just scoop it out with a knife or your fingers or whatever," O'Shea had said. "Food don't come finer than that."

Ben planned to join his family for dinner that night, and Martha had suggested that Eliza invite several friends to share the campfire after their meal. "We'll serve up some coffee and some sugar biscuits," she'd said. Eliza had invited Sam, Smithy, the Petersons, and Janie Marie. She had also asked Janie Marie to invite Caleb, if she saw him around.

It was early evening when a jubilant Ben rode into camp. "We held the livestock together all during the storm and that damned stampede just fine. Scared to hell, but Cal, he just kept on yelling things to keep us all right. Lordy, what a scare!"

"Is Caleb coming over, Ben? I sent word by Janie Marie." Eliza tried to keep her voice light.

"No. He wants to stay with the livestock tonight. But he says thanks to Mama and Papa for asking him."

Eliza fought keen disappointment mixed with anger. She had now made two attempts to right the wrong of the quarrel. She'd wanted to ride with Janie and Caleb that one day, and had had every intention to do so, but for Caleb's obvious coolness toward her. Now she had specifically invited him to join her and her family for a social gathering and he had refused. Once again, she resolved to forget this man who, more often than not, tormented her thoughts.

It was late that evening when the Landons and their guests gathered close to the fire. The women drew their shawls close; the men wore their greatcoats. It was cold. Stars glittered in a cloudless sky and it was hard to believe the violence that had struck this land a few hours earlier today.

"I hear those riders that suddenly appeared with the stampede were Pawnees, Stilly," Thomas said. "What's the word on that?"

"That's what O'Shea says. He's not sure what happened, but we're either damned lucky, or Pawnees figure we're worth saving. We don't know which is what."

"What does that mean?" Lucy Ann asked.

"Either the buffalo weren't heading for us anyway, in which case we were lucky," Stilly replied, "or if they were, and the Injuns knew it, they were able to head 'em off in another direction, and we were still damned lucky. Either way, it leaves you weak in the knees, knowing what could have been."

"I know about stampedes," Janie Marie said. "Those big ox can go crazy, and for no good reason they'll join up with the buffalo, and then they're gone for good. They'll move on across the land, wrecking wagons, killing other animals and folks too. If there's a team hitched up, whoa! Those wild-eyed creatures'll just plunge with the buffalo, pulling that little old wagon that leaps and jerks behind it like a toy until it cracks and buckles and smashes to smithereens. Sometimes you can turn them, like the Indians did today, but Ben, there's nothing in the world you or Cal or anyone in the whole world could ever do to stop them. They'll just run until their craziness is used up, but leaving scenes behind that'll stop your heart. Big wagons smashed to splinters and torn cloth, and barrels all broke up, and scattered tools, and guns, and bodies of folks who got trapped, or got thrown from the wagons and caught under the animals' feet. I'd say whatever happened today, we were so lucky, we can't know."

Sam stood up and stretched. "I just hope none of us experience what you've told us about, Janie. But let's forget about that, and go walking under the stars. It's sure a pretty night."

"And cold," Lucy Ann said as she drew her shawl tight. "You folks go ahead. I'm going on to bed." Martha and Thomas agreed it was too cold and too late. But Sam persisted.

"Come on, Eliza. Janie Marie. Ben. Smithy. Let's walk a bit."

Janie Marie shook her head. "I'd just like to sit here

for a while, Sam, and talk some women talk with Ellie here. I'm hopin' you'll understand."

Sam smiled as he doffed his wool hat and then put it back on. "Good night then, fair ladies. Come on, boys. Let's leave them be."

Janie Marie sighed as the men disappeared in the shadows. "He's a good man, ain't he."

"Who?"

"Sam. He's so damned decent, and good. And he sure loves a good time."

Eliza nodded. Janie Marie had something on her mind and it must have to do with Caleb. Eliza was silent. She felt stiff and guarded as Janie Marie picked up a small stone and worked it in the dirt close by the fire.

"Ellie . . . Cal . . . he likes you a whole lot." She laughed. "I knew that from the very first night back at Independence Camp. He told me some about you. Things that happened when you were both children. Fishing together, and racing horses and reading and things like that. He said he'd never forgotten you. I didn't like hearing it, but after I met you down at the river that morning, I knew why he liked you." It was quiet, and neither Eliza nor Janie Marie spoke for a time. When Eliza spoke, her voice was soft.

"But maybe we're not the same kind, Janie. Caleb and me. Maybe not at all."

"Well, I say you're thinking isn't right, and I say you're wrong. Real wrong. Now, I sure don't know what else to say, except I like having you as my friend. But I'll tell you another thing, since we're talking, just us. There's a man who loves me a whole lot and I saw him today. He was leading the warriors who saved us, well enough. And that says a whole lot to me."

"I thought that, Janie. I thought that right after it was over, and I thought what a feeling of love for another person that must be. I can't even put a name to it."

"You said it well. It's a good loving for another. And if I thought as you're thinking, then I could think Red Cloud and me—we're not the same kind of folks either." She smiled. "Well, I guess I'd better be saying good night. But Cal—he's not likely to come around if he thinks you're gonna toss him away."

Chapter 17

Patches of orange wildflowers and cactus, exploding with pink and yellow and creamy white blooms, covered the high plains. But a sudden rainsquall early this morning caused the trail to be slippery with mud and the going was slow.

Eliza and Lucy Ann had left the trail to pick wild onions, a treat when boiled with meat. Reaching the top of a small knoll, they saw small, scattered herds of buffalo, the bulls grazing apart from the cows and calves. The great, shaggy beasts looked tame today as they lumbered about, looking for grass and water, and they paid scant, if any, attention to the passing train. Different, indeed from the raging herds that had torn through the country-side some days ago.

"Stilly says we wouldn't make it to Oregon if it weren't for the buffalo," Lucy Ann said.

"Well, I'd say he's right," Eliza answered. "There's not a stick of wood to be seen, and we haven't seen any for days. Not even dry grass. But the chips do fine once you get used to them. And as Janie Marie says, the whiter the drier, and the drier the hotter cook fires you'll get. Without the chips we wouldn't have fire, and without fire we sure wouldn't have hot food and coffee and all of that."

"Stilly and George are forming another buffalo hunting party, come Sunday. There's talk they may hunt with a group of Pawnees."

"Hunting with Pawnees, Lucy Ann? Where did you hear that?"

"Mr. O'Shea's been in touch with them. He told Stilly, just last night, that our men may have that chance when we get close to the Pawnee village."

Eliza sighed. "I sure wish women could go."

Lucy Ann laughed. "You might want to go, Ellie. You seem to take to that kind of thing. But no thank you, I'd as soon stay in camp."

As the train was now making its way slowly down a narrow gully, Janie Marie appeared. "I'm borrowing a spare man to drive my wagon for a spell so I can walk with you," she said. "But first I'm going on a ways over there." She pointed to a place where a rushing creek made a sharp turn. "I won't be gone but a minute."

"We'll walk on slow," Eliza called out.

"You've gotten to know her some, Ellie," Lucy Ann said. "What's she like? I mean most of us know something about her, and—well, we all hear she's been a lady of—"

"No need to wonder, Lucy Ann," Eliza said in a firm tone. "Janie's one of the best." Eliza was pleased that Lucy Ann didn't pursue the subject further.

It wasn't long before Janie Marie reappeared, laughing, while slipping and sliding down a small hill and carrying a very small baby buffalo.

"Where on earth did you find that?" Lucy and Eliza asked, incredulous at her find.

"I heard the mama. Not far from where we were back there, and I could hear from the mama's cry she wasn't doing well. Sure enough I found her just beyond that little hill. She'd slipped and fell, and it won't be long before she's dead, but her poor baby here was trying to nurse with the mama dying. You know . . ." She stopped talking and drew a deep breath. "I'll bet the Evanses' cow

157

that's just come into milk with her own calf wouldn't know much different and would take on this little orphan baby."

Eliza looked closely at the animal and began to laugh. "It looks like a little old bear! With a beard!" All three women laughed until tears came to their eyes. "Come on," Lucy Ann said. "That's a good idea. After we set camp, let's take it to Lorene, and we'll just see!"

It was late in the day when the train came to a halt, and a short time later Eliza, Janie Marie and Lucy Ann walked over to the Evanses' wagon.

"Look at this, Mrs. Evans," Janie Marie said, petting the animal's shaggy head. "Orphaned, and no mama to feed it. What do you think?"

Lorene looked at all of them, surprise stamped on her face. "Do you think that would work? That our milk cow and her calf wouldn't mind?"

"I'll bet you my shoe it'll work," Janie Marie said. "Can we give it a try?"

Lorene smiled. "Let's!"

The four women walked out to the cow, contentedly grazing, her calf close beside her. Janie Marie set the baby buffalo down beside the cow, who stopped feeding as she and her calf appeared to study the little stranger. The cow sniffed the buffalo and the buffalo snuggled next to the calf, the calf then nuzzled the buffalo, and the buffalo began to nurse.

Janie Marie took ahold of Eliza's hand. "Ain't that something. I had a good hunch it might work. I sure do think that's something, indeed."

Some days later, Eliza saw the baby buffalo, following right along with the cow and the calf. Eliza smiled. She sure did like Janie Marie.

Chapter 18

By midmorning it was hot; hotter than any heat the emigrants could remember as, day after day, they treked under a sun that blazed from a clear, blue sky.

"Indian village on up ahead, Ellie. Pawnees. That's the word from up front." Martha, walking ahead of the Landon's wagon with Maggie McVey, turned and called back to Eliza who was driving *The Lone Eagle* today. Eliza heard the edge of worry in her mother's voice.

"It's all right, Mama," Eliza called back. "Remember, it's thought they're the ones who turned the buffalo away, so they must put some value on us!" Eliza knew she was the only one who knew for sure that Red Cloud was responsible for saving them all. "Besides, Mr. O'Shea's with them and that should make it all right."

Eliza knew that for a fact. Early this morning, O'Shea had ridden out of camp after advising Stilly not to skirt the Pawnee village, but to bring the train to a meadow a short distance away. O'Shea had then asked the Executive Committee if they would consider allowing the train to camp for a couple of days. It would be a fine chance to hunt buffalo with Pawnees. The Executive Committee had been pleased to agree.

"Understand," he'd said to the committee. "These

Indians'll welcome any of our people who might want to visit the village. In fact, a visit would be the courteous thing to do."

It was midday when the weary emigrants set camp. After tending to chores, Eliza gathered small mirrors, fishhooks, several combs, and ribbons together. Then she looked for Janie Marie, but Janie's wagon wasn't occupied. Eliza suspected that she had perhaps already gone on ahead to visit Red Cloud. So, late that afternoon, Eliza and her parents set out with many other folks to visit the village a short distance away.

It was a large village, with hundreds of buffalo skin tepees and lodges strung out for miles along the Platte. And it hummed with activity. Wooden racks holding strips of buffalo drying in the sun stood between many of the tepees and lodges. Older women tended to children and to fires; older men chipped arrowheads and worked on tools. A small group of younger men and women, naked except for their breechclouts, galloped into the village with whoops and laughter. Dogs and horses were everywhere.

But soon the noise and dust subsided as the visiting emigrants, along with some Pawnees, gathered in front of an enormous lodge. Here, O'Shea, Red Cloud, Two Bears, and an old, old man whose dark, wrinkled face looked like a polished walnut sat on a buffalo robe. Directly in front of the men were three gorgeous red, white, and blue wool blankets, upon which lay a half a dozen long ivory handled knives, their blades gleaming in the sun.

Eliza figured the old man was Thunder Eyes, the fine old chief O'Shea had spoken of. She also figured the blankets and knives were O'Shea's own gifts for these people he obviously enjoyed. The men now conversed, while smoking from a long, beautifully carved pipe.

On seeing the crowd of emigrants, Red Cloud immediately stood up. He then turned, said something to the other three men, and quickly walked through the crowd. All eyes followed him as he walked slowly and with purpose to meet Janie Marie.

Eliza could hardly supress her own gasp of surprise as she saw Janie, dressed in a beautiful white buckskin dress. A fringe at the hem of the dress, decorated with small, polished animal hooves and bells, came just to her knees. A necklace of blue, red, and green beads, quills, and glittering brass coins hung around her neck. And her hair, worn today in two long braids, was the color of wheat. She watched Red Cloud approach and she smiled.

She was beautiful, she was dazzling, and when Red Cloud offered her his hand, she took it and he led her back to the lodge. When Janie Marie spoke, she directed her words to Thunder Eyes. Red Cloud then spoke to Two Bears, Thunder Eyes, and O'Shea. All three men looked pleased and it appeared that an important decision had been made. Eliza knew what it was—Janie would become Red Cloud's wife.

Later that evening, Smithy walked over to the Landons' camp. Eliza sensed that she should tell him about Janie. When she'd finished telling him what she could, she smiled, expecting to see his wide grin. But Smithy didn't smile; his eyes were somber as he looked out at the evening sky.

That night Eliza dreamed of winter back in Kentucky. A fire glowed on the Landon's kitchen hearth, but it was cold inside the house. The branches of the cherry tree outside her window scratched against the window and someone whispered her name over and over. "Eliza! Eliza, wake up!"

She woke with a start, sat up, then smelled the odors of the inside of the close, musty wagon combined with

161

damp prairie grass and camp smoke. She heard the scratching again. "Eliza!" It was Janie Marie's voice. "Eliza, Please hear me. Please come!"

"Yes!" Eliza put her face close to the wagon cover. "I'll be there. Wait!" Quickly pulling her brown dress over her head and grabbing her shawl, she jumped down from the wagon to find Janie Marie waiting for her.

A thin streak of dawn showed in the east, and not far away Pawnee fires winked and glowed. Without saying a word, Janie Marie took one of Eliza's hands and Eliza felt a ring slipped into her palm.

"This here's a real pearl ring," Janie Marie whispered. "Mr. O'Shea gave it to me a long time ago. If you don't know it, and I guess you don't 'cause there's been no talk about it, but Mr. O'Shea's the one who bought me my gear so I could come out. He always said I was a real lady."

"You are a real lady indeed, Janie. But why are you giving me the ring, and are you going with Red Cloud? To be his wife? Please tell me. I've wondered ever since this afternoon when you left with him, and you looked so pretty and—"

"Shhh. Yes. I'm going with him and I'm leaving all my gear to you. I'm also saying good-bye." She laughed softly and Eliza heard her delight. "I'll be pleased and proud to be Red Cloud's wife. He sparks me, Ellie. Sparks me like no other man I've known."

Sparking! Eliza's smile was wry. So that's what Janie Marie called her passion for her man. And she obviously felt a great joy instead of the shame, confusion, and anger Eliza had felt that day when she and Cal had had their disagreement. But now a sadness welled up inside Eliza as she realized her friend was leaving. She didn't want Janie to leave. This woman, who knew so much and was so wise, was Eliza's best friend.

"You mustn't worry, Ellie," Janie Marie said. "I

162

figure love is love. It don't matter what the skin color is, or if some folks are different than us." She laughed. "That only means we look different to them, too. And love is love and I know Red Cloud loves me. I'll manage fine. Remember, I lived with Sioux, and if I'd had my own say back then, I'd never have left. But now I'm taking my own horse and some clothes with me and that's all. I want you to have the ring and take what you need or want from my gear. You can see that some of the other ladies take what they want. Lorene, and Maggie, and Lucy Ann."

"Oh, Janie," Eliza said, her voice soft and sad. "I don't want you to go."

"Please, Ellie. Be pleased for me. Mr. O'Shea is, and so is Cal. You must too 'cause it feels right to me, like nothing has in my whole life."

"Let's promise that someday we'll see each other again. Let's promise that, Janie."

"I promise you that." Janie Marie's voice was solemn. "And now I got to say something else before I leave. And that's this. Don't be so . . . so hard on yourself and Cal. A man's a man. And a man's got needs. Cal, he might have thought he loved me once 'cause I was . . . well, one of his first, and I was his only woman then and I liked that about him. But I knew he didn't really love me and I told him that. I told him I wasn't his kind. You are, though, and he knows that. And there's sure no sin, Ellie, in knowing how it feels to want a man and letting him know it too. When the feeling's right. You'll be knowing when that time is."

A silence fell between them. "Did Cal talk to you, Janie? About . . . about him and me?"

"All he said was you'd had a difference of thinking about something. And he only told me that after I'd hounded him as to why we hadn't seen him around. I figured out the rest. Ellie, I got to go now."

Eliza put her arms around Janie Marie and held her

close for a moment. Then she watched her walk away. A short time later the thud of a horse's hooves on dirt echoed, then the sound faded, and Janie Marie was gone.

Eliza ached to see Caleb. God, she wanted so to see him. If she could talk to him for just a little bit. It would be so easy to walk out to the herders' camp, just outside the circle of wagons. But what would she say to him?

Listen to me, Cal. I've been a ninny, and I'm sorry, and now Janie Marie's gone and I feel so sad and I want you to hold me. Please hold me, Cal. Or—Cal, listen to me. Janie Marie's run off with Red Cloud and she says it feels more right to her than anything has in her whole life. Are you sad too, Cal? I am so sad and I want more than anything in the world to tell you that. To talk to you.

But she didn't go to Caleb. Instead she sat down on a camp stool beside her wagon, and as she slipped the little ring on her finger, she thought about Janie Marie's words and she waited for day.

Chapter 19

The warm summer winds that blew across the great Platte Valley carried the sickening stench of rotting flesh. The specter of sickness and death gripped the emigrants as the trail took them past hastily dug graves and carrion-riddled remains of a horse, an ox, or a cow. Abandoned possessions dotted the land like forgotten toys. Cast iron kettles, mattresses, mirrors in heavy wood frames, cowhide trunks, spinning wheels, rocking chairs, churns, plows, beds, cradles, bake ovens, and books. Sometimes these things were picked up by passers-by; more likely not.

Handwritten signs appeared, written by folks who had treked here yesterday, or last month, or perhaps last year. POISON WATER. DON'T DRINK. Printed with wagon dope on a piece of cloth; the cloth tied to a stick stuck in the mud alongside a murky creek. Thus, the emigrants were advised of bad or good waterholes, and rank or sweet grass.

There were personal messages too, written on pieces of cloth or paper, or painted on rocks. And a shiny, bleached white animal skull informed a certain Scott Brown that Edward W. was waiting in Laramie, while words scratched on a rock directed Buck Burgess to rendezvous at Fort Hall with George Potter.

The messages fascinated Eliza and she wondered what had happened to the people who had written them. Had they met each other? She thought about Chad, Nancy, and Will Green, and she wondered where they were now. She wondered if Caleb was interested in the messages, and did he think about the folks who'd written them, too? Then she chastised herself for thinking about him as the ache in her heart refused to leave. It seemed, too, that it was worse now, because Janie Marie was gone.

Other members of the train missed Janie Marie too. Since the day she'd left, many of them had made a nice comment or two about her. Some of the women, of course, had clucked their tongues on learning she'd run away with an Indian, but it didn't amount to much. That was Janie Marie's business and everybody else had their own families and their own business on their minds. Everybody, that is, except Leonard Hagen.

"You shoulda stopped her, McIntyre," Hagen had said only that morning when he'd ridden up on his horse alongside Sam, who often walked with Eliza and was doing so today. "She's nothin' but a whore, but you shoulda stopped her anyways." Hagen spit on his knife blade, whipped it across his pants, and stuck it back in its sheath. Eliza shuddered, despising him.

"If I'd'a known," he continued, "I'd'a killed him. Killed the lousy, red sonuvabitch and maybe her too. If I'd'a known. And I'll tell you . . ."

"Hold on, Leonard," Sam said, keeping his eyes straight ahead. "Don't go saying things that could get you in trouble. It's none of your damned business what the lady did. She could do as she liked. Now hush your prattling and put your mind to the fine hunting trip we'll be taking."

The trip, so carefully planned back at the big Pawnee village, hadn't occurred. The great buffalo herds had drifted farther west. The hunters would have had to ride for days in order to find them, followed by taking time for

166

the hunt. It was decided that when the train came to a place where the herds were grazing, O'Shea would contact the Pawnees and the hunt would proceed. Yesterday the emigrants had once more seen herds of the beasts and the day of the hunt was close at hand.

"I'm takin' my boy." Hagen said, his voice a taunt.

"You're boy isn't old enough." Sam answered. "You know the rules, Leonard. Your boy's just a tad."

"We'll see about that," Hagen called out, turning his horse and riding away.

For the next two days, *The Oregon Roll* traveled and camped in a bleak country of barren hills and sand. But at the end of the second day, excitement and anticipation swept through the camp. O'Shea reported that large herds of buffalo had been seen, and he then asked Stilly to form the hunting party. Pawnees were also in the area, friends of Red Cloud, and these men would take the men on the hunt. They would also show them how to hunt with bows and arrows, which the Pawnees would provide. According to O'Shea, Red Cloud had asked his warriors to do this for him, as his expression of gratitude. The emigrants had brought him the beautiful woman who had become his wife. And Red Cloud had sent word that he had never felt such happiness and contentment as he did now with Janie Marie. O'Shea also told the emigrants that Red Cloud and Janie Marie were camped not far and planned to rendezvous with the train during the next few days. Eliza was elated at the prospect of seeing Janie within a short time.

Nearly all the men with the train wanted to go on this great hunt. Thus straws were drawn, and those fortunate at the draw were consumed with excitement.

It was after the evening supper and Eliza watched

167

her papa ready his big rifle. Thomas and Ben were two of the lucky ones, but Eliza didn't know about Caleb. Because tomorrow was Sunday, she'd decided she would visit him. She would be friendly, and try to act as if nothing had happened. If he took to that, then she'd suggest that they walk, or perhaps ride together, and she'd tell him how she missed Janie Marie and how anxious she was to see her again.

"I tell you, Ellie," Thomas said. "I talked to Ben and Cal before supper, and we're excited as all get-out."

"Caleb's going then?" She felt the sinking feel of disappointment.

Thomas grinned. "Sure, he's going. This is going to be a new experience for all of us. None of us have hunted with Indians, and to be able to go with Pawnees, well . . . that's something none of us dreamed would happen on this trek." Thomas Landon's eyes sparkled as he leaned his rifle against the wagon and lighted his pipe. He then looked closely at Eliza. "It seems Cal's not been around lately. Not since we first got to this valley and you two took your long ride. Did something happen to put you off from each other?"

Eliza shrugged. "It was something that was my fault, but I don't want to talk about it, Papa."

Thomas nodded. "Well, if you think enough about each other in a caring way, you'll work it out."

Eliza thought about her father's words. She cared. She cared enough to plan to visit Cal, straightforward and plain. But she also didn't want to appear as the fool. Maybe Caleb didn't care about her enough to be bothered. Maybe he hadn't given another thought to the quarrel that day, now a long time ago. If that was the case, it would be dreadful to visit him and have him be polite but treat her like air. No, she wouldn't visit him. Not at all. And once again, she struggled with the realization that she must put Caleb Pride out of her mind.

* * *

The next morning, before daybreak, the hunters gathered around a fire and sipped hot coffee while waiting for the Pawnees. But when Hagen joined the men, bringing his boy with him, Stilly looked directly at Hagen and spoke in measured tones.

"You know the rules, Leonard. Your boy's too danged young to go. Give him another couple of years. My God, man, I can't be responsible for a lad that young. None of us can. And riding with Pawnees and learning a whole new thing, hunting with bows?"

"He's gonna learn, and this is the best way," Hagen argued.

Stilly shook his head. "I'm sorry. I can't and won't allow it. I'm not taking my own boy, Jeremy, who's spoilin' to go, and he's some older than your boy."

"You gonna force my boy to stay and be a sissy like Pride's dumb boy? That boy don't do nothin' but bullwhack, paint pictures, and hang around the women."

The silence that fell over the group was cold as stone. Then Caleb spoke. "You sonuvabitch! You goddamned sonuvabitch!" Keeping his eyes on Hagen, he spat on the ground in contempt and he then started for him.

"Enough! Hold on there, Cal!" O'Shea boomed out, his tone hard and flat, as he strode out to Hagen and waved to Caleb to stand back. O'Shea then stood close to Hagen, nose to nose. "I can't figure you, Hagen," O'Shea said in a soft voice. "Except to know that you're bent on trouble. Now Peterson here says your boy don't go, then he don't. You can join us or stay, but cut the arguing. The captain's word goes, and you know it."

"You 'n' Peterson ain't boss, O'Shea." Hagen's voice was thick with rage. "Not when it comes to my boy. Since he can't go, then by God, we'll go ourselves. Just him and me."

169

O'Shea shrugged. "Suit yourself. That's not a smart thing to do in this country, but you're not gonna ride with us and bring your boy."

With a fury, Hagen turned on his heel, grabbed his boy's arm, and left. A short time later the Pawnee hunting party rode into camp, and with O'Shea and the Pawnees taking the lead, the hunters rode off.

It was hot that afternoon and a quiet time for the emigrants in camp. Martha had baked up a batch of bread, and she now sat in the small patch of wagon shade reading *A New Home*, a book with suggestions on how women might make their homes in the West comfortable and pleasing. Eliza had taken a washboard and battling stick down to the river, where she'd washed clothes and then weighted them down with rocks on the grassy bank to dry. Now, walking back from the river she passed Smithy, who sat on a camp stool, drawing. Eliza sat down beside him and watched him as he sketched Jeremy and Betsy playing a game of stick ball with Dog.

Smithy's hands moved fast across the paper, his head moved up and down as he studied his subjects for a moment, and then turned back to his work. He looked at Eliza once, grinned, tore a sheet of blank paper from his pad, and handed it to her along with a pencil. Eliza had never been good at drawing, but she would try.

Janie Marie's wagon was close by. Eliza and Lorene, not wanting to leave it behind, had seen that somebody had driven the wagon team since the day Janie had left. Looking at the wagon carefully, Eliza started to draw a picture of the pretty butterfly, but a few moments later she laughed. The butterfly she'd drawn was crooked and funny-looking, but it was also fun to draw, and soon she was engrossed in drawing the camp, the wagons, the people and animals, surrounded as they were by the barren hills.

Suddenly Eliza was struck with a sense of uneasiness. It was too hot, and insects buzzed and whined too loud while the nasal, high-pitched cries of hawks seemed to screech. She stopped drawing and shaded her eyes, watching the birds as they wheeled in the cloudless sky; their cries sounded so strange. She frowned. Were those the cries of hawks, or was it something else? She didn't know, but she had the keen sense that something was wrong.

Putting her pencil down, she looked at Smithy, who had also stopped his drawing and was holding his pencil in midair. Then, dropping his work, Smithy stood up and uttered a cry of such anguish that Eliza's skin crawled. She stared up at him, stunned, and then she scrambled to her feet.

"Smithy! What . . . what is it?"

The boy was silent and he leaned forward, his face strained, his eyes wide. Eliza followed his gaze, but she saw nothing except low rolling hills and sand dunes. Then Smithy cried out again, "Ahheee! Ahheee!" A hoarse, high cry, his face twisted and contorted. Eliza grabbed his shoulders and shook him. "Smithy! Smithy! Stop it! You . . ." But, tearing himself free of Eliza, Smithy started to run, and that's when Eliza saw a figure on horseback crossing the dunes and heading toward camp.

Eliza followed Smithy, walking slowly at first while trying to make out who was coming their way. It was when Smithy stopped running and held up his arms in a gesture of supplication that Eliza recognized Red Cloud. Eliza stopped, stupified, as Red Cloud dismounted, lifted a bundle wrapped in a buffalo hide off the back of his horse, and walked toward her. Eliza closed her eyes.

Oh God! Oh God! Blowing sand stung her face; she bit her lips and tasted blood as the sand dunes wiggled in dizzy lines and turned gray and black. Feeling her legs buckle, she forced herself to walk on until she met Red Cloud, and she met his eyes.

Eliza then turned and ran. "A blanket!" she screamed to the emigrants in camp. "Water! Whatever we have, bring it! It's Janie Marie! She's hurt! Oh God! Please help!"

On reaching the camp, Red Cloud laid Janie Marie down on a quilt in a patch of shade beside her little wagon. Eliza touched Janie Marie's beautiful dress, and her hair. A mud plaster, caked with dried blood, was smeared over her slashed throat. Red Cloud took a parflech from around his neck, and placed it on Janie Marie's breast. When he turned and looked at Eliza, she saw tears in his eyes. Then Red Cloud stood and left. There was nothing he could do here. Janie Marie was dead.

It was late afternoon when the hunters returned, and it was quiet in camp that evening.

Working in the shadows of lanterns and half-darkness, Martha, Lucy Ann, Lorene, and Eliza laid Janie Marie out, preparing her for her grave.

The rising sun reflected on pebbled clouds edged with gold on this early morning. All the emigrants had left Janie Marie's grave except Caleb, Smithy, and Eliza. Eliza was still working on marking a large rock with white letters: JANIE MARIE. RED CLOUD'S WIFE. Eliza looked up at Caleb. "Do you . . . do you know how old she was?"

"Maybe twenty. Nineteen or twenty." Caleb had an arm around Smithy's shoulders as they both stood, waiting for Eliza.

"I remember she told me she was seven when her folks came west, but I don't know what year that was," Eliza said.

"She was nineteen or twenty, Ellie. Still a young girl with a lot of living to do."

Eliza nodded as she carefully painted B. 1829, D. JUNE 1848. When she'd finished, she stood and listened to the wind blowing across the rimrock and bluffs. "It's a sorrowful wind this morning," she said. "It's a sorrowful wind mourning for Janie Marie." She looked up at Caleb. His blue eyes looked hard and she didn't think he'd heard her.

"We're riding in a few minutes," he said. "We'll meet you all later today at Chimney Rock."

Eliza put her hand on his arm. "You're looking for Hagen, aren't you."

"We're looking for her killer. At the same time we're looking for Hagen and his boy. A day and a night out alone is a long time out here. If we find Hagen, we've got questions. He headed south, in the same direction as where Red Cloud and Janie were camped and we know how Hagen's crazy and we know how he felt about Janie Marie going off with Red Cloud."

Eliza looked at Caleb closely. "You know more than that."

"Yes." His voice was bitter. "Red Cloud told a cousin of his who was hunting with us that Janie had left her and Red Cloud's camp to go berry picking. Red Cloud was dressing down an antelope in their camp. When she didn't come back as soon as she should have, Red Cloud set out to find her. He found her, all right. As you know, with her throat slit."

Eliza heard the catch in Caleb's voice. "Now we're riding, Ellie, and there's no time to spare. Red Cloud's with the Pawnees we hunted with yesterday. O'Shea says they plan to meet the man, Tomschini, and Tomschini's glad to ride with anyone who'll kill white folks."

"Oh God, Cal," Eliza cried. "I want to kill whoever did it. That isn't right, but I feel that way, I do."

They stood, quiet for a moment. "I understand, Ellie." Then he turned to her and at the same time Eliza spoke. "I've forgotten our silly quarrel, Cal. I hope you have too. Please take care of yourself," she whispered. "I'll be waiting for you at Chimney Rock."

Chapter 20

O'Shea led Clancy, Dooley, Sam, and Caleb through desolate country of cactus, sagebrush, and greasewood. Wind-burned country where scrubby conifers grew along sandstone bluffs and layers of rimrock were silhouetted against the sky. It was a silent ride except for the horses' hooves shuffling through the sand. Then O'Shea spoke.

"Hagen's got no wits," he said. "I've seldom seen a man with less wits. No man with any sense, who knows as little as Hagen knows about this country, takes a tad of a boy out to hunt. And Hagen doesn't know any more about Indians out here than a hind-sore bear." He shook his head. "God damn, we've been doing well except for him."

Clancy nodded. "There's often one bad pea in the pod, Paddy. I reckon he's the one on this train."

Caleb agreed, but he didn't say. Caleb wanted the silence. He wanted to think about Janie Marie with her tough beauty and her fierce desire for independence. He wanted to think about her feeling for folks like Smithy, and her pride in having Ellie for a friend. He also wanted to think about her love for Red Cloud, a man who loved her for what she was, not for what she did.

He remembered back to the time just before she'd left to go with Red Cloud. She'd talked to Caleb about it.

She'd known Red Cloud would be waiting for her at Thunder Eyes' village. He'd told her back at the Big Blue that he'd be waiting, and he hoped she'd leave the train and consent to become his wife. She'd told him that if her answer was yes, she'd be there, wearing her deerskin dress.

She'd also told Caleb how excited she'd felt about living again in country she'd loved a long time ago. And she'd told him about the beautiful dress she'd kept with her all these years. It was a dress one of the Sioux women had given her when she was a little girl, to wear one day honoring a husband. Well, Caleb thought. Janie Marie had worn the dress for a short time and she'd probably been as happy with Red Cloud as she'd ever been in her life. But then some goddamned bastard had found her alone, slit her throat, and that had ended her beautiful dreams.

"Hold!" O'Shea called out, interrupting Caleb's thoughts. The men reined in their horses at the edge of a bluff as O'Shea leaned forward in his saddle, his body tense and strained. Far out on the sandy plains Caleb saw a triangle like a dark smudge against the cloudless sky.

"I've seen that kinda thing only once before," O'Shea said. "Come on, let's ride."

The sun was high when they reached a tripod made of three wagon tongues poked straight up to the sky where Hagen's naked body was hung. A harsh wind kicked up swirls of sand below his bound feet; he'd been scalped and castrated. His bloody organs, tied around his neck, dangled over a bloodstained board with black letters that read THIS MAN KILLED RED CLOUD'S WOMAN. TOMSCHINI.

Caleb felt the gorge rise in his throat. He wiped his brow, slick with sweat, and looked at Dooley, whose eyes were closed. Clancy let out a low whistle. "Holy Jesus," he said while O'Shea picked at his teeth with a piece of stiff weed.

"Cut him down," O'Shea said, dismounting and

pulling an old buffalo hide from behind his saddle. Dooley cut the rope; Clancy cut off the sign and propped it against one of the wooden tongues. Then, wrapping the corpse in the buffalo hide, they tied it fast with rope.

"The boy, O'Shea," Ben called out. "What about the boy?"

"Tomschini probably has the boy and there's no point in us going after him and bringing us more trouble," O'Shea said. "We'll bury Hagen and then we'll ride back to Chimney. We got our own folks to worry about."

They buried Hagen on a sandy ridge, leaving the painted sign to mark the spot. Before the sun had slipped into afternoon, the men were riding toward Chimney Rock.

As he rode, Caleb pushed thoughts of Hagen out of his mind. He wasn't worth thinking about. He thought instead about Eliza. He thought about the curls of red hair framing her face and her green eyes that could laugh with delight or, and Caleb smiled ruefully, blaze with anger. He thought about her pleasure at seeing the herds of buffalo, and how she had enjoyed telling him about the buffalo wallows, and the black-eared jackrabbits. He was glad she'd said she'd forgotten their quarrel. He'd had enough of the misery of the past weeks when he'd deliberately avoided her. That was over now; he'd go to see her as soon as they reached camp and ask her to walk with him out to the Chimney. He'd also do his best to see that they didn't quarrel again. She had become his heart's desire, and if he was to win her, he mustn't sully her feelings in the least by his own immediate want for her.

It was midafternoon and the sunlight on the bluffs and towers of rocks was a brilliant pink, while one spire was thrust higher than the rest.

"That's the Chimney," O'Shea called out. "It's always damned impressive." A short time later, O'Shea yelled "Ho!" *The Oregon Roll* was camped on the meadow not far away.

Once in camp, O'Shea wasted no time. He walked over to the Hagen wagon, stayed a few minutes, then he asked Stilly to call a meeting. He told the folks he and his party had found Hagen hung, that the boy was nowhere about, and that it would be futile and a waste of time to look for him. He also told them about the sign. "We'll go with that," he said. "That's Tomschini's way. Now, tomorrow we got to get going. Any questions?" There were none.

But when Stilly asked for a volunteer to drive Mrs. Hagen's wagon, nobody stepped forward. "Dooley?" Stilly looked at Dooley, who usually volunteered for tasks. "How about it?"

Dooley shook his head. "I'm not feeling good toward those folks," he said. "Not even the missus. You're asking me, Mr. Peterson, not ordering me. I won't do it unless you order me to, and I'm hoping you won't do that."

Ben then stepped out of the crowd. "I'll do it for a couple of days, if it's all right with Cal," he said.

Caleb agreed. "What we might do is take turns, Stilly. Each of us herders could take, say, two days."

"Good idea." Stilly said. "Ben, you start then, and we'll rotate it with your men, Cal. The important thing is that we keep Mrs. Hagen's wagon and oxen in good-enough shape to keep 'em moving right along."

The crowd broke up. Caleb made his way directly to the Landons' camp, where he found Eliza pouring buttermilk out of a bucket that had swung behind the Landons' wagon all day.

"Have you been out to the Chimney yet?" he asked.

"No! But I want to know more about Hagen. I want to know—"

"Please, Ellie, no. It was probably the worst thing I've seen in my life. As O'Shea told everybody, 'Hung means hung,' and we're believing the Indian's note. Tomschini's. He took care of Hagen well enough, and now I have to believe, for my own peace of mind, that Hagen's the one who killed Janie. Now. Let's talk about walking on out to this place that we've been hearing about ever since we left Independence. In fact, I heard about it long before that from people who passed it going west, and then came back east."

"Well . . . Papa wants to go in a minute now. He was waiting until you all came in. We were all waiting, as a matter of fact. So why don't you and Smithy come with us? We're all going. Lorene and Clancy and the Petersons. And then we're having potluck at Stilly and Lucy Ann's. As a matter of fact, Lucy Ann just happened to mention to me that if you wanted to walk with us, you'd sure be welcome to eat with us, too."

"I'd like that, Miss Landon." Caleb grinned. "I'll get my boy and we'll be ready."

"It's made of marl," Thomas said. "I've read about it some. Crumbley, earthy clay."

"It's a marvel, isn't it." Martha's voice was touched with awe. "Sometimes I think on the sights we've seen and the fine folks we've met on this trek, and I . . . well, I'm glad we came."

"Let's climb on up," Eliza said. "Do we have time before supper, Lucy Ann?"

"We do. Come on, let's go!"

With Jeremy and Betsy whooping and yelling as they scampered on ahead, beckoning to Smithy to join them, the rest of the party followed. But Caleb and Eliza lagged behind.

"I'm glad you said what you did this morning," Caleb said. "I would have said something like that if you hadn't. Oh, Ellie, these weeks haven't been easy, and I've missed you and wanted to be with you more than I can say. And right now, I'll say that I'm not intending on having any more quarrels. That's not right, when there's feelings of care."

"It was hard for me too. I wanted to see you, to talk to you, and a couple of times I almost came out to the herders' camp to visit you. But then I didn't. And Cal, I have to say I miss Janie more than I ever thought I'd miss a soul in my life. But more than that, it makes me so sad to know that she was feeling so happy about living with Red Cloud, and then this . . ."

"I thought the same, Ellie. I thought about that a lot as we were riding today. But we have to get on, you know." He looked at her and smiled. "If you let me hold your hand, we'll talk some more about old Boone."

Eliza laughed as she grabbed his hand. "That's nice, Cal. That's real . . . say, it looks like Mr. O'Shea's been up there and is now coming back to camp." O'Shea, approaching Caleb and Eliza, tipped his broad felt hat at Eliza and looked at Caleb closely.

"There's always new names up on the Chimney," he said. "I always like to walk out and take a quick look-see. Keep an eye out Cal. I will too." And he walked on.

"What does that mean? Eliza asked. "To 'keep an eye out'? For what?"

Caleb shrugged. "Danged if I know. Maybe we'll find out."

Reaching the base of the huge tower, they were both amazed at the names left for others to read. "There's got to be a good hundred names and more," Caleb said, his soft voice reflecting his awe. "I had no idea, and it's clear, Ellie, that folks have used anything—wagon paint, axle grease, and even gun powder to write their messages for other folks to see."

"I like reading them," Eliza answered while walking slowly along the path. "Listen to this. Jim Boggs . . . and

179

Dutch Robb, back in '45, asks that Mary Boggs meet them in Laramie! Wouldn't it be fun, Cal, to get a message left on a rock? And Cal, if we put our names here, then people will read . . ." Her voice trailed off as she saw Caleb standing a little ways away, staring at words painted in black along the face of a long narrow space. Eliza joined him. " 'Max Pridentz,' " she whispered. " 'If you pass this way, look for me in Laramie. Clara McCabe.' "

"Cal! That's written to you, but you're white as sand!" She laughed, a tease in her voice. "Who's Clara McCabe? Someone who knew you by your old name?"

Caleb turned, his eyes wide. "No!" he said. "No! I don't know that person, not at all. But I won't put my name here. I won't." He then turned and started down the dusty path alone.

Eliza, caught with surprise, ran after him. "Cal, wait!"

Caleb turned. "You best stay with your people, Ellie. I've got to get back to camp and try to figure something out. I won't be coming for supper tonight. Please don't ask me why."

Hearing the anguish in his voice, Eliza nodded. "Of course, Cal. Of course."

"I'll be talking to you later, Ellie. One evening soon, I'll be coming on by." And with that, he was gone.

Eliza pondered the strange message all night. Clara McCabe. Who was Clara McCabe? Then she remembered O'Shea's words: "Keep an eye out," he'd said. And she wondered if that had anything to do with the woman's message. It had to. There wasn't any other explanation.

Chapter 21

The canyon echoed the sounds of the passing train. Whips whistled and cracked across the backs of the beasts, men cursed and shouted, wagon wheels creaked as axles ground against sand-filled hubs. Now and again folks called out orders to children, who fretted and cried.

Eliza was sick of it. She was sick of the dust and the sand and the smelly beasts and the foul piles of dung that she always tried to avoid. She was sick of the snorting animals and their dumb, shoving confusion. She was sick of worry about weather, food, and hostile Indians. She was also sick of the worry about Caleb—the latest being his reaction to the message back at Chimney Rock. Once again, she'd seen little of him these past few days. It was clear that he had something on his mind.

Reaching behind her head, Eliza tightened the knot that held a cotton rag over her nose and mouth and closed her burning eyes. One of these days she would ask him about Clara McCabe.

Now, on this early morning, stiff, gusty winds kicked up clouds of dust and it was already blazing hot. By noon, temperatures in this dry, sunburned land would be almost unbearable. Thus, it was with astonishment that Eliza noticed a deserted blacksmith shop where a sign read

TINWARE BY A. RUBIDUE. Two log huts, surrounded by mounds of stinking buffalo hides, stood beside the shop, and an Indian woman, wrapped in a blue blanket, sat in the doorway of one of the huts while three children played with a pack of wolflike dogs. Eliza stared at the woman. People would live here?

She turned to her mother, who was walking beside her. "Why on earth would that woman live here, in this awful country?"

"She's a man's woman, Ellie. She'll live wherever her man chooses to live."

Eliza was startled at the sharp tone in her mother's voice. "Do you think all women do that, Mama? Have you had to do that with Papa?"

Martha shrugged as she leaned into the wind and blowing dust. She then turned to Eliza and spoke in a loud voice. "We go where they go, don't we? If some of us on this train had had our own say, we might not be trekin' here this morning."

Eliza was taken aback. Just the other day her mother had talked about the wonderful sights they'd seen, and how much she liked all the people she'd met. Did her mother now regret her decision to come west? Eliza also wondered if, when she got married, she would go with her man anywhere he might choose to live. Doubt crossed her mind. She would never consent to live in a shack in a desolate canyon.

Reaching in her skirt pocket, Eliza felt a small clump of soft green-gray sage she'd dug early this morning. She would put the sage in a jar of water, and give it to her mother tonight. The plant's scent was wonderful, wild and sweet. Things like that made her mother feel better; new kinds of plants also meant the train was coming into a new kind of country, and a new kind of country meant they were getting closer to Oregon.

"Martha. Ellie. We're not far from Fort Laramie,"

shouted Thomas, who was driving the Landons' team of oxen. "Stilly thinks we should have a party. We'll have good reason, too. We'll be a good six hundred miles from Independence, and after Laramie we're getting close to the Wind Mountains and the Rockies. I tell you, we're getting closer to Oregon. Ellie, how about you taking the wagon for a ways while I walk with your mother."

Putting his arm around Martha's waist, Thomas looked at her closely. "You're needing some fun, M." Eliza smiled as she walked ahead to take the drive. "M" was her father's special name for her mother and he didn't use it often. But Eliza knew that her mother wasn't feeling well. It was her time of the month, and while Martha handled it better than many women on the trail, it was still difficult, adding its own dimension to the burden women felt regarding the dreadful lack of privacy. Addressing this most pressing need was accomplished by having several women, holding their long skirts wide, stand in a circle, thus providing the essential enclosure for a single woman or perhaps two or three.

"Now, I'm thinking," Thomas said, "that when we get to the Willamette Valley, we'll settle by a creek so nobody has to walk a mile and a day for water. And next summer, I'm planning on digging us a good well close to our kitchen door. From what I hear, M, we're moving right along, which means we'll be getting to Oregon in time to build a good place before the winter rains."

Martha laughed. "Oh, Tom, I'm looking forward to that. I'm already thinking about Christmas in our own house with a fire on the hearth and a fine meal served on a real table, where we can all sit together."

"It's going to happen, M. It's sure going to happen."

On June 2, O'Shea led *The Oregon Roll* into Fort Laramie. A big, squat fort built of mud and thick, whitewashed walls picketed with bastions at all four corners, it sat on the high, windy plains right in the middle of Sioux country. Clusters of tepees surrounded the fort. This was the place where Indians camped, visited, and bartered horses and pelts for dry goods, tobacco, alcohol, and beads.

It was a chaotic place. Trappers and Indians, hunkered close to the ground, called out bets and rolled the dice among piles of silver coins. Mountain men, wagon guides, and freight drivers milled in and among the emigrants; folks like the folks with *The Oregon Roll* came into the fort with their creaking wagons and beasts, tended to their business, then left. Few folks had it in mind to stay.

Goods were controlled by post sutlers, men who followed United States soldiers wherever they might be garrisoned. At Fort Laramie fresh-baked bread, cheese, butter, and milk were sold for the trail in enormous quantities, as well as being offered in small eating houses. Brisk sales of whiskey and rum took place day and night in dark grogshops. Grains and dried fruits, bacon and eggs, as well as horse tack, trail gear, and tents could be bought. Few emigrants left Laramie without spending cash, and taking advantage of emigrant needs, prices were high.

Martha visibly blanched at the price of flour, oats, and coffee, but she bought them nevertheless. Thomas, hoisting the big bags up into the wagon, tried to mollify her complaints. "It's what it is, Martha, and I'm pleased we have the money to buy."

"We'll be more careful with our sugar, Tom. I'm not paying two dollars for a mere cup of it, and that's what they're charging here."

Tom laughed. "I agree with you on that."

"When might Ben and Caleb be coming in?" Eliza asked her father.

"Probably not until after we've gone. They had a couple of lame horses and were planning on taking an

184

easy drive today. Looking then to reshoe them here. O'-Shea and Cal agreed to rendezvous tomorrow, late afternoon. So we won't be seeing them until then."

Eliza looked closely at the milling crowd. Might she possibly see a girl looking for a handsome young man named Max? But Eliza also knew there wasn't a way in the world to figure out when the message had been left on the rock. It could have been left last week or last year. But if anyone at Laramie was looking for a man named Max, that person wasn't letting herself be known, and as the Landons left the fort, Eliza was sure that the girl named Clara McCabe wasn't there at all.

Chapter 22

"Look ahead, now! Look on ahead and you'll be seeing the beginning of the mountains of shining stone, folks. I'm talking about the Rockies!" O'Shea turned in his saddle, his words carrying strongly across the windswept plateau. Men threw their hats in the air and the emigrants cheered. Soon this morning, *The Oregon Roll* would reach the Bitter Cottonwood, where they would camp overnight. And tonight they would have a grand party.

A sparkling clear stream ran past groves of cottonwood trees at the Bitter Cottonwood. There was an abundance of sweet grass, and chokeberries and gooseberries for the picking grew among clumps of willows. It was a beautiful place, spirits were high, and the emigrants were ready for good times when the train came to a halt at noon to allow time to prepare for the party.

But it was also here that the first ominous word of sickness rippled through the train. Mrs. Hagen and her three remaining children were sick. The word had come from Dooley, who had driven the Hagens' wagon the last two days. When Martha had heard of the woman's plight, she'd volunteered to ride with Mrs. Hagen today and tend to her needs.

It was midafternoon when Eliza walked over to the

Hagens' wagon. Eliza felt that her mother had done her share in helping Mrs. Hagen and she should now come home. Someone else could take their turn.

Eliza found her mother standing in front of a smoldering fire, lifting steaming cloths out of a pail of hot water. Eliza joined her and together they silently wrung the cloths and spread them on the grass to dry. Martha then waved Eliza away. "Go along, now, Ellie. I'll be along soon. Remember we decided to make creamed potatoes for the party tonight. Please take care of that." Martha pushed back a stray lock of her hair, and Eliza saw that her mother looked very tired.

"Mama," Eliza said softly. "You've been taking care of those folks all day, and now that we're here, can't you come on home?"

"Hush! Now, listen to me, Ellie. Mrs. Hagen needs help. She doesn't know about proper nursing care. She believes in blistering and bleeding. She also believes in witches. I found one with two large pins in it, stuck up on their wagon wall. And today I showed her how to wash her baby's diapers. That's what I'm doing now. She's been doing it the old back-hills way, drying them out and scraping them off, and reusing them again. No wonder the sickness has a hold of them. Now you go on home and make up the potatoes. It also occurs to me the water here is decent enough for some bathing. You might stick your big toe in and scrub it some."

Eliza knew what that meant. Her mama had scouted out the creek, found it fine for washing up, and Eliza, Thomas, and Martha must all find some time to wash themselves. But Eliza hated washing herself in a river or a creek.

"Why do I have to? I bet Ben doesn't, and lots of the other women don't either. Lorene's the only one."

"The other women aren't my business." Martha answered, her hands on her hips. "As for Ben, he's with

187

animals and other smelly men all day, and it doesn't matter. But I have a feeling, missy, that if your brother is showing up at the party tonight, he'll find time to take a dip with some soap. Now no more arguing, and get along."

Eliza knew better than to say another word. The look in her mother's eyes, and the hands on her hips were plain enough. Eliza turned, and left.

A clump of bushes hid a place in the creek where the water was clear as glass, but cold. Lorene was there, wearing her chemise and soaping herself. Eliza quickly pulled off her dusty trail dress and petticoat and slithered into the water, gasping at the grabbing chill. Ploughing through the water, she joined Lorene and they laughed, their teeth chattering, their skin raised in goosebumps.

"Sometimes I feel clean after these wash-offs, and lots of times I don't," Lorene said. "But it's a sight better than feeling you stink like a field hand."

"I like to think of a time when we all get to Oregon and we'll have our own washtubs and warm water, and we can get in and soak. All to ourselves, and with no clothes on at all," Eliza said before taking a deep breath, dunking her head in the water, and soaping her hair.

"You've got the prettiest hair, Eliza. Pretty as can be. Has Caleb ever told you that?"

Eliza caught the tease in Lorene's voice. "Not directly."

"Everyone who has eyes in their heads can see he likes you a lot. Wouldn't it be fun if you two decided to marry while we're trekin'?"

"Oh, Lorene, that's way ahead of me. I like Caleb a lot all right, but marry him? I . . . well . . ."

Eliza didn't want to talk about that. It was something she wanted to keep to herself. But she had thought she might talk to her mother. Had her mother felt for her father some of the feelings she felt for Caleb? Did she have those feeling of want? And more than that—why did her mama have only two children when a lot of women looked weary to death after birthing six or seven or more? Eliza knew there was an answer to that and—yes, she'd ask her mother soon when there was time for a real chat. Maybe when they got to Independence Rock, and if they had a layover day, there would be time for a quiet cup of tea and women talk. With a pang, Eliza remembered that Janie Marie had tried to talk to Eliza once, but Eliza had closed Janie Marie out. Now, if that were to happen, Eliza wouldn't do that. She'd talk with Janie and ask questions and learn things.

Eliza and Lorene, finished with their bathing, dried themselves, dressed, and walked back to camp. At the end of the campground, away from the wagons, Thomas, George, Clancy, and Sam were busy setting up a long table by placing boards on packing boxes. Lorene and Eliza walked up to watch them.

"Hey," Sam called out. "I know you two are going to be the prettiest ladies at the party tonight."

"We'll sure be ready to dance, Sam," Lorene answered.

"And I'll bet you my shoe we'll have a fine time," Sam replied.

Eliza frowned as she saw her father wipe his forehead and sit down on one of the boxes. He was pale, and he closed his eyes for a moment while taking deep breaths.

"Papa?" Eliza quickly walked over to where he sat. "What's wrong?"

He opened his eyes, smiled, and brushed her away. "I'm just tired, Ellie. You go on home and I'll be comin' along soon as we get all set up here. Go along, now. I'll be just fine. An old tough bird like me . . . I never get sick."

"I'll stay on here, Lorene, with Papa."

"No, you won't," Thomas replied. "You best get on back, fix the food for the dinner, and get yourself ready. I'll be just fine."

There was no arguing with him, and Eliza, feeling a gnaw of worry, walked back to the Landon's camp.

The big pot of creamed potatoes bubbled atop the iron grate above Eliza's cook fire. After adding salt and a handful of wild onions, they smelled heavenly. Satisfied with her dish and knowing she had a little time to herself, she would now dress for the party. Climbing up into the wagon, Eliza pulled the flaps shut, savoring her moments of complete privacy. Earlier today she had taken her pretty pink dress and her mother's blue dress from the clothes trunk and had carefully laid them on top of Janie Marie's satin patchwork quilt, which now covered Martha and Thomas's bed. Eliza smiled as she touched the quilt. Wherever Janie Marie might be, Eliza knew she would like what was happening this afternoon. Time to think about a party, and a little time to think about being pretty for a handsome man Eliza knew she loved.

Eliza quickly stripped off her clothes, bundled them together, and put them in a corner for a washing tomorrow. She then walked over to her mother's full-length mirror, that stood in its heavy oak frame at the end of the wagon, tilted her head back, and looked at herself. Pulling her long red hair back with one hand, she studied her freckled face and looked into her own green eyes. She slowly traced her fingers down her neck, stopping for a moment at her breasts before letting her hand trail down across her belly, and down her thighs, and she arched her brow as she stared at her mound of red pubic hair. She sighed, hearing her uneven breath, as she thought about Caleb. Caleb's face, browned by the sun and wind, his blond hair, his eyes as blue as the summer skies, and his smile and dimpled chin.

She felt joy and a passion she'd not experienced before as she thought about him holding her and caressing her. To have him touch her breasts, and her nipples, rigid now with want for him. To feel his tongue in her mouth, hot and probing. She longed to touch him—to run her fingers through his hair and kiss his eyes, his fine nose and mouth, and then kiss his chest and his belly. Eliza shivered. God, she wanted him. She ached with wanting him, and she smiled. He sparks me, she thought. He sparks me! And Janie Marie's words rang in her ears: *It's all right, Ellie, to want a man, and let him know it when the time's right.*

She shook her head and lifted her chin. It was time now to think about other things. Quickly putting on clean underthings, she slipped the pink dress over her head, brushed out her hair, and tied it back with a yellow ribbon, letting her curls cascade down her back. Then, taking a small leather-bound book and a pen out of an inside pocket of the wagon cover, she opened the front wagon flap, and jumped down. Knowing that her pot of creamed potatoes was close to perfection, she would catch up on her journal while she waited for her mother.

A shady spot beside the wagon provided a good place to sit, and after settling herself, she reflected that she hadn't written a word in her journal since the night at Chimney Rock. Now she wrote carefully, describing how she had come to terms with Janie Marie's death by feeling Janie Marie's presence from time to time. She also decribed Fort Laramie and the people there, paying attention to her description of the soldiers and trappers and their Indian wives. She wrote about her feelings for Caleb, and how she was looking forward to the party tonight. Then she closed her little book. Her journal entry, dated June 22, 1848, was the last entry she would write.

"Ellie?" Eliza looked up to see her mother walking across the clearing. Eliza stood and quickly walked out to meet her. "Ellie, you look so pretty," Martha said. "It's been a long time since I've seen you so dressed up."

"And you look tired, Mama. Real tired. Please rest now before you get ready for the party. The potatoes are done, and I have your pretty blue dress laid out on the bed."

"I'll rest some," Martha said. "But both the little Hagen girls and the baby died this afternoon and Mrs. Hagen's very sick. It's cholera, no doubt of that. Now, Ellie . . ." Her mother, seeing Eliza's horrified expression, put up her hand in warning. "There's no point in getting upset. We'll do the best we can."

Speechless, Eliza followed her mother as Martha climbed up into the wagon and rummaged around until she found a large jar of chicken broth. Pouring some of the broth into a small jar, she screwed the lid on tight. Then Eliza grabbed her mother's arm.

"Mama! You said it's cholera! Surely you aren't going back! You've been there all day, and you've got to rest. You look ever so tired. Besides"—Eliza heard the anger in her own voice—"those folks are nothing but trash. We don't even know them and I don't want you going back!"

Martha turned and looked at her daughter with surprise. "We might not know them, and they might not be as we think we are, but that woman needs help." she spoke in a quiet, but firm voice. "It's not like us not to help people that need help, is it, Ellie?"

"I don't know." Eliza's eyes flashed. "I don't feel that way about them at all. It's too bad about the little girls, but they're probably better off. I hated Hagen, Mama, and I still do, and I always will. I hope he burns in hell forever and I can't find charity in my heart for his ignorant woman. I hate your being with her and I don't want you to go back there. Let someone else do it, but not you!"

Eliza stopped talking and clapped one of her hands to her mouth, her eyes wide. This was the first quarrel she had ever had with either of her parents. Martha was quiet for a moment. When she spoke, her own eyes blazed with anger.

"I'm sorry for you, Ellie," she said. "But that poor, ignorant girl, who is only about your age, has been beaten . . . yes! Beaten by somebody, either her own people or her husband, all of her life. And she isn't right in her head. A thing I've suspected all along, and learned for certain today. But that doesn't mean we ignore her, and simply let her die. She's here, with us, all of us, in a strange land, not knowing for sure just where we're going, and she's very afraid. She's never lived a life like you've known, or as I've known. And she's lost all of her children, she's sick and needs help. Maggie will be with her tonight, but tomorrow I'm going back. Now"—her tone softened some—"there isn't time to talk more. You go along to the party. I'm going to rest a little, and later this evening, your father and I will put on our dancing shoes and join you all."

"To tell you true, Mama, when Lorene and I finished bathing today, I saw Papa helping to fix the supper table, and he wasn't feeling well. Have you . . ."

Martha nodded. "Yes. I saw him. He's tired, but he'll be fine. He was helping Stilly with one of the oxen. He'll be coming on home soon."

Eliza carefully moved her mother's dress, and then Martha sat down on the big feather mattress. She reached for Eliza's hand. "You're a fine girl, Ellie, and I understand how you might feel, but we'll talk about it another time. Maybe when we reach the Sweetwater, we can have a chat over a cup of tea." She smiled. "I have a feeling there's something on your mind. Something you might want to be telling me."

"I'm sorry for speaking to you as I did, Mama." Eliza sighed. "Well . . . I'll be looking for you and Papa later. I'll be dancing with Caleb. Maybe all night!"

Martha laughed. "Indeed it's time we had a talk," she said. "Now, go along. We'll see you later on."

What a grand night for a party, Eliza thought as she walked across camp toward the gathering crowd. The wind had died, the sky was cloudless, and there was a full moon. Eliza decided to forget the Hagens. There was no point in letting thoughts of those poor folks spoil her evening. Besides, Eliza couldn't remember when she had felt so happy. She knew it had been a long time.

Chapter 23

It was a feast like the folks hadn't had since leaving home. There was roasted buffalo; big bowls of rice pudding, baked beans, potatoes, fresh breads, pickles, relishes, cakes and pies, pots of coffee, and pitchers of milk. Whiskey was even allowed that night, a decision voted on unanimously by the Executive Committee.

As Eliza set her pot of steaming potatoes on the food table, she was keenly aware of Caleb, who was talking with George McVey. Caleb then walked over to Eliza, whistled, and grinned.

"I mean to say, ma'am, I don't think I've ever seen such a pretty lady."

Eliza looked around, astonished. "Why, who are you referring to, Caleb Pride?"

"Well now! I'm only thinking of a certain red-haired lady wearing a pink dress, with a yellow ribbon in her hair. Now I'm wondering if I could have the first dance with this pretty lady?"

Eliza laughed. "Oh yes, Cal. Of course!"

The long line of folks extended far out into the clearing as the weary emigrants lined up at the table, taking time now to enjoy each other with their own feast, some drink, and later the music and dancing. After helping themselves to the various bowls and platters of food, they sat down on camp stools, or on the ground, covered in spots with blankets or hides. And they ate.

Eliza and Caleb sat in a small circle with the Petersons, Evanses, and Smithy. "Where's Ben?" Eliza asked after swallowing a mouthful of Lorene's savory baked beans. "I haven't seen him for a couple of days, and I don't see him here."

"He's not feeling too well and he's resting up some. He says though he plans to be here later for the dancing."

A swift pang of fear flashed through Eliza's mind as she remembered her mother's words: *It's cholera . . .*

"What's wrong with him? He hasn't been sick since a long time ago in Kentucky."

"He's just tired, Ellie, and needs some rest. Don't worry about him. He's a healthy cuss."

"I don't like to bring it up, but it's said that Mrs. Hagen's got cholera," Lorene said, her blue eyes wide.

"I was talking about that with George." Caleb's tone was somber. "That's what he says. What do you know about this, Ellie?"

"Ummm. Mama said likewise. The children died, and I guess Mrs. Hagen has it, but Mama says we'll do the best we can, and we shouldn't get all worried."

Stilly nodded. "I came close to callin' off this party on account of their dying, but O'Shea said we should think of the living and go ahead with our plans. He knows how we've been looking forward to tonight."

Suddenly the music started; nobody wanted to waste time. Sam rocked back on his heels as he twanged on his harmonica, Danny pumped his accordion with gusto as Clancy grabbed his banjo, and Stilly his fiddle. In minutes the good times sound echoed across the big camp. Caleb and Eliza spun around, dancing the two-step, enjoying every moment of the prairie party. "Who are the lucky fellows tonight? Who have you promised your dances to?" Caleb asked.

Eliza tilted her head back and laughed. "Why, Mr. Pride. Why would you presume to ask, so early in the evening?"

Caleb's eyes crinkled with his smile. "I guess I was hoping you might consider dancing a lot of the evening with me. Maybe the whole evening?"

"Well, I want to dance with Papa. And I want to dance with Ben. But I guess I could get by just fine if I danced the rest of the evening with you!"

Then, laughing and clapping their hands in time to the beat, they joined a line forming a reel. As Eliza danced that night under the starry sky, she knew she would remember this night for the rest of her life; this was a special night, and right now her heart was filled with joy.

"Ten-minute rest, folks! Give us ten or fifteen," Clancy called out and Eliza was caught by surprise. "It's so late already? Cal, I haven't seen Ben. And I haven't seen Mama or Papa either." She frowned as she scanned the great, smoky campground. Lanterns, sitting on the long table and hanging from tree limbs, cast shadows on folks standing around campfires. Eliza's family wasn't there.

"Something's wrong, Cal. Somethings wrong and I've got to get home!" She started to run, fighting a sense of foreboding. The party wasn't important anymore. Nothing was important except finding out why her family wasn't at the party. But as she raced across the moon washed meadow, Caleb running beside her, she knew that sickness was the thing that had kept them away.

A lantern hung by the door of *The Lone Eagle* and Thomas climbed down from the wagon just as Eliza and Caleb arrived. The lantern's light reflected little orange spots off Thomas's glasses, and when Eliza saw her father's face, she knew that he was very sick.

"Your mama's sick, Ellie." Thomas Landon's voice was hoarse and faint. "And I have to say I've had better evenings myself. I'm sure we'll be feeling better, come morning. Now the evening's still young. You go on back to the party. Both of you."

"No. I'm staying here with you and Mama." Eliza's voice was firm as she quickly climbed the little stairs up into the wagon.

"My God, Mr. Landon." Caleb spoke in a low voice. "Surely you folks don't have cholera!"

Thomas nodded. "We've got it, Cal. Mrs. Landon's pretty sick. But we're tough folks. And as long as Ben and Ellie are . . ."

Ben! Caleb remembered back to this afternoon when Ben had ridden the herds in. That was when he had told Caleb he wasn't feeling good, and had declined to come to the party. A wave of worry swept over Caleb. I've got to get to Ben, he thought. But not a word to Thomas about it. No need to cause him and Mrs. Landon and Ellie that extra fret. Caleb hurriedly tipped his hat to Thomas as he started to leave. "I'm thinking you and Mrs. Landon will be feeling a whole lot better tomorrow, sir. Lots of folks survive this curse."

"Cal," Thomas said. "If you can spare Ben tomorrow, you'll send him over? His mother wants to see him, and so do I. We'd appreciate that."

"I will, Mr. Landon. I sure will."

Oh, Susanna! Oh, don't you cry for me. The music drifted through the night as Caleb raced out to the herders' camp. As he ran, he remembered the preacher in Harrisburg he had seen and heard, a long time ago. The preacher had said there wasn't any sickness out west. He'd said the air was good, and the water was pure. This country, west of Laramie, was the west. The preacher had lied.

Then the terrible thought came to Caleb that Eliza might get sick. That was an unbearable thought. The notion of something—anything—happening to her was unthinkable. After he looked in on Ben, he'd go back over to the Landons' wagon and help Ellie. With both of her folks sick, she was sure to need a hand, and tomorrow he and Ben would help her so the train could get on its way.

Caleb found Ben, wrapped in a blanket and curled up under a mess wagon, his eyes wide open, seeing nothing. Ben Landon was dead. Kneeling beside him, Caleb took one of Ben's cold, stiff hands and held it tight. "Oh my God, my God, dear Ben," Caleb whispered. "Dear, dear Ben!"

He stayed with Ben for a long time, and looking out into the night, he saw Ben's horse, Babe, hobbled not far from the herders' campfire. In the reflection of flames that licked in Babe's eyes, he saw a boy riding a magnificent chestnut mare named Red. The boy held a bloody gander's head high in his hand, twirling it again and again, like a salute. A time Caleb had never seen—a time he'd always wished he had.

The party was over. The music had stopped, the fires had died as the emigrants picked up their food dishes, their shawls, and coats and blankets to return to their wagons and tents. The silence of night lay over the camp, except for the Landons' wagon, where cholera had struck Martha and Thomas like a hand marked with death.

Eliza tended to her parents as they fought the agonizing cramps and the severe diarrhea coupled with wretched vomiting that fouled the wagon. Supporting their heads, Eliza forced them to sip water through their black and blistered lips. And as they lay, weak and quiet, or later, in a babble of delerium, she placed cool cloths on their fevered brows.

Later in the night, Eliza knew her mother and father were losing the battle. But she continued to wash them and desperately coaxed them to take water and chicken broth. She whispered to them, her voice hoarse and fierce. "Mama! Papa! You can't die! We're getting close to Oregon and you can't die. Mama, we're going to have tea at the Sweetwater. I want to talk to you. You can't die! Papa! You can't!"

Toward morning, Martha asked for Ben. "Where's Ben, Ellie?" Her voice was a whisper, but lucid.

"Ben's with Caleb, Mama," Eliza answered, holding a small lantern close so she could see her mother's face. "Ben's tending the herds. I'll get him for you in a while."

"No. I won't live that long. Ellie, you and Ben must get on to Oregon. As we had planned. And Ellie . . ."

"Yes, Mama. Yes. Ben and I will. I promise you."

"There's another thing. I've seen the light in your eyes when Caleb's around. If your heart feels it, pay it some mind. Like I did with your own papa. Caleb's a fine man, and . . ." She looked at Eliza for a moment as if she wanted to say more, then the light in her eyes faded, she sighed, and was gone.

"Ellie," Thomas Landon's voice was a bare whisper as Eliza took her father's hand, and kissed it, feeling the hot, dry, rough skin on her lips. "You and Ben . . . Ellie, you've got to go on. You know . . . there's money in the chest. Enough money for the both of you to buy good land. Buy lots of good land. That's what I was going to do. And . . ." He closed his eyes for a moment, then with great effort he opened them. "You and Cal . . . and Ben . . . try to stay together." And with those words, Thomas Landon was dead.

Eliza sat for a time in the wagon that reeked of the battle with cholera. She held her father's hand, her eyes wide as she stared at the flickering lantern, unaware for a time that she was surrounded by disease and death.

* * *

She heard the guards' signal of day and Caleb calling her name. She stood and walked stiffly to the front of the wagon and pulled the wagon flaps open. She looked at him, not comprehending, as he looked up at her. Stilly, Lucy Ann, Smithy, Clancy, Lorene, and Mr. O'Shea were there. But not Ben. Eliza then knew that Ben was dead.

Caleb climbed up into the wagon, grabbed her wrists, and held them tight. "Let me tend to them," he whispered, his voice rough. "Lucy Ann and Stilly want you to come with them and get some rest."

"No!" Eliza looked at Caleb, her eyes wild. She pushed her hair, heavy and wet with sweat, back from her face, and she ran her hands down the front of her dress, stained and filthy with vomit and mucous.

"There's nothing you can do," Caleb said. "There's nothing any of us can do. It's hit a bunch of folks. Mrs. Hagen and Dooley—they're both dead. You've done all you can do. Please, Ellie, go over to the Petersons' and I'll clean up here. Then I'll come and get you, and Lucy Ann and Lorene will help you lay them out, and Smithy and me—we'll help too, if you want."

Eliza drew away from Caleb as if she'd been struck. "No!" she hissed at him. "I won't go. Bring me Ben, Cal. I'll clean them myself. I don't want you or anyone helping me. You all go!" In the light of pale dawn, Caleb saw Eliza's cold, determined eyes and he knew there was no changing her mind.

A short time later, Caleb and Stilly brought Ben to Eliza. She then asked them to leave and she turned to her task. Several times as she worked, she remembered her father's words after the buffalo stampede. "When there's real trouble, you can't let go. Not then." She wouldn't let go. She would make her father proud of her, and do what had to be done. She quickly washed and cleaned the ravaged bodies and then dressed them in their best clothes. She was dry-eyed as she worked, even when she tied a pretty white ribbon in her mother's black hair.

It was midmorning when Eliza opened the wagon flaps and looked out at a sky where the sun was too bright. A little later, standing beside eight newly dug graves, Eliza placed branches of prickly cactus over her people, praying that this would keep the wolves away. The wind had come up, and as she tied her poke bonnet tighter, she was reminded of the time she had stood beside Janie Marie's grave.

At midday, the wagons were loaded and camp was struck. Both Ben and Sam begged Eliza to let them drive her wagon team, but Eliza flatly refused. Taking her papa's bullwhip, she watched O'Shea raise his arm, and whistle as the train started to move. She then looked around for a sign—one landmark she might remember if she ever returned. Clumps of cactus grew all through this limitless land. Ahead she could see the Wind Mountains and the Rockies, the great gateway to the Oregon states. But Eliza Landon knew she would never return to her family buried here in the vast windswept land where they had trekked on their quest of dreams.

Chapter 24

Bleached animal bones littered the alkaline flats surrounding the lake. Bones of oxen, horses, mules, cattle, and dogs had been drawn to the vile water and had died after drinking the stuff. A weathered sign driven into the crusted ground close beside the trail skirting the lake read POISON. ALKALI WATER HERE.

"Get on there, Big Moo! Get on!" Eliza cried, taking her whip to her lead ox. Big Moo was the ox that Caleb had given her after her family had died. Caleb considered the animal to be especially strong and smart; Eliza had named him Big Moo because of the animal's size and his bawl.

"Move on, Big Moo! You can't be thinking of stopping here! Move on!" she called out again, keeping her wagon moving ahead as *The Oregon Roll* worked its way along the shallow lake, heading for Bessemer's Bend on the North Platte where they would camp that night.

Oh Lord, Eliza thought, wiping her upper arm against her forehead and leaving a smear of grime and alkali dust on her face. She wrinkled her nose with distaste as she caught the strong odor of her own sweat and unwashed skin. Lordy, Lordy, to be able to take a bath.

The last time she'd bathed was more than a week

ago back at the Bitter Cottonwood. That time seemed like a very long time ago. A time when she had argued with her mother about a piddling matter such as having to bathe in the river. A time when, as she had dressed that late afternoon, she had taken time to pay attention to herself and had wanted to look pretty for the party. A different time then, when her worries had been niggling. Now, all of that seemed silly and foolish. Now, haunted by the memory of the sickness that had taken her family, her heart felt torn and her worries were different. What was important now was facing each day with a new resolve—reaching the Oregon country. Today this meant another day of treking across a sun-scorched plateau, dotted with patches of alkali. Mean stuff that could kill people and animals alike.

At the nooning, earlier today, Eliza had worked on her oxen, wiping their big dusty gray faces with one of Ben's cotton shirts. It had bothered her at first, using the shirt like that, but she'd told herself if it worked to keep the alkali from caking up into hard, sun-baked rims around Big Moo's and the other animals' noses, mouths, and eyes, well, that was putting a piece of good cloth to good use.

Now, this afternoon, as the emigrants treked on through smothering dust, Eliza looked on ahead over the rolling hills and saw the Sweetwater Mountains. Patches of snow were scattered across the higher peaks. Would she see snow before reaching the Willamette Valley? She couldn't imagine anything more welcome than that. Snow. So clean, and so cold.

She then turned her thoughts to tonight when she would join the Petersons after supper. Lorene was bringing a special fruitcake as a desert, and Sam was sure to start folks singing if he brought his harmonica. Tonight would be the first time since Eliza's family and Dooley McVey and the Hagens had died that there would be thought given to fun. While Eliza didn't feel ready for that kind of thing, she knew it was time.

It was late in the day when *The Oregon Roll* came to Bessemer's Bend. Tomorrow the train would cross the Platte and the folks would say farewell to this great dun-colored river that had served as fine guide but difficult companion to the emigrants since they'd first reached it two months ago.

A grove of cottonwoods offered a fair campground, and after setting camp the men got busy caulking the wagons, making sure the seams were tight. Sam inspected *The Long Eagle* with care and then patched two seams with thick tar. When he finished, he looked at Eliza with a gentle smile. "I'm looking forward to this evening," he said. "I hope you are too."

"It will be nice," she said. "Taking our minds off ourselves a little."

As she walked across camp toward Stilly and Lucy Ann's, she stopped for a moment and watched a group of children playing hide and seek. Their high-pitched shrieks, laughter, and shouts sounded good. But it was then that Maggie's frightened shouts broke over the camp.

"Danny! George! Come quick! Our team got to the water, and they're sick! They're sick as can be!"

Hitching up her skirts, Eliza turned and ran back to her wagon, where she jumped up inside and yanked the lid off one of her big food barrels. Lifting out a large hunk of bacon, she tucked it under her arm, jumped down from her wagon, and raced over to the McVeys' camp. Danny, George, and Sam were working with one of the stricken animals; Stilly, Caleb, and Clancy were with the other.

Both oxen lay on their sides, their tongues lolling out of their mouths, their eyes rolling in their heads as they gasped for breath.

"Here," Eliza shouted, thrusting the bacon to Danny, who rammed it onto the end of a stick. Then, while George held the animal's mouth open, Danny forced the bacon down the its throat, followed by sloshes of vinegar that Sam dumped from a large jug. Caleb, working calmly but quickly with Stilly and Clancy on the other animal, had done the same thing. That done, they watched the animals for a few moments. If anything could save the two miserable beasts, it was this. Maggie, standing between Danny and George, had tears in her eyes.

"I don't know, Maggie, if it'll work," George said. "But it worked before when Clancy's ox got in trouble."

"It should work, George," Clancy said. "We got to them soon enough."

The big ox head showed big teeth; it grinned and its big eyes glowed green, and then it coughed and its head crumpled and disappeared in the night as Sam and Smithy jumped out from behind the Petersons' wagon into the circle of folks sitting in front of the fire.

Maggie laughed—Oh, Maggie laughed while the children squealed with delight at the game of make-believe. Sam and Smithy both bowed. Smithy grinned, while holding the big stick that he and Sam had rigged up by wrapping wads of newspaper with a cloth, and attaching it to the stick. Smithy had then painted this "head" as a cow's face, while Sam had used willow branches to form horns.

"Those two oxen of yours, Miss Maggie," Sam said, "are doing just fine." Everybody laughed and cheered, and Maggie looked livelier than she'd looked since she'd lost her boy.

Lorene passed out slices of fruit cake, laced with brandy, and Lucy Ann and Eliza poured steaming coffee into cups, followed by a pitcher of thick cream. Many of the folks had gone on to bed, but the McVeys, the Evanses, Eliza, Caleb, Smithy, Sam, and O'Shea sat around the Petersons' fire, which flared like small orange curtains shutting out the night.

Eliza, sitting next to Caleb, leaned back against his arm, warm feeling and strong. She looked closely at these people who were now so important to her. Stilly and Lucy Ann. Lucy Ann's belly large now with child, due in just one month, and Lucy Ann excited about having her baby born in the Oregon states.

Stilly's face reflected distant thoughts as he sat with his arm around Betsy, the pretty child with brown curly hair and large brown eyes. Betsy had had her tenth birthday yesterday. Stilly and Lucy Ann had given her a horse that Stilly had bought from a Sioux at Fort Laramie. When the Petersons had sold their place in Pennsylvania, Betsy's horse had been included in the sale and neither Stilly or Lucy Ann had forgotten the sorrow in their daughter's eyes. Betsy was ecstatic with the little broom tail, a beautiful roan she called Streak.

Sitting between Betsy and Lucy Ann was Jeremy, a good-looking lad who looked a good six inches taller than when they'd left Independence. Next month Jeremy would turn thirteen.

Eliza's gaze fell on Maggie, George, and Danny, who sat close together and were quieter than they used to be. Good-hearted, easygoing folks, and Eliza was delighted to see Maggie's cheerful face tonight. Next to the McVeys were the Evanses. Clancy and Lorene, steady, generous, and cheerful. And also rich, but it never seemed that way. Clancy hoped to start a school in the Willamette Valley. "It's important," he'd told Eliza once, "that education out in the Oregon states not be confined to the missionaries." He had also told her that teaching children seemed to be a good thing to do.

Then there was Sam. Sam, who always wanted everybody to have a good time. And Sam, along with O'Shea, knew a certain amount of doctoring for both folks and animals. Eliza watched him now as he blew softly on his harmonica, playing a tune everybody liked: "Long Time Ago."

Yesterday Sam had walked with Eliza for part of the day and she'd learned that he'd lost his wife and three-year-old boy to typhoid, just over a year ago. He'd then sold his house and the newspaper he'd owned in Decatur, Illinois, and had decided he'd come west. Sam's plans were to establish himself at the northern end of the Willamette Valley in a little town where he hoped to start another newspaper.

Smithy sat next to Sam. Where had this silent boy with the brown unruly hair, the big eyes, and the wide grin come from? Eliza often thought about that. Smithy had obviously gone to school because he could read and write. And Smithy wasn't so shy anymore; he no longer ducked his head or worried so much about Dog as he used to. Eliza often remembered the words her mother had said; Smithy was wise and lucky to have found Caleb Pride.

Eliza held Smithy's drawings and paintings in high regard. She had carefully packed away the pictures he'd given her—drawings of her family, of Caleb, and Dog, and recently he'd given her a new painting of her wagon with the great eagle on it.

Sitting next to Smithy was Paddy O'Shea, the man they all counted on. To Eliza, O'Shea remained mysterious and she continued to hold him in awe. He knew so much, yet he talked very little. And now with her family gone, he often came by in the late afternoon, after the train had set camp, and he'd ask how she was doing, and did she need any help. Eliza always said thank you, that she was doing just fine.

Thoughts of her family were always there. Her grief had, at first, seemed unbearable, but as she faced each day with a determination to see that day through, determination became her ally. She also remembered, time and again, her father's last words, "buy land . . . good land . . . lots of good land . . ."

Within the last few days, she had given thought to her future. Aside from surviving and getting to Oregon, she must have a plan for herself. She had thought about returning to Independence and going to a seminary, but that idea, along with becoming a "go-back," brought on a melancholy. She thought of going to California, where, in the Sacramento Valley, she would buy land and perhaps find a school that suited her future needs. She didn't feel comfortable with that idea either; she had no interest in going to California. Her heart was set on the Oregon country, and she kept coming back to her father's plan. This plan suited her well and this was the plan she would stay with.

With that decision made, she began to feel better. In the Willamette Valley she would claim as much land as was allowed, and then buy land to add to her claim. She would build herself a good house, develop a fine farm, and maybe raise some cattle. If there was a thought of Caleb in her mind, she pushed it aside. She had her own life to think about and she had no idea what Caleb's plan might be. It was something she had wanted to talk to him about, a long time ago, but there had never been time. Just as there had never been time to talk about old Boone. She smiled. For some reason that didn't seem so unimportant, and she wondered why.

* * *

"How much longer do we have to put up with it?" Clancy asked the question that was on everybody's mind—putting up with the alkali. Eliza turned her attention to O'Shea.

"Off and on all the way to Fort Boise," he answered. "After that, it depends."

"Depends?" Stilly asked. "Depends on what?"

"Depends on what you folks think about an idea I've got." O'Shea had everybody's attention. Drawing his great coat around his shoulders, he looked around the fire, meeting the emigrants' eyes. Then he spoke slowly. "Everybody dreads crossin' the Blues. At best it's one helluva—excuse me ladies, but it's a hard crossing. Then, after crossing the Umatilla River, we've got the trek on down the Columbia Plains. Dry land not a whole lot different from this, all the way to The Dalles. At The Dalles we're going to either take the Barlow Trail over the Cascades, or we'll take the Columbia down to Fort Vancouver and Oregon City. Now you've all heard that river trip's wicked at best. It can be done, and we'll do it well, if that's what you folks decide is best. But let me tell you an idea I've got where we could avoid those Blues, and the Columbia."

He paused, reached into his coat pocket, and took out his pipe and an old leather tobacco pouch. He untied the pouch and carefully shook a little tobacco into the bowl of his pipe. Tamping the tobacco down, he lit his pipe and drew deep, savoring the heady smoke. Then he spoke.

"After we leave Fort Boise, we come on to a river called the Malheur. Now, if we should cut west there at the Malheur River, we'd go over a piece of desert and come out at a river called the Deschutes. The Deschutes isn't a whole long ways from the Cascade Mountains that separate this desert from the Willamette Valley. Now, crossing the Cascades'd be tough, I'm not denyin' that, but the thing is, once we're across, taking a southwest route, we'd come out at the southern end of the valley. There'd be no crossin' the Blues; there'd be no Columbia to worry about." His words were measured and slow. "It would be crossing the patch of desert to the Cascades and then crossing on over to the valley. Stephen Meek did it a couple of years ago, but got lost. If we decide to do it, we're *not* gonna get lost. I know the country some, and I wouldn't suggest it if I thought it wouldn't work."

Visions of crossing the Blues raced through Eliza's mind. She'd heard about the terrifying experiences; how chains and ropes, wrapped around huge trees and anchored to wagons, would often snap, sending wagons careening down a steep hill, a canyon, or a ravine, smashing the wagons and all the goods to smithereens. She had also heard about storms that came, even in late summer, bringing snows that stranded folks, and the folks had died of cold and starvation. And there were always the stories about unfriendly Indians.

"Well," Stilly said. "We've got some time to think about this, so let's think."

O'Shea nodded. "Clancy, you brought up the alkali and I figured it was a good time to tell you about my idea. But I'll also tell you this. Both ways, there's desert and alkali. Both ways there's mountains to cross."

"I'll say right now, Paddy, I'm for your plan," George said. "I'm for cutting across to the Cascades." Maggie silently nodded her head, while looking into the dying fire.

"I agree with George," Sam said. "I'll go with your plan. Avoid crossing the Blues."

"I'm for it," Danny said. "If Ma and Pa are, count me in."

"Let's think on it," Caleb said. "The rest of the folks should be told, Stilly. And Paddy, we should all take a good look at your map. Then after the idea's had time to sit, we can take a vote."

It was late when the small party broke up. Hugging themselves to keep off the chill, their voices were soft as

211

they said good night and walked off to their wagons and tents. Caleb took Eliza's hand as he walked with her over to *The Lone Eagle*.

"Tomorrow I'm riding with you when we cross the river," he said.

"I can do it, and I want to, Cal. Janie Marie took her wagon across, and so can I. But I have to say I think it's fine if you ride with me."

Caleb slowed his step. "We're getting close to the Sweetwater, Ellie. And Independence Rock. When we get there, let's find us a place with some pretty flowers and a little creek. Maybe we can take a picnic, and spend a little time."

"There hasn't been time like that for a while. Oh Cal . . ." Her voice broke. "I miss my papa and mama and Ben. My God! I do!" She stopped and raised a clenched fist up to the sky.

"When I look up there at night, I think of God," she cried, tears streaming down her face. "A God I'm supposed to believe in! And then I think of my people. My good people, and when I think of what happened to Janie Marie, I wonder if there's a God at all. And if there is, is he a just God? To my mind, I think not."

Caleb gently drew her to him. Holding her close, he caressed her hair, and not speaking, he held her as she wept. When she stopped crying, he lifted her face to his, and his voice was soft. "If there is a God, Ellie, and I generally think there is because good things happen too, good things will happen to you and me."

"Good things haven't happened for a while." She wiped her tears and smiled a little half-smile. "No, that's really not true, is it. We were able to save Maggie's oxen, and we sure had a fine time tonight. Thank you, Cal. Thank you for listening to me. I'll be looking forward to a good crossing tomorrow, and then we'll be leaving this river." She sighed. "We'll be leaving this country where my family is buried, and I don't suppose I'll ever be back."

Chapter 25

Hawks silently glided in the pearly gray dawn, and cotton-woods showed black against the sky as the emigrants prepared to cross the Platte. Among other duties, wagon tops now had to be folded back and anchored tight. This would prevent the chance of a stray gust of wind catching the hempen fabric, dizzily spinning the wagons, dumping them, and throwing screaming passengers into icy waters, to be swept downriver to watery graves.

Eliza, astride Babe, took her place in line behind the Evanses' wagon. Babe nervously pawed at the ground, blew, and tossed her head. Eliza leaned over the big palomino and talked quietly in her ear, while rubbing her golden brown neck.

"Good girl, Babe. You'll be doing fine." Then, hearing Stilly's whistle, she kneed Babe hard. "Get on there, Babe now. Get on. We got to go." She talked quietly and steady, while urging Babe through the slippery shallows. Suddenly they were in deep water and Eliza felt the river surge and pull against Babe. Babe strained her neck, lifting her head high, while struggling to keep her footing on the quivering, jelly-like river bottom.

Eliza knew it was quicksand, but refused to think about it now. Pulling hard on the reins, she forced Babe to stay close to Big Moo, whose rasping bawls seemed to propel her forward, forcing the rest of the team as they strained against the swift current. Panic, sure and swift, rose in Eliza's throat as she was suddenly engulfed in a world of snorting animals and the terrifying roar and hiss of sand-laden waters sweeping against *The Lone Eagle*'s huge wagon wheels.

Then Babe foundered and Eliza shuddered, fighting her terror and her desire to scream for help. *When there's real trouble, you can't let down. Not then, Ellie. Not then.* Her papa's words cut through to her, and leaning over Babe, she forced her voice to be as steady as she possibly could, while she yelled in Babe's ear. "Babe! Babe! Up! Up! Come on! We're almost across!" At the same time she saw a hand reflected in the big splashes of water and bright sun. It was Caleb's hand, sure and steady on the throat-latch of Babe's harness as Babe steadied herself, and re-gaining her balance, she snapped her head up and plunged ahead through the shallows and on to dry land. Eliza saw, right beside her, Big Moo and the oxen team haul her dripping wagon ashore.

"You did it, Ellie, you did! Good job!" Caleb shouted. Eliza, muddy water streaming from her dress, fell forward in her saddle and flung her arms around Babe's neck. Looking over at Caleb, astride Sweetface, she smiled. "Thanks, Cal. You helped too."

The Oregon Roll left the parched, alkalied country and came to a land of stinking, steaming marshes strewn with animal bones. Swarms of flies and mosquitoes tortured the emigrants and animals. Again, the presence of buffalo helped ease the folks from the itching, burning bites when O'Shea passed the word that the pesky, persistent insects shied the smokey, chip-fed fires. Small fires were built even inside the moving wagons, but still the children fretted, and the animals were often driven to a frenzy. The train moved fast to get through this cursed place.

Then, on leaving this country, the emigrants found themselves again in a dry land where, for two days, clouds of grasshoppers appeared. Fat clattering things that clung to the animals and people, and swarmed on the ground to be crunched by boots, hooves, and wagon wheels. Late one afternoon Eliza saw big trees throwing out arms of deep violet shade while a girl, dressed in a pink dress, danced on a shimmering lake. Eliza shook her head, knowing she was seeing a mirage. But she thought about her pink dress with the white lace collar. That dress had been very important to her once; now she couldn't think for sure where it was, or if she even had it. The pink dress didn't matter anymore.

Chapter 26

A humped shadow, dim and vague, appeared against the horizon of dawn. As the train moved on, the hump became distinct and by late morning Eliza and the emigrants watched it with keen eyes.

"Ellie." Eliza turned and waved at Caleb, pleased to see him. But why was he riding up here with the wagons? He never did that; his place was at the rear of the train, riding with the herds.

Quickly dismounting, he fell in step beside her, while leading Sweetface. "Let me take it," he said, indicating her quirt.

"I can drive my team, Cal. Perfectly well."

"Well, let me just give you a little rest." She looked at him, puzzled, but she handed him her quirt. "What brings you up here this morning?"

Caleb grinned. "See that?" he asked, pointing west toward the looming shadow.

"I've been watching it for a while now. It's Independence Rock."

"Independence Rock means the Sweetwater and good drinking water for our animals and for us."

She laughed. "I know. The rock looks like a big turtle, doesn't it."

"It does!" They both laughed, and then Caleb

looked serious. "There's something I want to ask you." He paused, plucked a piece of tall weed loose, and appeared to study it closely while he walked.

"Well . . . ask." Eliza's tone was slightly impatient; her thoughts were on getting to Independence Rock and having a bath in the Sweetwater with Lorene and Lucy Ann. They had already made their plans.

"What are you going to do when we get to the Willamette Valley in Oregon?" Caleb looked at her intently. "We've never talked about that."

"No," she said. "We haven't. But now that you ask, I can tell you I don't know exactly where I'm going in the valley, but I intend to stay with Papa's plan. I figure to buy land on top of my claim and build a good house and have a good farm. Maybe raise some cattle. That's what I intend to do."

"H'mm." Caleb nodded thoughtfully. "You know, I have the same thing in mind. For Smithy and me." He and Eliza walked on in silence for a few moments before he spoke again. "Let's pull on over," he said. "Let these folks behind us go on ahead. I want to ask you something and I don't want to be walking when I ask."

"We mustn't dally, Cal. I can't wait to get to that good water up ahead."

"What I've got to ask won't take long," Caleb said, while moving her team off to the side of the wide trail and motioning to the folks behind to go on ahead. "We'll catch up soon enough." He then whistled, called her animals to a halt, and turned to her. When he spoke, his voice was soft with an edge of worry. "This sure isn't the kind of place I had in mind for asking what I'm going to ask, but I don't want to wait for the right place. That isn't important anymore. What's important is what I'm going to ask and what you're going to say." He cleared his voice twice, took off his battered straw hat, and held it at his side.

"My God," he said. "I'm as scared as an old hen that

knows a fox is in the barnyard. Well, I just got to say it now." He paused and again looked at her intently. Eliza, noting that the last wagon in the long line had passed, frowned.

"Say what, Cal? We have go get back in line. You know how much Stilly hates for folks to pull out like we've done. And I'm anxious to beat all to get on to the Sweetwater . . ."

"I love you, Ellie." Caleb's words came with a rush. "Oh God, I love you so much, Ellie, I can't say it enough. And I'm asking you to think about marrying me."

Eliza stared at him, wide-eyed, aware for a moment of the squeaking wagons, the muffled shouts as the train moved on up ahead. She blinked, her eyes burning from the wind and alkali dust. Raising one hand, she tried to wipe the tears away, leaving a smear of grime along her sunburned cheek.

It wasn't supposed to happen this way. Not like this! Not standing out in a barren, dusty country, a no-man's land and listening to a declaration of love and a marriage proposal from the man that she adored. But it was happening, and she felt her head giddy with joy. Clapping her hands over her mouth, she laughed with delight.

"Oh, Cal," she cried, "Oh Cal, Lordy, I'm so happy I could burst. The right place? You said this wasn't the right place? It sure isn't. Where's the soft moonlight, and the sweet-smelling flowers? All of those romantic notions a girl thinks about. And me . . . I should be wearing a pretty flowery dress, all sweet and clean." She laughed again as she grabbed his arm. "Look at me, Cal. Just look at me. I'm sunburned as all get-out and my eyes are the color of red ants. I'm covered with alki dust, my hair's a tangle of mess, my hands are calloused and hard, and I need a bath so bad I stink to high heaven and it's a sure pity. And here you're asking me to marry you, and I can't remember when I've been so happy. Yes! Yes!"

Caleb threw his hat up in the air, grabbed her, and

whirled her around. "Yaahooo! Yaahooo!" he cried. Setting her down, he cupped her chin in his hand and turned her face up to his. "You might take a good look-see yourself, Eliza Landon." His voice was soft. "'Cause I'm not looking like any prize. But does that matter? Does that matter at all?" His eyes were tender and he smiled. "Oh Ellie, no. That doesn't matter. What matters is what we feel, and what matters is that you love me enough to marry me."

Suddenly Eliza's world of parched earth and blazing sun, of noise and dust and worry and awful sorrow, hung suspended. Her heart quickened as his lips brushed her forehead, and trailing a forefinger lightly down the side of her face, his mouth gently sought hers. Then, drawing her close to him, she responded, parting her lips, tasting him, while feeling the sudden rush of need for him. Slowly she pushed herself away, and she laughed, her laugh trembling, her voice low.

"I do love you, Caleb Pride. I do indeed."

Caleb's smile was a smile of joy that Eliza had never seen in her life. She reached up and touched his lips with her fingers. "Cal, did you know that your eyes are as blue as the summer skies? Did you know that I've thought that ever since we were children?"

Caleb laughed. "And did you know that I almost didn't have the nerve to speak up today? Do you remember, back at the Platte, when I asked that we find a pretty place for a picnic up ahead at Independence Rock?"

"I do. I do indeed."

"Well, that's where I thought I'd ask. I wanted to wait until we got to a pretty place. But when I asked O'Shea where that pretty place might be, he laughed and said there wasn't much pretty until we get to the Bear River up in the Rockies. I couldn't wait that long, Ellie. I just couldn't wait. Now, I got to ask you though . . . when?"

"When what?" He saw a sparkle of tease in her eyes.

"When can we get married? When will you marry me?"

"Cal, we might be the only train between Independence Missouri and the Pacific Ocean that's traveling without a preacher. And we got to have a preacher. I guess we'll have to wait until we find one."

"Fort Hall," Caleb said in a firm voice. "There's got to be a preacher at Fort Hall. Or at least a Justice of the Peace or some kind of marrying man."

"Fort Hall sounds awfully bleak. Fort Hall's probably not a whole lot different than Laramie. What do you say to waiting until we get to the valley? Yes! Let's wait until then. I want our wedding to be real nice, Cal. And you know if we take the cutoff Mr. O'Shea told us about the other night, we're going to get there a sight quicker that we'd thought."

Caleb was quiet for a moment. "Put that way makes me think I'm going to vote O'Shea's way, and forget about crossing the Blues. But if you want to wait until we get there, we'll wait. Then we'll do it up right and maybe even have us a party. Do you think Stilly and Lucy Ann will stand with us?"

"Oh yes. I'm sure they'd be pleased, too."

"Can we tell everybody? I want to shout it to the world!"

Eliza thought for a moment. "Well . . . I know Mama and Papa and Ben would say yes, and Janie Marie would be tickled to the tips of her toes. And seeing as how you're so anxious . . . I say yes, too!"

Again Caleb grabbed Eliza and whirled her around. "I'll be seeing you this evening, my darling girl. At Independence Rock. Soon as I'm through with the animals, I'll be comin' on by."

"And maybe, Cal," Eliza said, her green eyes sparkling with laughter. "Maybe tonight we'll have some time to talk again about old Boone."

Caleb threw back his head and laughed. "Oh Ellie, I haven't forgotten that."

Eliza then turned, and flicked her quirt over the backs of her team. "Get on there, Moo, get on! We got to get ourselves to Independence Rock."

Throwing his hat up in the air, Caleb caught it, turned, and waved as he jumped on Sweetface and galloped back to the rear of the train.

Chapter 27

Independence Rock on the Sweetwater. How many times had these bone-tired emigrants heard of this place. This great camping place where the Sweetwater River offered fresh clear water, and the enormous bulky rock provided shade.

The Oregon Roll, arriving midafternoon, set camp, allowing the travelers a small bit of leisure time. Eliza thought she would burst with joy as she quickly took care of her chores. She could hardly believe what had happened today and she silently repeated Caleb's words again and again. *Oh God, I love you so much, Ellie . . . and I'm asking you to think about marrying me!*

Yes! she thought, I'm going to marry Caleb! I'll be Caleb's wife! Eliza Pride! Mrs. Caleb Pride! Sorting through her food boxes, she tried to think of something special to fix for supper that night when Caleb would be eating with her. But game had been scarce, and Eliza settled on mixing up a batch of cornpone and bacon. She would open a jar of her mother's plum preserves to add a touch of festivity, and she would be waiting for him, bathed, refreshed, and wearing a clean dress.

Grabbing a chunk of soap, a towel, and her clothes, she hurried to meet Lucy Ann and Lorene at the river.

Lucy Ann had sent Betsy to find a place—a place where clumps of greasewood provided a bushy screen and Betsy would act as a lookout, affording the bathers a more relaxed sense of privacy.

Eliza couldn't wait to meet with her friends, and the thought of a dip in the river seemed heavenly after the long travel through the sunbaked alkali land. And did she have a wonderful surprise to tell her friends? Yes, she could hardly wait.

As she approached the river, she saw Lorene splashing with vigor in the sparkling waters. Lucy Ann stood close to the shore, up to her knees in water, but no farther. Both Lorene and Lucy Ann waved. "Come on, Ellie, come on! Water's cold as snow, but it sure feels good," they both cried while Betsy stood, stoically close by, keeping her eyes out for a possible intruder.

"I can't wait!" Eliza called out, quickly peeling off her dusty trail dress. Then, wearing her chemise, she laughed with delight as she ran into the river, and quickly lathered herself, feeling her skin pebbly with goosebumps.

"Lordy," Lucy Ann said with a laugh while venturing farther into the water, "I used to be plagued with such modesty, I never thought I'd be doing this kind of bathing 'cause of my big stomach. But not now. Not after that stretch of awful dusty trekin' we went through."

"And how I yearn for a real bath," Lorene called out. "I swear that's the first thing I'm going to do when I get my place out in Oregon. Take a real hot bath in my own washtub."

"And I have a surprise!" Eliza cried. The words tumbled out, quick as could be; she couldn't hold back for another minute. "And I can't wait to tell." She laughed as she untied the ribbon that held her long hair back in a knot off her neck. She shook her head, her green eyes dancing with joy.

"Tell! Tell!" Lucy Ann, Lorene, and Betsy all clamored, their voices rising in unison.

"Cal and I are going to get married! He asked me this morning!"

Shrieks of joy echoed off the rocks as the women gave each other cold, slippery, goosebumpy hugs.

"When? When?"

"Not until we get to the valley," Eliza said, breathless with elation. "But when we get there, we're going to do it right. We'll all be there and we'll have a splendid party. Oh Lordy, I'm so happy I could just—I don't know what." Skipping her hand against the water, she sent a spray over Lorene's head. Lorene shot a fat spray back, and then Lucy Ann splashed them as they frolicked and laughed and shrieked while playing in the Sweetwater River.

"Lucy Ann," Eliza called out, her voice coming in short breaths. "Will you and Stilly stand with us?"

"We will, you know we will."

"And Lorene, you told me once how you love to play the organ. Well, I'm not going to get married without organ music. Will you play?"

"I will, I will indeed. I'll play with a song in my heart, for you and Cal."

"Betsy . . ." Eliza walked back to the shore. "Will you be my flower girl? You'll wear a pretty dress and carry a basket of flowers." Betsy giggled and ducked her head, suddenly shy. But then she looked at Eliza, nodded, and smiled. "Yes," she said. "I'll be your flower girl."

"It's all settled." Eliza gave Betsy a hug. "And you'll be the prettiest flower girl that ever was."

Then, splashing themselves as they left the river, they dried and dressed. "I can't believe this has happened," Eliza said. "I have to keep talking about it."

"Do," Lucy Ann said as she and Lorene both laughed. "Yes, do tell us more."

"Well, he just rode up this morning as I was walking along and we were talking about this and that, and he just . . . he just asked me."

"I knew he would, Ellie," Lorene said. "I knew that a long time ago. Anybody would have to be blind not to see how much that man loves you. His eyes just melt when he sees you, and he watches you all the time."

"I . . . I didn't know that. I knew he liked me well enough, and I . . . you know I . . . since Mama and Papa and Ben died, there's been lots of other things for me to think about." She sighed. "Well, it's time now to think about other things. Let's take our dusty old clothes back to our wagons and then let's walk up to the rock and read the names. It isn't far, and we've got time before supper."

"Let's. I knew we would do that," Lorene cried. "I'll bring some good wagon dope so we can add our own names."

A short time later, they all met again to walk up the trail to the rock. "I just wish my family was here," Eliza said. "They'd be shining with joy 'cause they sure loved Cal. And Janie Marie, too. Whoa, can't we all see Janie Marie, fixing me up all fancy?"

"Ellie," Lorene suddenly exclaimed. "I wasn't thinking at all. What about a dress? Heavens, if you need one, I've got a whole trunk full. And I have a particular one in mind that would look real pretty on you. It's white with little pink and green flowers, and it has real pretty lace at the neck."

"And you can carry my yellow parasol," Lucy Ann added.

Eliza, walking between her two friends, put an arm around each of them. "Lucy, the first time I ever saw you, back at Independence, you were sitting by your wagon, under your parasol. It fits you. I want to see *you* at my wedding, carrying your parasol. But I sure might borrow a dress, Lorene. I don't think Cal's going to want me to

225

take the time to order cloth all the way from back east and then have me take the time to make it up. And my best dress—the pink one that I wore back at the Bitter Cottonwood—I don't think I even have it anymore."

"Mama!" Betsy, who had gone on ahead, now came racing back down the trail. "I see Mr. Edwards's name!"

"Well, my heavens, Betsy Lou, let's just see." Lucy Ann turned to Eliza and Lorene. "George Edwards lived not far from us, back in Pennsylvania," Lucy Ann said. "He was the one who gave Stilly and me the first idea of coming out. What fun this is, coming on to his name."

Eliza smiled. Wouldn't it be something to come onto a name of someone you knew.

The huge rock was strewn with names. Some smeared on with wagon dope, others carefully printed with paint. ALLISON WEAVER, OREGON HERE I COME FROM BOSTON IN 1846. JACOB WEAVER, BOSTON TO OREGON IN '46. And Mr. Edwards's name. GEORGE EDWARDS, PENN TO THE OREGON STATES. 1845.

"Come on!" Lorene laughed. "Let's add ours. I'm not going to let this chance go by." In moments the three women and Betsy were busy inscribing their names and dates. ELIZA LANDON, JULY 1848. Who might read that, she wondered. Who might care? It was fun thinking that for hundreds of years her name would stay, just as she'd printed it on the face of the rock, joining other names of folks making the long trek west.

Then, as they turned to leave, Eliza bent down to read one more message that caught her eye. A message that left her stunned. There it was again! Another message just like the one she and Cal had seen at Chimney Rock! MAX PRIDENTZ LOOK FOR ME AT FORT HALL. CLARA MCCABE. Eliza felt her heart slide to the pit of her stomach. What in God's name did this mean? She shook her head, trying to clear her mind.

"C'mon, Ellie," Lorene called from the trail on ahead. "We'd best be getting on back to camp."

Eliza sat down on a big slab of flat rock, bent over, and untied her boot. "I've got a rock in my boot," she called back. "You all go on and I'll be coming. Don't wait." She waved at her friends.

"We'll walk slow," Lucy Ann said. "So come on, and catch up."

"I'll be coming along." Eliza sat very still for a moment, trying to clear her thoughts. Looking out toward the Rocky Mountains, she saw peaks gleaming against the great blue bowl of sky. After a moment or two, she got up and walked over to the place on the rock where the message was written and she read it again, hoping she had perhaps misread it. But it was there and there was no mistake and no pretending it wasn't there. Now Eliza knew she needed to hear from Caleb about the woman, Clara McCabe. Who was she? Why was she so anxious to meet Max Pridentz?

Eliza's cornpone and bacon sizzled slowly over her cook fire. Sitting in her mother's rocking chair close by, Eliza watched the sky turn red and gold over the big cleft in the Sweetwater Mountains; the cleft known as Devils Gate. That is where they would trek tomorrow.

The wind had come up, sending dark clouds scudding across the sky. Long shadows played over the Sweetwater and Eliza got up from her chair to get her shawl. She tried to think about tomorrow; she tried to think about Caleb's wonderful words today. But it didn't work. Her mind was closed in on the strange messages.

Questions now came to her mind that she had not thought of before. Why was it that she knew nothing about Caleb's life, from the time he'd left Kentucky until she had met him back in Independence? Why had he changed his name? What had happened? As far as she knew, people changed their names when they had been in trouble and they didn't want anyone to know who they

227

really were. She thought back to what he'd said when he'd told her family that nobody knew him by the name of Max Pridentz and he'd refused to tell them why. She thought back to Chimney Rock, and how upset he'd been when she and Caleb had discovered the first message. As Eliza pondered the matter, it became clear to her that his change of name and his refusal to explain why had a direct connection with the girl, Clara McCabe. She also knew that Caleb owed her an explanation. If she was to become his wife, she had a right to know; she would ask him tonight, straight out.

"Ellie!" She looked up to see him striding toward her. He had on his light tan buckskin pants and his best shirt, the one with the fringes and thrums. He waved and broke into a run. "I'm coming on by," he called.

A feeling of love for this man, so powerful it brought the sting of tears to her eyes, swept over her. But the cloud of the message she'd seen today made her shiver, and she drew her shawl close. She stood up to greet him, forcing a smile.

He drew her to him and kissed her tenderly. "Ellie," he whispered in her ear. "I can't believe it. My God, I thought this afternoon would never end and I couldn't wait to get here and be with . . . Hey," He stepped back and looked at her again, his eyes puzzled. "What's wrong? You've got a bundle of worry on your face."

Eliza held his gaze. "Yes, Cal. I do." She drew herself up as tall as she could, steeling herself against the questions she must ask him, feeling the stiffness in her neck and spine as she then said what she had to say. "I walked to the rock this afternoon. And I . . . I saw another message written for you. Just like the one back at Chimney. Only this time Clara McCabe asks that you meet her at Fort Hall. I have to know, Cal. Now. And you must

228

understand that. Who is Clara McCabe? Why are you so affected by her name?"

Caleb's face had gone white, and the light had gone out of his eyes as he stared at her. He blinked and turned away and neither of them spoke for a time. When Caleb broke the silence, his voice was flat and hard.

"I'll say this much, Ellie—there's things about me you don't know. Things I can't tell you about. Not yet. Maybe not ever. But I'll try and tell you something about Clara McCabe." When he turned back to her and searched her face, Eliza's heart went out to him; she could hardly bear to see him so hurt, but she had to know about the strange message. She silently nodded, meeting his gaze, direct.

Folding his arms across his chest in a stance Eliza had never seen him use before, he took a deep breath before he spoke. When he did speak, his voice was toneless, without expression. "Some time ago . . . a year or so after I left Kentucky, I worked in a tannery up in Pennsylvania run by a family named McCabe. They knew me as Max Pridentz. Clara was the youngest, a crippled girl with blond hair. I felt sorry for her because she wasn't treated right. I never got to know her well, but one day she found me in the office where I did bookkeeping and I told her then I hoped to go out to Oregon someday. She asked me if I'd teach her how to read, and I said sure. But I never did 'cause she never came back until the day I left, and . . . ." He paused, and again turned away.

"Yes, Cal. Please go on."

Facing her again, he continued. "I'd changed my name by the time I got to Independence, mind you, and it was there, last year, in January that Mr. O'Shea came into Moody's and asked me, out of the clear blue, if I knew a fellow named Max Pridentz. He went on to tell me he'd met a girl coming west named Clara who was looking for the fellow Max. Max Pridentz. I told Mr. O'Shea that I didn't know of a fellow by that name and he seemed to accept that. But I've always thought O'Shea knows I'm Max. If he does, he's the only person who knows that, Ellie. Except you. Now." Again he took a deep breath, and Eliza knew that what he was telling her was painful beyond what she could imagine. "It's my thinking that Clara's somewhere out here in the Oregon states. Mr. O'Shea told me he thought she'd taken up with an Indian and was living around Fort Hall. I'm also thinking that as Clara came west she left messages for me, as folks are want to do, hoping I might come on by. That's all there is. That's all there is, Ellie. There sure wasn't anything ever . . . nothing ever . . ." He spread his hands out in a helpless gesture. "We were only children, and I only saw her close twice. And even if we'd been older . . . well . . . I'd never have seen her in that way."

"Does she know you changed your name?"

"No. She couldn't know. I left there and I was still Max. And I never saw her again."

"Will you *ever* tell me why you changed your name?"

"Oh! God! I don't know!" She heard the anguish in his voice. "It doesn't have anything to do with the here and now. And not with you, Ellie! Never you! If it ever had anything to do with you, yes! I'd tell you. Please let's not talk more on this. Not when we've got such good things happening to us. Please!"

A silence fell between them. Eliza was vaguely aware of frogs croaking down by the Sweetwater; it was a sound she always liked. Reaching up, she touched Caleb's face, and as she held his face, dear to her beyond her own feelings, beyond herself, she saw tears in his eyes. She touched his lips.

"No, Cal," she said gently and her eyes held a pledge. "We won't talk about it again."

* * *

Thunder crackled and lightning danced against towering granite peaks west of the Sweetwater, while up on the dark slopes of the Wind River Mountains, forest fires raged. Then the rains came.

Eliza lay in her bed, listening to the storm and thinking about what Caleb had said. Finally, unable to sleep, she got up and placed her rocking chair at the front of the wagon. Pulling the wagon flaps open, she sat down and watched the storm.

There's things about me you don't know. Things I can't tell you about yet . . . Maybe not ever. His words echoed over and over in her mind. Maybe someday he would tell her what it was that troubled him so much—a thing, an event that had happened when he was young and it had to do with Clara McCabe.

But now, Eliza knew she had to let it be. Whatever it was, she had to put it away and forget it, and she had to stop wondering about Clara. If she didn't, her love for Caleb would become sullied and tainted by her doubts and distrust. And above all, she was resolved to stay with her pledge. *We won't talk about it again,* she'd said. She silently vowed to keep that pledge.

The next day *The Oregon Roll* moved on up the Sweetwater through the narrow stone walls at Devil's Gate to the open sage-covered country of the South Pass. The emigrants didn't say much as they treked along the wide dusty trail; most of them were unimpressed. But Eliza turned to Lorene, who was walking with her that day.

"Think of it, Lorene! We're at the top of the whole continent! Eight thousand feet above the Pacific Ocean!"

"I like that notion," Lorene said.

"Look close! Ellie! Look close!" Caleb called out as he galloped up to Eliza and Lorene. "I had to ride on ahead and be with you for just a minute. Just think, from

231

here on, all of the rivers and streams flow west to the Pacific Ocean."

Eliza laughed. "I wonder if it will be easier for us, coming on down the other side."

They all laughed, then Caleb whistled and rode back to the rear of the train.

Chapter 28

"I tell you, that baby's coming today, Ellie. Mark my words and say they're right." Maggie McVey chuckled as she and Eliza together wrung out a pair of Danny's heavy cotton pants and lay them beside numerous other garments on the grassy riverbank to dry.

It was a beautiful morning in the Rocky Mountains where the train was camped at the Bear River for two days. And what a sight to behold. The Bear River, running through an emerald green valley where drifts of wildflowers made a spectacular show of blue, yellow, pink, and white.

"Now that we know she's going to have her baby in the Oregon states, I doubt there'd be a prettier place to have it born than here," Eliza answered, looking at Maggie, who pressed her fists against the small of her back, leaned and stretched, while looking up at dark-forested mountain slopes and snow-covered peaks.

"Hmm. You sure speak the truth. And being as today's Sunday . . . well, that's a good enough day to be having a baby, and with the added layover tomorrow, that'll give her time to get a little rest. And we all need it. Folks and animals alike."

"True enough, Maggie. From what Caleb says, lots

233

of our wagons and gear are needing repair. I'm going on over to Lucy's this afternoon. Soon as I'm through baking up some bread, and I'll be taking her some."

Maggie nodded as the two women walked back to camp. "You'll let me know, Eliza, when you'll be needin' me to help with the birthing."

"I will. No doubt of that."

Returning to her wagon, Eliza kneaded a batch of bread dough on her wagon seat, placed the dough in a bread pan, covered the pan with a clean cloth, and set it in the sun to rise. While waiting for her clothes to dry and her bread to rise, Eliza sat down to alter one of her mother's dresses. Taking in the waist and letting down the hem would give Eliza one more dress to wear.

It was midmorning when Eliza gathered up her clothes at the riverbank and took them back to her wagon, where she stashed them, placing pieces of flannel on top. She would take the flannel with her over to Lucy Ann; it would come in very handy when the baby came.

"No more spirits, folks! Now that you're all in the magnificent Oregon states, there's no drinking of spirits allowed!"

Eliza shaded her eyes and looked out at the grassy clearing where a preacher stood on a stump. He'd ridden into camp yesterday, a tall man with a big face and small eyes. Both he and his horse had looked weary and Stilly had told the man he was welcome to stay over with the train for a day. This pleased many of the folks, who were anxious for some preaching, and the man was treated with generous hospitality. Now he had the clear attention of many of the emigrants, who stood, or sat on campstools or on the grass, listening to him preach.

"That's absolutely right! And it was the great people of the Oregon Territory who voted it right! No more liquor will touch our lips! No more giving it away, either to Injuns, who crave the evil stuff. Now, I'm telling you . . ."

Eliza sighed, finding the preacher's words irritating. Picking up the pile of flannel cloths and two loaves of her fresh bread, she walked over to Lucy Ann's. Lucy Ann, seated in a chair in the shade, was patching a pair of Jeremy's pants. On seeing Eliza, she smiled and stood up.

"I'm so glad you're here, Ellie. What with our men gone hunting, and Betsy and Smithy riding with some of the young folks, it's going to be a long day."

"I'm glad Jeremy got to go with Stilly and Caleb," Eliza said. "How are you feeling? Maggie's sure you're going to have that baby today."

Lucy Ann nodded and took a deep breath. "Maggie's dead right. This baby's coming today, or my name isn't Lucy Ann Peterson. But I'd sure like to walk a little. Help it on its way. Maybe we could walk down by the river and watch the spring."

Steamboat Spring, located in the Bear, was a place where every few minutes a fountain of water shot high into the air. It was a strange place, the surrounding waters making a chugging noise not unlike a steamboat. It was a place all the emigrants talked about seeing long before they arrived, and after they'd seen the gushing waters, they talked about it long after they'd left.

"Whatever you feel like doing, Lucy. But we don't want to walk too far."

"It's good to walk after riding in the wagon the past few days. I don't like that a whole lot." She laughed then, noting her own awkward, splay-footed gait, and she spoke in short, breathy sentences.

"Lordy, Ellie. I'll tell you, I'll be glad when this baby's born. It's getting to be a heavy one."

Taking Lucy Ann's arm, Eliza walked slowly, matching her pace, as they walked across the meadow and down to Steamboat Spring, where the waters rolled and bubbled and snorted and gurgled. Then, suddenly a huge spray of water spouted up high, glistening silver and gold in the sun before dropping back into the roiling river.

"Isn't that something!" Lucy Ann exclaimed, seating herself carefully on a large, flat rock. Silently, they watched the mysterious waters and another spout. "Just think, Ellie," Lucy Ann exclaimed. "Just think about the things we've seen on this long trail out to the Oregon states. Things we'll be talking about for the rest of our lives."

Eliza nodded. "I've thought about that, too. I used to keep a diary of sorts. I'd write down things that happened, things we'd see, and some of the feelings I had. But I haven't picked it up since Mama and Papa and Ben died. I never gave it a thought, in fact, until right now. But we'll sure have our stories, Lucy. Stories to tell our children and grandchildren. And you'll have a fine story, having a baby while traveling out."

Lucy Ann took a deep breath. "You know, each time we women have a baby, there's some chance. And I've gotten a little nervous, I guess, this time. With no doctor, and not even a midwife . . . well, I guess I have to say I'm feeling a little uneasy."

A sudden cold pang of fear struck Eliza. No, nothing would happen to Lucy Ann! Lucy Ann was strong and healthy, and Eliza and Lorene and Maggie would help her have this baby and she'd be just fine.

Lucy Ann laughed. "Besides, it's been a long time. Betsy's eight now, and Stilly and I had decided, after we had her, that two was enough."

"Lucy, I have to tell you . . . I don't understand that. It was something I was going to talk to Mama about, but I never did. How does that be? Why do some of you have only two children and others have more than they want?"

Lucy Ann laughed. "Lots of times it's plain good luck, Ellie. But with me, shortly after Betsy was born, my own Mama gave me a book about all of this. *The Private Companion of Young Married People,* and Mama said to me, 'Lucy,' she said, 'if you're going to keep your man from

236

jumping on you every time he has it in mind, read this. Both of you.' Well, we did, but then I also use other things. A good syringe, and ergot, ground up real fine, seems to work with me. Then last fall, after Stilly and I'd decided to make this trek, I got lazy, and . . . guess what!" She patted her enormous belly. "I've got the book, Ellie. I'll loan it to you and . . . when . . ." She suddenly whinced, but then held up her hand as if to caution Eliza. "No," she said. "Not yet. I want to think about something else for a minute or two. Something fun . . . something we'll be looking forward to. When it's time to go back, I'll let you know."

"Well . . ." Eliza said. "Let's talk about what we're all going to do when we're living in the valley, close to each other. Let's talk about Christmas. I'll be Mrs. Pride then, Lucy, and Cal and I'll have you all over to our house for sharing Christmas dinner. We'll have a real table to eat on and candles all around. Now, tell me what do you suppose Betsy and Jeremy might want for Christmas?"

Lucy Ann laughed. "Jeremy's wanting a new Kentucky rifle just like Cal's. Ever since he laid eyes on that rifle, he's talked about having one of his own. If Stilly agrees, that's what we'll be getting Jeremy. And Betsy? Betsy . . ." Lucy Ann whinced again, her face now white as chalk.

"Lucy!" Eliza grabbed Lucy Ann around her waist.

"You don't need to tell me, Ellie, and I'm not going to argue with you. This baby's on its way."

It was hot and close inside the Petersons' wagon, the heavy wagon cover allowing only for a flat dim light. Maggie, Lorene, and Eliza were now with Lucy Ann, who lay on her bed. Wet with sweat, Lucy Ann counted. "One . . . two . . . three . . ." She counted over and over again as she pulled hard on a long string of knotted cloths Stilly

237

had tied to the headboard. The labor contractions had now increased in speed and intensity.

Eliza nervously eyed the clean cloths stacked beside her, and she smiled as she saw the nice pile of baby clothes—flannel wrapping sheets, little cotton shirts, sacques, belly binders, and a stack of new diapers. Kettles of hot water bubbled on the fire outside, tended by Maggie. Lorene bathed Lucy Ann's forehead and face with cool, wet cloths, while Eliza messaged Lucy's feet.

"Lucy, if it gets bad, do you want us to give you some laudanum?" Eliza asked.

"No!" Lucy Ann panted. "I'll not take it. Opium's . . . opium's bad for a baby. But please!" Her voice was hoarse. "Please! I don't want Stilly and the children to know about the pain and all." Again, she gripped the knotted cloth, her knuckles white, her eyes wide. "My God!" she cried. "It feels like hot, heavy things are comin' down all through me! Promise! Don't let Stilly and my children see any of the birthing."

"We won't! We promise we won't, Lucy!" Eliza said. "By the time they get back, you'll have that baby, and you'll be resting, just fine. You've got the three of us to help you, and you just keep on pushing and soon you'll have that child in your arms."

But as Eliza watched Lucy Ann, straining, her eyes bulging with pain, she was afraid. Could she and Lorene and Maggie do the birthing right? Could they do what they must to help her birth the baby and not do anything wrong? My Lord, if only her mother was here. Or a doctor, or a midwife.

"Help me! Help me!" Lucy Ann's cries were desperate. Suddenly Eliza knew what she had to do. Standing at the foot of the bed, she grabbed Lucy Ann around her hips and pulled her toward her. "Let your legs go, Lucy. Come on, drop them! Lorene, count with her. Help her think about counting. Let's all count! One . . . two . . ."

Maggie, carrying a bucket of hot water, climbed back up into the wagon and joined them. "One . . . two . . . Come on, Lucy." Lucy Ann's harsh, panting voice joined them as she pushed, half crying now, as she tried again and again to push her child from her womb. Then she let out a long moan and a cry.

"Ah, Lucy!" Eliza cried. "I see the baby's head and it's got a whole lot of black hair." Then, grasping the baby's shoulders as Lucy Ann continued to work, gasping and groaning in her labor, Eliza gently pulled the slippery baby out and laid it on the bed between Lucy Ann's legs. Maggie quickly tied off the umbilical cord, snipped it, and picked up the baby, who let out a loud wail. Eliza reached out and took Lucy Ann's hand. "Oh, Lucy, you've got a beautiful little girl."

Maggie cut the umbilical cord, then washed the baby, wrapped her in warm flannel, and handed her to Lucy Ann, who, with raised arms, lay ready to receive her child. For a moment Lucy Ann studied her baby's wizened, red face, opened the blanket, and looked at her closely. Then she smiled, closed her eyes, and slept.

Eliza looked at Lorene and Maggie. "We did it!" she whispered. Lorene and Maggie nodded.

"Lucy Ann did it," Maggie said with a smile. "We helped. Thank the good Lord everything went all right." The three women then hugged each other in the close, hot wagon that smelled of sweat, of blood, and of birth.

They stayed with Lucy Ann that afternoon, quietly cleaning the wagon, and starting some supper. Lucy Ann would be hungry when she woke up, and Stilly and the children would be starved. Eliza walked out to the meadow and picked some bright pink and yellow flowers, which she placed in a jar beside the bed. Lucy Ann would like that.

It was late and the sun was low when the women made themselves a pot of tea, sat down outside the wagon, and chatted. Every now and then one of them would climb up into the wagon and look at the mother and child, who both slept.

Toward evening Stilly, Jeremy, and Caleb returned. Stilly joined Lucy Ann, who was now awake and nursing her baby. Stilly looked at both of them with an expression of exquisite tenderness. A few moments later the baby, apparently satisfied, stopped nursing, and Lucy Ann handed her to Stilly.

"She's a wonder, Lucy," he whispered. "She's our Oregon girl. Remember when we started planning our trip?" They both laughed softly. "And then you learned you were with child?" he continued. "I didn't want to come west then, but you insisted. Now, I'm glad. Yes, I'm so glad. You choose her name, Lucy. You decide."

"Ask Jeremy and Betsy to come and meet her, and then we'll all decide," Lucy Ann said.

After Jeremy and Betsy were sitting inside the wagon, Lucy Ann asked them all what they might think of calling her Cecilia Louise.

"I like that," Stilly said. "I like that name. It's a pretty name, and it fits her just fine."

"Can we call her Cece?" Betsy asked with a little laugh. "Cecilia Louise is awfully fancy."

Lucy Ann smiled and looked at Stilly and Jeremy. "What do you think? Should we call her Cece"?

Jeremy nodded solomnly while Stilly thought for a moment. "You can call her Cece," he said. "That's a nice name too, and a good idea, Betsy. But I think I'll call her Cecilia Louise."

Standing outside by the fire, the women now started to leave. "Wait," Stilly called out. Eliza turned and looked at him, framed in the wagon opening, holding his tiny baby daughter, his face wreathed in a gentle smile. Stilly raised his arm. "Thank you," he called out softly. "Thank you all very much."

Chapter 29

Bees hummed among thickets of willows, wild roses, and goldenrod in the valley bottom lands where the waters of the Port Neuf River sparkled clear. Wind-blown grasses, rippling silver and brown, covered the surrounding hills. Three nobby, sage-covered buttes stood as dark shadows against a cloudless sky. *The Oregon Roll* had come to the high country of Snake River, a plateau of desert, dry rocky canyons, and giant waterfalls; the land of the plateau Indians—the Paiute, Bannock, and Shoshone.

Early morning dew still glittered on the sage as the dirty gray wagons rolled up to the whitewashed mud walls of Fort Hall.

"Take some care with your planning, folks," O'Shea had advised. "I'm thinking we won't cross Snake River and go into Fort Boise. The old river's high, and I'd like to avoid crossing by staying on the south bank. Unless there's objection, we'll wave at Boise and roll on. So Hall's the last place of settlement we'll be going through until we get to The Dalles, or the Willamette Valley, depending on which route we take."

While at Fort Hall, Eliza, in spite of her vow to forget Clara, paid some attention to the girls she saw. Girls she

241

figured to be about her own age buying goods, loading wagons, tending to animals and helping children. But she saw no sign of a blond, crippled girl watching for someone passing through. Eliza then reasoned that Clara was probably no longer at Fort Hall, and besides, if she'd taken up with an Indian, she'd have a different life to tend to; Max Pridentz should no longer be on her mind.

It was at the Raft River Crossing, a place where a trail leading to California broke from the Oregon Trail, that the emigrants met a group of Mormons. The emigrants with the two trains enjoyed a nooning together, and Eliza chatted with two young women who were anxious to reach their destination.

When the two trains parted, Eliza watched the Mormon train as it swung off toward the southwest. She thought back to the first trail junction she'd seen, months ago. The vision of the two evil-looking men came to her, sharp and clear. The one-eyed man and the man with the burned head. She shuddered, and shook her head, trying to rid herself of the memory. But someday, after she and Caleb got to the valley and were talking about treking out, she must remember to tell him about those fellows. It wasn't important now. Now it was important to get on across the Snake Plains.

Day after day, in the dim light of each new dawn, the emigrants would strike camp and start the day's roll. By midmorning the sun blazed from a cloudless sky as the people treked through thick dust, churned by every hoof, every boot, and every wheel that crossed this barren land. There were days when the emigrants walked along bluffs high above Snake River gliding silently below. There were days when a piece of shade under a twisted juniper tree or a patch of tall desert grass was a welcome sight.

Some evenings brought dry camp in long purple shadows, with no water and no cook fires. Some evenings the people decided to travel on, and they would walk all night, passing outcroppings of obsidian that glittered under a full moon. During night treks, the oxen stepped slowly, voices were soft, and the children slept. Then, setting camp at dawn, the emigrants would sleep until midday and prepare to roll again late in the afternoon.

Eliza thought about O'Shea's idea of crossing the desert to the Cascades, instead of crossing the Blues. If they crossed the mountains, there would be cool shady forests, creeks with clear, cold water, and banks of wild-flowers. But Eliza had faith in O'Shea, and if she had a say, she'd vote to take the cutoff. She wished she had a say.

The men would vote on O'Shea's idea when they reached a camping place east of Fort Boise. If the vote favored O'Shea's plan, O'Shea and Caleb would scout on to the mouth of the Malheur River and then, following the river, they would head west, scout that country, and wait for the train at Malheur Lake. If, on the other hand, O'Shea and Caleb decided that the desert crossing was too dangerous and not worth the risk, they would double back and meet the train at the mouth of the Malheur; *The Oregon Roll* would then cross the Blues.

O'Shea had no qualms about taking Caleb and leaving the train. The Executive Committee had unanimously agreed that Stilly would act as guide and Clancy would be acting captain. Both men were smart and capable and, with O'Shea, had studied maps of the area. The train would do just fine.

"When I was a boy once, I . . ." Eliza looked up to see Caleb, reining in Sweetface. Grinning, he dismounted and walked along beside her. "It's a tough go along here, isn't it," he said. "What do you think? Should I vote to cross the desert, or the Blues? What would you do?"

"I was just thinking about that and I've made up my own mind. Let me know what you decide."

"So." He laughed. "You won't say until I say.

You're a scamp, Miss Landon. Well, let me tell you a funny story I thought of this morning. One that ought to tickle your bones out here in this danged heat. Now, when I was a boy . . . after I'd left Kentucky, I was a drover for a while. Back in Pennsylvania. And sometimes I stayed in taverns at night where I heard old men tell lies. This is how they talked, and this is what they said." Caleb squeezed his eyes shut, and made his voice thin and little.

"Yup. Yup. Yup Pap. Yonder, beyond the Massooree River, and yonder, beyond them high mountains of bright stone, there's shinin' mountains so high you cain't ever see the tops, and snows so deep, you cain't walk. And folks trekin' there get so danged hungry they et their shoes. Ain't no lie, Pap."

Eliza laughed so hard tears came to her eyes. "Oh, Cal, I love that story. What else did they say?" She was delighted. This was the first time she'd heard Caleb talk about that time in his life.

"Oh, they'd tell lies all night about how hard the trek was out here, and each fellow always tried to outdo the other in telling tall tales. I liked hearing them talk though, 'cause even then I knew I was going to come out here someday."

"Tell me some more about that time. Where were you when you first knew you'd be coming out?"

"In Harrisburg. On my way to buy myself a pair of boots with copper toes. A preacher was standing up on a porch with two Indians about the age I was then, and the preacher was talking about coming out here and 'carrying the word of the Lord to save the Indian heathens.' I was spellbound! I listened to every word he said. Of course I couldn't go; I didn't have the money, and I wanted money. Even back then I didn't want to be poor when I got to Oregon. But I bought my boots that day, and I remember thinking after buying them how proud you would have been of me."

"Ah, I like that. You thinking about me. I would have been proud of you, too. What happened to the boots?"

Caleb laughed. "Well . . . I've grown some since then, and . . ."

Eliza heard the change in his voice and saw his frown. "I don't know," he said. "I guess . . . well . . . those boots may have ended up with Clara McCabe. I don't know what happened to them."

Remembering her vow not to question Caleb about Clara, Eliza quickly changed the subject.

"Lucy Ann's sure doing fine. And doesn't Cece look just like her mama with her black hair and dark eyes. When Cece smiles, I swear I see Lucy Ann's dimples. What a pretty baby, Cal. And how fine it is that Lucy and Stilly plan on having her baptized when we get to Oregon and we're to be her godparents."

"Yes," Caleb answered. "I'm real proud of that, Ellie."

"So am I, Cal. So am I."

The echo of roaring water signaled that *The Oregon Roll* had come to Salmon Falls on the Snake River. On the bank below, naked Indians hurled barbed lances into the churning waters, spearing enormous salmon whose silvery scales flashed in the sun.

Stopping briefly at a nearby Indian village, the emigrants bartered mirrors, fish hooks, shirts, skirts, hats, and tobacco for fresh salmon. Late that afternoon, after setting up camp, they buried their fish under the coals of the cook fires, baked them, and while feasting on the succulent pink flesh, debated with relish whether the great salmon of Snake River or buffalo hump, found back on the plains, yielded the better meat.

* * *

Now came days of gray skies and drenching rain as the people moved through country recently swept by a wild desert fire. When the rains ceased, the sun reappeared, bright and unrelenting over a scorched land. Twisted limbs of burned sage stood as grotesque statues against the clear blue sky. Thank the good Lord, Eliza thought, that we didn't come through here a few days ago. She knew it would have been impossible to escape the terrible blaze.

But the land began to change, and when the emigrants passed by small streams with willows and cottonwoods growing along the banks, Stilly brought the train to a halt.

"Set camp, folks," he called out, his voice high with joy. "We've made it across the Snake Plains, and we'll soon be passin' by Fort Boise." Cheers split the air. "Now," he continued, "after supper we're calling for the vote. We'll either cross the desert to the Cascades, or cross the Blues. You all know what Mr. O'Shea thinks is best, and if we vote his way, he and Mr. Pride will be leaving us tonight to see firsthand if taking the Malheur is the best thing to do."

The meeting was called to order for one piece of business only. "Those in favor of Mr. O'Shea's plan to cross the desert to the Cascades, say aye," Stilly called out.

"Aye!" The men's shouts sounded unanimous.

"For the sake of formality, is anyone favoring taking the Blues?"

Silence. "Well, it's clear to me, then, that we go with Mr. O'Shea's plan. Now, he and Mr. Pride will leave us later tonight, and while they're gone, I'll be acting as guide; Mr. Evans will be acting captain until we meet Mr. O'Shea and Mr. Pride at the Malheur Lake. Any questions? Anybody got anything to say?"

"On to the Cascades!" The shouts rang through the camp. "On to Malheur Lake!"

Caleb slipped his arm around Eliza. "Are you pleased with the vote, Ellie? Did it go your way?"

"It did. And also . . . all of you voted for Mr. O'-Shea's plan. It seems to me that's important, too."

"It is. Now, if things go the way he thinks they should, we'll be in the Willamette Valley before the fall rains."

"Sometimes that seems like a long ways away." Eliza sighed. Campfires winked and lanterns inside tents glowed a warm orange light as she and Caleb walked toward her camp. "The tents look nice," she said. "Almost like little homes. They look a sight better to sleep in than the dusty, dark wagons."

"If we were going through Fort Boise, I'd buy you one," Caleb said. He looked at her, silhouetted against the evening sky. He loved to look at the silky, smooth curve of her cheeks, and her soft, sensuous lips. For the first time on this trek, he wanted to be rid of the everlasting camp and all the folks and animals and noise. He, too, was sick of the eternal dust and worry about weather and people and animals. Other folks' animals.

He longed to be alone with his beloved Eliza and he often thought about what it would be like to live in a real house and share a real bed in a bedroom, and sit at a real table and share a kitchen-cooked meal with her. No more hunkering down on campstools around an open campfire; no more lingering goodnights, and then a return to his own cold camp. No more lying in his blankets thinking about her . . . thinking about her with an ache in his groin that he couldn't help because of wanting her.

His voice now was rough when he turned her to him. Taking her chin in his hand, he looked into her eyes. "Someday, Ellie . . . someday soon now, you won't need to think about sleeping in either a tent, or a wagon 'cause we'll have a house of our own with a bedroom and a fine big bed beside a window where we can look out at the stars and the moon peeking in and out of tall fir trees. Oh Ellie, I love you more than I thought a man could ever love a woman."

When he kissed her, Eliza felt the heat of her own passion for him surge through her limbs. "And me, Cal! I'm so full of love for you too." She laughed softly and ran her hands through his hair, pulling his head down to her and kissing him, her lips parted. Then, gently pushing him away, she sighed. "I'm glad we're taking the shortcut, Cal. 'Cause we're going to get to the valley sooner, and we're going to be ready to get married, we are."

"We are at that," he whispered. "I'll miss you in the days ahead, and I'll be waiting for you, Ellie. At the lake they call the Malheur. I'll be waiting, oh yes, I'll be waiting."

Then he turned, and walking across the campground, he remembered the first camp of *The Oregon Roll,* back at Independence. They had come a long ways since then, over a thousand miles. He, too, had come a long ways since then; he had the love of Eliza Landon. He smiled to himself. If there's a man alive who's as lucky as me, he thought, he'd have a danged hard time proving it. And he laughed softly as he walked over to join O'Shea.

Chapter 30

Eliza eyed the big Shoshone village with interest. Clusters of willow huts, covered with woven mats, formed tight circles. Platforms, built atop sturdy sticks, held long racks of salmon drying in the sun. It was a busy place. Black-eyed children romped between the huts and around the platforms. Women, wearing buckskin shirts that came to their knees, tended cooking fires where fish stews simmered in woven grass pots smeared over with pitch. Salmon, buried under beds of hot coals, steamed and baked. A few old women, their gnarled fingers moving fast, sat in the shade of raggedy cottonwoods. Chatting and laughing among themselves, the women wove long grasses and reeds into cooking vessels, baskets, and mats.

The Oregon Roll stopped there at noon for a rest and perhaps some trade, before moving on through lava and granite highlands toward Fort Boise. The emigrants mingled freely among the Indians, some of whom spoke broken English while holding out baskets packed with fish-cakes, dried salmon, grasshoppers, crickets, lizards, and boiled rats. All for sale or for trade. Eliza was delighted to trade two mirrors, three fish hooks, and a cotton shirt of Ben's for two large pinegum-coated baskets for herself, a pair of small rabbitskin moccasins for Cece, and beautifully beaded moccasins for Smithy and Caleb.

Eliza, pleased with her trade, started over to join Lorene, who was bartering with a young Indian woman. Angry shouts caught her attention. Four Shoshone men were arguing with a tall, naked Indian—a huge, unkempt man with burs and weeds clinging in his long, matted hair. The big Indian was angry, and he spat out his words with contempt. Two white men stood beside him. Eliza was astonished to see that these men were the same men she'd seen back at the Santa Fe Junction, months ago. She frowned and stared at them. The one-eyed man, now wearing an eye patch, and the man whose head looked like a prune, caused a shudder to course down her spine.

Suddenly a splatter of stones sprayed the big Indian as a group of Shoshones, men and women, advanced toward the three men. The Shoshones held rocks in their hands and they shouted. The two white men quickly mounted their horses and one of them shouted to the Indian, "We're riding on." The big Indian shouted something to the Shoshones, then leaped on his horse and the three men galloped out of the village.

Eliza shook her head. Evil men, they were. She wished she hadn't seen them on this pretty day. She then turned her attention to Lorene, who had her eye on a beautiful white ermine cloak. Lorene was offering the Indian woman a diamond brooch, but the woman wasn't interested.

"Stay?" Lorene asked the woman. "Please wait?" The woman nodded and Lorene turned to Eliza. "Try and keep her here, Ellie. Please. I've got an idea."

Eliza pointed toward the scene of the recent ruckus. "Why the trouble?" she asked.

"Tomschini," the woman said. "Trouble is Tomschini. He comes now with two white men. Bad men. They come here this morning. No. We don't want them here. We make them leave."

250

Tomschini! That was the name of the man O'Shea had told the folks about back at the big Blue. That was the same man who, it was said, had killed Hagen. "Will they come back?" Eliza asked the Shoshone woman. The woman shrugged. "How to know? Tomschini rides where he wants. Looking now for Paiute. If he finds Paiute, he'll kill him. Bad white men are looking for a white man. If they find white man, probably kill him. Probably not be back here."

Lorene reappeared, holding two dresses, one of white and pink organdy, the other of a blue brocade. On seeing the dresses, the Indian woman's eyes glittered with pleasure and the barter was made: Lorene had the ermine cloak, the woman had the dresses.

Running their hands down the white fur, Eliza and Lorene exclaimed on its luxurious softness and exquisite beauty. "It's the most beautiful thing I've ever seen," Lorene said. "Clancy told me, before we left home, that when I saw something out here I wanted, I should try my luck at Indian trade. This is the first thing I've seen that I wanted, and I did it. I think it's a fair trade, too. For both the Indian woman and me." She laughed. "Lordy, I don't know when I'm ever going to wear it, but it's wonderful fun to have."

"Something will come up and you'll be glad to have it," Eliza said. "I'll bet you my shoe on that." Then she turned serious. "Did you see the bad-looking Indian and the worse-looking white fellows?"

"Umm. I did. Men I wouldn't care to come across. But they've moved on, and by the time we all set out again, they'll be long gone."

Eliza shrugged, wishing she had Lorene's calm sense. Lorene was right, she told herself. The three men would be on their way and why would they be interested in any of the folks with *The Oregon Roll?* Eliza decided she'd be better off forgetting the incident.

"That's the first trouble we've come on, seeing Indians argue like those fellows back there," Clancy said. The wagon train had left the village, Clancy and Stilly at the lead.

Stilly stared straight ahead; when he spoke, his tone was soft and thoughtful. "I didn't like the looks of it, Clancy. I remember seeing that one-eyed fellow and his prune-faced pal back at Independence the day before we set out. We saw 'em again at the Santa Fe junction. They weren't to my liking then and they weren't today. With them starting out on the same trail as us, I decided to find out something about them. So . . . while most folks were busy trading, I scouted around and found a Shoshone who spoke some English. I asked him about the arguing and who those men were. The big Indian is Tomschini. Remember O'Shea telling us about Tomschini, back at the Blue?"

Clancy nodded. "That'd be hard to forget!"

"Ummm. It seems Tomschini is riding with those white fellows who came up from California. All three of them are looking for somebody. Tomschini's looking for a Paiute; the two white fellows are looking for someone named Max Pridentz. Yeah, Clancy. The Indian I talked to even had the name of the white fella those men are looking for. Now I've heard that name, Max Pridentz, but I can't remember where and that bothers me. I'm thinking O'Shea might know, or maybe Cal. It seems important though, and I don't know why."

"Max Pridentz," Clancy mused. "Doesn't mean a thing to me. But I'll tell you . . . I'm not anxious to run into those three. I'd just as soon let them go their way and we'll mind our own business."

"They're not interested in us," Stilly said. "They're looking for those particular men. According to the Shoshone, the white fellas are going on over the Blues. Maybe they think they'll find their man over there. The big Indian's on his way to anywhere he thinks he might find the Paiute. I don't think we'll see them again, but that's not to say we shouldn't keep an eye out."

On a windy morning three days later, billowy clouds scudded across the big bowl of sky as *The Oregon Roll* stopped for a moment on the bank of the Snake River. The emigrants looked across at Fort Boise, turned back to the trail, and treked on.

Eliza's heart now quickened as she realized she'd soon see Caleb again. On reaching the Malheur River, with no sign of Caleb and O'Shea, Stilly didn't hesitate. Raising his arm for a left turn, he and Clancy led the string of dirty gray wagons off the main trail. Now, following dim, dusty tracks, the emigrants started across the desert, heading west.

Eliza's wagon was first in line that day, behind Stilly and Clancy at the lead. A hot wind whipped over the land, snapping up loose leaves, small branches, and swirling dust. On seeing an Indian village, nestled in a grove of quaking aspen and cottonwoods up ahead, she wondered if Stilly might bring the train to a halt and call for an early nooning. She hoped not. She was anxious to get on to Malheur Lake.

The village was located in a pretty place. The Malheur River sparkled as it tumbled through a big meadow while plumes of goldenrod nodded in tall grass and aspen leaves flashed silver green. All around the village, children laughed and played. Some of the women were busy at the cook fires, some were scraping rabbit skins, and several men worked with horses in a corral that stood in the shade of old cottonwoods. Now, seeing the wagon train approach, the villagers stopped their tasks and play. It was then that Eliza saw a young white woman leaning against the wattled fence. A white woman, living out here in this desolate land and living in an Indian village! How strange.

The woman watched as the creaking train approached. When Stilly and Clancy were within earshot, Stilly halted the train, waved his dusty hat, and shouted against the wind. "Hello!" he called. The woman nodded, but didn't move. "Excuse me, ma'am," he called again. "How far are we from the Malheur Lake?"

The woman looked back at the corral, shouted something to one of the men who stood watching the train, then walked out to meet Stilly. A white apron covered the skirt of the woman's faded blue dress, which barely came to the tops of her boots—men's boots, well worn, but sturdy. The boots had copper toes. The woman had a slight limp, and after she'd left the patch of shade, she took the poke bonnet that she carried and put it on, covering her blond hair, which gleamed in the sun.

Eliza's mouth felt like cotton and her heart pounded as she knew, for dead certain, that she was looking directly at Clara McCabe. She knew it as well as she knew her own name. It all fit. The blond hair, the limp, and the copper-toed boots . . . living here in an Indian village. She started to call her name, but something stopped her; she would wait.

"Not far," the woman replied to Stilly's question, looking at the folks with curious eyes. "Just keep going on this trail. You'll be getting there yet today. But there's nothing out there. No white folks. No settlements. Nothing at all. Why're you coming this way?"

"We're on our way to the Willamette Valley, ma'am. Our guide thinks the desert route's shorter than crossing the Blues. He's out there scouting the way now. He and another of our party. You haven't by chance seen them ride by? It would have been sometime last week."

"White folks never come here, mister. But about a week ago I heard a couple of riders ride by in the night. Maybe that was them."

Stilly nodded. "Thanks, ma'am." He put on his hat, touched its brim, and turning, he whistled to start the train. Eliza still said nothing, but as the train moved on, she turned and looked back. The woman was still standing there, watching.

"Clara?" Eliza called back at her. "Clara McCabe?" But her call died in the wind rattling the branches of the old cottonwood trees. The woman waved, but she appeared not to hear.

Chapter 31

A morning mist shrouded the big lake while, close to the marshy shore, cattails and reeds showed brown and green. Caleb pulled a pot of boiling coffee off the cooking grate and set it aside; its aroma mingled with smells of fresh cornbread O'Shea had taken out of the Dutch oven. Taking a deep breath, Caleb stood and inhaled the pungent odor of the morning sage. To the east a streak of dawn was stretched like a band of pewter in the sky. It was going to be a fine day, and according to his figuring, *The Oregon Roll* should be coming in from the Snake River today and he would be with Eliza again.

Caleb liked this country and he wanted to share it with her. There was something about it; something he couldn't put a name to, but he wanted to see more of it and he was glad O'Shea had decided the folks could make this trek across to the Cascades. Meanwhile, while waiting for the train to arrive, he and O'Shea would ride out toward the great long peak called Snow Mountain and see country they wouldn't have a chance to see once *The Oregon Roll* arrived.

Finishing breakfast, the men cleaned up camp and stashed their gear in their tents. Caleb wrote a short note, saying he and O'Shea would be back in the afternoon.

Then, pinning the note to his tent, he and O'Shea mounted their horses and started to ride.

They rode easy, over country sprinkled with mountain mahogany, juniper, rabbitbrush, and tall sage; Snow Mountain glowed pink with the first flush of dawn. At the crest of a ridge, they stopped. To the east, rimrock lay like layers of gold in a land of great canyons, chasms, and ravines. To the north, a grove of white-trunked aspen shimmered in the morning light, and beyond the aspen Caleb saw a valley where a sparkling stream meandered through meadows and tall green grass waved in the morning sun. Caleb caught his breath; he'd never seen a land like this. His skin tingled and felt pebbly as he realized this was land he wanted for his own.

"By God, Paddy, I sure like that valley."

O'Shea laughed. "You're only looking at a small part. A little valley out here in the middle of the desert. It's no place to settle down, if that's what you're thinking. Come on. We'll ride on up Snow Mountain a ways. I'll show you something else."

Partway up the face of the mountain they came to the rim of a shallow canyon, where O'Shea reined in his horse and turned to Caleb. "Now look at that, Cal." O'Shea's face was creased with a grin. "Look at that 'cause I doubt you'll see another sight like this again in your life."

Below them a glittering stream, flanked by clumps of juniper, pine, and aspen, threaded its way along the canyon floor. Beyond the canyon was the desert, and beyond the desert were mountain ranges where patches of snow gleamed pink and gold. A word didn't come to Caleb; he couldn't think of anything fitting to say. He felt giddy with joy and he wanted Eliza to see it too. Oh yes! He wanted her to feel the same way. But, he told himself sternly, what was there for his feelings? He was on his way to the Willamette Valley where he'd wanted to go ever since

257

he'd heard of it, years ago. What on earth would he ever do here? This country was far from anything and any people, except maybe a few roaming Indians. And farm out here? Impossible! Eliza would think he'd gone daft if she knew he had even the remotest notion of settling here. After all, there was nothing to settle to—nothing to farm, no forests to provide wood for shelter, and no white folks at all. He shook his head to rid himself of his foolish illusion.

"Huh!" O'Shea suddenly grunted, squinting his eyes and pointing out to a roll of dust moving slowly through the desert. "I hadn't thought we'd see what we're seeing now," he said. "I wanted you to see the canyons up here, but look at that. That dust means Indians on the move, dragging plunder and wickiups. A friendly bunch. Paiutes. Part of the Shoshone nation that used to wander from the Snake way down to the Rio Grande. They live off the desert, they do. Wandering with the seasons; followin' rivers downstream in winter to trail back up in summer. Always looking for food, water, firewood, and shelter. When they wear down a campsite, they hide their gear. They'll be coming back. They travel far that way."

"Doesn't look like there's many," Caleb said.

"Hell no, Cal. Paiutes are split up into little groups. We're probably looking at a man and his wife, or maybe several wives. Children and grandparents. Maybe a couple of aunts and uncles, and a few cousins. But that's all. Desert's too hard to feed big tribes, so the Paiute, they stay in small groups, like what we see. Fella by the name of Old Eagle is still chief of the whole tribe. His son, Tall Singer, and Tall Singer's cousin, Gray Squirrel, saved my life some years back. That's how I come to know some of these things."

Caleb knew by O'Shea's tone that he wanted to tell his story, and Caleb was pleased. He had learned a lot from this man and he listened carefully to whatever he had to say.

The two men sat astride their horses in silence for a moment while O'Shea dug out his pouch of tobacco, filled his pipe, lit it, and took a long pull of smoke.

"I was after beaver," he said, his voice soft. "Up in the Blues. One winter something got ahold of me and I was sick. God A'mighty, I was sick. And there must have been twenty feet of snow and so cold the stars and moon and sun could have froze and turned the world dark as a pile of black cats! Well, sick as I was, I stumbled into a trapper's cabin, thinking I'd be dead and froze stiff before that day was gone. But next thing I knew, from the floor where I was curled up, aching and sweating and chilled with fever, I saw two young bucks in bark leggins and long fur coats standing in the door, snow whirling in around 'em. These two young pups stared at me, came on in, built a fire, and stayed until the storm let up. Then they carried me out, got me on my horse, tied me there, and we went a ways, I'll say, before we came to their village. Now, you know Paiutes don't use tepees, Cal. They live in huts that look like upside-down bowls made of sticks. Well, they put me in one of them and they laid me on a pile of rabbit skins and covered me with rabbitskin blankets, which, by the way, there's nothing in this world to beat. The women fed me porridges made of nuts, and teas made of herbs, and they had me use their sweat lodge that's nothin' more than a little wickiup. They used sage branches to sprinkle water on red hot stones that sat in a little fire pit inside, and . . . hell! I got well! That's where I got to know Old Eagle and his people."

O'Shea puffed quietly on his pipe, his blue eyes thoughtful under his shaggy brows. "You remember Tomschini, the Indian who claims to have taken care of Hagen?"

Caleb nodded. "Can't say I'd exactly forget him."

"Well, Tomschini had a little sister, Wyula. When him and Wyula were real young, they were brought to live with Old Eagle by a white man who claimed to be their pa. Tomschini and Wyula were wild ones, they were, and as they got older, the wildness stayed. Neither of them took to living as Paiutes and having respect for their beliefs. And they never fit in real well. Wyula was real easy on the eye though and right about the time I was living there, Tall Singer took her as his wife. But then Tomschini and Tall Singer didn't get on. I remember the day I left there, there was a fight between those boys. And while I know now something about Tomschini and his ways, I've never heard a word about Tall Singer. Never knew what happened to him."

"You haven't seen any of those people since you left?"

"No. But I didn't leave right after getting well. I plain didn't want to leave. In the spring, when the ice was off Snake, we caught salmon day after day. Thousands of them. What we didn't eat was smoked and dried, and I tell you Cal, what a time! Relatives and families came from all over for a festival with dancing and singing and gambling and other games. Until then I'd wondered where Tall Singer got his name. But when I heard him sing, I didn't wonder anymore. He was a tall lad and had a voice that I've never heard the likes of before or since."

O'Shea was quiet, looking off at the little coil of dust. "That summer I went with the tribe to gather seeds. They take seeds from everything, you know. Cattails and desert sunflowers and ricegrass, and the women shake them to get the ripe seeds and then they roast 'em, dry 'em, and store 'em in baskets they've rubbed with pitch and clay to make tight."

"They don't hunt and eat meat?"

"Hell no! Except rabbit. They eat rabbit. Paiutes learned, a long time ago, how to live off little desert creatures. Now, come fall, in another month or two, they'll be traveling to the low ranges of the Blues where they'll gather the pinon seeds, and that's when they'll hold their rabbit drives. That's something to see! They make nets of nettles and milkweed. High nets and hundreds of feet long, set where they figure the rabbits will run. The young bucks drive the rabbits into the nets and then club them to death. Hundreds of them 'cause those rabbits mean food. Cooked, dried, whatever. And the women sew the skins together in long strips to make the most beautiful cloaks and blankets you'll find. That's what they wear in winter. Except for the skins they don't bother much with clothes."

O'Shea took a deep pull on his pipe before continuing. "I tell you all this, Cal, but other folks don't know about that time. It was, hmm, maybe five–six years ago. And there was a woman there I loved a lot. A pretty little squaw with soft brown eyes, and she sure loved me. But after that year I knew I couldn't live her life, and she couldn't live mine, so I left. But the dust out there is her people. Paiutes passing through."

Both men were quiet as the roll of dust disappeared into the colors of desert and sky.

"Well . . ." O'Shea turned in his saddle. "If we had time, we'd ride on up to the top there." He pointed to the top of the mountain. "I've only been up there once, and I tell you, you can't believe the world you can see. Everything from the mountain peaks of the Cascades and California, to lakes and a little patch of desert . . . pure white sand and . . ." The high-pitched sound of a horse's whinny interrupted O'Shea. "What the hell?" He turned abruptly toward the sound. A broomtail roan stood on a small rocky point not far away. Poised and alert, the men rode toward the horse. Suddenly O'Shea stopped and let out a low whistle as he held up one hand. "I'll be damned, Cal! Looks like we got us a hurt Indian. Hurt bad too, I'd say."

The Indian lay on his side under the shade of a large juniper tree. A deep gash on his forehead extended to his left ear, which was nearly severed from his head. He was naked, his body bruised with streaks of bloody welts, and the skin exposed to the sun was burned and blistered.

"Jesus! God Almighty!" O'Shea muttered. "He's a hurt one, he is! We've got to get some water to him."

With care they rolled the man over. The man groaned and tried to open one of his swollen eyes as O'Shea cradled his head and Caleb held a water jug to the man's mouth, wetting his blood-caked lips. Caleb judged the man to be about his own age, a tall man with high cheekbones. Scraps of blue feathers were still twined in his braids.

"We'll be taking him back with us, won't we, Paddy?"

"Yeah! But . . . hmm. I tell you . . . hurt as he is, I think I recognize this man." O'Shea's words were soft. "This Indian, Cal, if I've not gone crazy, is Tall Singer. We'll be taking him with us, sure enough."

The Indian moved his head again and tried to open his eyes. "Tomschini!" he whispered.

Startled, O'Shea leaned down close to the Indian. "Tomschini did this to you?" The Indian again tried to open his eyes. "Yes! His tone was urgent. "Clara! Clara!"

"Clara?" O'Shea asked.

"My woman. Clara. Please . . . get her and our babies. Don't . . . don't let Tom . . ." He sighed and turned his head away.

Caleb felt the blood leave his face and he looked at O'Shea, whose expression was impassive. "Come on, Cal," O'Shea said. "It doesn't matter right now who Tall Singer wants. We got to get him back to camp 'cause he needs some tending to." Together they lifted Tall Singer onto his horse, tied him into the saddle, and started to ride back to camp.

Caleb knew now that his path would soon cross Clara McCabe's. It was time to tell O'Shea about the McCabes and what had happened to him long ago.

262

"You know, Cal," O'Shea said, interrupting Caleb's thoughts. "I was thinking back to a particular fight between Tall Singer and Tomschini. After Wyula had become Tall Singer's wife, Tall Singer's family, including Wyula, went to dig camas root one day. When they returned, they found the bushes around their camp covered with coyote carcasses. Now Paiutes believe good spirits dwell in the coyote, and Paiutes never kill them. When Tall Singer's people saw all of those coyote bodies, including pups, draped over the bushes, they were angry and grieved. But Wyula and Tomschini burst out laughing, and Tall Singer struck Tomschini. Tomschini then took after Tall Singer and the two of them almost killed each other before a couple of fellas broke up the fight. Now I suspect there's been bad feelings between those two, Tomschini and Tall Singer, all of this time. And if Tall Singer's woman is now the woman he calls Clara, well . . ."

Caleb nodded while looking straight ahead. "I have to tell you, Mr. O'Shea. I have to tell you something about myself that nobody knows about. And I have to tell you now, while I'm feeling I can."

O'Shea said nothing as Caleb, his face without expression, his voice flat, told what had happened to him years ago in Pennsylvania, and why he thought the girl, Clara, had been looking for Max Pridentz.

"She liked me well enough, I guess," Caleb said. "And she maybe thought if we happened to meet out here, it would be a good thing. But I always figured you knew Max was me, Paddy. From the first time you came into Moody's back in Independence. And I'll not forget how you threw the two McCabes offtrack when you told them you'd heard Max Pridentz had gone to California. But I'll kill them if I ever see them, Paddy. It's a fact."

O'Shea took a deep breath. "I understand that, Cal, but I tell you now that there's no point in going after evil folks if it's only going to bring you more trouble. And

263

that's what I figured back at Independence. Sure, I figured Max was you. The girl gave me an account of you that was clear as day. She also told me she'd heard a likely description of two men, a one-eyed fellow and a man with burn scars on his head, who were traveling west. Now she didn't tell me the men were her brothers, and she didn't know if they were looking for Max, but she wanted to let Max know the men had come out west, just in case. But Cal, you got to tell Eliza."

"No!" Caleb's cried. "I can't do that! She knows some about Clara and that's all she needs to know. I still feel the shame, Paddy. I don't want Eliza to know."

O'Shea shrugged. "It's your business, Cal. But you've got a tough job ahead of you. After we get back to camp and find out from Tall Singer where Clara lives, I'm going to ask you to go fetch her. We got to do that for Tall Singer. One of us has to go get her, and I'll be better off in camp, tending to him and watching for any trouble Tomschini might bring. One way or other, Clara will be in our camp for a day or two, and she'll be meeting Eliza."

Caleb nodded, his voice heavy with worry. "I'll think of something, Paddy. And I'll ride to get Clara, as you ask."

It was toward evening when the men rode up the spine of a long ridge and looked down on the familiar wagons camped along the big lake. The herds grazed contentedly in the tall grass, smoke from the train's cook fires rose in tall spirals, and sounds of talk and laughter echoed across the land.

"No need to say anything to the folks about Tomschini, Cal. No point in causing worry before we hear what happened from Tall Singer. As soon as we find out where Clara is, you'd better ride. I'll ask Stilly to call an executive meeting to make sure nobody objects to a layover day tomorrow. That ought not to bother folks too much out here by the lake."

Caleb nodded. "I'll be leaving tonight," he said. "Soon as I find out where I need to go." Caleb felt sick at heart. For days he had looked forward to seeing Eliza. And Smithy, too. Elation and joy had been with him all day today as he'd thought ahead to having dinner together and telling them about this strange country that he felt something for, but didn't know why. And most of all he wanted to hold Eliza in his arms, and kiss her and caress her and tell her how he had missed her and how much he loved her; he wanted to feel her slender body pressed against his . . . but there was nothing he could do. He must do as O'Shea had asked.

He also knew there was nothing he could say to Eliza until he returned to camp with Clara. Then he would tell her what he must. O'Shea was right. As he rode, his heart felt like stone and he wondered if she could still love him, as she did now, once she learned the story. He doubted it very much.

Thus, the two men, leading the little broomtail roan bearing Tall Singer, slowly rode down the high ridge, through the big meadow, and across the grasslands toward camp.

Chapter 32

Eliza, as well as the other emigrants, were elated to reach Malheur Lake. Earlier that afternoon, Caleb's note assured the folks of his and Mr. O'Shea's intentions to ride that morning and return to camp in the afternoon. Therefore, it was with high spirits that preparations were made for a pleasant evening ahead, and Eliza set her own task as fixing a fine supper for Caleb, Smithy, and herself.

She looked around her, liking the particular feel of this place. She liked the looks of the enormous, sparkling lake with big marsh beds scattered along the otherwise grassy shore. Birds were everywhere. Great white pelicans, blue herons, and horned grebes, plovers, sandpipers, finches, and snipes. Eliza had no idea what many of the birds were, but she was delighted to recognize swans, ducks, hawks, geese, song sparrows, and meadowlarks. She stood, fascinated, as she watched the large birds dive in the water for fish while the smaller birds pecked around the shore and darted among the gray-green bushes and tall reeds. Watching birds in flight, and listening to their calls, she wondered if the same kinds of birds lived in the Willamette Valley. She hoped so.

Cattails grew in thick clumps at the edge of the lake. Snapping off a few of the long stalks, she carried them back to her camp and arranged them in a large pottery crock. She set the crock on the ground beside her wagon. The effect of the mottled crock, the brown cattails, and their long, strappy leaves against the worn wagon wheel was pleasing to her eye.

A sense of exhilaration swept over her. She would soon be with Caleb, yes, but there was something else. Something about being here beside the big lake that she liked. She wondered how Caleb felt about this land. He'd been here for a day or two and had had opportunity to see more of it than she had. She would ask him tonight.

She would also give Caleb and Smithy the moccasins before dinner. Then after dinner, when she and Caleb were alone, she would tell him about the woman she'd seen back in the Indian village by the Malheur River. It was important that he know.

The rollicking strains of "Old Dan Tucker" drifted out over the camp. Eliza smiled. Sam loved his harmonica, and he loved the dancing. He hoped folks might feel like dancing tonight. He'd spoken of it, earlier, shortly after the train had set camp and he'd stopped by *The Lone Eagle* to ask Eliza if there was anything he could do to help. There wasn't, she'd said, giving him a big chunk of butter she'd just taken out of her bucket, which hung from the end of her wagon.

"Thanks, Ellie," he'd said. "You know, we've left the misery of the Snake Plains behind and we're heading straight on to the Cascades. Meeting up with Mr. O'Shea and Caleb here at this pretty lake later today and with everybody feeling fine, we might as well have some dancing." Eliza had agreed. And wouldn't it be grand, she now thought. In only a few hours, she'd be dancing with Cal, sashaying around the glittering lake in the moonlight. Thinking about that made her feel giddy with happiness, and it was then that Betsy's loud shouts interrupted her fantasies.

"Here they come! Here come Mr. O'Shea and Mr. Pride! They're riding off the ridge out there! And they're leading another horse too! Come and see! Mama! Papa! Everybody! Come and see!"

Shading her eyes, Eliza saw that Betsy was right. Eliza quickly lifted her stewpot off her cookfire and set it aside. She then climbed up into her wagon, put on a clean apron, and tucked a small, white desert flower in her hair. Now she felt as ready as she could, to meet Cal.

A crowd had gathered to meet the two men, and as Eliza hastened to join them, she frowned. Caleb was indeed leading a horse with a rider, slumped low. What did this mean? Who would be out here in this desolate country, far from settlements, and far from the main trail? It could be a trapper, she reasoned. Or perhaps a mountain man, a guide, or an Indian. Well . . . the women would tend to the man this evening and tomorrow he'd no doubt be on his way.

Lucy Ann, carrying Cece on her hip, joined Eliza. It was a large crowd now; everybody had gathered around and were waving and calling out "Hey, hey. Howdy, Mr. O'Shea and Mr. Pride!" Eliza thought her heart would burst with joy.

Then, as the men got closer, the cheers and calls died, and except for the creaking saddles and jingling bits and spurs, there was silence. Side by side, the two men rode into camp, Caleb leading a roan bearing a naked Indian. Eliza flinched and she heard gasps of horror as the crowd saw the Indian's bruised body, his blistered skin, his lips black with dried blood, and one ear nearly severed from his head. Twice he tried to lift his head and open his eyes, but each time he failed and his head fell forward against his chest.

O'Shea reined in his horse directly in front of the people, while Caleb, leading the roan with the injured Indian, rode on, his eyes searching the crowd. When he saw Eliza, he looked at her intently, his eyes not leaving hers. It was then that Eliza realized that Caleb wasn't going to stop. Running out to him, she walked beside Sweetface. "Cal?" Her voice was high with worry. "Cal? What's happened?"

His face was pale as he smiled a thin smile. "I'll be seeing you later, Ellie, but not tonight. You'd best be hearing what O'Shea has to tell you all now."

"Oh Cal," Eliza cried. "Why not? I . . ."

"I can't say more, Ellie. It's best you go back and listen to O'Shea."

Eliza was stunned. There would be no dinner with Caleb tonight. She wouldn't be able to give him the moccasins and tell him how much she had missed him. She wouldn't be able to tell him about the girl she was sure was Clara McCabe. Beyond that, she wouldn't feel his loving touches, his kisses, his strong embrace. Hurt, angry, and suddenly despondent, she turned and walked back to the crowd. She tried to reason with herself, telling herself something of great importance had come up. Something to do with the Indian. All she could do now was wait. She then turned her attention to O'Shea.

". . . and he's hurt pretty bad," O'Shea was saying, still seated on his horse. "I'll be putting him in my tent and I'll tend him while the rest of you go about your business." O'Shea then looked out over the crowd, his gaze coming to rest on Stilly. "Stilly?"

Stilly raised his hand. "Here, Paddy. I'm here."

O'Shea smiled, took off his sweat-stained hat, and wiped his brow. "How did the trek go? Any problems?"

"None at all. We trekked on through just as fine as could be. But we're glad to be here and meet up with you and Cal, I'll tell you that."

"Good. I wasn't worried. And we're glad to see all of you too. Now, can I meet with the Executive Committee tonight? A short meeting, right after supper?"

A murmur of agreement rippled through the crowd; the men of the Executive Committee all affirmed that they would be there. The emigrants then talked quietly among themselves, speculating on what was going on as they walked back to their wagons, their tents, and their cook fires. It was clear that there were questions regarding the Indian; it was also clear there would be no dancing that night. The sight of the hurt Indian and O'Shea's request had cooled thoughts about good times that evening.

Eliza and Lucy Ann walked back to the Petersons' wagon, where Lucy Ann put Cece in the little cradle she'd brought from Pennsylvania. "It's strange," Lucy Ann said, straightening and looking at Eliza. "Something's wrong. Is it me, or do you feel it too?"

"I feel it," Eliza said in a soft voice. "There's something wrong and it's not just a hurt Indian."

Later that evening members of the Executive Committee met in front of Caleb's tent. O'Shea, who rarely participated in discussion unless asked, and only voted when called on to break a tie, stood off to one side. Stilly didn't waste words.

"I've talked with O'Shea and he feels it would be better for the Indian if we lay over tomorrow," he said. "What's your feelings?"

"Fine with me," George said. "I'm sure Maggie would agree. Another day or two of rest here beside the lake—you've got my vote."

"And mine," Clancy answered. "But what the hell, Stilly? Who's the Indian? What's happened?"

Stilly deferred to O'Shea. "Paddy?"

O'Shea stepped forward. "The Indian talked a little to Cal and me. He's Paiute. He's been knifed, horse-whipped, dragged by a horse a fair ways, then left for dead. Yesterday, he thinks."

270

"Who would have done a thing like that?" Clancy asked.

"I'm not sure yet. But this man's a decent fellow. I knew him once, some years back. Name's Tall Singer."

Clancy shrugged. "I vote we stay. Give the man a chance."

"Sam?" Stilly asked, a flash of a connection racing through his mind. This Paiute who had been beaten and left for dead . . . could he have been Tomschini's victim? Was Tomschini somewhere around here? Stilly felt uneasy. It was important that he talk to O'Shea right after this meeting.

"Sure," Sam said. "It won't make a lot of difference if we get to the valley a day or two later than we'd planned. As Clancy said, let's give the man a chance. Let the animals rest here where there's good grass, and as for us—we'll have a day to hunt and fish."

"Good," O'Shea said. "Now, Caleb's with the Indian at this time, and he asked that I tell you he also votes to stay. And I sure appreciate you all supporting my request."

There were no more questions, Stilly thanked the men, the meeting broke up, and Stilly walked over to O'Shea. "I need a word with you, Paddy."

"Let's talk on the way over to my tent," O'Shea answered. "Soon as the Indian's able, I want to talk to him some more."

Stilly then told O'Shea about the incident involving Tomschini back at the Shoshone village. O'Shea listened intently. "Tomschini found his Paiute, Stilly." His voice was grim. "Now, Tall Singer'll recover well enough in a few days, but the worry is this. I don't know if Tomschini thinks Tall Singer is dead, or still alive. Tall Singer says Tomschini cut the drag rope, and left him. I sure don't want the big bastard poking around looking for him. We need to keep a sharp eye out, Stilly. Tomschini's a damned crazy man."

271

O'Shea was quiet for a moment and then he sighed. "There's another thing I need to ask you, Stilly. Tall Singer's asked for his woman and children. Caleb's going to get them, soon as he learns from Tall Singer where they are. We think they may live in the village we passed back there on the Malheur River, but we need to make sure. I'm thinking of asking the Executive Committee to consent to another request."

Stilly nodded, but said nothing.

"Tall Singer's not gonna be well enough to travel alone, on his own, for a while yet. Whiskey laced with opium's giving him some relief, but he's still in a helluva lot of pain. Problem is I don't want to lay over after tomorrow. So—how do you feel about taking Tall Singer, his woman, and children on with us for three, maybe four or five days?"

"Fine with me, Paddy. I'll ask the Executive Committee tomorrow, after Caleb's back. Now . . . another question on another matter. Does the name 'Max Pridentz' mean anything to you?"

O'Shea shrugged. "Don't know," he said. "Should it?"

"Back at the Shoshone village, two white fellows were with Tomschini. They'd ridden in from California together. Ridden in with the big Indian. The white men were the same two we saw back at the Santa Fe junction not far from Independence. The one-eyed fellow and the one with the wrinkled head. They're looking for this fellow, Pridentz, and they were heading over the Blues. Maybe they think that's where this fellow is, I don't know and don't care. But thing of it is . . . I've heard that name, and I'll be damned if I can remember when. I thought you or Cal might know."

O'Shea looked up at the wash of stars as the scene back at Independence camp came to his mind. It was right after the Landon family had arrived. "Max! Max

272

Pridentz!" Eliza had cried out. O'Shea remembered how he had heard her greeting and he'd been startled. But he also remembered that nobody had paid it much mind, being busy as they were with their tasks at hand. Stilly's wagon, however, had been close to where Caleb and the Landon family had met. Stilly was the man Thomas Landon had first approached; Stilly had certainly heard Eliza's greeting. Stilly didn't remember that right now, and that was fine with O'Shea because Caleb didn't want his story known. O'Shea would do what he could to honor that.

"I'll give thought to the name," O'Shea said. "But you say those fellas were the same fellas we saw back at the Santa Fe Junction and they for sure were heading for the Blues?"

"Yeah. That's what the Shoshone told me."

O'Shea nodded. "If I think I can help you with the name, I'll let you know. I'm asking that you keep this talk between us, Stilly. It's best that way." Stilly agreed, and the men parted.

Sleep didn't come to Eliza that night as images of the wounded Indian and Caleb's face, worried and distracted into another time, came to her again and again. Questions raced through her mind. What had happened? What was wrong? Why had Caleb avoided her? What was the problem with the Indian? Why did events surrounding the Indian seem to be secret? Finally, wrapping a shawl around her shoulders, she climbed down from her wagon and stood in the night.

The wind had come up and loose clouds scudded across the face of a full moon. The big lake looked wrinkled and black with little silver waves. Coyotes bayed, one followed by another, and an owl hooted. Then, over by Caleb's tent a horse nickered as somebody moved

273

through the shadows. Startled, Eliza watched as a man mounted a horse. She recognized the man as Caleb, and she gasped as she saw him take his quirt to Sweetface and ride hard out of camp.

She waited, listening to the echo of the horse's hooves. A few moments later she saw him in the moonlight, and she watched him ride up the ridge and disappear. A great sadness and foreboding enveloped her as she stood very still. She listened to the water slap against the shore and she wondered what kind of business would call Caleb out of camp in the middle of the night. Where would he be going in this desolate country? Of course it had to do with the Indian. Then, a glimmer of an idea came to her. The Indian village, back at the Malheur River, could be the closest Indian village to this lake. That village might be the Indian's home. And the Indian just might be Clara McCabe's man! Had Cal ridden off to see Clara and to tell her what had happened? That seemed quite possible, and the longer Eliza pondered this notion, the more the idea fit. No one, of course, except Caleb, Mr. O'Shea, and the Indian had the answers. Tomorrow Eliza would go to visit Mr. O'Shea.

She found him, camped as usual, some distance from the main camp. Wearing his battered broad-brimmed hat, an old shirt with holes in the sleeves, and a pair of britches that had seen better days, O'Shea was obviously intent on enjoying this layover day in casual dress. Eliza approached him tentatively, yet resolved not to show her caution. She watched him for a moment as he shoved a batch of biscuits into his Dutch oven.

"Good morning, Mr. O'Shea," she said, her voice firm.

O'Shea straightened and smiled at her. "Morning, Miss Landon. I was sort of expecting to see you this morning. Coffee?" He held up a steaming pot. "And please sit down." He indicated that she sit on a camp stool close by the fire.

"Thank you," Eliza said. "And yes, thank you. I'll have a cup. That would be nice."

O'Shea picked up a cup, poured it full, and handed it to her. "Well," he said, arching one of his thick brows. "You've not come to visit about the weather now, have you?"

Eliza shook her head. "No, sir." She took a sip of the boiled coffee. It was stronger than any coffee she'd tasted before, but she liked its pungent bitterness. "No," she said. "I haven't come to talk about the weather. How's the Indian?"

"He'll recover, given a little time."

"Mr. O'Shea, Caleb rode out of camp late last night." Eliza fixed her gaze straight on him; she spoke quickly and to the point. "I didn't see him to talk to after you came into camp, and it was obvious that he didn't want to see me. I want to know where he's gone and when he'll be back."

O'Shea scratched the nape of his neck and looked at Eliza as if he was seeing her for the first time. Eliza held his gaze. "You know, Miss Landon . . . it's sure . . ." He sighed and shook his head. "He's gone to fetch the Indian's woman." His voice was flat and direct. "He should be bringing her in later today. Her and a couple of children."

"Did he have far to go?" Eliza watched O'Shea's face carefully. "Did he by chance ride back to the Indian village we all passed by? The one on the Malheur River?"

O'Shea shrugged, his face impassive. "That could be the village," he said. "But you'll be seeing him soon, Miss Landon. I can tell you that, but I can't tell you more." He then quickly stabbed a fork into pieces of thick bacon, cracked several eggs into the hot grease and stirred them, then took his biscuits out of the oven.

"Breakfast?" he asked, while serving up a plate.

"Thank you, Mr. O'Shea, but no. I must be getting back."

O'Shea nodded. "You won't mind, then, if I take this to our guest, the Indian."

"No," she said, standing and smiling at O'Shea. "Thank you for telling me what you could."

Walking back to her own camp, she was now convinced that Caleb had indeed ridden back to the village on the Malheur River. Mr. O'Shea had indicated that and it made sense. Of course Caleb hadn't wanted to talk to her last night. He'd have known then he was going to go get Clara, not an easy thing for him to have to do. And if Clara was the Indian's woman, and he brought her back here, wouldn't it be possible that Eliza would learn the whole story behind Clara McCabe?

It was possible, and the more Eliza thought about it, the more she knew it was probable. But now knowing, or at least having an idea, that she in all probability would learn his story, she felt doubt creep into her mind. It was plain that the memory of whatever had happened to Caleb caused him unspeakable pain. Was it necessary, then, that he tell her? Was it necessary that he recount something that obviously brought him a particular agony? She remembered his torment back at Independence Rock. *There's things about me you don't know. Things I can't tell you about yet . . . Maybe not ever.* She remembered his anguished eyes. Would knowing his story make any difference about how she felt about him? No, indeed not. How in the world could it? The more she thought about him feeling forced to explain, the more she decided against wanting to hear him out. She didn't need to know right now. There would be time for that. Perhaps after they got to the valley and after they were married, he might feel comfortable telling her. Yes, she thought. There would be time.

* * *

It was a day for chores, this extra layover day. Eliza took a pile of dirty clothes to the lake, where she joined several women banging their battling sticks on skirts, aprons, dresses, shirts, pants, and underclothes. Slapping the heavier garments on rocks, the women helped each other wring the clothes and then they laid them on the grass and weighted them with stones to dry. Finishing that task, Eliza walked back through camp. Lucy Ann was busy with Cece, Lorene was mending an ugly rent in the Evanses' wagon top, and Maggie was reading the book of Martha's that most of the women had now read—*A New Home*. Many of the men and older boys were out hunting; some of the women and children were fishing in the lake.

It was a quiet time, but it was hot and the air was flat. Thunder rumbled and some folks spoke of a coming storm. Feeling restless and out of sorts, Eliza walked down to the lake shore, where Smithy was working on a painting of a large swan. Eliza looked closely at Smithy's work—the long, straight neck, the large, black bill, and the white plumage. "It's beautiful," she said. Smithy looked at her and smiled.

Then, looking around at the surrounding country, a thought struck her—what fun it would be to explore this land with Caleb. And as she idly watched the livestock grazing on the tall meadow grasses, it also occurred to her that this country was a paradise for animals. How odd, she thought. But as she looked at the sky, pebbled with pink and white clouds, she felt a strange elation and she knew it was connected to this country. She liked this land. A lot. But then she chided herself. Why should she feel this way for a place that was far from any kind of civilized living? And what on earth would she ever do here? Cal would think she'd gotten addled in the brain if she told him how she felt. Still . . . she would see more of this country, and not with the slow-moving wagon train. Nor would she wait for Caleb. She'd take Smithy, Betsy, and Jeremy with her this afternoon and they would ride a ways. She knew they'd like that.

Kneeling beside Smithy, still working on his swan, she posed the question. "How about riding today?" Smithy grinned and nodded his head. "Good," Eliza said. "I'll see if Betsy and Jeremy want to go too. How does later this afternoon suit you?" It suited Smithy just fine.

A few moments later, as she walked back from the lake, she saw Mr. O'Shea, astride his horse, talking with Stilly. O'Shea pointed out toward the big mountain called Snow Mountain, Stilly nodded, and O'Shea rode out of camp. Stilly started to walk over to O'Shea's tent, but then turned and quickly walked back to his own wagon. Eliza reasoned that O'Shea had told Stilly where he was going and had asked him to keep an eye on the Indian. That meant that for the next few minutes anyway, the Indian would be alone. And if the Indian was well enough to talk, and if he spoke any English, as Eliza had a notion he did, she might learn from him who his woman was.

She shivered. Would she dare go into Mr. O'Shea's tent and speak to the Indian? As far as she knew, no woman on this trek had put a foot inside that tent. But Eliza, resolved to find out about this matter, took a deep breath and hurried across camp.

The front of Mr. O'Shea's tent was closed, and as Eliza walked around to the back, she felt her heart pounding. She wasn't afraid of the Indian; it was entering Mr. O'Shea's private tent, without his permission, that bothered her. If she found the back flap closed, she would be unable to go in, and in a way, she hoped this would be the case. But the back flap was opened enough to allow in fresh air. Hesitating for just a second, Eliza stepped inside. Smells of astringents, medicinal barks, opium, hides, and tobacco filled the close space, and in the dim, orange light she saw the Indian lying on a pile of buffalo robes. His head was bound with a clean white cloth, his eyes were puffy but no longer swollen shut, and the blisters and cuts on his body had begun to heal. He turned his head and looked at her.

"Is Clara here?" he asked. "Is she here? Blue Bird? Little Bear? Are they safe?"

Eliza touched his arm. "They're not here yet." She spoke softly. "But I'm sure they will be soon."

"I told O'Shea and the blond one. Tomschini must not find them." He looked at Eliza with beseeching eyes.

"He won't. Mr. O'Shea and . . . the blond one won't let that happen. Can you tell me . . . does Clara live in the pretty village by the Malheur River?"

The Indian looked at Eliza closely. "Who . . ."

"I'm the . . . I'm the blond one's woman," she replied. "My name is Eliza. The blond one is called Caleb."

The Indian nodded, while keeping his eyes on her face. "Yes," he said. "Yes. We live by the Malheur."

Eliza looked at the man for a moment. He was very tall and slender. Bits of blue feathers were stuck in his long braids. He had high cheek bones and smooth, ruddy skin. Once he recovered from his dreadful wounds, he would be a handsome man indeed. Eliza touched his arm again, smiled at him, then left.

Chapter 33

It was midafternoon when Eliza, Smithy, Betsy, and Jeremy left camp and rode through the meadow out to the ridge where they reined in their horses and looked out over the countryside. Eliza drew in her breath, swept again with a sense of exhilaration as she saw a land of canyons, rimrock, and chasms, set against the beautiful Snow Mountain. A flock of geese suddenly appeared and flew over Malheur Lake. Their shadowed pattern moved on, steady and serene.

"I like it here," she said to the children. "What do you all feel?"

"It's too big and too empty," Jeremy said. "I'd rather be seeing lots of trees."

"Me too," Betsy replied.

But Smithy smiled and nodded his head. Smithy agreed with Eliza; he liked this country too.

"Come on!" Eliza called, laughing and pointing out to sprinkles of bright color that carpeted the lower land. "Let's ride. I have my magnifying glass so we can see things in the flowers we couldn't otherwise see."

Drifts of blue and yellow and white flowers grew as tall as their horses' chests. Dismounting, Eliza handed her glass to Betsy and showed her how to hold it so she could see the silvery hairs on the stems and the veins of the leaves. They walked on through the tall grass, taking turns with the glass while examining the flowers, marveling at the intricate designs and patterns. It was while Jeremy was examining a purple flower with tiny yellow sacks and a beak that Eliza suddenly felt a change in the air. "We should start back to camp," she called. "Storm's coming on."

Moments later the sky had turned to a nasty yellow and the wind had come up, whipping big swirls of loose twigs, leaves, sand, and dust.

"Come on!" Eliza shouted. "Now! We've got to get home! Storm's coming on quicker than I'd thought."

Mounting their horses, they rode hard, back to the long ridge and down to the meadow on the far side of camp. While riding across the meadow, Streak suddenly whinnied and, rearing back, threw Betsy to the ground. Streak then raced on. Bringing Babe to a halt, Eliza dismounted and knelt beside the child, who sat moaning and holding her ankle.

"Smithy!" Eliza shouted. "Go get Streak! She's probably headed for camp, so you shouldn't have trouble. Jeremy, ride with him, but then you get on to camp and tell your mama and papa what's happened out here. I'll bring Betsy in with me."

Betsy's ankle was now turning an ugly blue and beginning to swell. "I've got to bind that, Bets," Eliza said as she stood, up, pulled on her own petticoat, clamped her left boot on the edge of the dirty hem, and yanked hard. Ripping off a strip of cloth, she wrapped it tight around Betsy's ankle, tucking in the loose end.

"There! That ought to help some until we get back. Lean on me and we'll get you up on Babe." When Betsy stood up, her face was white with pain. Putting her arm around the girl's waist, Eliza started toward Babe, who stood, patiently waiting.

Then without warning, Eliza felt the sting of dust and sand against her face, and looking out toward camp, all she could see was a dark brown wall that filled the sky, bearing down, fast.

"Dust!" Eliza cried. "Dust storm!"

In seconds dust and sand beat on Eliza and Betsy like millions of needles, at the same time blinding them and clogging their mouths and noses. "Lie down!" Eliza screamed, choking on her own words. "Lie down!" She heard Babe's high whinny, and then Babe was gone, galloping away from the huge dark wall. But Babe wasn't a worry to Eliza right now as she flattened herself down in the grass against Betsy, and flung one arm around the child. She and Betsy would wait it out. She prayed that Smithy and Jeremy had been able to get back to camp before the storm had hit, and she also wondered where Caleb might be.

It seemed like a long time had passed as she and Betsy stayed flat in the grass, their bodies assaulted by the roaring wind, sand, and dust. A very, very long time.

The noise started as a different sound and far away. One that Eliza, her ear pressed against the ground, was vaguely familiar with. Listening, and listening, she felt her blood turn to ice as she heard a cadence of thunder, swelling and coming closer. She heard the terror in her voice as she screamed. "Stampede! Stampede! Oh, my God!"

The earth began to shake as Eliza stood up and jerked Betsy to her feet. Putting an arm around her waist, Eliza dragged her, both of them screaming, as they stumbled and lunged a few feet before they collapsed on the ground.

"Get up! For God's sake, Bets—" Eliza cried as horses, oxen, and cattle, shadowed in the brown air, moved closer with a deafening roar, and at the same time she heard Betsy's blood-chilling scream. Eliza stopped her own cry. Betsy couldn't run! And even if she could, there was no place to run to. There was no protection; nothing between them and the crazed beasts, and there was nothing Eliza could do. Nothing at all. Eliza put her arms around the hysterical child and held her tight. We'll die, she thought. This is the way . . .

Suddenly, above the thundering hooves, a volley of gunshots rang out, and through the thick, orange dust, Eliza saw a blur of men, their pistols held high, racing on horseback to turn the stampede. A rider, wearing a kerchief over the lower part of his face, brushed by Eliza, an arm reached down as Eliza frantically pushed Betsy up, and she then saw Caleb's wild, red-rimmed eyes. Eliza stumbled and ran, trying to get farther away from the frenzied animals. Then, in the awful world of dust and roar, she saw another rider, and she screamed as she thought one of her arms would be yanked out of its sockets, as she, too, was jerked up onto a horse. After hearing the rider cry out, "I've got her, Cal," Eliza knew she was riding behind Mr. O'Shea.

They rode on, she and Mr. O'Shea, through a fouled air that smelled of animals' bodies and sweat and breath, and on and on through the terrible wall of dust.

"Smithy and Jeremy!" Eliza cried. "I sent them—"

"They're back in camp," O'Shea yelled back.

Thank God! Thank God, the boys were safe. Now as she held on to Mr. O'Shea, her arms around his waist, she leaned her head into his buckskin coat and she felt the warm wash of tears on her face.

The rains came, quelling the dust. Thunder cracked and sheets of lightning lit up the camp beside the big lake as O'Shea and Eliza rode into camp.

"Paddy! Ellie!" Caleb's desperate shouts rang out as he ran through the curtain of rain toward O'Shea. O'-

Shea quickly reined in his horse, dismounted, and reached up to help Eliza. The moment Eliza's feet touched the ground, she felt Caleb's arm around her, supporting her, holding her close.

"Dear God, Ellie!" He pressed her to him as Eliza fought to stop her trembling, and the awful gasps that kept rising in her throat.

"Smithy? Where's Smithy?" she asked.

"He's fine. He's inside the tent. Oh, thank God! Ellie! Thank God! Thank God!" he said again and again, his voice rough and strained. "My God! To lose you—I couldn't . . . I couldn't . . ."

She gagged and spat out mud and grit, and she clamped her teeth together to stop their chattering, but she couldn't stop. "Betsy? Is Betsy . . ."

"Betsy's all right. She's with Lucy Ann and Stilly. Come."

Once inside Caleb's tent, Caleb wrapped her in a buffalo robe. "I'm going over to O'Shea's for a moment," he said. "I'll be coming right back." Eliza nodded while pressing her face into the robe's dark curly hair and smelling its stale gamy odor. Still trembling, her teeth still chattering, she closed her eyes for a moment, took a deep breath, then looked around. Her eyes slowly adjusted to lantern shadows dancing on the canvas walls, and her stunned gaze then fell on Smithy, wrapped in a blanket and sitting in a corner.

"Oh, Smithy!" She stood up and, dragging the buffalo robe with her, walked over to sit beside him on a large wooden packing crate. Smithy's eyes were wide and wild. Eliza put her arms around him, and as she held him close, she could feel sudden tremors run through his thin body. She held him quietly for a time, and as the tremors quieted, it occurred to her she could never imagine this boy's own terror.

It was then that Caleb reappeared, holding a bottle

and two small glasses. "Here," he said, offering her a half-filled glass. "It's brandy. I got it from Paddy. It should help warm you some."

"No, Cal," Eliza waved the glass away. "None for me, I think, and none for Smithy. We'll be doing fine." She then turned and looked closely at Smithy. "You got back here before the dust came?" Smithy nodded, and Eliza was relieved to see that his eyes were calm. Then she turned to Caleb. "Did you bring back the Indian's woman?"

"I brought her back, along with two children. We rode into camp just before the dust storm came up. That's how I learned where you and Betsy were. Jeremy told us. He and Smithy were already here, but scared to hell." He looked at Eliza intently as he continued. "The woman I brought back and her children are with the Indian now. The woman, Eliza, is Clara McCabe." He watched her, his eyes level with hers.

"I know," Eliza said, hugging herself under the heavy robe. She still found it hard to talk easy. "I saw her, Cal. Back in the village when we came through. I knew it was her . . . I was going to tell you. Is she . . . is she all right?"

"Yes. She's all right." Caleb frowned. "Ellie . . . there's . . ." He paused. No. Eliza thought. I can't let him tell me what he thinks he must. Eliza was then aware of the silence of a spent storm; a silence broken only by dripping water and a lone coyote's cry. Smithy stood up, rummaged through some things, and picking up a drawing tablet, he began to draw. Seeing that sort of return to a quiet time, Eliza knew she had to get out of her drenched clothes. And now that her trembling had stopped, she'd be able to walk back to her wagon alone.

"I'm going on home, Cal. I'm all right, and I need to get out of these wet things."

Caleb nodded. "I'll walk with you. After you're in

dry clothes, we'll come back." He put an arm around Smithy and hugged him close. "When we come back, I'll build up a good fire and fix all of us a hot supper."

Walking across camp, Eliza looked up and saw torn clouds racing across the big-faced moon. Little orange spots of light from the wagons and tents dotted the darkness while the long grasses, flattened from the rains, gleamed silver in the moonlight. Caleb, his arm around her as they walked, suddenly stopped and turned to her.

"I have to tell you something, Ellie. It can't wait."

"Don't. Please, please Cal!" Eliza cried, fighting the feel of tears. "Whatever it is, it's a thing that causes you a whole lot of pain. And I know it has to do with Clara McCabe. But please, don't tell me. Please!"

"No, Ellie. I must. You see, this is something I must say. There won't ever be a time in our lives when it will be easy. I must tell you now." She heard the urgency in his voice and she was silent. If it was that important for him to tell her, then he would, and she would say nothing more to stop him.

"When I was a boy . . ." He paused for a moment and cleared his throat. "When I was a boy, after I'd left Kentucky, I worked in a tannery owned by McCabe. I've told you that, Ellie, and how I talked to the young girl, Clara, a time or two. Well, Clara had two brothers. And one day those brothers took Nellie, and they killed her by dipping her in a vat of boiling grease, and then they . . . they took me and they . . . they violated me. They . . ."

Eliza looked at him, uncomprehending, her eyes wide. "Oh my God!" she whispered. "Caleb! Oh! My dearest love! I . . ."

"Please wait. I have to tell you more."

"Yes. Whatever, Cal . . . whatever you say . . ."

"I need to tell you that if it hadn't been for Clara, those boys would have done worse things to me 'cause it

286

was Clara who saved me by dumping a bucket of boiling water on one of her brothers and I grabbed a firepoker and slammed it into the other boy's face, and then I ran. I ran and I ran, for days it seems, and a while later, maybe the next week . . . I don't know, I stopped running, and I changed my name 'cause I didn't ever want to think about what had happened to the boy, Max Pridentz. I couldn't ever be him again. And I never talked to anybody during that time. Not any more than I had to. I was so shamed . . . I was so full of shame, I swore nobody would ever learn about what happened to me. I also swore that if I ever met up with those brothers, I'd kill them, Ellie. Now I've found Clara, and I've learned from O'Shea that Clara's brothers are somewhere out here in the Oregon states. It seems that they might be looking for me. One man wears a patch, the other has burn scars on his head and—"

Eliza gasped and grabbed Caleb's arm. "I've seen them!" she cried. "I've seen them twice!"

Caleb looked at her, not believing he'd heard right. "You've seen them?" His voice was a whisper. "You couldn't . . . how . . . No! I . . ."

"Listen to me! Yes, listen to me, Cal! I saw them first at the Santa Fe Junction, just out of Independence, and we were stopped there, waiting for the train ahead of us to turn off. Yes! I saw them. And I said to Lucy Ann I hadn't ever seen such evil-looking men. And then I saw them last week, back in the Shoshone village! They were there with the big Indian, Tomschini! Oh Lordy, Cal, they're not far from here!"

Caleb shook his head. "No, Ellie. According to O'Shea, they've gone on over the Blues. Now, they're not real smart fellows. Not keen at all. I knew that when I was a boy and Clara tells me the same thing. She says they'll probably think about hunting for me when something brings me to their minds, but otherwise they like as not to give me any thought. But I tell you, they're the worst scum that ever walked this earth, and if they happen upon me or you, I'll kill them. I'll kill them sure as I'm telling you this, and I'm not so sure I want that for you."

"Maybe not. Maybe you don't want that for me. But I'm your woman, Cal. And I always will be. There's no denying that, Caleb Pride."

Caleb took her in his arms and held her close. "I can't tell you how I feel. I can't tell you how I dreaded having you find this out about me. It's been a curse, Ellie, that's always in the back of my mind, never leaving me, never letting me be free. And I don't know if I'll ever be free of it. How can I know?"

"You can begin to know by knowing how much I love you, Cal. You can begin to know by sharing that awful pain with me. Because knowing this doesn't make me love you less. It makes me love you all the more and it makes me want to help you forget it and learn how to be free of that unspeakable curse."

He laughed softly, his voice uneven. "This is a start, Ellie, and I'll say it again. I can't ever tell you enough, how much I love you."

He kissed her tenderly, and as they held each other close, the sound of a man singing floated across the camp. The man's voice was beautiful, strong, and clear.

"That's Tall Singer," Caleb whispered, lifting Eliza's face and looking into her eyes. "I'll bet he's singing a song of joy because he's reunited with his family, he's alive, and he's with the woman he loves. If I could sing, I would, because I'm also with the woman I love."

That evening, as Eliza, Smithy, and Caleb sat around the campfire, Eliza gave Caleb and Smithy the moccasins, and Smithy then showed Eliza the drawing he had made that evening. It was an exquisite drawing of the country they had seen from the top of the ridge today—the pleated chasms, canyons, and folded mountain ridges, shadowed under blossoming clouds. She smiled and put her arm around him. What a gift this boy is, she thought. A gift to Caleb, and now to me.

Later Caleb and Smithy walked with Eliza to her wagon, they all said good night, and as Eliza fell asleep in her wagon, she could still hear Tall Singer's song.

The next morning a rosy sun bathed the high desert plains and winked over the sparkling lake. The air was fresh and pungent with the smell of wet dust and sage. Beads of water, reflecting prisms of light, stood on the cattails' strappy leaves; meadowlarks' songs filled the air.

The herders, led by Caleb, set out to round up the livestock, scattered by yesterday's storm and stampede. Tall Singer told them where he figured the animals had gone, and following Tall Singer's advice, the men found all of the livestock, including Babe and Streak. It was just after noon when the men returned with the herds. Stilly then called for a short meeting of the Executive Committee; decisions were agreed to and once again it was time for *The Oregon Roll* to move on. Whips cracked, cattle bawled, horses nickered and blew, and the children called out and laughed. Eliza looked toward the front of the train, where O'Shea and Stilly rode in the lead. Tall Singer, who was still recovering, rode in O'Shea's wagon, driven today by Caleb.

"All ready?" O'Shea called out. "All ready, folks? Let's roll!" Then he whistled, raised his right hand, and the long wagon train slowly circled away from Malheur Lake and headed northwest toward the Deschutes and the Cascades.

"You're sure you want to walk?" Eliza, quirt in hand, turned and asked Clara, standing beside her.

"Walking's never bothered me yet," Clara answered. "Yes," she said. "I do."

Chapter 34

A late August moon beamed down on the long line of tattered wagons tilting and lurching across the high desert. The wagon wheels, now dry and skewed, creaked as they ground against the coarse sand and crushed the brittle sage. The herders, dark figures slouched low on their horses, kept a watchful eye while sounds of coyotes' cries echoed off Snow Mountain, now far to the east. Night treks were quiet treks, voices were soft; night treks were also cold treks, offering relief sought from the brutal heat of the day.

Tall Singer, recovered from his wounds, now rode at the lead with O'Shea and Stilly. Before the train had left Malheur Lake, Tall Singer had urged O'Shea not to take the southwestern trek, but instead take a more northerly route that stayed close to small rivers and streams. He had told O'Shea that with steady traveling, by the next full moon they would come to the river the white men called the John Day. Following the John Day north for three days, the train would turn west and cross a short mountain range with forests of large, red-barked pines. They would then descend to the Deschutes plains. There had been no dispute to Tall Singer's plan and tonight was the night the train should reach the John Day.

Walking in the moonlit dust beside her wagon, Eliza

looked up at the sky, strewn with stars. She liked traveling under the path of the Milky Way. And Clancy, who knew a lot about stars, had taught some of the folks how to look at the heavens and identify Cygnus the Swan, Lira and the summer triangle, and the great square of Pegasus, the winged horse.

"Eliza." Eliza was startled to hear her name, and what a strange call. She stopped. "Yes?" She turned. "Who's calling me?" No one answered and she shrugged. Oh Lordy, she thought. I'm beginning to hear things, like they say you do. She shook her head, turned, and waved at Smithy, who was driving Caleb's wagon behind her. Smithy waved back. Surely if he had heard somebody calling her, he would let her know. Eliza laughed and gave herself a little lecture. Nobody would be calling her like that. It was a voice she hadn't even recognized. Silly girl, she whispered. But she wished, as she often did, that Caleb could walk with her instead of having to ride with the herds.

Her thoughts now turned to Caleb and Clara and Tall Singer. The emigrants knew part of the story. They knew there had been trouble between Tall Singer and the big Indian, Tomschini. They knew that Tall Singer and Clara hadn't wanted to return to the Indian village where they had lived. Instead they wanted to travel with this wagon train, and taking their children, they wanted to cross the mountains to the Willamette Valley. That presented no problem to these people, who liked the tall slender man. They liked his gentle ways, and his singing voice that had an intoxicating beauty. And following Clara's name for him, everybody called him Tall.

The emigrants also liked Clara, a pretty young woman with large brown eyes and blond hair that she wore braided and wrapped around her head. Clara kept a stern eye on her children, Blue Bird, the little girl she called BB, and Little Bear, nicknamed LB.

Eliza's thoughts were especially keen on the talk and

events of that day when Clara, holding Blue Bird by the hand and carrying Little Bear on her hip, had walked with Eliza. During the heat of the afternoon, she had told Eliza something about herself, and about the boy she'd known as Max.

"Well," she'd said, "first thing is this. And I'm real anxious that you and Max . . . I mean Caleb, know this. Ross and Earl aren't my brothers. They're not kin at all. I don't have family except for Tall and my children. Now, years back, my ma and pa and me lived not far from those folks, the McCabes. Mr. McCabe had this tannery, but he and Mrs. McCabe, they didn't have any children. Then my folks, they died of fever, and Mr. and Mrs. McCabe took me in. Folks around there got to calling me McCabe's girl, and the name stuck. Now the McCabes were good enough folks, and when Mr. McCabe's sister and her husband died, they left two orphan boys, Ross and Earl, and Mr. and Mrs. McCabe took them in too. So, those two aren't McCabes at all. I don't know what their last name is. I didn't ever hear it said. But even back then, when we were children, those two boys were trouble. Then one winter Mrs. McCabe died and things didn't get a lot better for me. And I hated those boys. Lordy, I hated them. They were always poking me and teasing me about this." Clara kicked out her crippled leg. "And they said bad things. Twice they tried to do bad things to me, but Mr. McCabe, he caught them and beat the tar out of 'em, but that didn't do much good. And I knew soon enough, after Max—I mean Caleb—came there that they had their eyes on him and would do something bad to him. Anyways, after Max—Caleb—ran away, I ran away too 'cause Mr. McCabe was real sick and I knew those boys would get me, considering what I—Caleb and I had done, me dumpin' the boiling water on Earl, and Caleb smackin' Ross in the face with the poker."

Eliza turned and stared at Clara. Then she snapped

292

her quirt and yelled at Big Moo. "Gee! Gee! Big Moo!" Big Moo slowly turned while the rest of Eliza's oxen, following Big Moo's lead, pulled *The Lone Eagle* off the trail.

"Please! Please, Clara! Tell me what happened to Caleb," Eliza said while waving another party on. "It's something I don't . . . I don't understand. Caleb . . . he told me he'd been . . . well, violated. I don't understand that, and I can't bring myself to ask him about it."

Clara looked at Eliza, her brown eyes intent. "Are you sure you want to know this?"

"Yes! I need to know, Clara! I . . . well, I don't . . . as I said, I don't understand, and there's nobody else I could ever ask."

Clara frowned as she looked down at her daughter standing beside her. "You run along now, BB," she said. "Stay with the folks and I'll be catchin' up soon enough." Blue Bird nodded and skipped into line with George and Maggie. Maggie took the child's hand, waved, and walked on.

"She's not old enough to understand," Clara said. "But I don't want her even close to hearing what you've asked me to tell you. Now, I'll tell you the story, Eliza, but then I don't want to talk about it ever again." She looked at Eliza, her eyes flat but intense.

Eliza nodded. "You have my word."

Eliza's eyes never left Clara's face as she listened to Clara's story. Eliza's eyes, stretched wide, felt like cracked glass, and once she clapped her hand to her mouth, stifling her cry. When Clara had finished, Eliza walked out to rimrock, where she looked down at a silver ribbon of a river, fringed with olive green. Kneeling on the dry, sandy ground, she put her head in her hands and she sobbed. It was sometime later when she felt Clara's hand on her shoulder and she heard her soft voice.

"He's alive, Eliza. And he's so fine. A lot of that has

to do with you." Eliza turned, tears streaming down her sunburned cheeks, her eyes anguished.

"Oh, my God! My God! It's a wonder he isn't . . . he . . . isn't crazy! Oh Lordy, Clara! I swear to you! I swear to you if I ever see either of them—either of those men—I'll kill them! I'll kill them! I will! I will!"

"I just pray you never see them again. Not ever."

Eliza was quiet as she stood and watched the line of wagons move on. Then she and Clara, still holding LB, walked back to the trail. Eliza flicked her quirt lightly at Big Moo and *The Lone Eagle* was soon back in line. She tried then to turn her attention to Clara, who told her more about herself and how she had come west.

She told Eliza how she had worked in a hat factory in Philadelphia. She was then hired by a judge and his wife, wealthy Philadelphia people, who had a grown son. Their name was Shaw. These kind folks also planned to come out and Judge Shaw knew of a superb guide, Mr. O'Shea. Thus Clara left the east with these people and came west.

"Durin' that trek, two things happened that sure changed my life. Mrs. Shaw taught me to read and write, and that's why it was nice, writing my own name for the boy I'd known as Max, to see, figuring he might be passing by. The other thing that happened to me was me meeting Tall. I met him at Fort Hall. It was Judge Shaw who brought him to our camp. He and Mrs. Shaw thought he was a fine man. But it was Pips who considered Tall the best man he'd met in his life. And Pips and Tall came to be good friends."

Clara laughed. "Then one day, Tall seemed to just take notice of me. Pips used to tease me, saying it was my blond hair Tall loved. And Tall just took to me like nothing you've seen, and I took to him, and so . . . I stayed with him. No marrying 'cause he was of course married, and the Judge couldn't do that. And so it was that I went to live with him back at the village you all passed by."

Eliza, feeling some relief from the anguish of Caleb's story, was now caught up in Clara's story. "I knew that was you," she said. "Cal had told me something about you. About your blond hair, and he told me about his boots. Your boots." She pointed at Clara's dusty, worn boots. "Aren't those the same boots?"

"They sure are. I found them after he'd run, and I took them. I've worn them perfectly fine ever since."

"Well," Eliza said, "when I saw you wearing those boots, I knew you were the Clara who'd left the messages for Max. That, your hair, and your limp that . . . Oh, Clara, I'm sorry."

Clara shrugged and put her hand on Eliza's shoulder. "Don't feel bad," she said. "It's something I've had all my life. One leg didn't want to grow like the other, but it's all right. It's never seemed to get in my way, or slowed me down. I'm just thankful to the Lord that my children didn't take after me. That happens, you know."

"It does, and then it doesn't. Your two children are pretty, Clara. Real pretty."

Clara smiled with pleasure. "I think they'll get by. But now I'll tell you about the rest. Ohhhhh!" She sighed. "I tell you it's mighty nice to have someone to talk to."

Clara then told Eliza about Tomschini's sister, Wyula, who had been Tall's wife, but then had run off with a Bannock. After a number of years, though, she'd left the Bannock, and returning to Tall's village, she'd asked Tall to take her back into his house.

Clara laughed. "I was living with him then, and our children were babies, and I told Tall if he took Wyula in, he'd be saying good-bye to me and our children for good. Tall wasn't keen on that, and besides he'd told me, before I started living with him, that he wasn't interested in keeping the practice of having another woman. I was enough, he said." She laughed again, her brown eyes flashed, and Eliza was struck with the thought that Clara reminded her of Janie Marie. And the more Eliza listened to Clara and got to know her, the better she liked her. She knew that she and Clara would become good friends. Clara continued her story, telling Eliza that after Tall had turned Wyula away, Wyula had gone to her brother, Tomschini. When Tomschini had learned that Tall had refused to take Wyula back and then learned that Tall was living with a white woman, Tomschini had set out to settle matters himself.

"He came to our house," Clara said. "Just a couple of days before you all passed by. But Tall made it real clear that he wouldn't take Wyula back. Tomschini left and we thought the matter was done with."

She went on to tell Eliza about how Tall often rode out by Malheur Lake looking for wild horses, which he then caught, brought back to the village, broke in for riding, and then either traded or sold to other Indians and, in recent years, to white folks.

"So, I didn't worry about him being gone," she said. "He's often gone, camping out there, way beyond the lake, and riding on, all over this land. That's been his life. He's been here where we are now, and he's gone over the mountains to the valley at times. He likes it that way. That's his mind, and it's fine with me. Lots of times he'll meet up with his own people, or other tribes he's known all his life.

"When he goes to the valley, he visits Judge and Mrs. Shaw and Pips, and that's where we're going to live. On land not far from them. Judge Shaw is buying it for us, and we pleased as all get-out. You see, Tall's thought a lot of, by everyone who knows him. So when he's gone for a long time, it's not a worry to me. It's funny, though, when I saw you all coming by, I came real close to asking you to watch for him. Then I figured you had things on your minds, and I didn't. But you know if Caleb and Mr. O'Shea hadn't come on to Tall, he would've died."

"How do you know?" Eliza's voice was high and

anxious. "How do you know that Tomschini won't come after Tall? Especially if he finds out he's alive. How do you know that any more than Cal and I know about those two brothers?"

Clara shrugged. "We can't know. But we got to get on with our living and Tall says that the best thing for us to do now is get over to the valley and settle in. Same as you and Caleb. We all have to live the best way we can." Clara put her hand on Eliza's arm. "And remember this. Those men—Ross and Earl—are slow thinkers. Real slow. They'll probably not think to look for Caleb unless they hear something that reminds them of him. Otherwise they won't. If I was to figure it out, I'd figure they probably met up with Tomschini somewhere, got to talking to him, and when they learned he was looking for Tall, they remembered the boy, Max . . . I mean Caleb, and they decided then to go looking for him again."

Now, walking on in the moonlight, Eliza tried to comprehend all of Clara's story. She knew she would never question the matter further with Caleb. The thing that had happened to him had now become her own sorrow too. She also knew now why Caleb had never wanted her to know anything about his past life, or about the woman named Clara McCabe. It was ironic that this woman had become her friend, and she was the only one who shared with Eliza the knowledge of Caleb's terrible curse.

"Eliza!" Again, she heard her name. Again, it sounded peculiar and she didn't recognize the voice. And again, she stopped and looked around. "Yes?" she called out boldly. "Yes? Who's calling me?" Again, nobody answered. She turned and walked back toward Smithy.

"Did you hear somebody calling me?" She looked at him closely. Smithy shook his head.

Eliza drew her shawl tighter. "Smithy . . ." Her tone was sharp. "If you do hear somebody call me, please point out to the person that I'm right on ahead." She felt cross and apprehensive. Why would anyone play a game with her like this? If it happened again, she would ask Lorene, who walked three wagons ahead, to walk with her for a ways. But as the train moved on, she didn't hear her name called again.

It was after midnight when Stilly called out. "Strike camp, folks. We're at the John Day River, right where we should be."

Eliza drew a long sigh of relief. She was exhausted. She knew it was partly because of the story she had heard from Clara yesterday; the story had never left her mind. And she had been worried as an old she-bear all night, dead certain that somebody had called her name. Knowing now that nobody had, she wondered if she was going daft. Folks did. She'd heard of that. Men and women, gone all crazy as they'd treked.

She felt jittery and she noted with care that she and Smithy were camped close to Clancy and Lorene. Before she got into bed, she drew the front flap of her wagon cover tight. She also made sure her father's rifle was within easy reach. But with all the precaution and her own fatigue, her sleep was fitful as she dreamed about a young boy, a fire in a firepit, and two men, one with a burned head and one with only one eye.

Chapter 35

It was a week later and *The Oregon Roll* moved through a barren country of dry gulches where great columns of rock rose from enormous brown hills whose flanks were scarred and seamed and dotted with stunted thorn bushes and juniper. The train, treking at night and keeping their course west, came to a small river where Stilly signaled a halt.

"It's time to rest," he called out. "We've been traveling without a layover for over a week. We'll be staying on here tomorrow, we'll roll the day after."

Early the next day Eliza awoke and watched the rising sun tip the barren hills with red. A few minutes later she saw that the hills were smeared with streaks of red, pink, gold, and bronze. Strange colors, strange country, she thought as she started up her cook fire. A coyote broke the quiet of the early morning and Eliza smiled. It was a beautiful day. The air was cool, and she felt again the sense of exhilaration she had felt back at Malheur Lake.

The glimmer of an idea had come to her mind. Last night, as the folks had treked, she had heard her name called out again. She had willed herself not to react, but instead she had walked on. If somebody wanted to catch her attention, that somebody would call her again. That somebody did, and Eliza was now convinced it was Smithy. She was convinced he was trying to speak, and she must be careful as to how she might ask him about it. A big question in her mind was if she should say something to Cal. She knew how Smithy loved to surprise him with things he could do. Catching fish and then fixing suppers for him at the end of the day; giving him drawings he'd done, especially for him. Eliza also had an idea as to why Smithy was trying to speak, but she had to think about it. Think it out. In the meantime, today was not the day to say anything to Caleb. If it was Smithy's grand surprise, Eliza should guard it well, and today she and Caleb and Smithy should make the most of this layover day.

Taking a deep breath, she stared at the striped hills. Yes, they were odd. What could have made them that way? Tall would know. Tall knew everything about this country. And herein lay the key to Eliza's thoughts about Smithy.

Two nights ago, Tall had told stories to some of the emigrants as they had sat around the campfire. He'd told them about a time when the Cascade Mountains had been an enormous ring of fire mountains surrounding vast inland seas. He had said that ashes from the flaming mountains had covered the land, and as the mountains thundered and blazed, they had spit out streams and rivers of hot rock.

He had told one story about a hulking, lopsided mountain so high its peak had rarely been seen. But after becoming a fire mountain, it puffed so much it had blown in on itself and it had had no top. Coyote had felt sorry about the mountain losing its top and had given the mountain two beautiful lakes, divided by a wall of great pines.

Tall's last story had been about a boastful boy who told everybody he knew that he could do everything bet-

300

ter than any other boy in his village. One day Coyote asked the boy not to be so boastful, but that didn't stop the boy. Year after year, the boy boasted about how he could kill bears, and wolves, and coyotes and people too, with his bare hands. When Coyote heard this, Coyote talked to the boy and told him he must not talk that way. But the boy still didn't listen to Coyote and continued to boast. This made Coyote angry, and Coyote took the boy's voice away from him so the boy could never talk again. As the boy grew older, he realized that he would never know certain things because he couldn't ask questions. He would never know why rabbits were brown, and sometimes black, and why Coyotes had pointed ears. He would never know why stars sometimes fell at night, and why rivers flowed certain ways. From that time on, the boy was called Fool Boy.

After Tall had finished his story, many of the folks had clamored for more. But Tall had said it was late, and he would tell stories again, another time.

Eliza had looked closely at Smithy, who had sat between her and Caleb. Smithy's eyes had been fixed on Tall Singer, and he hadn't moved. Eliza put an arm around the boy. "That was a good lesson story, Smithy," she'd said. "For boastful boys and girls, and grown-ups, too. I don't think there are any boasting folks traveling with us on this train." But Smithy hadn't shared with her his usual easy smile.

Now, Eliza set her coffeepot down on the cooking grate, and walked over to Smithy's camp. "They're strange, aren't they," she said, gesturing out toward the hills. "I'll bet Tall can tell us why they have those stripes. Let's ask him later today."

Smithy nodded, but he didn't look at Eliza, nor did he smile. Eliza put her hand on his shoulder. "Come and

301

ride with Cal and me today," she said. "It's a beautiful morning with the sun on the hills, and that river looks like it's got a lot of good fish." Smithy shook his head.

"Well, then how about coming on over to my camp and keeping me company while I fix us some breakfast. Caleb should be here soon."

Smithy nodded and stood up; Eliza waited while he got his drawing pad, pencils, and paints. Eliza was now convinced that Tall's story bothered the boy. Today she would find Tall and ask him to explain the story to Smithy himself.

A short time later Eliza pulled fresh biscuits out of her Dutch oven and at the same time she heard Caleb's shout. "Ellie. Smithy." Looking up, she saw him striding toward them, a smile on his face. Her heart quickened, as it always did when she saw him come to her like this. She stood up, Caleb grabbed her, kissed her, and then gave Smithy a hug.

"Let's go riding today," he said. "Let's see what makes this country look this way." He gestured out toward the striped hills, poured himself a cup of coffee, and looked at Smithy. "Hey! What's the trouble with you? Your face is as long as old Dog's on a cold morning! Come on! We'll go riding, and we'll do a little fishing, too. We'll see if we can catch bigger fish than Ellie. We haven't had time to do that for a long time."

But Smithy shook his head, then pointed to the hills and to his drawing pad, pencils, and paints. "Do you want Cal and me to stay in camp?" Eliza asked. "We don't have to go riding. We can stay in camp just as well and have a good look around."

Smithy shook his head, indicating that they should go. "Well then," Caleb said. "When we come back, we'll have a fine supper, and find out from Tall why the hills are striped. I'll bet he'll have a good story to tell." Smithy nodded, and Eliza was pleased to see him smile.

It was midmorning when Eliza and Caleb left camp. In spite of the lovely morning and the fine day ahead, Smithy was foremost in Eliza's mind and she turned to Caleb. "Cal . . ."

"We should think about sending Smithy away to a special doctor or a special school." Caleb said. "I think it's time we talked about that, Ellie. As soon as we get to the valley, we should look at that."

"I'm pleased to hear that. Yes, we should look into it. Clancy might know though, Cal. We could ask him this evening."

"Good idea, Ellie. We'll do that, you and me."

They rode on, following the river through open country, stopping at a grove of cottonwoods growing along the riverbank. After setting out a picnic lunch, Eliza looked out at the river and sighed. "You know, Cal. Any school we send him to will be a school far away. In the East. There aren't schools like that yet out here."

"I know. I've thought of that, a lot."

"And before we do that, we've got to make sure he feels good about himself. That, to my mind, is important. He's got to have that."

"He will. This trek has done him a world of good. He's learned how to think for himself, and how to think about other folks, too." Then, coming up behind her, Caleb put his arms around her. Eliza felt a tingle of pleasure as his mouth gently brushed against her neck. "He and I can trek back," Caleb said. "And if we do, I'll be thinking at times about this delicious soft place here on your neck."

Eliza laughed. "And you'll probably get enjoyment out of your trek, too."

"Sure. We both will. Once a man's done it, he can sure do it again."

Eliza turned to him, reached up, and pushed back a lock of his hair. She looked at him, her green eyes warm with love while her voice held a tease. "You might want to trek back east, Caleb Pride, but not me. The only place I'd think on going back to would be the place around the Malheur Lake. And I don't know why I'd be going back there except I liked it. And I've wanted to ask you, ever since we were there, how you felt about that country. But there hasn't been time. So . . . now I'm asking. What did you think of it?"

Caleb was quiet for a moment. When he spoke, his voice was soft. "Lordy, Ellie. I liked it there! I've not ever seen a place I liked so much. I even had crazy thoughts on putting down out there, but I thought you'd think me daft."

She laughed with delight. "That's so strange because I tell you, when I watched the animals grazing on the tall, sweet grass, the thought came to me that it was a paradise for them. But it's far. Far, Cal, from everything people like us need. Stores and towns and folks."

"It's a notion to keep. You know for a fact that country isn't going anywhere. Even if we are."

Then, cupping her chin in one hand, he looked deep into her eyes. "You can't know, Ellie, you can't know how different I feel since telling you about . . . about what happened to me. It's like a hundred years have been peeled away from my mind. I love you so much, and you accept me, knowing all that, knowing . . ."

Placing a finger on his lips for a moment, then standing on tiptoe, she took her finger away and gently kissed him. "Not much worse can happen to a boy, Cal. Not much worse."

"I don't intend to bring it up again," he said. "Not unless there's reason to. There's too many good things happening to us, and we don't need to think about it again. But I had to tell you how I feel . . . so . . . free . . . knowing that you know."

Then, placing his hands on either side of her face, he kissed her, and Eliza felt the fire of want for him, and the sweet ache, as she took his tongue in her mouth and willingly pressed her body against him, delighting in the feel of his strong legs against hers and aware of the want he had for her too.

"Oh, Cal," she whispered. "I wish we could be married, right now!"

"You can't be wishing that more than I," he said, his voice soft and a little uneven. She pulled away from him, and with her index finger, she traced down the side of his face, kissing his eyes, and his nose, and kissing him again, quickly on his mouth. "Yes," she said. "It's a fact that I want you, but it won't happen, Cal. Not until we're husband and wife, good and proper." She laughed. "Tell me . . . do you think everybody has a trouble with this . . . like we do? Do you think that Lucy Ann and Stilly did? And Maggie and George?"

"You bet I think they did." Caleb said with a smile. "Remember, it's supposed to be the original sin. Sure they struggled with wanting each other."

"It's a puzzle," she said. "You love somebody so much you ache to have them, but something holds you back and won't let go. And yet . . . it's scary too, letting yourself go and be taken . . ."

"No! Oh Ellie, please don't be afraid. I don't want you to ever be afraid of me. And I would never, never . . . take you. I promise you that. I also promise you that our life together will be a fine life. I can't live long enough to be able to do all the things I want to do for you, and for Smithy, and for our own children too."

"And I . . . I feel that for you," she said. "Yes, I do."

"Look." She pointed to a yellow leaf caught in a backwater. "I don't ever want to be like that leaf. Whirling round and round, and not going anywhere. We won't let that happen to us, will we?"

Caleb laughed. "No," he said. "We sure won't. Come on, Ellie. Let's see who can catch the biggest fish."

It was late that afternoon when Eliza and Caleb rode back toward camp with eight trout laid in Caleb's fishing basket. Riding slowly along the river, Eliza smiled. It had been a splendid afternoon. The terrible thing that had happened to Caleb so many years ago was as resolved as it ever could be. It was a good thing that he didn't want to talk about it again, unless there was reason. And it was time now to put the matter away and leave it. On the fine, bright side, they would both talk to Clancy tonight about schooling for Smithy. Eliza felt especially pleased with that thought. Looking at Caleb riding beside her, she playfully swatted his arm.

"Just like when we were children," she said. "Back in Kentucky. I caught the most fish!" They both laughed, and rode on.

Small columns of smoke rose from the cooking fires. The shouts and laughter of the children mixed with the tones of talk. Fires crackled, cook pans thunked, all the familiar sounds and sights—and then there was Sam, playing "Oh, Susanna." Good camp sounds of evening that Eliza knew she would remember all her life.

They rode past George, bent over a wagon wheel. George straightened. "I need a little help, Cal, if you've got time. Wheel's bent." Caleb dismounted Sweetface, hobbled her, and walked over to help.

Eliza decided to stop by the Petersons and ask them if they would like some trout for supper. She would visit with Lucy Ann for a moment, see how Betsy was doing with her sprained ankle, and take a peek at Cece.

She found Betsy cooking dinner while keeping an eye on her little sister, who lay in her flannel-lined cradle and made soft cooing noises. Eliza picked up the baby.

"How's your ankle, Bets? I see you still have it bound up. It should be getting better soon, I think."

"It's some better, but I still can't walk much, and I have to stay in the wagon while we trek."

Eliza could see that her ankle was still swollen. "You don't give it a chance to heal," she said. "I see you out playing games with the other children at the end of the day. You can't expect it to get well that way."

"That's what Mama says. And every day I say that to myself, but I get so tired of not being able to play. Mama won't even let me ride Streak."

"Don't whine, Betsy," Lucy Ann said, joining Eliza and taking a quick look at Cece. "It doesn't suit you, and as long as your ankle's swollen like that, you're going to have to ride in the wagon. I don't want to hear your complaints."

Startled, Eliza looked at Lucy Ann, who rarely talked in such cross tones. She looked uncommonly tired. "Smithy was here, Ellie," Lucy Ann said. "Not too long ago. Looking for you and Caleb. I think he was going down to the river. He had his drawing pad and pencils and he headed that way."

"I'll go find him," Eliza said. "But Lucy, Cal and I brought back some fish. I'll clean some and send some over. You look tired. Real tired."

"I am tired. We're all tired."

Eliza gave her friend a hug. "I'll see you later, after I find Smithy."

It was a cool evening and Eliza thought she should walk over to her wagon and pick up a shawl. But no, she didn't want to take the time. Besides, she felt a sense of urgency as she walked quickly through camp, passing Caleb and George on the way.

"Cal?" She called out. "Have you seen Smithy?"

"Nope. But wait just a minute and we'll go find him." Eliza stopped, feeling impatient now as she

307

watched Caleb and George ease the repaired wheel down in place. Caleb then waved off George's thanks and joined Eliza. "He's probably still down at the river, finishing off a drawing."

"I know. That's what Lucy Ann said. But he's usually waiting for us, and I'm . . . well, we'll go find him."

"And you'll tell him you caught the most fish." Caleb looked at her, his blue eyes twinkling with laughter.

"I will! I'll tell him that, and I'll tell him that if he'd come with us today, he probably would have caught the most fish."

Finches and red-winged blackbirds flitted among clumps of willows growing along the riverbank; the pungent smell of late summer hung in the air. But Smithy was nowhere to be seen. He should be here, Eliza thought. He should be here, his head of tousled brown hair bent low over his work with Dog sitting patiently beside him.

Eliza felt tiny pinpricks of fear along her spine, and when she looked at Caleb, she saw worry in his eyes. Caleb frowned. "Smithy?" he called, his voice loud. "Smithy!" Dog's high yelp from downriver caused them both to feel a flooding sense of relief.

"He's down there, Ellie. Come on, let's go! I'll bet he has a fine painting of the hills."

But something was wrong. Smithy, on knowing Eliza and Caleb were close, always came running with Dog. Caleb sensed it too; she heard it in his voice. "Smithy? Smithy?" he called again as he started to run.

Icy fear gripped Eliza as she ran. She told herself that nothing could happen to Smithy. Smithy had never wandered like some of the children did. He wasn't fond of water so he wouldn't have been tempted to swim, or even wade in the river. Indians? Not likely. But then the big Indian, Tomschini, flashed through Eliza's mind, and as she raced on, behind Caleb, stumbling over rocks and pushing aside willows, she cried softly to herself, her words hoarse and ragged. "Dear God, dear God! Please!

Please let him be all right! Please dear God! Please . . ."

They found him in a place where the grass grew tall. A golden butterfly sat in his touseled brown hair, an ant crawled around his open mouth, and his eyes were wide open as if he was looking at the sky. His drawing tablet and one of Caleb's floppy old hats lay by his side. His left leg was big and black with two tiny holes of snake bite in his calf. Dog, his head laid on Smithy's chest, whimpered, and didn't get up.

"Oh, my God! My God!" Eliza heard her own wail, thin and high, as she saw Caleb pick up the boy.

"Smithy! Smithy!" Caleb's anguished cry echoed over the hills as he picked up the boy and held him close, his face twisted with the agony of terrible grief.

This isn't happening, Eliza thought. This isn't happening to us, and not to Smithy. God wouldn't take Smithy away! He wouldn't! Bending over, she picked up his writing tablet and clutched it hard, letting the paper cut into her index finger and into the base of her thumb, welcoming the slight hurt. She couldn't give in. Not now. She glanced at the drawing, an exquisite drawing of the hills with their shadowed streaks and the words *The Painted H* printed underneath. A piece of paper fluttered in the grass. Eliza picked it up. It was a small, crude self-portrait of Smithy, wearing Caleb's hat, with the caption, in Smithy's handwriting, *Fool Boy*. Eliza closed her eyes for a moment and then put the paper in her skirt pocket. Caleb didn't need to see it. Not ever.

Many folks gathered at Caleb's wagon that night. As they sat by the fire, Sam played "Shall We Gather by the River" on his harmonica. Later, Betsy put her head down on her knees and sobbed. Jeremy, blinking hard against his own tears, put his arm around his sister; it was very quiet in the camp.

Eliza left the fire once, walked to her wagon, and

opened her mother's oak chest, removing the linens and china that were wrapped and packed inside. She shook out two linen tablecloths and carefully lined the chest. Returning to the campfire, she talked briefly to Clancy and George, who walked back to Eliza's wagon and returned with the chest.

"Ellie." Caleb's voice was ragged with grief. "You think a lot of that chest. I know you do. You've talked to me about where you'd be putting it in our house in the valley. Please . . ."

"The chest is better off holding Smithy, Cal," Eliza's voice was firm. "You can make me a new chest."

It was dawn when they buried the boy on a grassy place close to the striped hills. Eliza printed his name on a large stone. SMITHY. AGE ABOUT 10. DIED AUGUST 28, 1848. SNAKEBITE. Caleb and Jeremy talked a little about Smithy. Caleb told the folks how he'd found him in a barn back in Illinois, and what a splendid artist he was. Jeremy talked about how much he loved to go fishing with Smithy even though Smithy always caught the most fish.

And then the wagon train started to roll. Twice Jeremy walked back to get Dog, who kept returning to Smithy's grave. Then, as they treked, Eliza heard Tall's song.

It is above the Milky Way that you go;
along the flower trail;
There is dust from the whirlwind;
the whirlwind on Snow Mountain;
That is where the rocks are ringing;
they ring your name in the mountain.
They ring the name of Smithy,
never the name of Fool Boy.

Chapter 36

Caleb was no longer captain of the livestock. After Smithy's death, he'd met with the Executive Committee and asked to be replaced. He had his own wagon to drive, and he felt it would be fair to turn his duties over to Danny McVey, who had become a capable herder. The Executive Committee had agreed to Caleb's request and Caleb now drove his wagon in line behind Eliza's, walking with her most of the days.

The Oregon Roll now traveled through an open forest with little underbrush under the red-barked pines. Long shafts of sunlight filtered through trees so tall it made a person dizzy to try to walk and look at the treetops at the same time. It was a quiet trek where sounds of the jostling, creaking wagons were muted by the cushioned pine of the forest floor.

Coming out of the forest and crossing a meadow, Eliza saw butterflies. Brown and white butterflies, tiny, bright blue butterflies, and butterflies with golden wings.

"I feel like Smithy's traveling along with us," Eliza said to Caleb. "I like to think that."

"I've got to quit thinking about him suffering," Caleb answered. "I can't get it out of my mind."

Eliza took a deep breath. "I have to tell you some-

311

thing, Cal. Something I figured out this last week." She put her hand on Caleb's arm and looked at him. "I think Smithy was about to talk, just before he died."

Caleb stopped and looked at Eliza, his eyes puzzled and intent. "Whatever do you mean?" he asked softly. "What are you telling me?"

Well . . . it was strange. It was during a night trek . . . the night we got to the John Day River. I . . . I heard someone call out my name. I did, Cal. Someone called out 'Eliza' sort of slow, and sort of, well, now that I've thought about it, it was a shy, a real shy sort of a sound. In a million years, Cal, I wouldn't have thought it was Smithy. Then when I heard it again, somebody calling my name, I walked back and asked Smithy if he'd heard it too. But Smithy, you know how he always did, he just shook his head. Then, when I didn't hear it again, I decided I'd been hearing things. But then, the night before he died, a night we were treking again, I heard my name called again, and I believed then it was him. I'd thought about telling you, but I decided that this was a secret, the most important secret Smithy ever had, and he wanted to surprise you. Later, when we talked to Tall, I put things in place, and now I'm sure I'm right."

She reached out and touched his arm. "Come on, we can walk while I talk." They walked on, their steps measured and slow, as Eliza continued. "This is what I think. Tall's story about Fool Boy bothered Smithy. But I also think that story made him determined to talk. It was like it unlocked something in him, but he didn't know how. I mean, if Smithy knew he could talk, he wouldn't just start talking like you or me, or Jeremy or Betsy, or anybody. He'd have to . . . learn, sort of. Learn, all over again. And I think he was . . . well, practicing those couple of nights."

Caleb was quiet for a time and then he whistled softly. "What you say makes me feel real happy. That

312

Smithy knew he could talk. It also makes me feel sad because he never had a real chance."

"Well, think then about what Tall told us. About how Smithy came to see him after we'd left, and he'd wanted to know why the hills were striped. Tall's story must have tickled Smithy. He'd have liked the notion of the cloud spirit who decided that this country needed color. He'd have liked the idea of the spirit telling Coyote to find a boy who could paint the hills, and when Coyote did, Smithy would have especially liked the thought that the spirit gave the boy the big brush made out of a wild horse's tail. And how he must've enjoyed listening to Tall tell him about how the boy then painted the hills the colors we see today. Then, remember, Tall said when Smithy left Tall, after hearing the story, he had a big grin on his face."

For a few moments Eliza and Caleb walked in silence. When Caleb spoke, his voice was soft, and Eliza saw a faint smile on his face. "And what else do you think?" he asked.

"Think on this. We were all so curious about the striped hills. Now, if Smithy had the notion he could talk, and then he learned the story about the hills, I think he might have planned on telling us the story that night. That's how he wanted us to know. So, I think his thoughts about himself must have been good that afternoon."

Again there was a silence before Caleb spoke. "I see," he said. "Well, Ellie, I'll say this, and that's that your telling me these things about him sure makes me feel better."

Later that same day, the train moved through a high country of big meadows, surrounded by pines, and the emigrants got their first glimpse of a string of snow-clad mountain peaks. Mt. Hood, St. Helens, Adams, Jefferson, Washington, and the Three Sisters. They were looking at the fabled Cascades. The last barrier separating these weary people from the Willamette Valley.

313

Shouts and whistles rang through the air. Men threw their battered, sweat-stained hats in the air, and women waved their faded poke bonnets. Caleb grabbed Eliza and spun her around and kissed her; Stilly held Cece high. "We're getting there, Cecilia Louise. We're getting there, my Oregon girl!"

Chapter 37

Eliza smiled. A nooning on the Deschutes River could hardly be better than this day in early September. Small white clouds floated in the sky; song sparrows and meadowlarks, perched on tree branches and atop juniper trees, filled the air with melodies. Caleb had just ridden out of camp with O'Shea, Stilly, and Tall to scout the waters, looking for a good crossing. If they found one close by, they hoped to get the wagons across yet this afternoon.

"Mama's real sick, Aunt Ellie." Startled, Eliza looked up from cleaning three trout she'd caught last evening, to see Betsy hobbling toward her. Betsy was carrying Cece.

Eliza frowned. "Your mama's sick? Lordy, Bets, your mama's never sick." Eliza put her fish in one of the baskets she'd bought back in the Shoshone Indian village, placed the basket in her wagon, and wiped her hands on her apron. "What's the trouble?"

"I don't know," Betsy said, holding the squirming baby who had started to fuss.

Eliza held out her arms. "Let me take Cece, Betsy. Now, tell me what's wrong."

As Betsy handed Cece to Eliza, Eliza saw the fear in Betsy's eyes. "She started feeling bad this morning and

Papa made her lie in the wagon. I was riding in there too because of my mean old ankle and I was taking care of Cece. Then we got here, and Papa left with Mr. O'Shea and Mr. Pride and Tall. It was after Papa had left that Mama started throwing up and I think she's got fever now. It's like the sickness of the bloody flux. I decided I'd best come and get you."

A rush of foreboding and dread swept over Eliza. There were times when fever, even out here away from the cities, claimed folks. Not like back home, but when it struck, it could be deadly. Symptoms were well known. A dreadful fatigue, followed by wretched body aches, dysentry, headaches, and nausea with high fever. Thinking back, Eliza realized that Lucy Ann had looked unduly tired these last few days. Eliza forced herself to be calm.

"Well, Bets," she said, "let's see what we can do. We'll make her feel better real soon. Where's Jeremy?"

"He went fishing with Mr. McIntyre and some of the others."

On reaching the Petersons' wagon, Eliza handed Cece back to Betsy. "You wait here," she said. "No sense in you and Cece being around your sick mama." Climbing up the steps into the wagon, Eliza was assailed by the stench of sickness. She found Lucy Ann lying on the bed, curled up tight and shaking with chill, her skin hot to the touch.

Quickly gathering up some of Cece's things, Eliza joined Betsy. "Bets, I want you to take Cece and these things that she'll need and go over to Mrs. McVey's. I don't want you or the baby here at all. Scoot now, and go!"

Betsy looked at Eliza with frightened eyes, her lower lip trembling. Eliza put her arm around her. "There's no need to worry or cry. Your mama's a fighter, and we'll get her back on her feet real soon." Betsy silently nodded, and clutching Cece and the things Eliza had given her, she hobbled across camp toward the McVeys'.

A bucket of cool wash water stood under the Petersons' wagon. Grabbing the bucket, Eliza carried it up into the wagon, where she tended to Lucy Ann, who had been struck, full force, with fever.

"Where's Cece?" she whispered once, opening her fevered eyes.

"She's fine, Lucy. She and Betsy are at Maggie's. Here, you've got to have water and some of this." Lucy Ann swallowed a spoonful of thick syrupy medicine Eliza gave her, took small sips of water, then fell back on her pillow.

"I can't even take care of my baby, Ellie." Tears welled up in her eyes and Eliza took one of Lucy Ann's hot, dry hands. "Your baby will do fine, Lucy. Please don't worry. Your job is to rest and get well."

"Eliza?" Clara stood outside the wagon, holding two large jars that she set on the wagon floor. "Mrs. McVey told me about Mrs. Peterson's bein' so sick, so I hurried and got these made up. One's a broth and the other's tea. In my way of thinking, they do better than some of the medicines we give to folks."

"Ah, this will be wonderful, Clara. And it's not that there isn't a pack of medicines. I found castor oil, and quinine, and hartshorne as well as rum and laudanum and peppermint. But I'm thinking your broth and tea will do her just fine. Thanks, Clara. Thanks a lot."

"I've never known that broth there, or the tea either, to fail. I learned to make the broth when I was a child, and the tea, I learned from Tall's people. She's doing all right?"

"She'll be fine. She's a fighter, and I know she'll be fine."

"Let me know if there's a thing I can do to help."

Lucy Ann had now fallen into a fitful sleep, and as Eliza sat down in the close, hot space, she silently prayed that God not take this good woman. She would make it, Eliza told herself. With rest, she would be fine. But as she

317

listened to Lucy Ann's fast, shallow breathing, she felt the cold chill of fear.

It was a little later when Lorene appeared, holding her white ermine cloak. Climbing up into the wagon, Lorene laughed softly. "I tell you, Ellie, if this pretty thing's going to do anyone any good on this trek, it'll do some good for Lucy Ann. When she's feeling better, she can wrap herself in this and feel like a queen."

Eliza smiled. "You think of everything, I swear."

"Well, it's nice to make folks feel good. You do that, and so does Lucy Ann." She then sat down on a box next to Eliza. "I'll stay with you," she said. "Four hands sometimes work better than two and we sure aren't going anywhere near a river crossing today."

That afternoon Lucy Ann went into a delirium and her breathing was shallow as she cried for her baby, and babbled incoherently. Her fever didn't break.

It was toward evening when Stilly, Caleb, O'Shea, and Tall returned. It was too late to move camp, and when Stilly learned how sick his wife was, his face turned the color of cold ashes. "We'll roll when Lucy Ann's feeling up to it," he told O'Shea. "We're not going anywhere 'til then."

It was cold that evening and stars glittered in the dusk of twilight as Caleb walked with Eliza back to her wagon. Throwing his great coat over her, Caleb held her close as they walked. "She'll make it, Ellie," he said. Lucy's tough."

"She's sick as can be, Cal. I just pray the fever will break tonight, the way it's supposed to. Sam came by this afternoon. He says there's nothing we can do that we haven't done, but I could tell, he's worried."

"She's going to make it." Caleb's tone was insistent. "She'll pull through."

"Lordy, Cal, I hope you're right. I can't bear the thought of losing her. We've lost enough folks on this trek. To lose Lucy Ann would be . . ." Eliza's voice broke.

"You can't be thinking that way, Ellie. You've done what you can do. Now, please. Try to think ahead. We're getting close to the valley and this trek will be done with. Think about building our own place! We'll build it not far from the river where you can see the beautiful water, and there'll be tall fir trees, and sunshine and meadows full of flowers. Try to think about those things tonight, please."

Eliza nodded. "I know, and I feel good when I think about that, and I think about it a lot, I do. You and me, and Stilly and Lucy Ann, and Lorene and Clancy . . . all of us, living close to each other and settling in."

"That's been our plan, and it won't change. It's not going to change, Ellie." He tenderly kissed her goodnight.

That night as Eliza tried to sleep, it wasn't the sick, delirious Lucy Ann who came to her mind. It was the image of Betsy, hobbling across camp, holding Cece.

The pink dawn of morning faded to cloudless skies, and when Eliza walked over to the Petersons' wagon, she felt a great wash of relief. A smiling Betsy was cooking breakfast, and she held up a pan of fresh cornmeal bread.

"Mama's ever so much better," she said with a lilt in her voice. "Have some of Mrs. McVey's bread, Aunt Ellie. She made it especially for us this morning. And Cece and me, we stayed the night, and Mrs. McVey told me stories about fairies and goblins, and we had a good time. And mama . . . she's doing just fine."

Jeremy, a big grin on his face, was rubbing down Streak, and it was then that Stilly, holding Cece in the crook of his arm, left the wagon.

"Oh, Ellie, what a relief. What a relief. With your good nursing too. Her fever broke in the night. Soaking wet she was, through and through. But Jeremy and I got her wrapped up in clean quilts and she slept a good calm sleep. I tell you . . . well, I just thank you, Ellie. You and the others. Lorene is visiting her now."

He then sat down on a camp stool and started spooning a thin creamy mush into Cece's tiny mouth. "And I'm enjoying this little princess this morning, I am."

"But Mama wants to move on today," Betsy said, while spearing chunks of bacon with her fork. "So Papa says we will."

Eliza frowned and looked at Stilly. "Are we?" she asked, surprised. "Can't we stay over one more day? Give Lucy a day of rest? It shouldn't hurt."

"Lucy's the one," Stilly said. "She's anxious to get on our way. Anxious to get to that valley. Sure, I wanted to lay over one more day, but she won't hear of it. So, we're leaving right after the nooning today."

"And I get to help Papa drive the wagon across the Deschutes," Jeremy said. "Riding Streak, too."

A sudden gust of wind caught Eliza's untied bonnet, lifted it off her head, and sent it spinning through the air. Jeremy leaped up and caught it and they all laughed. "I guess we'll never get away from the stubborn old wind, will we," Jeremy said.

"It doesn't seem that way, but it's supposed to be some better in the valley," Eliza said. Then she turned to Stilly. "Let me have Cece today, Stilly. Caleb can take my wagon across while I ride inside with the baby. Then I'd like to keep her for the rest of the day so Lucy will have the day to rest."

Stilly looked at Betsy. "What do you think, Bets?"

Betsy shrugged. "If Aunt Ellie wants to, and if Mama says yes, then sure enough."

Stilly laughed. "Well, if Lucy says yes, Cece is yours for the day. Until we set camp tonight."

Eliza smiled. "I'll ask her."

Eliza found Lucy Ann sitting up in bed and wrapped in Lorene's ermine cape, while sipping a cup of Clara's herbed tea and nibbling on a sugar biscuit. Lorene was sitting in the small rocking chair, and both women looked

320

expectant, as if waiting for her. Eliza laughed with delight. "Don't you look grand, Lucy!"

"I'm glad to see you, Ellie!" Lucy Ann said, her voice was husky, and she coughed, but her eyes were clear and it was obvious her fever was gone. "Whew! I'll say I feel every inch a queen! And isn't this the prettiest thing you've seen in your life?" She smiled ruefully. "But I'm a naked queen with ruined clothes, and I'd just as soon not go through that fever again."

"We don't want you to either," Eliza and Lorene said in unison.

"Lucy, let me take the baby today," Eliza said. "That will give you a good day of rest."

"Well . . ." Lucy Ann hesitated and looked up at the wagon cover, where a miller flitted against the light. "That would free up Bets some. And Stilly says she's eating fine, and Lordy, I'm glad for that. It's probably not a bad idea. Why don't you take her when we're ready to cross and keep her until we set camp tonight. I should be feeling a lot better by then."

"Good. I'll come and get her. I'm so relieved to see that you're better, Lucy. Now, I'd better be getting back. Got to get ready for the crossing and we sure know what that means."

Lorene rolled her eyes and sighed. "We sure do! Pulling . . . the . . . wagon . . . top . . . back." They all laughed, feeling lighthearted at Lucy Ann's speedy recovery.

Lucy Ann held up her hand. "This wagon top stays put! Stilly says it's a calm day, and if we take it down, the light would sure hurt my eyes."

"That's exactly why I think we should wait another day, Lucy," Eliza said as Lorene nodded in agreement. "Give yourself a day of quiet, before we roll."

But Lucy Ann shook her head. "I'm so much better, and I'm so anxious to get there, as is everybody. It won't do to stay over another day. Getting to the valley can't happen soon enough for me."

Lorene stood up. "I have dresses to spare, Lucy. After we get across, I'll bring some over to you. And now, I'm on my way, too. Keep the cloak for a while. It looks beautiful on you, and when you're up and about, you can give it back to me."

"Thanks," Lucy said, smiling and snuggling into the white fur. "I'll see you on the other side of the Deschutes."

Flat slabs of rock jutted out into the river, providing a launching platform for the wagons, now lined up and ready to cross. Eliza walked over to the Petersons' wagon, where Betsy handed Cece to her. Taking a quick look inside the wagon, Eliza was pleased to see Lucy Ann, lying in bed, still wrapped in Lorene's ermine cloak. "You're looking ever so much better, Lucy. Better even than this morning. Don't worry. I'll take good care of Cece."

Lucy Ann waved. "I'm feeling lots better, too. I may even be ready to dance tonight. Anyway, I'll see you on the other side."

Eliza laughed. "You're making a fine recovery, Lucy. It's got something to do with Lorene's cloak."

A short time later Eliza carefully positioned her faded, blue parasol over a pile of quilts that she had arranged on the floor of her now topless wagon. With the wagon top down, the sun was bright and scorching hot. She then put one of her poke bonnets over the baby's head, and as she sat down on the quilts, holding Cece, she realized that she hadn't ridden in her wagon during a river crossing since before crossing the Platte. She much preferred riding Babe and taking her wagon herself, but her reward today was having Cece and knowing Lucy Ann could rest without this particular worry.

Then Caleb was there and it was time to go. Caleb

whistled and called out the now familiar calls. Big Moo bawled and threw her big head about as Caleb flicked his whip, urging her to take the lead in pulling the wagon across the big, flat rocks into the water.

Eliza watched Caleb work the oxen, and in moments, she felt the swift waters catch the wagon bed. She sucked in her breath and held Cece tight. Deceptive water. Never a good sign.

"Caw! Caw! Get on there, Big Moo!" Caleb shouted, his voice firm and loud. Big Moo's bawling got louder, but then the big ox lurched ahead and Eliza felt the wagon surge, steady, and pull well against the sucking current. It seemed like a long time, though, before Eliza felt the wagon tilt back a little, as the wheels touched ground. Her team then hauled the dripping wagon ashore. Eliza knew the water was rougher than Caleb had expected, but if he was concerned, it didn't show as he grinned up at her.

"Let me hold Cece, while you climb on down," he said. "Then I'm going back over. That water's danged swift, swifter than we thought. I'll be helping the others and the herds." He laughed. "I tell you, Ellie, Big Moo hates water worse than any animal I've seen. But when she knows she could be in trouble, she does better than any animal I've seen."

Then, holding Cece, who made little sticky baby sounds and coos, and waved her tiny fists in the air, he smiled. "You're sure a pretty one, you are," he said. "And your mama and papa are coming on across, right about now." It was then that Eliza looked back across the river to see Stilly and Jeremy, Jeremy proudly riding Streak, as he helped drive the Petersons' oxen into the water.

Suddenly a gust of wind whipped down on the water, making little silver ripples on the surface and catching the Petersons' wagon. The big wagon tipped, and then slid downstream like a crazy ship before coming to a stop, caught on a rock.

"Stilly! Lucy!" Eliza screamed as Caleb thrust Cece into Eliza's arms, shouting "Oh my God!"

Now, the foundering oxen, desperately trying to regain their balance, could quickly worsen things by pulling the wagon farther into the river. But Stilly, who had reached the wagon, crawled up on the wagon tongue. He had to cut his team loose. He would worry about them later, but now he had to stabilize the teetering wagon, and he knew he could count on help coming his way as several men, including Caleb, Tall, and O'Shea, on their horses, were trying to reach him. Eliza, holding Cece, felt her skin prickle with spasms of fear as she watched Stilly take his knife out of its sheath and expertly cut the rope that bound his flailing animals to the wagon. But during this time, Jeremy was urging Streak to swim downstream toward the wagon.

Looking up, Stilly saw his boy. "Jeremy!" Stilly cried. "No! Go on! Get on across!" Streak, losing his footing, foundered, making big silver splashes before regaining his balance. The big roan then swam to shore, alone. Clancy, standing on shore and prepared for such an incident, heaved a rope out over the river.

"Catch it! For God's sake, catch it, Jeremy!" Jeremy's head bobbed up in the water; he grabbed the rope, hung on for a moment, then disappeared. Sam, rope in hand, raced down the riverbank to try to find Jeremy, while Clancy ran downstream and threw the rope to Stilly. Stilly caught it on the third try. Eliza breathed a sigh of relief, knowing that when Caleb, O'Shea, and Tall reached Stilly, the four of them could hold the wagon against the current while Clancy and the men on shore pulled the wagon across to safety.

Then Eliza's eyes widened in horror as she saw Lucy Ann, wrapped in the long cloak, try, for some insane reason, to reach Stilly. Stilly had started to wrap the rope around the wagon tongue, then distracted for a split second, he looked back toward Lucy and lost his precarious foothold on the slippery tongue. His blood-chilling scream rent the air as the rope snapped from his hands and leaped like a wild thing before coming down on the water with a small, sparkly splash. Stilly surfaced once, his face reflecting unspeakable horror before he was swept out of sight.

At the same time the wagon, with its tongue popped up and skewed to the sky, was jarred loose from the rock and the big thing spun around, skidded, and slipped this way and that way as it shot down the river. Eliza saw Lucy Ann, naked, her long, black hair reaching her buttocks, as she clung to the side of the wagon and then she too disappeared in an explosion of water and wood as the powerful current smashed the wagon to bits on a rocky point downstream.

A few minutes later, broken clouds still moved across the sky, a meadow lark sang, and when the stunned folks looked out at the river the only hint of something strange, something wrong, was an ermine cloak, caught on a willow, gleaming white in the afternoon sun.

Chapter 38

Wind-torn alpine trees dotted the bleak lava fields high in the mountain pass. Turkey buzzards wheeled in thin, clear air. The bulks of the North and Middle Sister loomed dark and brooding with patches of rotting snow on their upper flanks. Looking north, the emigrants saw the white peaks of Mt. Jefferson, Washington, and Hood. To the west, beyond the lava plains and down the mountain, through the dense fir forest, lay the Willamette Valley. To the east, lay the land of the Deschutes. *The Oregon Roll* had reached the summit of the Cascades.

For ten days the emigrants had labored, pulling and pushing their wagons as they moved up through the piny flats of the high country, then crossing long uphill stretches of coarse, volcanic pumice dust and scrawny pine.

Now, having reached the top of the pass, shouts and laughter echoed against the rocks. But to Eliza, the sounds of joy were harsh and cruel as she fought the image of Lucy Ann. Lucy Ann, naked, her black hair swinging against her buttocks as she had desperately clung to the spinning wagon amid the big, silver sprays of water that had burst high in the air like thousands of diamonds.

She heard in her mind, again and again, her own

ragged scream of terror . . . "Lucy! Lucy Ann!" as, clutching Cece, she had run beside the river, only to stand, numb and silent, staring out at the sparkling Deschutes as it had tumbled swiftly downstream, past the gleaming fur, caught on the willow tree. And Lucy Ann's voice still rang in her hears. "I'll see you on the other side! I'll be ready to dance tonight!"

Dear God, Eliza thought. Dear Lucy Ann. To be so debased at the end of her life. She thought of her own family who had died privately, even in their agony of disease. Smithy had died privately, too, in the company of his beloved Dog. Janie Marie? Eliza couldn't know, and thank God for it. But the image of Lucy Ann, stripped and naked, screaming incoherently before she had disappeared in that explosion of wood and water, tormented Eliza day and night. That, and the brutal memory of the bodies.

It had been the next day before the men had retrieved them. Betsy, Jeremy, Stilly, and Lucy Ann. Water-soaked, bloated beyond recognition, and rank with the smell of rotting flesh. Those who had buried them had hurried. Then *The Oregon Roll* had moved on.

Now, at the summit of the Cascades, Eliza stood holding Cece and she looked out over the bleak, wind-swept land. She felt Caleb slip his arm around her waist. "The trek's brought us sorrow, Ellie. No question about it."

Eliza nodded. "It's like I can hear it in the wind, Cal. Like now. The wind whistling and blowing over this bare, wild country brings me a feeling of sorrow. It's like they're the winds of sorrow."

"But we're almost there," Caleb said. "Think of that, and we have a whole new set of things to think about. Getting married for one, and I'm glad to tell you that Paddy O'Shea is tickled to stand with us. Then finding our land. Finding the place where we want to live should be an exciting thing. There's a whole lot of good things ahead of us."

"I know that, Cal. And I'll feel better then. I know I will." She looked down at Cece, whose rosy face was framed with black curls, her long eyelashes looking like a little fringe against her round cheeks. Cece was her child and Cal's now, as if she had been born to them. There was no question of that.

Caleb reached down and gently touched one of Cece's cheeks. "She's a pretty one, Ellie. We'll do well for her." Eliza nodded while absently watching Dog lope over the rocks in pursuit of something he thought he could catch. Dear old Dog, Eliza thought as a wry smile crossed her face. Cece and Dog, gentle reminders of family and folks Eliza and Caleb had loved so much.

Descending the mountains, the emigrants moved through thick, dark forests, coming at times to places where the sun rarely shined. Eliza found no joy in this trek, gloomy and dark beyond what she had ever known. Twice they camped beside glittering lakes, and one day they came to a river called the McKenzie, and many people exclaimed on its beauty as it rushed down the mountain toward the Willamette Valley. Eliza thought it was pretty, but it was another river, and it brought no peace to her mind.

Following Tall, *The Oregon Roll* wound through woodlands where vine maple flashed their blaze of red and gold leaves; a country thick with deer and game, a country where fish caught in the wild river were the color of rainbows. And then on a day in mid-September, the train came out of the mountains and Clancy, who was captain now, whistled, calling the folks to a halt.

"There it is, folks!" It was O'Shea's voice that boomed out as he pointed to the west. "There's the land of milk and honey, the Willamette Valley! It's here you all wanted to come to, and it's here we are now!" He turned in his saddle, smiled, and touched his hat like a salute.

Green. Green. Even in mid-September, this valley was green. A green valley laced with rivers and streams; a green valley with groves of magnificent oaks, stands of pine and stately cottonwood, broken by vast meadows and grasslands. A green valley where, off to the west, the emigrants could see the range of low mountains separating this land from the Pacific Ocean. A beautiful, green valley that these weary folks would now claim as home.

As *The Oregon Roll* moved on, they passed a few scattered homesteads. Women settlers, startled by the passing wagon train, left their kitchens or their gardens and, while wiping their hands on their long white aprons, hastened out to meet the emigrants. Men shaded their eyes, put down their tools, or left their fields, to join their women in greeting. What a joyous time it was. The men shook hands, and clapped each other on their backs; the women hugged one another and the children looked at each other with shy smiles.

"Where you all from?" the settlers asked. "How long have you trekked? You come from the east, and not from the north! You came across the *desert?* And the Cascades? Hmm! Hmm! How many folks did you lose?"

"We come from Illinois," some of the emigrants answered; others said they'd come from Missouri, Ohio, Virginia, Kentucky, and New York. "We've been trekking for six months," they said. "But we made up time. About one month, coming by way of the desert. Yes, we lost folks. Fourteen, all told."

Many of the settlers invited the emigrants to stay, to eat, to camp on their land. Some accepted the offer. When the others started to move on, the settlers gave them food. Bags of onions, potatoes, carrots, turnips, and beans; baskets of fresh blackberries, raspberries, and huckleberries; and jars of sparkling honey, jellies, and jams. Then with shouts of good-bye and farewell, the wagon train moved on to a place on the banks of the Willamette River. It was here, at this place called Ten Oaks, where they set camp in a grove of sprawling oak trees.

Late one afternoon several of the emigrants gathered around a big campfire. Clancy spoke first. "This valley's the prettiest sight I've seen in my life," he said. His smile was broad. "I'm sure where I want to be." Lorene laughed. "I'm glad, Clancy Evans, because I'm not interested in going a whole lot further."

Maggie, who stood between Danny and George, had tears in her eyes. "It cost us a child," she said. "But it might have cost us more if we hadn't come." George nodded while putting his arm around her. "We have to think about it that way. And this valley here will be home for us, and for Danny, and Danny's future wife and their children, and on and on, for the next hundred years. That's why we did it. That's why we came. For us and for them."

O'Shea held up his hand. "I have to say this," he said. "You folks have been a fine bunch. Now you'll be breaking up soon, some of you heading further west, some going north or south, some staying right here. As for me, I've got to get back to the states, and after Cal and Eliza's wedding, I'll be leaving you all. So this is the time I'd like to say again, you're a fine bunch of folks."

"Why don't you stay?" somebody called out. "Stay the winter, at least." O'Shea shook his head and smiled. "I'm not real fond of this valley," he'd been heard to say more than once. "It's too danged wet, and sometimes it's even too green." He didn't say that today though. He just said he had to get on back.

"Will you be coming here again?" Lorene asked.

"Sure! Sure!" O'Shea answered. "In a couple of

years I'll be bringing some more folks out, and I'll be looking to see you all then."

That evening Caleb, Eliza, Tall, and Clara met with O'Shea. "Tomorrow Tall and I are leaving camp early to visit an acquaintance of Tall's and Clara's," Caleb said. "A man by the name of Shaw. Judge Nathan Shaw. I learned yesterday from Tall that this fellow will no doubt be tickled to marry Eliza and me, and Ellie and I are hoping to get married within the week."

"You set the date, Cal, and I'll be there. Until then, I thought I'd scout on down south a ways. Awfully pretty country in southern Oregon. But you let me know by tomorrow, and I'll be coming back for your wedding. No doubt of that."

Caleb smiled, obviously pleased. Tall then pointed to a long forested ridge, barely visible against the sky. "The man, Shaw, lives out there. We will stay the night on land I plan to take my family to." Tall looked at Eliza. "If you want to come, I know you would be welcome to stay with the people named Shaw."

"A fine idea, Ellie, how about it?" Caleb asked.

Eliza looked at Clara. "Are you going?"

"No. I want to see them, but I don't want to ride all that way right now with Little Bear and Blue Bird. You go on though, Ellie. You'll get on with the Shaws real well."

Eliza shook her head. "I think not."

"What would you think, then, if I see land to my liking?" Caleb looked at her with a question in his eyes. "Land I'd want to claim for us. Wouldn't you want to see it too?"

"All this country is pretty." Eliza heard her voice, so soft, so terribly soft. "If the land suits you, Cal, I'll no doubt like it too."

She turned away, fighting the terrible urge to cry. Oh Lordy, she hated this feeling. She hated the rush of tears that always seemed to push against her eyes; she hated the flatness inside her head. Again and again she asked herself why she couldn't accept the drowning back at the Deschutes like the others had. Lorene had. Lorene, who right afterward was unable to eat or sleep, was smiling again, and making plans about settling in the valley. Maggie too. Maggie was busy planning her garden for the spring. "Starting with the sweetpea seeds I've brought with me. I'll be planting them in February," she had said. And Clara, who had been really quiet for some days even though she hadn't known the Petersons well, was now talking about the house she wanted Tall to build and the garden she wanted to tend.

"It will sure be a sight easier to grow things here than out at the Malheur," Clara had said. "Growing season's short there. Winters are cold. I'm looking to have my own garden, like those gardens we all saw coming this way."

But Eliza had been unable to overcome her melancholy, and now thoughts of Caleb leaving tomorrow seemed overwhelming. It was then that Clara put a hand on Eliza's arm.

"I've been giving something some thought," she said. "And that's that you need a cradleboard for Cece. I talked to Tall about it a couple of days ago, and he's just about finished making a frame. I was going to finish it for you, but why don't you do it yourself? I'll show you how."

Eliza forced herself to listen to Clara. As she listened, the idea became appealing. A cradleboard for Cece. How nice. With a cradleboard, she could strap Cece to her back and carry her like the Indian women did. It made good sense, and suddenly this seemed important for her to do.

"We'll lace it good with oak twigs and cover it with cloth," Clara said. "You must have something we can use. Wool, or good cotton. Tall's people use tanned deer hide, but since we don't have that . . ."

Eliza laughed. For the first time in weeks, she laughed. "No, Clara. We haven't had time to tan hides, and you're looking at a woman who doesn't know how."

"Well," said Clara, smiling at Eliza's laugh, pleased that she could have caused it. "When we have the time, I'll show you how. But now a good piece of cloth will do."

Eliza brightened at the thought. Yes, she had the cloth. One of her papa's old flannel shirts. And now she would put it to good use.

The next morning Eliza woke up and thought about the things she had to do. She also know realized, for the first time, that if Lucy Ann were here, she would tell her to put her sadness away. Her own life had to go on, she would say, and above all, she would expect that Eliza take very good care of her child, her beloved Cecilia Louise. Today then, Eliza figured the most important thing to do was to follow Clara's instructions and make the cradleboard.

Ah, Caleb thought as he rode with Tall. The magnificent rolling hills of the Willamette Valley. Looking west he could see the coast range, and to the east were the foothills of the Cascades. It was magnificent country, no doubt of that, and he was glad to have this opportunity to ride with Tall, who obviously knew where he was going.

They rode to the northeast, and Caleb's thoughts now were on land he might like well enough to claim. He and Tall had ridden a fair way when Tall reined in his horse. "That land," he said, pointing out toward grassy hills butting against heavy forests, "is good land, with good water. That is where I plan to live. I made that plan two years ago, and last year when I was here, I talked to Judge Shaw about it. I didn't know then that I would be here so soon." Tall smiled. "But now, here I am."

Caleb nodded. "It's sure pretty country," he said. "Real pretty. And you're right, Tall. I could figure on living out there. Are there folks living close by?"

Tall nodded. "Indians are scattered all over."

Caleb knew that. Molallas, Santiams, and Calapooyas. Tribes that fished the streams, gathered fruits, nuts, and roots, hunted the woods, thick with game, and were considered friendly people.

"There is also a place beyond the Shaws. We will pass it on the way to the land I hope to own. That place is owned by a man named Connors. He built a large house on it as he waits for a woman to join him."

"People will settle here, Tall. No question of that."

Tall nodded. "If you choose to live out here, Shaw and his wife will not be far. Clara and I would not be far either, and as you say, there will be more people coming to this country. Soon there will be many more."

Now, Caleb saw, off in the distance some ways, what he assumed was the Shaws' place. A big, two-story log house, flanked by two large oak trees. As the two men rode closer, Caleb smiled. Small paned windows sparkled in the afternoon sun, and a garden of dahlias, marigolds, hollyhocks, and yellow roses grew in front of the wide front porch. Ah, he whistled softly. This was the kind of a place he would have; this was the kind of house he would build for Ellie.

Suddenly a dog barked and a tall, gray-haired man walked out from behind the house, stood and looked at the riders for a moment, slapped his thigh, and burst out with a booming laugh. "Tall Singer!" the man cried out. "You've come back, by Jove! You've come back. Maudie, Tall's here."

A woman appeared at the front door, paused for a moment while drying her hands on her long apron, then walked quickly across the porch and down the steps.

"Tall," she called out. Caleb saw that she was a plain-looking woman, tall and angular, with gray hair tied

334

back in a knot. Her wide-set blue eyes flashed with joy, and her smile was wide as she took Tall Singer's hand in hers. "You're here to stay, Tall? And Clara?"

Tall's handsome face revealed pleasure as he smiled. "Clara is at the Ten Oaks camp by the river. She and our boy and girl. And yes. We are here to stay." He then introduced Caleb to the Shaws. He liked them both very much.

It was light and airy inside the house. The many windows allowed for the bright afternoon sun, and the heavy doors were opened wide. Maude led them through a large front room with dark, polished furniture, carved and spooled; richly patterned rugs covered part of the heavy-planked floors and bouquets of flowers spilled out from vases and urns.

Following Maude into a dining room, the three men sat down at a long oak table. In a few moments Maude returned with a pot of coffee and a large plate of cheese, pickles, and coarse bread with a thick salty crust. Sitting down with the men, she leaned across the table and placed her hand on Tall's. "The land!" she exclaimed. "Nathan has claimed the land for you. For you and Clara."

Judge Shaw smiled for a moment, but then he frowned. "The land laws are confusing, Tall. Congress now officially recognizes us as the Oregon Territory. That happened just last month. But the land laws fail to address the question of Indian ownership. So, acting as you asked me to last year, I acquired over a thousand acres in your name, Clara McCabe's name, and any children you two might have."

Tall Singer smiled. "Thank you." He turned to Maude. "Thank you. I am also pleased. Clara will be pleased too. She is very anxious to see you again. We will be good neighbors. Now, please tell me what has happened here this past year."

"You should know that Henry Connors died,"

Maude said. "He'd brought in a string of horses from down river, and one of them was a mean devil. A black stallion that he wanted to break especially for his lady, who had requested such an animal. His lady, Lydia Wells, was planning on coming out this last year, you know. Well, one day Henry had the horse out, working her, and she threw him. It was a dreadful accident. Nathan found him, but not until some time after the fall. Nathan got him here and I nursed him, but poor Henry didn't regain consciousness and died a day later."

"And his woman? What happened to her?"

"I don't know. Nathan wrote to her, and . . ."

"I told her the land was hers for the having since Henry had proved it up admirably. She wrote back that she might come out here one day, but right then she was enjoying life in San Francisco. So, we have yet to lay our eyes on Miss Lydia Wells."

Tall nodded. "Now, how are my own people? How are the feelings between your people and mine?"

Nathan and Maude were both quiet for a moment. Then it was Nathan who spoke. "You both surely know about the tragedy that occurred last November? The Cayuse slaughter of the Whitmans out at Waiilatpu?"

Caleb nodded. He had first heard about it last spring, before *The Oregon Roll* left Independence. Early in the trek folks had talked a lot about Dr. Marcus Whitman, the man who had established a mission in the Cayuse and Walla Walla country. The man had been murdered by Indians. It was said that Dr. Whitman's wife and twelve other white folks had been murdered too, including two little boys who had lost their parents on a trek west and had been living with the Whitmans. It was said that the slaughter had continued for over a week. But Caleb knew no more about it than that.

"I am not proud of that, Nathan," Tall said. "I know of no one who is. But I do not know what has happened since that time."

336

"Word of the tragedy reached our legislature just as they were convening in December at Willamette Falls. A company of riflemen was immediately authorized to capture the murderers, but the territorial government had no means to fund it. A loan commission, made up of Jesse Applegate, a certain Mr. Lovejoy, and a Mr. Curry was appointed, and a letter was sent to Mr. James Douglas, chief factor of the Hudson's Bay Company at Fort Vancouver, asking for funds. Well, with Douglas and the HBC under British rule, Douglas couldn't do that, but the good man did advise that a military force, under the leadership of Peter Skene Ogden, chief factor at Fort Vancouver, had been sent to negotiate for the release of fifty-three women and children, held captive. Because of Ogden's superb frontier knowledge and his years of experience in working with Indians, he was successful."

"That may be." Tall's voice was grim. "But I have heard that there was much sickness among my brothers in that country. I have heard that my people were angry with this man, Whitman, because many of them did not want to learn the white man's ways. Ways they felt were being forced on them. It is trouble like that that excites my own enemy, Tomschini. And I will tell you about Tomschini another time. But when Tomschini hears of trouble such as that, he will take his own revenge on white people as well as on any of my people whom he considers as friendly with the white man. These are the things I fear, Nathan."

The Judge nodded. "You hear correctly about the sickness. Terrible epidemics of measles and dysentery swept through the tribes, killing hundreds of people. There is also great fear now by your people that the white people will take land without fair treaty. That is a credible fear. It's my belief that, in general, the white people, settlers, politicians, and missionaries alike aren't handling these matters well."

"I hear there has also been trouble here, in this country," Tall said. "Do I hear the truth?"

Caleb was startled. He had thought relations between the Indians and white settlers here in the valley were friendly, and with mutual respect, both people lived in harmony.

Nathan shook his head and sighed. "Unfortunately you hear the truth. Just last March, a party of Klamaths and Molallas tested the mettle of Richard Miller, a good man who lives in Champoeg County. This war party surrounded Miller's home, and the settlers, frightened indeed, reacted by forming a group of vigilantes who pursued the Indians to a place on Abiqua Creek where they gave battle. Two Indians were killed. Not content with that, some of the younger white men took up battle the next day, killing seven Indians, one of them a woman. And now the white men who participated in this dreadful event refuse to discuss it. They are ashamed, and rightfully so."

"I have little patience with this kind of thing," Maude said, her voice stern, her face solomn. "We white people must recognize the Indians' rights. We must understand why they are fearful as we continue to intrude into the land. We must be careful and not insist on pushing our ways onto these people. I strongly disagree with the missionaries in this respect. And if we move on to their land without proper negotiation and treaties, there will be more bloodshed."

Tall nodded. "There is much that both people must learn from each other. Thank you for telling me what has happened." He then turned to Caleb and smiled. "You are as quiet as I have known you to be. Why don't you ask Nathan the question you need to ask him? After you settle that, we should ride. I want to see my land before dark."

Caleb nodded, awed by this man, his wife, and Tall—people who knew a lot about this country and the politics of events. He looked at Judge Shaw. "Sir, I'm looking for a man to marry me and my Eliza Landon.

Might I ask you, sir, if you would perform our marriage?"

Judge Shaw leaned back in his great carved chair and laughed. "By Jove! I'd like that!" He slapped his thigh. "God Almighty! I'd like that a lot! And when are you thinking of marrying?"

"Could we give my Eliza and yourself, sir, a week?"

"A week it is then. And Tall, Pips should be home by then."

"Pips!" Tall cried out. "Pips will be home?" He smiled broadly.

"Pips is our son," Maude beamed as she looked at Caleb. "He's been away for two years. Studying at Harvard University."

Tall nodded, his face creased with pleasure. "You will find him a good man, Caleb."

The Judge laughed. "You couldn't pick a better time for a wedding celebration, Mr. Pride. With our boy coming home, we're already planning a party for all of the valley people. And your wedding will be reason enough for a grand event."

"Before you two leave," Maude said, "let me ask you, Mr. Pride, if you and your wedding party would like to come on out here a day before your wedding. I well remember how it was, trying to bathe and ready oneself for a celebration while in camp. And how I yearned for a real bath!"

Caleb was overwhelmed. Here he was, sitting in the grand home of these folks whom he liked a lot; folks he knew Eliza would like too. This good man seemed delighted to marry him and Ellie, and now this generous woman had offered her house so he and Ellie could prepare for their wedding day in style. Added to that was the notion of a real party to follow the wedding, and then on top of all that, he was about to ride out to take a look at the very land he might well claim as home for himself and Ellie.

Caleb grinned. "I . . . I didn't expect to find all this. Yes, we'll come on out. And very pleased to do so, I must say. Thank you. This is a kindness we won't forget. Thank you. But let me say, there will be five of us. Our friends the Evanses, and our guide, Padraick O'Shea. And there will be lots more folks coming for the wedding. Will we be a trouble?"

"No, not at all," Maude said. "We'll be looking forward to having you here, and we'll have a fine party."

After riding east for some ways, Caleb and Tall both reined in their horses as they looked up on a hill where, standing in a grove of oaks, was a large rambling log house.

"That's Mr. Connor's place," Tall said.

"Poor fellow," Caleb answered. He looked at the place closely, wondering for a moment what would happen to it. And he toyed with the idea of inquiring. But no, the setting wasn't right. It was too open out here. No forests, and no river close by.

The two men rode on through country with wide meadows and fields where groves of oaks spread out graceful limbs—country where a river ran, swift and clear. Early that evening they rode in country where fir trees grew tall, and rich, dark green sword fern, mixed with gold and crimson vine maple, wove a tapestry of magnificent color.

Caleb was elated. This was much like the country he'd dreamed of. Yes, he would file his claim for this land, six hundred and forty acres of valley with open meadows for planting his crops, and forest and the river close by.

Later, as he and Tall hunkered down beside their campfire, Caleb smiled. What a fine place to raise a family. With Tall and Clara and the Shaws not far. It was everything he'd dreamed of, and more. But a notion picked at his mind.

"I got to ask you, Tall. How do you feel about me wanting to claim land next to yours? After the talk today with the Shaws, I have to ask that."

"White people must have land too," Tall said. "Nobody lives on this land, Caleb. Nobody is forced to leave. I will be pleased if you claim it as yours. Clara will be pleased too."

"Thank you, Tall. Thank you for bringing me here."

Chapter 39

Eliza didn't need to be convinced that the country Caleb had found was country he should claim as their own. She also saw no reason why Caleb should delay in filing the claim while she prepared for her wedding day.

"I'm busier than a china merchant, Caleb Pride. There's lots of things that need to be done." She smiled down at Cece as she strapped her in the cradleboard. "Land you like, I'll like. We've already talked about that."

After these past weeks, she sounded like herself again, and Caleb was delighted. Maybe it was the thought of preparing for her wedding in style, and a real wedding party. Maybe it was the notion of soon having her own home. She didn't say, and Caleb didn't ask; he was pleased and relieved that she'd come out of her melancholy.

Thus, early one morning Caleb hitched his faithful oxen to his wagon, told Eliza he would meet her at the Shaws' place, kissed her good-bye, and left the Ten Oaks camp. Seeking out the county clerk, he laid claim to land in the County of Yamhill of the Oregon Territory, paid three dollars for a marriage license, then drove his wagon and livestock out to the land that was now his. Once there, he pitched his tent and made a bed of fir boughs, covering them with thick quilts. Next to his tent, he built a small lean-to of cedar poles, covered with branches. This would be home for himself, Eliza, and Cece while he built a small, one-room cabin for the winter.

The emigrants who had come west with *The Oregon Roll* were breaking up. Clancy had staked his claim on land not far from Ten Oaks; George and Maggie, along with several other families, had headed farther west and Sam had gone north to see about getting a job with a newspaper called *The Oregon Spectator*. Few of the folks who had come out with the train remained with Eliza and Caleb at the campsite. But everybody planned to meet out at Judge Shaw's place on September 28.

The day before the wedding was a beautiful day. O'Shea left camp early, driving *The Lone Eagle* and Eliza's faithful team of oxen, with Big Moo at the lead, out to the Shaws'. After the wedding tomorrow, Caleb would drive the big wagon, with Eliza and Cece riding inside, home.

Now, Eliza turned Cece over to Clara, who would care for the baby until after the wedding. Then, mounting Babe, Eliza rode over to the Evanses' camp. She, Clancy, and Lorene, following Tall's directions, would ride out to the Shaws. As the three of them rode slowly out of camp, Eliza looked back at the big campground. Dry leaves and acorns covered the ground; sunshine streamed through the huge oaks and there was the pungent smell of trees, old leaves, good earth, and the river. Eliza was caught for a moment with joy, anticipating her life ahead. It would be a good life, she thought. A very good life for Caleb, and for Cece, and for herself.

"Caleb, wilt thou have . . ." Caleb stood tall, his hair trimmed neatly to just below his ears. He wore a fashionable suit that Clancy had insisted on loaning him—a suit made of black broadcloth, complete with a white linen shirt and a black cravat. In his left hand he held a small gold ring he had bought when passing through Fort Hall and had kept carefully tucked away. That would be his gift to his bride today. O'Shea, dressed in buckskins decorated with blue and red quills, fringes, and thrums, stood beside Caleb.

"Eliza, wilt thou have . . ." Eliza, wearing Lorene's dress of white cotton lawn sprinkled with blue flowers and trimmed with white lace, stood with Lorene by her side. Today Eliza wore her heavy auburn hair swept up and held in place with two tortoise combs. A rosy hue touched her high, rounded cheeks; her green eyes sparkled.

"I, Caleb, take thee, Eliza. . . . I, Eliza, take thee, Caleb. . . . With this ring . . ." Caleb smiled at her as he held out the little ring, and he saw her eyes, wide with surprise and joy.

"Those whom God hath joined . . . I pronounce that they are Man and Wife." Lorene dashed over to a piano that stood in the corner of the big living room; the men whistled and stomped, and the folks called out, "Best to you, Ellie and Caleb! God be with you both!"

A feast lay before them in the dining room. Platters of venison and beef and ham; bowls full of beans, tomatoes, squash, and potatoes; and piles of corn on the cob. This was followed by cakes and cookies and pots of coffee. But there were no spirits or liquor on the table or sideboard; prohibition was the rule.

"A toast to Mr. and Mrs. Pride!" O'Shea's voice rang out over the laughter and talk as glasses of grape juice were raised.

"A toast to my beautiful bride, Eliza Pride!" Caleb called out, and again the glasses were raised.

"A toast to all of you folks who made the trek across," Judge Shaw's voice boomed with delight. "And a welcome to all of you to this magnificent valley."

344

"A toast to all of you, especially to Tall and his good wife, Clara!" Pips Shaw lifted his glass.

Then, once again the good times sound of "Oh, Susanna" started the folks dancing as Eliza and Caleb danced the first dance together, whirling around the room as the folks clapped and sang. Eliza laughed with delight. "Oh, Cal! I'm so happy! I'm so happy!"

"You look so beautiful! My beautiful Ellie!" Caleb looked at her with adoring eyes, and then he whispered in her ear. "Let's not stay too long, Ellie! Let's not!" Eliza felt her face flush as she looked at him and smiled. "We won't, Cal," she said.

All that afternoon, laughter and music rang out from the Shaws' house. Eliza, dancing once with Pips, told him how much she liked their house.

"Well," Pips answered, "I hope you'll find this country as much to your liking as this place. We all certainly do."

"It's beautiful country. No doubt of that. And both Mr. Pride and I are anxious to settle in. Now, tell me, Mr. Shaw. What is it that you do?"

"I study and draw plants. I'm called a botanical artist. Sometime next year, or the year after, whenever I think I have enough good work, I'll bundle up my drawings and head back to the East Coast, where government folks in Washington are anxious to see what grows out here. But for some time to come, we'll be neighbors." He looked at her and smiled. "And I'll wager you won't find fault with our land."

"I hope not, sir."

"No, Mrs. Pride. Not 'sir'! My name is Pips. And I'd like to call you Eliza, and your husband, Caleb, if I may. Now, what say you to that?"

"Of course. That's easier, isn't it, Pips." She liked him. An easygoing young man with thin blond hair and a neat mustache. How lucky Cal and I are, she thought, to have these fine people, the Shaws, and Tall and Clara as neighbors.

As the beat of the music changed, Caleb approached and smiled at Pips. "I'd like to claim my bride, sir," he said. Pips bowed. "It's been a pleasure, Eliza Pride. A pleasure, indeed."

"Eliza Pride," Caleb said, taking her in his arms and leading her in a polka. "Say, I like that sound. And I ask you now, why don't we say our good-byes and go?"

Eliza nodded. "Yes. We'll say good-bye to Mr. O'-Shea, to Judge and Mrs. Shaw, and then let's go home, Mr. Pride."

They found O'Shea standing on the porch with Pips and the Judge. Caleb clasped O'Shea's hand and held it for a moment. "God A'mighty, we'll be looking for you, we will. Eliza and me." O'Shea laughed. "Promise me then, Eliza Pride, that you will call me Paddy, and not Mr. O'Shea?"

Eliza and Caleb both laughed. Caleb's expression then changed. "We'll be expecting you to stay at our place." Lordy, he thought. How much he would miss this man.

O'Shea looked closely at Caleb. "You're damned lucky, Cal," he said, drawing Caleb to him for a moment. O'Shea then turned to Eliza. "And you're a lucky woman, Eliza Pride." Eliza smiled as she shook his hand. "I know that, Mr. O'Shea. And thank you for being such a good friend."

A short time later, amid shouts of good-bye and good luck, Eliza climbed up into the wagon and Clara reached up and handed her Cece. Whip in hand, Caleb whistled, and with Big Moo still at the lead, the oxen team started to pull *The Lone Eagle* down the narrow, dusty road that led to the Prides' land.

It was almost dark when they arrived at the camp Caleb had made in the grove of tall cedar and firs. Eliza fed Cece and put her in a box lined with fir boughs and flannel. Setting the box inside the tent, Eliza looked down at her for a moment. Cece, who had been passed around among loving, admiring folks all day, was now sound asleep. Tomorrow Eliza would bind her in the cradleboard and then, with the baby on her back, she would ride with Caleb and take a good look at their land. Now there were other things on Eliza Pride's mind.

She smiled as she went to Caleb and stood before him. Caleb drew her to him. "I can't say it enough, Ellie. I love you. I cherish you." He held her face between his hands and looked into her eyes. He touched her cheek with his index finger and he traced down her face to her throat. He bent his head and kissed her gently, his breath warm on her face. "I say this to you. When I close my eyes, my darling, I see you. Always there. When my eyes are open, I still see you. Always there. You are never far from my thoughts. Never."

His fingers trembled as he worked at the small buttons on the bodice of her dress, and he smiled at her when he saw her dainty white slip, edged with lace. He traced his finger over the top of her breasts, and Eliza drew in her breath and looked up at him, her eyes wide, feeling such pleasure. She put her hands behind his head and ran her fingers through his hair.

"Oh, Cal," she whispered. "I love you so."

Caleb gently slipped the ribbons of her chemise down over her shoulders, cupped her breasts to his mouth, and ran his tongue over her nipples. Eliza arched her body back, pressing her thighs against him, feeling his heavy maleness thrust between her legs.

"Cal, I didn't think it would be like this," she said, her voice low and uneven. "I'm aching with want for you." She laughed. "Yes, I am."

Caleb lifted her and laid her down gently on the

quilts he had arranged over layers of fir boughs. This was their first bed together.

"Yes, my darling. It's like this. Between you and me."

Eliza's passion rose to a height she'd never dreamed she possessed as he entered her and she felt, in the superb joy of loving him, amazement at the moment of her ecstasy. She cried out to him, as he did to her, and again, and again, they were joined. Again and again Eliza felt the exquisite pleasure of loving him, and then they slept.

The next morning Caleb leaned over her and gently brushed her curls back from her brow. "Before Cece wakes up, I want to tell you something," he whispered. "I used to wonder if this day would ever come, Ellie. And I used to think at night, how it would be. I wanted you so, but I didn't want you to be afraid. And I don't think you were." His eyes twinkled with a smile.

"No, Cal," she whispered. "I wasn't afraid." She smiled at him. "I was wanting you, Cal, and it was . . . well . . . loving you was beyond what I'd ever thought it would be."

"I want to promise you two things," he said. "I will always love you, Ellie, and I will do well for you and for Cece and for our own. You won't ever want. You'll be proud of me, Ellie. I promise you will."

Eliza smiled. "I'm already proud of you, Caleb Pride. And maybe today we can find time, after we've tended to things, to talk again about old Boone."

They both started to laugh, and as they held on to each other, laughing with pleasure, Eliza heard Cece's soft peeps of her own welcome to the new day.

Chapter 40

December 31, 1852

The shiny black buggy, drawn by two big roans, whizzed over the frozen road. "Go fast, Papa!" Cece cried, keeping her eyes half-shut and lifting her rosy face up into the cold wind. Eliza, holding three-year-old Ben Pride in her lap, laughed as she watched the snowy fields whiz by.

"Yes, Cal. Go faster!"

Caleb whistled and snapped his whip as the buggy rounded a swooping curve skirting a snowy field. "I thought you'd like this buggy, Cece. You and Mama, and Ben."

"A fine Christmas present, Cal," Eliza answered, listening to the rumbling wheels and the squeak of the rich leather seats. "And riding in it makes me feel like a true lady."

Caleb chuckled. "Shouldn't take a buggy ride to make you feel like that, Ellie. A true lady you are. Everybody in the valley knows that."

"Hmm." Eliza buried her chin in the blanket. "Speaking of ladies, I've got two things in mind. One is that our own little lady, Miss Cece, will enjoy being at the

Shaws' New Year's party tonight. Don't you think, Cece?" Eliza put an arm around her and gave her a hug.

"Oh, yes! I will and Lela will have good things to eat and tell us stories and we'll all play games."

Lela Perkins was Maude Shaw's hired girl who had come to the Willamette Valley two years ago. She had lost all of her own family on the Oregon Trail to cholera, and when Maude and Nathan heard of her plight, they had hired her immediately. Lela was an excellent cook and she enjoyed children. She also helped Maude with the schooling Maude now provided in her big house for the few children who lived in the upper valley.

"And speaking of ladies," Eliza continued. "I'm curious, as we all are, to meet Lydia Wells tonight. Maude says Miss Wells was here last week, looking over her place, and she plans on moving into her house right away."

"She's got a big place to come to, and a place that needs lots of work. I hope she's got a heart for farming, Ellie. If she doesn't, she's going to be in for a surprise. Nothing's been done to the place since before we came, and that's over four years ago."

"Clara and Maude and I talked about that just last week. We'll all help, Cal. The best we can, and it'll be nice having a woman closer to all of us. I'm planning a tea party next week to honor Miss Wells. Unfortunately Maude can't come because she's going to Portland with Nathan. But Clara's coming, and we'll have a fine time."

"Well, she'll have a hearty welcome tonight," Caleb said. He then turned to look at Eliza and winked. "I'll bet you my shoe, Mrs. Pride, that with Sam and Clancy and Lorene and all of the valley folks coming to the Shaws', well—it'll be a fine party we'll be having to welcome in 1853."

It was amid a flurry of greetings that the Prides arrived at the Shaws'. After seeing his family inside the house, Caleb drove his buggy down to Nathan's big barn.

Clouds had come up and snow was falling. Small, dry snowflakes that meant colder weather here in the valley.

Caleb thought about the evening ahead, an evening that promised to be exciting. Nathan had recently returned from Portland, where he had met with two men who presumably knew a lot about valley agriculture. Nathan was excited about some grafted fruit trees these gentlemen were selling and Caleb, always eager to learn more about valley farming, was interested too. Would fruit trees thrive here, or should Caleb and Eliza put their thoughts and money into raising more wheat? Caleb hoped for guidance to that question tonight.

A single lantern hung in Nathan's barn. As Caleb led his horses inside, he was startled to hear heavy breathing. He was more than startled to see a woman rubbing down a huge black horse. Caleb tipped his hat. He didn't recognize the woman at all. "Evening," he said. "My name's Caleb. Caleb Pride."

The woman, using a gunny sack for her work, barely glanced at him as she moved her right arm back and forth with powerful strokes. "Pleased," she said. "Can't put this horse of mine away wet. I'm Lydia Wells. I understand you and your wife will be neighbors of mine."

"Yes, Miss Wells, you're dead right. And my wife and I are looking forward to that."

Caleb quickly slipped the harnesses and bridles off his animals and guided them to two empty stalls next to Miss Wells. He then set to work, rubbing down his own animals. Twice he glanced at Miss Wells, who worked silently, as if he weren't there. She was a tall, big-boned woman with heavy black hair, and the shadows from the lantern reflected on an angular face.

"You're from San Francisco?" he asked.

"New York. Until five years ago when I answered Henry Connor's ad in a newspaper asking for a woman to come west to the Oregon, marry him, and share farming profits. I did. Came out by boat to San Francisco. Learned he'd died, and I stayed on in California. I paint pictures, you see. Don't get me wrong. I farm too. Farmed all my life till I decided to come west. But I made my own way in San Francisco by painting pictures of folks." She laughed. A thin, dry laugh for such a large woman. "I've got a pile of paintings, Mr. Pride." She then stopped her rubbing, put her gunny sack aside, pulled on a dark cloak, and headed for the barn door. "I'll be pleased to meet your wife, Mr. Pride." Then she was gone.

Caleb chuckled. A good sort of woman, he thought. A no-nonsense woman who would fit in well with the valley folks. Eliza would like her. So would Clara and Maude.

Candles glowed in every window of the Shaws' big house that late afternoon while guests continued to arrive, sharing rousing greetings and news. Eliza was delighted to learn that Clancy had recently opened his school in the small midvalley town of Ten Oaks, and that Sam's newspaper, at the other end of the valley, was going well. "I'll be extending circulation out here before long," Sam said, looking pleased. Caleb was also enjoying himself, having sought out Nathan and several other valley men, who were discussing valley farming policies.

Maude, finding Clara, Eliza, and Lorene visiting together in the front parlor, asked them to come with her to meet Lydia Wells. "We were wondering when Miss Wells would arrive," Lorene said.

"We were. We're all anxious to meet her," Eliza agreed, and Clara nodded.

"She'll be a real welcome sight to this valley," Clara said.

Maude laughed. "Come with me to the kitchen, then. Miss Wells insists on helping Lela and she's a bit

352

reluctant to come out here and meet our friends. Perhaps you can persuade her otherwise."

On seeing Lydia, Eliza's first reaction was one of surprise. What a big woman, she thought. A big woman with a plain face and thick black hair and blue eyes. "We're all hoping you'll like it here," Clara was saying in Clara's warm, welcoming voice. "And we're all—"

"Mama! Come and see what we're having for dinner." Blue Bird and Little Bear came running into Maude's kitchen. Clara held out her hand to her children, and hushed them with her fingers on her lips. "You're being rude," she admonished them. "This is our new neighbor, Miss Wells."

Lydia stared at the children, their skin the color of dark honey, their large brown eyes, and their dark hair. She looked at Clara, her eyes sharp. "Those yours?" she asked.

"Of course they're mine." Clara sounded taken aback. Mine and my man's. Their names are Blue Bird and Little Bear."

"Pretty children. And their papa—his name?"

"Tall Singer. He's Paiute. Come and meet him, Miss Wells."

"He's here?" Eliza caught the tone of surprise in Miss Wells's voice.

"He's here indeed," Maude answered in an even voice. "You must meet him, Miss Wells. Along with our other guests. Come now, let's leave the kitchen. It's time for those who want to change their clothes to do so."

But Lydia shook her head. "No," she said. "I'd rather stay here." She laughed, but there was no humor in the sound. "I don't, what do you say out here . . . 'mix' too well with strangers."

"We hope you won't consider us as strangers for

353

long," Lorene said. "Well, I think I'll be excusin' myself and dress for the dancing later on." She laughed. "Those of us who live far, like my husband and I do, have the distinct privilege of staying the night. Clara and Tall and Clancy and me and Eliza and Cal and the newspaper man, you'll be meeting them all, Miss Wells."

As Eliza, Clara, and Lorene walked back to rejoin the party, none of them said a word. Eliza wondered if they felt as she did, a keen disappointment in realizing that Lydia Wells wasn't what she had expected at all. Then, remembering what her mother used to say, "folks come as all kinds, Ellie. All different kinds of cloth, and we're better off to accept them all," Eliza decided she would try to like Lydia and she would try to become her friend.

A short time later Eliza, taking Caleb's hand, walked upstairs to their room to dress. "Did you meet Lydia Wells?" she asked.

"I did. I met her out in the barn. She was rubbing down her horse, and we chatted some."

"What did you think of her?"

"Well, I guess she's different, but she's fine. I figure she'll fit in all right, and you and Maude and Clara will like her. And you?"

"I thought her strange, but I guess I agree with you. She's probably a good soul. Please, Cal. Dance with her tonight. She doesn't look like a lady who has a lot of dances claimed."

Caleb laughed. "I'll do that, Ellie. I'll dance with all the ladies."

Eliza sighed. "It's nice having Lela in charge of the children for a while. It's the first time we've not had them with us."

"Nor us fussing over them," Caleb added.

Walking over to the small-paned window, Eliza looked out at the fading light of the winter day. Suddenly the old image of a long line of tattered, gray wagons came to her mind. It was a familiar image that came to her at odd times. Wagons lurching and swaying through tall grasses and down steep gullies and across deserts of sand and rock. Sounds of the creaking wagons, cook pans thunking, crackling campfires, and children's shouts. And faces. Stilly and Lucy Ann, Jeremy and Betsy, Smithy and Ben and her mother and father, and Janie Marie.

Eliza smiled as she unbuttoned the bodice of her wool traveling dress. Just yesterday she'd known for a fact that she was pregnant again. Now, as she stood in this warm house, full of friends and joy, she promised herself that if this child were to be a girl, she'd name her Ann Marie, taking names of the two young women she'd loved so much. She also decided that as soon as she and Caleb returned home, she'd tell him her special news.

Feeling Caleb's arms around her, she leaned back against him. "I like your warm breath in my hair. Oh Cal, I think you're so fine."

Caleb laughed softly and kissed the nape of her neck. "I have to wonder, Ellie, if there's a man on this earth as lucky as me."

Eliza turned to him. "And I, Caleb Pride, I have to wonder likewise. I can't imagine there's a woman alive who's as lucky as myself."

It was a dazzling party. Music—three fiddlers and two harmonica players, one valley man played a banjo, another man beat on a drum, and a woman played Maude's piano with skill. Eliza, wearing a pink silk dress trimmed with white lace, wondered if she'd ever heard such splendid music as she whirled through polkas, waltzes, and reels.

Delicious odors of food wafted from the dining room, where Maude's dining table was laden with roast meats, platters of squashes, potatoes, and breads followed by cakes and cookies and puddings and pies. Flasks of brandies and sparkling decanters of wine and spirits sat on the sideboard; prohibition was no longer the rule.

Lydia, holding a glass in her hand, wearing a bright red tafetta dress with purple velvet trim, stood by the sideboard. Nathan and Maude stood with her, visiting. Eliza, taking time out from the dancing, joined them. "I'll tell you again, Miss Wells, how pleased we all are to have you here in the valley."

Maude nodded. "You couldn't have better neighbors, either, than Caleb and Eliza. And beyond their place, up the river a ways, is Clara and Tall's place."

"That's good," Lydia said. "I like living alone but I also like knowing there's folks not too far."

"I'd like you to come to tea with Clara and me next Thursday," Eliza said. "Maude, are you sure you can't come?"

Maude shook her head. "I'm off to Portland, as planned, with Nathan. But I want to have you all here sometime next month."

"I guess I'm not much for tea, but that'll be nice," Lydia answered. "And I'll be askin' for advice from Mr. Pride, too." She spoke slowly, her speech slightly slurred. Eliza wondered if perhaps she had had too much to drink. But maybe she spoke that way naturally.

It was then that Caleb appeared and, offering his arm to Lydia, asked her for a dance. "No," Lydia said. "I . . . I don't dance. I never learned how."

"Ah, Miss Wells. You have the best teacher here in the valley," Eliza said.

"I'd agree to that," Nathan said with a chuckle. "And if you're seeking advice, all of us here in the valley are ready to help you with most anything you might want. But now, for the rest of the night, you ought to enjoy yourself and dance some. Dancing with Cal's a good way to start."

"Give me a try," Caleb added, a gentle tease in his voice.

Lydia shrugged. "I'll give it a try then . . ."

Lorene, wearing a beautiful blue silk gown, walked over to join Eliza, Nathan, and Maude. "I'm glad Miss Wells is dancing," she said. "Clancy's planning on asking her, too."

"Maybe Clancy will have better luck than I had," Nathan said. "She flat out refused to dance with me, but between us all standing here, we got her to dance with Cal."

"Lorene, do tell us more about Clancy's school," Maude said.

"Please do." Eliza's eyes sparkled. "I haven't seen it for months. The last time I was in town was the Fourth of July for your party. And you were all busy working on it then." Lorene laughed. "Well, as you know, it's come up from that windowless log cabin in town. Now we've got two windows and good benches and desks and I keep a jar of goose quills sharp and ready for Clancy." Lorene laughed. "And have we learned things, Ellie. Why, I've learned how to make ink by squeezing juice from those oak balls that lie around on the ground in the fall. And Clancy makes pencils by pressing lead bullets flat and then sharpening the lead. I've also knitted balls and braided rawhide ropes for the children to play with. They work. They work real well, and Clancy—well, I've never seen him so happy."

"And you, Lorene," Eliza said. You're glowing. Now, tell us what you hear from Maggie and George."

"I saw Maggie just last month when they came to town. Danny's married and he and his wife are expecting a baby. The McVeys like the country of southern Oregon a whole lot. The only problem is the Indians there are raising a ruckus, but other than that, they're doing fine."

"Eliza Pride . . . may I have this dance?" Eliza turned to see Pips standing before her, a smile on his face.

357

Whirling again around the room, Eliza frowned as she saw Lydia dancing with Caleb. In spite of Caleb's fine, strong lead, Lydia stumbled, and when she stumbled a second time, Caleb had trouble keeping her from taking a fall. Following that, Lydia walked away from Caleb and left the room. Eliza disliked the little scene. It was as if a small cloud had fallen over this otherwise splendid party. Make the best of it, she told herself.

"I hope our new neighbor will be happy here," Eliza said to Pips.

"I think she will. She's a farmer, she says, and she's also an artist. Taught herself. She paints portraits and pictures of folks, and folks doing things."

"Like Smithy!" Eliza said, delighted at this news. "Oh, Pips, how grand. I'll be anxious to see her work." Now that added something different to Miss Wells. Maybe she was a fine painter and didn't have a lot of time for much else. Eliza felt better, and later this evening she would again seek her out and ask her about her paintings.

"She told Mama that the only way she could make ends meet in California was because a fellow in San Francisco happened on to her work, liked it, and commissioned her to work for him. Ha! Now I say that's pretty fine. But there's a rub. Seems that this fellow was a tavern owner, and he wanted Miss Wells to do nothing but paintings of folks who came to his places. Folks drinking, talking . . . whatever. I don't know many women who could handle that, but from what I've seen, Miss Wells probably handled it just fine."

"Well, Pips let's hope she doesn't find our valley too dull."

The music had stopped and a brief silence fell over the crowd as Nathan stood before his guests. "It's almost midnight, my friends," he said. "I ask that we all raise our glasses in a toast to 1853. And I ask that we all join in singing 'Auld Lang Syne.' Then we'll eat and dance untill dawn!"

Cheers rose from the crowd and Eliza saw Caleb striding across the room to join her, two glasses in hand. Raising their glasses high, the valley people toasted 1853 and then the singing began . . . *Should auld acquaintance be forgot* . . . Caleb suddenly stopped singing and bent to whisper in Eliza's ear. "You know, my darling, you're the most beautiful woman in the valley."

Eliza felt herself blush, and she laughed. "Goodness, Mr. Pride." Then, standing on her tiptoes, she whispered, "And you still make a girl blush."

" 'Oh, Susanna'! It's time for 'Oh, Susanna'!" Eliza heard the laugh in Sam's voice. "C'mon folks with *The Oregon Roll!* Let's show them how we can dance!"

Eliza, dancing with Caleb to the lively, familiar tune, saw Lydia again, standing by the sideboard, watching the dancing. No, not watching the dancing, rather watching Caleb and herself. Eliza felt self-conscious, but when she looked again, Lydia had gone. Nor did she reappear that night, to join the revelers at the Shaws' grand party.

The next day the skies were clear and the snow-covered land sparkled under the bright sun as the Shaws' guests prepared to leave. Good-byes took time. Many of the folks were reluctant to part; it would be a long time before they all got together again.

Hot bricks, heated on the Shaws' hearth and wrapped in wool, had been placed on the floor of the Prides' buggy. Just as Eliza, Caleb, and their children were settled and ready to leave, Lydia appeared, astride her black horse.

"I'm looking forward to Thursday, Mrs. Pride," she called out, her voice loud and hoarse. "You're not so far, either. The other day when I was at my place, looking things over, I heard something that sounds like a bell come over the hill. I figured later that sound's got to come from your place."

Eliza laughed. "I had no idea the sound carried so far. That's an iron piece that I whang on when Cal's down at the barn or working out in one of the fields. I hope it doesn't cause you bother."

Lydia shrugged. "No." Her eyes were now on Caleb. "I'll be asking for advice and expecting it too," she said with a laugh. Then she waved and galloped off.

Caleb flicked his whip lightly and the Prides left for their long ride home, not far behind Lydia Wells.

It was afternoon when the Prides' buggy sped across the northern valley floor, blanketed under the fresh snowfall of the previous night. Patterns of dark green and white showed on stands of the great firs and pines that covered the surrounding hills. There were now three "places"— places where people lived and worked the land at this end of the valley. Lydia Wells's place was the first place that a traveler on the road would pass by; on over the wooded hill stood the Prides' place, and farther on, up a draw, was where Tall and Clara lived. Caleb idly wondered how many more people might be here in another year.

Eliza, seeing that Cece and Ben were sound asleep, let her thoughts drift back to the party last night. What fun it had been, seeing so many friends. A time of joy, enriched by her own knowledge that, come next summer, she would have another baby.

On up ahead now, atop an oak-covered hill, Eliza looked at the Connors' place, now to be occupied by Lydia. It was a big, ungainly-looking place, built of logs. The windows were small, so the inside must be awfully dark, Eliza thought. Too dark for an artist to work in. A stone chimney with part of the top gone stood at one end of the house. "Now that's a place that needs tending to," Eliza said. "And it's a lonely-looking place if I ever saw one."

"There's never been much living there, Ellie. Mr. Connors died, you know, shortly after he built it."

"I couldn't help but see, Cal, that Lydia had trouble dancing last night. I was sorry for the both of you. Especially you."

Caleb's answer was slow in coming. When he spoke, his voice was low. "Miss Wells, Eliza, had had far too much to drink. And you're right. The dance with her didn't go well."

Eliza was surprised. She'd never heard Caleb criticize another woman for anything. "But then," he continued, "I figure maybe she's having a hard time feeling right with all of us out here. Maybe she's a person we're going to have to get used to and then we'll like her well enough."

For a reason Eliza couldn't immediately define, a feeling of deep melancholy swept over her. Mulling it through, she realized that she had figured Lydia Wells would be far different from the woman that she was. She had thought that the woman coming up from San Francisco would be youngish, and pretty, and perhaps like . . . perhaps like Lucy Ann. And while Eliza had never thought of herself as being a prude, she hadn't liked seeing Miss Wells stumble as she had when she'd danced with Cal, and she hadn't liked her slurred tongue. She also knew that she didn't feel the anticipation of company when she thought of Miss Wells joining her and Clara for tea next Thursday. Enough of that, she sternly told herself as she remined herself again that folks are folks. And they were all from all different kinds of cloth.

Seeing Cece and Ben stir, Eliza gave Cece a gentle poke. "Let's sing," she whispered in Cece's ear. "Let's sing 'Old Dan Tucker.' "

A few moments later Eliza, Cece, and Caleb were singing some of their favorite songs: "Old Dan Tucker,"

"Auld Lang Syne," and "Home Sweet Home." Their voices echoed up to the patterned foothills, with Ben's small, high tones mingled in. Eliza smiled. She'd be glad to get home.

Chapter 41

"So, you've taken a liking to our valley, Miss Wells." Caleb, who had just come in from the fields, his face ruddy with the cold air, stood in the doorway of the Prides' living room and smiled at Lydia and Eliza as they sipped hot tea in front of the big fireplace.

"I'm pleased with the advice you gave me yesterday," Lydia said. "You know a lot about farming. You grew up farming, like me?"

"Yes, and then no," Caleb answered. "Now, if you ladies will excuse me, the animals don't know it's going to snow, and I've got to tend to them." And then he was gone.

"Where did you and your husband come from?" Lydia asked.

"Kentucky. We both came from there. We came out here in '48." Eliza reached down and patted Dog, who lay at her feet. "And this old fellow, he came too," she said. "All the way." She stood and walked over to Smithy's drawing of *The Lone Eagle,* which hung on the wall close to the fireplace. "This dog here belonged to the little boy who drew that," she said. Caleb found them both—the boy and the dog, back in Illinois, and adopted them. He named the boy Smithy. Smithy died of snakebite, back on the John Day River, but we still have Dog. If Smithy had lived, we know he'd have been an artist. Like you." Eliza hoped that Lydia, seeing Smithy's work, would offer information about herself, something Eliza was finding hard to accomplish because Lydia appeared intent on learning all she could about the Prides.

Lydia had no comment to offer regarding Smithy's work. Instead she continued with her questions. "You both came here right from Kentucky?" she asked.

"Oh, no. Caleb left Kentucky when he was just a tad of a boy. He was a drover for a while then he did all sorts of things. He worked on farms and for smithies, and he even worked in a tannery for a time."

"A tannery? Where?"

"In Pennsylvania. Somewhere in Pennsylvania. I'm not sure just where."

"And you all met back in Missoura. In Independence?"

"Eliza? Ellie?" Eliza heard Clara's familiar call.

"Ah, that's Clara." She turned to Lydia and smiled, feeling a sense of relief. It would be easier to visit, now that Clara was here. Maybe the two of them could draw out Lydia a little and get to know her some.

"Excuse me. I'll be right back and we can all have tea."

Moments later Eliza and Clara entered the room. Clara's twined blond braids gleamed in the afternoon sun, her smile was wide. After remarking on the cold weather, Lydia turned directly to Clara. "Eliza was telling me about Caleb and her coming out," she said. "And you . . . you're from Kentucky too?"

"Oh, no," Clara said. "No. I'm from Pennsylvania, and I came out as far as Fort Hall, years earlier than Eliza and Cal."

"I see," Lydia said, staring for a moment at Clara's lame foot before averting her eyes. "And you say . . . you're husband . . . is the Paiute fellow, Tall Singer."

Clara nodded. "And you've met our two children, who'll be going down to Maude Shaw's school, come next fall." Clara's smile was one of delight. "Tall and I are so pleased. But tell us, Miss Wells. Tell Ellie and me about yourself."

"Don't call me Miss Wells. I asked the same of Eliza here. It's easier to call each other by first names. Now, as to myself . . ." Lydia then recounted the story of how she'd answered Henry Connors' ad; how she'd learned of his death while in San Francisco, and how she'd stayed in California and painted pictures. "But then one day I just said to myself that place of Mr. Connor's was here and it was mine and I might as well have it to live in. So I contacted Judge Shaw and the next thing I knew, I was hightailin' it to Oregon and this is where I intend to stay, except for a trip now and then back to San Francisco. I tell you both, that's some place. You ought to go there someday."

"Well, we hope you'll like our valley," Clara said. "And we're all anxious to help. You just let us know when and what to do and somebody will be with you to help get it done."

Lydia suddenly stood up. "I best be getting on," she said. "Thanks to you for a fine tea and company. I'll be lookin' to see you both soon."

"I'll walk down to the barn with you," Eliza said. "Excuse me, Clara . . ."

"You'll do nothing of the sort," Lydia said. "I can make my way myself. You stay here with your company." Lydia then put on her dark wool cape and left.

As Eliza and Clara watched her walk out toward the barn, Clara sighed. "I have to say, Eliza, I don't care a lot for that woman."

"And I have to agree, but it makes me sad, Clara. You and I had both looked forward to another woman living here, but she's very strange."

Neither Clara nor Eliza said a word for a few moments, and when they spoke, they spoke about when they might plant their sweetpeas.

"In early February, Ellie. That's what Tall says." Eliza nodded. "That's what Cal says, too." And then they sat down in front of the fire to enjoy another cup of hot tea.

The skies were a dark gray and a cold northwest wind had come up. "There's a feel of snow in the air," Caleb said, standing bareheaded with the wind ruffling his hair as he looked up at Lydia, mounted on her horse. "You're sure you'll be all right?"

"I've been riding alone most all my life," she answered. "No point in worrying about me." She then raised her hand. "Good-bye, Mr. Pride."

As Lydia rode home from the Prides' place, she rode under a bruised sky. When she felt a spatter of snow on her face, she blinked back tears in her eyes, and she shouted once, "Oh my God!"

It was dark when she got home. Lighting a lamp in her kitchen, she stoked up the fire in her big wood stove. Then, lamp in hand, she walked down a long dark hallway to a back bedroom where piles of her paintings were stacked on the floor. Quickly, she rifled through the stacks—paintings of people. Old men and young men and boys. Old women, young beautiful women, and little girls. People playing in parks, people gathered in streets. And then there were paintings of people in pubs, taverns, and bawdy houses. Men and women—drovers, pimps, whores, freight drivers, miners, roustabouts, gamblers— white men, Chinese, Mexicans, and Negroes. Wild, vivid scenes, done in brilliant blues, reds, purples, and black. Sensuous paintings that brought to life these people who drank together, played together, and sometimes killed together. From this stack, she found the painting she sought, and holding her lamp close, she removed it from the stack.

Taking it with her, she returned to her kitchen and sat down at her kitchen table, bare, except for a bottle of whiskey and an unlit lamp. She propped the painting against the lamp and poured herself a glass of whiskey. She sat at the table for a long time as two images came to her, over and over again. One was the handsome face of Caleb Pride with his blond, windblown hair, his keen blue eyes, and his dimpled chin. The other was the image of the crippled woman, Clara. Not badly crippled, just enough so one noticed her slight limp.

Every so often Lydia's gaze fell on the painting. It was a painting of three men. A large Indian with unkempt hair was flanked by two white men. One of the white men wore a patch over one eye; the other man's wrinkled head looked like a prune. Lydia sat at her table long after the fire in her stove had died, and her bottle was drained, pondering on what she now knew.

Toward dawn, she walked to her bedroom, and when she lay down, she was keenly aware of her intense feeling for Mr. Pride. Her heart pounded, her mouth had gone slightly dry, and she felt an ache between her legs, an ache of desire that Lydia Wells had never before felt in her life.

Chapter 42

Early one morning in late August 1853, Eliza looked out her kitchen window and smiled. The river sparkled with sunshine as it tumbled past the green willows and cotton-woods. What a fine day Caleb and Nathan would have in Portland. What a fine day it would be to put up blackberries, picked just the day before. It might also be a fine day for birthing a baby, but Eliza would be just as happy if this child would wait for Caleb to be home, day after tomorrow.

In the pale pink of early sun, Eliza walked softly across her kitchen to peek into the bedroom where Cece and Ben lay sound asleep. Returning to her stove, she poured herself a cup of coffee and patted her swollen belly, feeling the sudden movement of her child. At the same time a spasm of pain coursed through her lower back and she winced. Yes, she thought. This child could easily be born today.

Looking upriver, Eliza saw familiar smoke curling against the pale blue sky. She wondered how Clara was doing, housebound as she'd been with Little Bear and Blue Bird, who had been very sick with measles. She wished Clara could come today, if Eliza needed her to help with the baby's birth. But Eliza then sternly reminded herself of her luck in having Lydia ready and willing to come.

Carrying her coffee, Eliza walked out on to the back porch and plopped herself down in a chair. Dog lay at her feet. Eliza liked sitting here where she could see the river, and now she found herself thinking about Lydia.

A strange woman, indeed. A brusque, uneven woman who, until recently, hadn't returned to visit the Prides. Nor had she ever accepted an invitation to dinner or tea. She was also a woman who had never, as far as Eliza knew, invited folks to her house.

The only times Eliza or Caleb had had contact with her was when they passed her place on the way to the Shaws, or on the way into town. They would then stop and inquire as to how she was, and ask if she needed anything, or if she needed help. Her answer was always no, she was getting along just fine. Eliza had asked, twice, if she might see Lydia's paintings, but Lydia had never opened her door to Eliza. She'd never invited her in to her house.

Then, for some reason, about a month ago, she had started coming around. She would often arrive early in the morning and she'd stay all day. Some days she helped Eliza with her washing, and her cooking, and her garden, but she usually wanted to help Caleb tend to the animals, the crops, and the fences. She was nice enough to Cece and Ben, but Eliza thought she was ill at ease with children, and she felt sorry for her, knowing that.

One day Caleb complained. "She's help, Ellic, but I don't need it. She should be tending to her own place. She hasn't set crops out, and she's not done a thing that I can tell."

"She means well, Cal. She's real different, I know. But I think she's taken a liking to us."

* * *

369

Eliza reached down and patted Dog, took another sip of her coffee, and eyed the piece of iron, her "calling piece." The sound of the triangle being whanged was powerful. Not only could Lydia hear it, but so could Clara and Tall, who had a similar device at their place. Eliza often felt a closer presence with Clara and Tall when, on hearing its clanging tone, she knew one of them was fetching their own.

An odd worry came to Eliza. Her nature, when these feelings occurred, was to sit quietly and figure them out. She thought back to her talk with Cal, a couple of weeks ago when he'd driven home from Nathan's with the news that two men, Mr. Adams and Mr. Hastings, would be in Portland with boxes of grafted fruit trees to sell.

"It's a chance for Nathan and me to talk with these men, to see the trees and consider if we should buy," he'd said.

"Cal, you've got to go," Eliza said and she'd laughed. "You look as excited as a child. You must go."

The notion of growing fruit trees had been with Caleb ever since last winter, and when he'd talked it over with Eliza, her enthusiasm had equaled his. Nathan and Maude were also interested, and the two couples had spent hours talking about growing orchards of Golden Cling peaches, Winesap or Gravenstein apples, Bartlett pears, and Black Biggereau or Royal Ann cherries.

"You must go, Cal," Eliza had urged. "I'll get along just fine. If I need help, I can always whang on the calling piece for Clara. Remember, Ben's birth was easy enough, and chances are that this baby won't even decide to come until after you're back."

But then measles had hit Clara and Tall's children, and Clara was needed at home. Maude and Caleb had then tried to talk Eliza into staying at the Shaws', but Eliza had balked. "We've got our animals to tend to, and I don't want to leave our place," she'd said, and Caleb knew she meant it.

370

Caleb then decided that he wouldn't go. On learning that, Eliza was angry. "You're being like a silly boy, Cal. And you're treating me as if I've got no ability to take care of our children and myself. If need be, I can just as well deliver the baby, and you know that. Now, get on with you."

Lydia had then learned of Caleb's concern. "I've heard you're not anxious to leave here, with Eliza expecting her baby most any day," she had said as she helped Caleb fit a shoe on a horse. "I agree with you, too. She'd better have someone with her. Tell her to whang on that piece of iron if she needs me and I'll come riding on up."

Caleb was silent for a moment. He then stood and looked at Lydia closely. "Have you . . . have you any experience with birthing?"

Lydia had laughed. "Why, sure. Being raised on a farm, you learn all of that when you're but a child yourself. Rest easy, Caleb. Should the . . . should the child come while you're gone, I'll help her. Don't fret with that. You and Judge Shaw should be enjoying your trip."

At Caleb's insistence, Eliza had agreed to use her calling piece to fetch Lydia if Eliza started feeling birthing pains. Very early yesterday, Caleb had left with Nathan, for Portland. He would be home late tomorrow and Eliza hoped her baby would wait for one more day.

It was hot in Portland, but Caleb was intrigued with this country he was seeing for the first time. Yesterday he had enjoyed listening to Nathan as they had passed by the great Oregon Falls on the Willamette River. And when they'd passed through Oregon City, Nathan had pointed out John McLoughlin's fine house. He'd also told Caleb of McLoughlin's role with the famous Hudson's Bay Company and the importance of the fur trade. Caleb found Nathan's instruction excellent, and a fine tonic for his unreasonable worry over Eliza.

Since leaving home, he had been plagued with a worry he'd not felt for her before. Several times he berated himself for leaving her and then he would rebuke himself, reminding himself that she wouldn't want him to carry on so. She would want him to think about the exciting task that lay ahead, meeting the men who were promoting the grafted fruit trees. She'd want him to be planning their fine orchards that, come spring in another year, would be bearing fruit. Apples, pears, and peaches. He also told himself again and again that Eliza was very capable of handling all family matters—tending to animals and crops and running the house. Further, he reminded himself that Ben's birth had been easy. With Clara's help, she'd had the baby in a short time, and later that evening, she'd been up some and about. No, he told himself, there's no need to be worrying so, and with Lydia ready and willing to help, Eliza would do just fine.

Caleb was impressed with Portland. He was impressed with the number of wood-frame houses, and shops and stores, churches and taverns. He was impressed with the two sawmills he saw, and a fine-looking flour mill. But he was especially impressed with the port. It was here that he saw the great masts and rigging of merchant vessels, anchored in the Columbia River. Ships that had crossed the dreaded and dangerous bar where the Columbia met the Pacific, and had then come upriver to Portland. Ships that brought goods and emigrants from the Atlantic coast and ships that brought goods from Europe. Ships that, once loaded with furs, would sail down the great river to the Pacific and from there to ports all over the world.

Portland, however, boasted of no hotel as yet, and Caleb and Nathan made their way to the public boardinghouse where Nathan stayed when doing business in town. "It's better than the inn at the other end of town," Nathan said. "Someday soon, a man's going to catch the notion of building a fine hotel here. But until then, Mrs. Logan's place will suit us just fine."

Caleb liked the looks of the place, a large, frame house, sporting a new coat of white paint. Roses, zinnias, and marigolds blooming in a well-tended front yard.

A short, plump woman with a warm smile walked out on the porch to greet them. "How nice it is to see you again, Judge Shaw," she said. "I have your rooms ready, and your letter told me you had an engagement at seven-thirty this evening. Supper will be served promptly at six o'clock."

Nathan smiled and introduced Caleb. "He'll be as taken with your good food as I am, I'll bet. Is Johnny around?" Johnny was Mrs. Logan's fourteen-year-old son. A boy Judge Shaw liked and hoped to help educate.

"You missed him by a hair," Mrs. Logan said. "He left just a bit ago to ride out to his cousin's place for the night. But he'll be back tomorrow. Before you and Mr. Pride leave." Mrs. Logan then turned to Caleb. "Johnny took a message from your cousin, Mr. Pride. She said she'd see you later this evening, and she hoped your journey had gone—"

"I . . . I . . . what?" Caleb stammered, not comprehending. "I don't understand, Mrs. Logan. I don't have a—"

"Well, for pity's sake! Johnny doesn't often get messages wrong. All I know is that I was out shopping and when I got home he told me a woman had been here looking for you, and when you weren't around, she said she was your cousin and she'd look to see you this evening."

Caleb laughed. "Well, if I've got a cousin looking for me, it's sure a surprise."

Mrs. Logan nodded. "We'll ask Johnny tomorrow. In the meantime, let me show you both to your rooms." She then led the two men inside, through a wide foyer, and up a flight of carpeted stairs. Nathan's room was at the opposite end of the hall from Caleb's; both rooms were comfortable and clean. The men were both pleased.

"Supper's only an hour away," Mrs. Logan reminded them. "And I've got the best blackberry pie you've had in a mighty long time." Then, handing Caleb and Nathan their keys, she turned and went back downstairs.

A bright blue counterpane and a vase of marigolds made Caleb wish Ellie could be here. Then he stood, sniffing the air. He smelled an odor he didn't like, but he didn't know why and he didn't know what the odor was.

He walked over to the window and opening it to let in fresh air, he stood, looking out at small clusters of houses, some smaller, some larger than Mrs. Logans, all with their own pastures for cows, horses, chickens, and pigs. He blinked, amazed and puzzled as he saw down the way a large black horse exactly like the horse that Lydia rode. He then turned from the window. That was it. The smell in his room reminded him of her. He'd noticed it occasionally when she happened to stand close to him, and once last week, she had brushed up against him as he stood, calculating the number of cherry trees he might plant on land close to his house. He'd been annoyed by that. Almost an intentional brushing of herself against him, but then he'd discounted it and forgotten the incident until right now. He now knew what the odor was. Whiskey and a woman's face powder or perhaps a perfume.

He shrugged. A guest of Mrs. Logan's who had stayed here in this room, or perhaps Mrs. Logan herself must carry the same odor as Lydia. But then he thought about the strange message Mrs. Logan had given to him. And the odd coincidence seeing the horse. He stood, absently rubbing his chin, and then he brought himself up short. Psh! he told himself. Stop this nonsense. The boy was obviously confused, lots of other folks ride big, black horses, and the odor belonged to another boarder or to Mrs. Logan. Tomorrow he would ask the boy about "the cousin," and the matter would be cleared. Right now he would turn his mind to fruit trees and questions he needed to ask of Mr. Adams and Mr. Hastings tonight.

Promptly at seven that evening, Caleb and Nathan walked down Mrs. Logan's front steps, heading for a tavern named the Ship's Inn. It was here where they would meet the two men. Nathan was ecstatic, and Caleb knew he would be too, if it weren't for his continuing gnaw of worry over Eliza.

On this August evening, the sun was just slipping behind a forested hill as Caleb and Nathan walked down Portland's busiest street. The Ship's Inn was a decent enough place, with two large rooms. Walking in, Caleb smiled to himself. He hadn't been in a tavern since leaving Independence and the Silver Moon. He found the heady aroma of tobacco, whiskey, rum, and beer pleasant, and he finally began to relax some and look forward to this evening.

Both Mr. Adams and Mr. Hastings were easy to spot. They were well-dressed men and obviously not part of the drinking crowd. They had also secured a small private room where the four of them could conduct business without interruption. And they had with them two large wooden crates packed full of small, grafted trees.

Two hours later, sated with information about fruit trees and excited beyond their dreams, Caleb and Nathan paid Mr. Adams and Mr. Hastings two hundred dollars, and walked out of the Ship's Inn with both crates— containing two hundred trees.

On reaching the street, Caleb, for no particular reason, happened to glance back at the tavern. There, seated at a table behind a murky window, was Lydia Wells. Caleb sucked in his breath and stopped.

"Cal, what's wrong?" Nathan asked.

"Look! Look, Nathan! Back there at the tavern. Look at the woman sitting , , ," But now the woman was gone. "I swear it, Nathan! I swear to God I saw Lydia Wells sitting at the window and she was watching us. God A'mighty! I swear it, I do!"

"Cal, calm yourself. Calm yourself. Now think. What on earth would Lydia be doing here in Portland? I've never even heard her mention the place. If we were in San Francisco, well, that would be a different matter. And why would she be here anyway? She's standing by to give Ellie a hand if need be."

"I don't know. But I have to go back to the tavern, Nathan. I've got to go back and see."

"Well, I'll come too, Cal. Of course, I will."

The Ship's Inn at this hour, on a Saturday night, was crowded with seamen, drovers, and freight drivers—not unlike tavern folks Caleb remembered as a boy. Caleb's eyes quickly swept over the crowd of carousers, noting that there were few women, and no sign of Lydia Wells, nor was there a woman here who resembled Lydia.

Approaching one of the saloon keepers, Caleb posed the question. "Was there a woman, sir, in here earlier? A tall woman, with black hair?"

"A large woman," Nathan added. "Rather plain-looking."

"Women come and women go," the bartender said, a slight smirk on his face. "We don't keep track of 'em here."

Nathan put his arm around Caleb's shoulders. "You're tired, my friend, and I know you're worried about Ellie. Come on, let's head for Mrs. Logan's have a drink in her parlor, then hit the hay. We'll get up mighty early tomorrow, and start for home."

Caleb nodded. "I must be going daft, Nathan. First I hear about a cousin coming to see me, and I don't have any cousins, and then I'm seeing people who aren't there." But he laughed. "I'll sure take you up on your suggestion, and don't we have something to drink to, the both of us. Won't Maude and Ellie be proud."

It wasn't one drink that Caleb and Nathan enjoyed in the quiet warmth of Mrs. Logan's parlor. It was four or five, and by the time the two men were ready to go upstairs to bed, they were both feeling the effects. Caleb laughed. "Lord Heavan, Nathan, I haven't been so pleasantly tight since I was a young whippersnapper and living in Independence. It's fine tonight, but I'll bet you my shoe I'll regret the drinking tomorrow."

Nathan nodded as he carefully put out the parlor lamps. Handing a small lamp to Caleb, he took one for himself. "Careful now, Cal. We got to watch our step." Tiptoeing up the stairs, the men bade each other good night and went to their rooms.

Caleb set his lantern on a small table, and blew out the light. He then stood at the window for a moment and looked out at the dark town. The moon was full and it reflected on the waters of the great Columbia River. For a few moments, Caleb reflected on how far he and Eliza had come. He remembered their discussions about "the Oregon" many years ago, and how they'd talked then about what it might be like. He liked those thoughts. He liked feeling he and Ellie were moving on. Not getting caught, as she had said once when coming out, "in the backwater of a drift, and not moving at all."

It was with a start that Caleb saw a woman standing below the house. The scene was so uncanny, he felt his eyes stretch wide, his mouth went slack, and he couldn't move. The woman was tall and she was big, and Caleb was sure without doubt that this woman, for some crazed reason, was Lydia Wells. He had no idea why, but that didn't matter. Nothing mattered except he knew that he couldn't wait until tomorrow to leave for home. He would explain to Nathan later. Right now he had to confront this woman and he had to leave tonight. He had to get home.

Chapter 43

By midmorning Eliza felt no more pain, and as she washed her bucket of blackberries, she breathed easier. Cece and Ben were tending to chores in the barn; when they were through, Eliza would send them up the hill to pick more berries.

But another strong pain grabbed her. A pain so strong that she gasped. "Whew!" she said aloud to herself. "I guess I was wrong. This baby's coming today after all!" A few moments later she felt another big push of hurt, accompanied by a rush of water down her legs. Hurrying now, she picked up the iron rod and whanged it on her calling piece. There! Lydia would hear that. Then she quickly stoked up her fire, put the kettle on, and made sure that all the things she'd need—flannel blankets, binding strips, diapers, and shirts—were on hand. Another pain followed, causing her knees to buckle. She patted a stack of soft, clean cloths to be used in the birthing and she felt reassured. Lydia would be here soon, and with her help she would deliver this baby.

When the next pain gripped her, she panted as she lay down on her bed and reached for the pulling rag Caleb had made for her. This baby's in a big hurry, she thought. And I might have to deliver it myself.

It was then that she saw Ben, his eyes round with worry at seeing his mother lying on her bed and moaning with pain. Eliza laughed weakly, and took his hand. "I hadn't planned it this way, Ben, but it can't be helped. If Miss Wells doesn't get here quick, I'll be birthin' alone." She ground her teeth together to stop another cry. Lordly she didn't want Ben to see all of this.

"Ben, you get Cece, and then you both go down the road to the big, mossy rock. No further, now. And you both wait there for Miss Wells. Go, now!"

Ben's face twisted and Eliza saw tears in his eyes. "I don't like Miss Wells," he said.

"That . . ." Again Eliza clamped her teeth together, forcing herself not to cry out. "That can't be helped, Ben. Now go! You go now and get Cece."

Ben nodded, wiped at his tears with his shirt sleeve, and scampered out of the room. Eliza now lay, working alone with her awful torment, while hearing her own cries. Then, in a sudden burst, she pushed as she'd never pushed in her life, and she realized she'd birthed her baby. At the same time, she saw Cece standing beside her, wide-eyed.

"I can help you, Mama!"

Eliza nodded. "Hand me the knife, Cece. Quick!"

Cece ran to the kitchen and came back with a knife, which she handed to Eliza. Eliza sat up and shook her head, steading herself as drops of sweat fell from her forehead onto her tiny new daughter. Clamping her teeth tight, she tied the cord and cut it with the knife. "Pick up the baby, Cece. She needs to cry."

Cece picked up the slippery child and Eliza smiled as she lay back on her bed and heard the thin bleat of life. Then Cece picked up a flannel blanket, wrapped the child, and handed her to Eliza, who took a deep breath and closed her eyes. She would clean her baby in a few minutes, after she rested a little. She then put the child to her breast and whispered, "Ann Marie."

It was a short time later when Eliza opened her eyes to see Cece, still standing beside her. Eliza smiled. "You did very well, Cece," she said. "Where's Ben?"

"In there." Cece pointed to the living room. "Want's to see you're all right."

"In a moment." Instructing Cece on what to do, they both carefully washed the child. "Cece, you're doing ever so fine. Let me ask you, before Ben comes in. Did . . . what happened to Miss Wells? Did she ever come?"

Cece shook her head while looking at Eliza with somber eyes. "No," she said. "She didn't come at all."

A maze of thoughts ran through Eliza's mind. Anger, outrage, suspicion, and intense dislike. What would have happened if Eliza had really needed her? Had needed her, perhaps, to save the child, or even herself? As Eliza lay back down on her bed, cradling the tiny girl, Ann Marie, she knew she didn't care at all if she ever saw Lydia Wells again.

Caleb dressed quickly in the dark, opened the door of his room, tiptoed down the stairs, and let himself out the front door. His intent was to find the woman. But the woman was nowhere to be seen. Caleb walked up and down the street, he circled the house time and again, and then he began to feel foolish. Could he have seen an illusion? Could he be going daft?

Letting himself back in the house, he returned to his room, walked back over to his window and looked down into the yard. There was no sign of anyone, let alone a woman he knew. But Caleb was certain it had not been an illusion. In fact, ever since he'd arrived here, he'd had the strong feeling that something was wrong. There were too many signs for him to ignore what his heart now told him to do. Go home. Leave now. Write a note to Nathan explaining what had happened. If Nathan thought him crazed, so be it.

On leaving Portland, Caleb rode past Oregon Falls and up the Willamette River. He rode like the wind, galloping over wild, rocky roads, knowing that Sweetface couldn't last at this pace and somehow he had to have another horse.

It was getting on toward day when, seeing the glimmer of lantern lights ahead, he shouted, "A horse! Please! Trade me a horse!" He was astonished when, approaching the place, a man and a woman stood in front of a house. The man had a horse ready; the woman held a lantern and called out God speed. As Caleb dismounted Sweetface and jumped on the fresh mount, he could only shout, "I'll set it straight back to you soon as I can. Name's Caleb Pride. I live on up the valley." And he rode on.

Jumbled thoughts came to his mind. But the one thing he knew was that if his senses served him right, Lydia Wells was crazed. As he galloped on, under the scattered morning stars, he thought about the boy who had fled from the tannery and the McCabes. He pushed that terrible memory out of his mine and he cried aloud to himself. Get home. Get home. Get home. Get home. The words fell with the cadence of the horse's hooves, on and on.

It was dawn as Caleb raced like the wind past the Shaws place. He wouldn't stop there. It would take time. But he would stop at Lydia's house.

He rode up to the big log house, dismounted, and beat on the door. Getting no response he rode down to her barn; her horse was gone. She was either with Ellie, where she belonged, or she was in Portland.

Riding on with a fury, he crossed the ridge, tore past his fields of ripened, golden wheat, and arrived home just as the sun was rising behind Tall Singer's hill. The first thing he saw was Cece, standing very still, staring at him, while holding a bucket of water that she'd obviously drawn from the well. Caleb leaped from his horse, grabbed her, and held her tight. He didn't say a word, and when he drew away from the child and looked at her face and saw her smile, he knew Eliza and Ben were all right. Striding into his house, he saw Ben, sitting at the kitchen table, eating breakfast, and he then saw Eliza, sitting in her rocking chair, nursing a baby. Caleb fell to his knees, buried his head in her lap, and held her hand as if he would never let go.

Late that same day, Caleb took another peek at his new baby daughter. "Ann Marie," he said softly, a tired, thin smile on his face. "I like that name a lot."

After supper that evening, after Ben and Cece were in bed, Eliza and Caleb talked. They couldn't put the pieces of this terrible puzzle together, but Eliza's voice was firm when she told Caleb she never wanted to see Lydia Wells again. "She's caused us trouble, Cal, and I can't countenance that. I think she's a tormented soul, and I don't know why, but it's not up to me to know, either."

"Torment can cause evil in folks," Caleb said. "I should be sorry for her, Ellie. But I'm not. The one thing we might not ever know is if the woman I saw in Portland was her. I might be wrong, you know. Lydia might have gone to San Francisco, and well . . . I might have been seeing things." But Caleb knew in his heart that the woman he'd seen had been Lydia Wells.

Nobody in the upper part of the valley or in town was surprised when they learned Lydia Wells was no longer around. Nobody was surprised or sorry when, later that fall, they heard she was back in California.

"I'd just like to believe that she was never here. Never one of us," Clara said one day when she and Eliza were sitting outside in the warm October sunshine. "She was a strange one, Ellie. So strange, she didn't belong here."

"And we all think of ourselves sometimes as 'strange,'" Eliza said, and she and Clara both laughed. "As my mama used to say," she continued, "everybody's a little touched in the head at times." They laughed again. "But as Nathan and Maude have said, she never felt comfortable here."

"Well, you all are getting into the fruit tree business, and having other things on your minds is good."

Eliza smiled and patted Clara's hand. "Let's have some more tea," she said. "It's good for you, now that you're wanting another child. From what you say, this tea's supposed to help you in that way."

Chapter 44

Early in the morning on December 31, 1857, Eliza got out
of bed, slipped off her long flannel nightgown, and
dressed—muslin underclothes, long, cotton stockings knotted at her thighs, a muslin petticoat, a blue wool dress, and
brown leather boots, laced high. She then opened the door
of her bedroom and walked into the kitchen, where a fire in
the big iron wood stove crackled and popped. Caleb had
started it up before going down to the barn. Glancing out
her kitchen window, Eliza saw that a light snow had fallen
last night, barely covering the branches of the fruit trees.
Orchards of cherries, apples, and peaches that she and
Caleb now raised. Eliza smiled. What a beautiful day for
the Prides' New Year's/Reunion Party.

Eliza moved quietly as she fixed a pot of coffee,
mixed up a batch of biscuit dough, and cut thick slabs of
bacon. She wanted the children to sleep as long as they
could this morning because tonight they would be up very
late. She smiled, anticipating the day ahead.

By midday, company would start to arrive, and by
early evening many of the people who had trekked west
in 1848 with *The Oregon Roll* would stand together in the
Prides' big living room and lift their glasses high with a
toast to the New Year of 1858 and to the kinship of '48,
ten years ago.

Eliza was especially excited this year because Paddy O'Shea was coming. Paddy had never returned to the valley as he said he would. Instead he had gone south to the Sacramento Valley where, according to a letter he had written to Eliza and Caleb two years ago, he had bought "considerable land." Last fall, the Prides had heard from O'Shea again when he wrote:

. . . I have married a pretty widow lady named Mary, who has a daughter the same age as Cecilia. Her name is Abigail, and we call her Abby. I'm now settled down and living in a real house. We'll all be coming to your New Year's party this year, and looking forward to it too! There is a thing Mary and I would like to talk to the both of you about. A proposal for you to consider.

Neither Eliza or Caleb could imagine what O'Shea had in mind. "We'll just have to wait and see, Ellie," Caleb had said. Eliza could see he was tantalized by what the proposal might be, and oh, so pleased to be seeing his old friend again.

Breakfast was now ready, and she could hear the children talking softly as they dressed. Then the back door opened and Caleb came in, stomping his boots and slapping his gloves against his wool pants. Eliza laughed. "Lordy, Cal! You and Ben! Cold weather brings out that high color in both of you! Your cheeks look like polished apples!"

Caleb grabbed Eliza around her waist and nuzzled his cold face against her neck. "How do you like that for an answer!" he said. "And is it cold! About as cold as it gets here in the valley. It won't hurt if Ben and I lay in a little more hay for all of the folks' horses. We can do it quick, right after we eat." Eliza agreed, and in a few moments the children came in, sleepy-eyed but excited about this day.

It was a busy morning, even though much of the work was already done. Yesterday eight-year-old Ben had helped his papa in the barn, making sure there would be plenty of fresh hay for the additional horses expected today. Ben had then cut armloads of small pieces of oak for the kitchen fire. Five-year-old Ann Marie had helped Cece, who was now ten, make up sleeping cots in the big sleeping room off the main house for guests who would stay the night. And Eliza had taken special care fixing the guest room for Mr. and Mrs. O'Shea. She'd made sure the white lace counterpane was spotless and smooth, and she'd arranged dried, ruby red rosehips and little cedar boughs in a small vase that she placed on the bedside table. Cece had baked batches of sugar cookies and Eliza had roasted a large turkey and ham. Maude Shaw was bringing roast beef and rolls, and Clara was baking several pumpkin and mincemeat pies. While it was the Prides' party, none of the guests would arrive empty-handed, and by late this afternoon Eliza's long oak table would be set with a glorious feast. Now there were last-minute details to pay mind to.

Right after breakfast, Eliza and Cece took glasses and plates out of cupboards while Ann Marie counted out the silverware. Then all three of them set fresh candles in Eliza's three brass candelabras and fixed a big bowl of pinecones, topped with a red ribbon, for a grand table centerpiece.

At midday Eliza looked around her big front room, where small-paned windows allowed streams of sunlight. Large braided wool rugs covered the puncheon wood floors; gleaming brass andirons sat in the enormous stone fireplace where a fire crackled, warm and bright. Smithy's pictures of the trek west, starting with scenes from Independence and continuing to his painting of the Painted Hills, hung on the log walls.

Eliza's family was ready, too. Caleb, wearing a black broadcloth suit, a white shirt with a stiff, high, white collar, black velvet vest, and black cravat, looked handsome and prosperous. Ben, who looked a lot like his papa with his blond hair and dimpled chin, wore a white linen shirt with full, long sleeves, a red velvet vest, and long dark pants. Ann Marie, whose red curls framed her round, freckled face, had on a blue cotton dress with a collar trimmed in white lace. Cece's dress was made of peach silk, tied with a yellow sash, and she wore a yellow ribbon in her dark hair. And Eliza's dress for this important day was of blue silk, with an embroidered collar and a red sash.

"I hear bells!" Ann Marie suddenly cried out. "I do! I hear bells!"

"I do, too!" Ben cried. They all heard them then, tinkling bells, coming closer. "It's Paddy!" Caleb said, striding out of the room and on to the big porch. "I know it's Paddy!" The whole family followed him and stood listening to the sound of the bells coming closer. Then, coming up over the hill, came a large, black carriage, pulled by a team of four prancing horses decked out with harness bells.

What a welcome it was with shouts and laughter and much exclaiming, and shaking hands, and introducing all around of the dark-eyed beauty, Mary O'Shea, and her daughter, Abby, whose eyes sought Cece, the child she had heard so much about.

Following the O'Sheas, other folks arrived. Cheers greeted Tall, looking handsome and regal, dressed in white buckskins, and Clara, whose dark blue dress accented her beautiful blond hair. Twelve-year-old Little Bear and thirteen-year-old Blue Bird both wore buckskins, decorated with tiny blue beads and white shells.

Cheers greeted Clancy and Lorene, who arrived in an elegant carriage. Clancy was dressed much like Caleb, and Lorene wore a red silk dress and diamond earrings. Then came the McVeys, and hoots of joy and cheers

388

greeted George and Maggie and Danny, who was accompanied by his wife and their children, George and Maggie's grandchildren.

The next carriage brought the Shaws. And again, the big house rocked with greeting as Judge Shaw walked in the big front door with Maude and Pips. The last guest to arrive was Sam McIntyre, and what a greeting Sam received.

What a fine party—merriment, good food, games, music, and laughter echoed through the Prides' big house all afternoon and evening. At midnight Caleb called for the first toast. "To the New Year!" he called out. "To 1858! And to our good guide, Padraic O'Shea, his lovely wife, Mary, and daughter, Abby!" Cheers filled the room as glasses, filled with wine, whiskey, or sherry, were raised.

"To *The Oregon Roll* and 1848!" O'Shea called, lifting his glass. "And to Caleb Pride and his lovely wife, Eliza, and their family, Cecilia, Ben, and Ann Marie!" Again glasses clinked. "And now, folks, I'd sure like to hear from those of you that came out in '48! I'd be pleased if you'd give me a word of what you're all doing!"

It was agreed, and Clancy started by saying he was pleased with the new school he'd built in town. He then beckoned to Maude and asked her to tell the folks about their plans to start a boarding school for the upper and mid-valley children. Maude, beaming with pleasure, outlined this plan that would provide schooling beyond the eight grades provided now. This news was met with cheers. The valley people considered education for their children a high priority, and support for such a notion ran strong.

When George was called on, he talked about living in the southern part of the valley, where "the grass is always green, and Danny and Irma Jean live just next door." Maggie nodded, her face wreathed in a smile.

"What's going on with the Indians, George?" the

Judge asked. "I know Table Rock Treaty of five years ago didn't help much."

George winced. "It's peaceful right now, but we don't relax a whole lot. I don't have a whole lot of faith in treaties working right."

Eliza glanced at Maude, who stood tight-lipped, not saying a word. Eliza knew very well Maude's opinion of treaties. "We're slowly pushing the Indians into little reservations," she had said more than once. "We lull them into 'peace' by giving them money and blankets and shirts and alcohol. But that will never compensate for what we are taking from them. Their land." However, Maude said nothing today. Today was the Prides' party, and she would not interject her own remarks at a time of festivities.

"Tall Singer!" O'Shea called out. "Let me hear from you!"

Tall came forward and looked at the people gathered in the big room. "I will not speak of treaties, because this is not the time. I will tell you, O'Shea, that Clara and I live not far from here. Our two children are now growing up and another child will be born to us in June." A smile creased Tall's handsome face. "We are pleased about that." Murmurs and soft laughs drifted across the room, while some of the women turned to look at Clara, whose dress concealed her slightly swollen belly. Tall then joined his wife, and O'Shea asked Sam to speak up.

Sam grinned and walked to the front of the room. "How about telling you I've started my own newspaper, Paddy! *The Oregon Gazette!*" Everybody cheered. "And how about asking all of you to help me with a story I plan on doing for September, commemorating the trek of '48, ten years ago. I've been taking notes here, all the latest news about where you're living and what you're all doing. I've also talked to Pips about doing a sketch or two of all of us that I'll be using. What say you to that?" Sam's

390

request was met with whistles and shouts of approval. Then, when Sam was through talking, Caleb asked O'-Shea to tell everybody about himself and what had happened to him since September of '48.

Paddy O'Shea's story was brief, but Eliza thought a lot more lay behind the facts than what he told today. He told how he'd been bit by the gold dust fever back in '49, and instead of guiding another group out to Oregon, he'd gone to California where he'd "had a little luck" with mining the gold, and he'd bought some land in the Sacramento Valley. During this time he'd met the widow, Mary, whom he had married. Once again glasses were raised as the folks drank another toast to the marriage of Paddy and Mary O'Shea.

And then it was time for the good times sound as Sam tuned up his harmonica, Danny and Pips picked up their fiddles, one valley neighbor picked up an accordion, another strummed the guitar, and the dancing started with "Oh, Susanna."

At around two o'clock in the morning some guests left, while those who lived far away—Sam, the McVeys, and the Evanses—stayed over, to leave the next day. The O'Sheas would stay until the following day, January 2.

In the late afternoon of the next day, Paddy, Mary, Caleb, and Eliza sat down in front of the fire in the Prides' front room. Everybody else had gone home; Cece, Abby, Ben, and Ann Marie were busy with other things; and now it was time for the grown-ups to talk.

"Sam's story should be a good one," Caleb said. "I'll be anxious to see it next fall."

"And Pip's sketches of all of us should take real well." Eliza laughed. "Think of that! All of us on the front page of Sam's paper, come September."

"Talk of next fall brings me to what Mary and I want

to talk to you about," Paddy said. "And I'll ask it straight out. What would you both think if you, Caleb, should leave here in March and not be home until . . . hmm . . . October?" O'Shea looked at them closely from under his thick brows.

Caleb looked puzzled. "There would have to be a damned good reason why, Paddy. That's a helluva long time to be away from my family. Damned long!"

"Well," Paddy said, "remember the Malheur country?" Eliza glanced at Mary, who was sitting very straight, her blue eyes intense.

"Sure! We remember the Malheur. We talk about it, now and then," Caleb answered.

"We do, Mr. O'Shea. Yes, we remember it very well."

Paddy laughed. "Will you ever come to calling me Paddy, Eliza, instead of Mr. O'Shea, like you did when you were a slip of a girl on the trail? Well, no matter. What does matter is this. That country, the Malheur country, is the best cattle country this side of California, and north. I've been back several times since we all came through, and each time, I thought about how you took to it, Cal. Then last year I took Mary with me, and by God, she took to it too!"

Mary smiled. "Paddy's right," she said. "And you both need to know that my father brought cattle into California from Texas some years ago. I'm familiar with cattle, and I know what good cattle country looks like. When Paddy took me out there, well, I'll say to the both of you, I haven't seen country that's better suited. There isn't a place I know of where the bunchgrass grows as it grows out there."

O'Shea nodded. "Nobody has thought about that country in this way yet. Nobody I know except Mary and me. And we're thinking of doing something about it. Like taking cattle out there. And we're not talking about a small herd. We're talking about big herds we've already bought. Longhorns, and some high-bred shorthorns. Fifteen hundred head in all. We bought them from a cattleman in Texas, and now we're looking for a man to join me and drive the cattle from Bell County, Texas, out to the Malheur. We're offering you the job, Cal. We're prepared to pay you well."

Caleb's heart raced as he listened to Paddy speak of that country—country he'd never forgotten. He looked across the room at Eliza, who appeared to be entranced with Paddy's offer.

"Now, if you take this job, Cal," Paddy continued, "you'll be foreman, and you pick our men. You know a helluva lot more about trailing cattle than I do. And as I say, we're prepared to pay you well; we'll pay you a flat one thousand five hundred dollars for your work."

There was silence in the room. The big clock in the corner struck four, and off in the kitchen there was the muffled rattle of pans.

When Caleb spoke, his voice was soft. "Whoa! I can't give you an answer, Paddy. Eliza and I need to think about it. It means me being gone for a long time, and I'm not sure . . ."

"Cal!" Eliza shook her head and lifted her hand. "We may need to talk about it, but you being gone for a time shouldn't be a trouble."

"Let me say one more thing," Paddy said, looking at both of them. "If things work out as they should, and Mary and I have no reason to believe they won't we'd be asking that you consider going in with us as partners. Now this would be separate from the cattle drive. The money we pay you for herding the cattle wouldn't have a thing to do with any partnership we might consider."

Mary nodded. "I have to say that I wanted to meet both of you before we made the offer. That has now happened, and I'd be as pleased as Paddy if you agree."

393

"We have the money," Paddy continued, "and we'll have the cattle, and we'll buy the land. But we would prefer to operate with partners, and we can't think of anybody on earth we would rather have working with us."

"Eliza," Mary said. "I have to remember to tell myself that this place is far. How might you think about that?"

"It's a notion that doesn't bother me, Mary. Not at all. If this is what we all decide to do, being far won't be a problem." She then looked at Caleb, whose eyes were on her. "Let's think about it, Cal," she said. "Let's give it some thought."

Even as she talked, Eliza's heart raced. The memory of that country touched her deep. There were times here in the valley when she'd felt a longing for that land that she couldn't identify. True, nothing very good had happened out there. There had been the awful dust storm and the terrible stampede, but still there was something. She remembered how happy she'd been standing by the big, marshy lake and watching the hundreds of birds. She remembered the feeling of freedom she'd felt as she'd walked into the meadow and looked out over the vast grasslands, with the beautiful Snow Mountain off to the west.

That night after everybody was in bed, Caleb held Eliza close. "I don't know, Ellie," he whispered. "It's a long time to be gone. Too long for me to feel good about."

"Go, Cal! You must! I know you want to, and I want you to go! I can manage, just fine. And while you're gone, we'll both think about Mr. O'Shea and Mary's offer. But I'll tell you now, Caleb Pride," she said, laughing softly, "aside from lying with you, nothing I've ever known in my life makes my heart race like the thought of that land!"

* * *

The answer to the O'Sheas' offer of the cattle drive was yes. The plan for the Texas-to-Oregon trip was well made. Caleb and his men would meet Paddy in Bell County, Texas. Paddy would have fresh horses ready; all the necessary equipment and the herds would be ready to roll. After a day or two of rest, Paddy, Caleb, and the herders would start the long cattle drive back to Oregon and the Malheur country. Mary would meet them there, having ridden up from California with several vaqueros and a cook. Camp would be ready for the men coming across the country; Caleb would stay with them for a day or two while discussing details of the potential partnership. He would then come home, where he would confer further with Eliza and the final decision would be made. But there was little doubt in anybody's mind what that decision would be. The Prides would sell their place in the valley, and come spring of next year, they would move east of the Cascades.

It was a dark, blustery morning on March 12. Slanty rain beat on the windows of the Prides' cabin where, at four-thirty in the morning, Eliza and Caleb were up. A fire crackled in the cookstove, as well as on the big hearth in the living room. After Eliza and Caleb had eaten their breakfast together, Eliza got the children up.

Caleb knelt and held Ben close. "You mind Mama, my fine boy. And I'll be thinking of you every day. Don't forget to give Sweetface a ride now and then, and rub her down well."

Ben nodded solemnly, proud that his papa had given him a new rifle just last week; prouder yet when Caleb had told Ben he was a "danged fine shot."

"I will, Papa. We'll do just fine. Better give Dog a good pat on the head." Caleb laughed, bent over, and patted old Dog.

He then picked up Ann Marie, who laughed when her papa nuzzled her neck. "You'll be havin' some teeth right soon . . . there!" he said and laughed, pointing at the place where she had just lost two front teeth. Ann Marie ducked her head into her papa's coat. "I'm going to mith you, Papa," she said softly. "But we'll do fine."

"I know you will. And when I come back, my pockets will be full of surprises." Putting the child down, he again knelt and held Cece, who clung to him, her arms around his neck.

"I'm proud of you, Papa! And like Mama and Ben and Ann Marie say, we'll do just fine!"

"I'll be looking to hear some new fiddle tunes, missy," Caleb said. "Keep on with your lessons with Pips. He's a good teacher."

Cece nodded. "I will, Papa. I promise I will."

Caleb then turned to Eliza. Taking her face between his hands, he looked deep into her eyes. Everything they needed to say to each other had been said. "I'll write," he said. "As often as I can. I love you, Ellie, and come October"—he paused, his blue eyes twinkling, "I'll be coming on by!"

She nodded and smiled. "And when you come on by, Caleb Pride, we'll talk again, about old Boone!"

Chapter 45

October 1858

Clara peered out the window of her cabin. Dark clouds were piled up above the fir trees; there was chill in the air. BB and LB had just gotten home from Maude Shaw's school and were down at the barn with Tall, unloading hay they had harvested last month. Winter feed for Tall's horses. Tall was proud of his animals, magnificent roans he had bred during the last seven years from the broomtails he had brought over from the Malheur country.

Tall had done well. His reputation as a breeder of fine horses and a fair businessman had brought him financial success as well as recognition among the many settlers who now lived in the valley. Tall was also a generous man. Last June, when Ben Pride had turned nine, Tall had given him one of his roans for his birthday. It was a beautiful animal, a blood bay with a black tail and mane. Ben had been ecstatic, and he'd named his horse Roan.

As Clara stood looking out the window, she thought ahead to next week when she and Tall would take their children and a string of Tall's horses and ride into town.

Clara looked forward to that, a three-day event. It would take all of one day to get there, and they would stay with the Evanses that night. The next day while Tall was busy, Clara would visit with Lorene and do some necessary shopping. Clara smiled. Lorene and Clancy had't yet seen Clara and Tall's four-month-old baby, John. And oh, my! The Evanses' house was so grand! Lorene had lots of fine furniture that she had had shipped all the way from the East Coast around Cape Horn to San Francisco, and then by freight wagon here. Beautiful things—silver and chrystal and fine china; beautiful rugs and furniture with velvet seats; and a grand piano that was such a beautiful thing—well! It was always fun to visit Clancy and Lorene.

Then, on the way home, Clara and her family would stop to visit the Shaws. With Pips home from one of his treks, it would be a lively time for all. There Pips would be, pen in hand, drawing pictures. And Pips with his fiddle, playing "Nelly Bly," "Wait for the Wagon," and always "Oh, Susanna."

Clara turned from the window and looked at John. She still had time to take the baby and go pick huckleberries for pies to take to the Prides on Sunday, the day when Caleb was expected home. What a homecoming that would be! Merriment of family and friends, a table spread with delicious food, and many glasses raised in toasts to his return.

It was time Caleb came home, Clara thought. Last March was a long time ago. Just last week, when Clara and Eliza were visiting, Eliza had told Clara how much she wanted him home. ". . . and the children are so excited, Clara, I can hardly keep them calm. They still ask me to reread his letters, and they love to read Sam's story about all of us, and look at the sketch Pips did. Especially the sketch of their papa. Cal will be pleased with the story, too." She'd laughed. "Right there on the front page. I think what he'll like best is the part about how he drove cattle all that way from Lexington to Philadelphia when he was a child."

"Folks sure like to read about us," Clara said. "Trekking out here in '48!"

But Clara had worried about it, and Tall had put her worry in his own words. "It was not wise, Clara. What if the brothers, who at one time were looking for him, should see the story? I do not feel good about it."

Clara had said nothing about her worry or Tall's words to Eliza. Over the years the terrible thing that had happened to Caleb had never been mentioned again. Clara thought that with the passing of time and events— Caleb and Eliza developing their ranch, building their beautiful home, having their own babies, socializing with other folks here in the valley—that dreadful time had no doubt faded in their minds. If so, that was fine, but it wasn't so with Tall.

While Tall never talked about his fear of Tomschini, he was always alert to the possibility of his return. Since coming to the valley ten years ago, Tall had yet to leave his family alone. When he rode into town, his family went with him. When he wanted to visit his people, east of the Cascades, he took his family along. Clara also knew that Tall had not been pleased when Caleb had decided to take the job with Mr. O'Shea. It meant, he had said, being away too long. And every three or four days, since Caleb had left, Tall had ridden over to the Pride place, stayed awhile and helped Eliza with a thing or two, and then ridden home.

Often on Saturdays or Sundays, the whole family would drive over to the Prides, or Eliza would bundle her children in her buggy and drive over to visit Clara and Tall. And while Tall and Clara disapproved of Caleb's accepting O'Shea's offer, neither of them knew that Eliza had been the one who had insisted he go.

Now Clara leaned over her baby and slipped her

index finger into one of John's tiny hands. She laughed, feeling the small surge of strength as John squeezed her finger then turned his head to her and smiled. Clara felt her whole being swell with love for this boy. She had felt the same way about Blue Bird and Little Bear, but this baby was different. Her other two had been active babies; this boy had a quiet nature and, much like his father, seemed content with himself.

Clara often watched John as he studied his surroundings: a reflection of sunlight on the log rafters of the cabin; a piece of bright cloth, or beads; his parents, his brother and sister, whatever caught his attention. Outside, he would lie for long periods of time, propped up in the cradleboard while his mother washed clothes, or gardened, or gathered berries. Without fussing, he would watch the great boughs of the fir trees swaying gently in the breeze, or the huge, billowy, slow-moving clouds against the sky, and he would laugh as the chattering squirrels ran up and down the trees, and then turn solemn as he watched birds soaring in flight.

John looked like Tall. Much more so than either Blue Bird or Little Bear. He had Tall's handsome face, and thank the good Lord, he wasn't crippled! Clara had worried about that. With each child, from the moment she first suspected she was pregnant until the child was born, she had silently prayed that her children wouldn't be born as she had been, with a withered leg and twisted foot.

It was Tall who had insisted that this boy be called John. John McCabe. "All of our children will live in the white man's world, Clara. Just as I live a white man's life now. BB and LB might want to change their names when they grow older. If they do, they have my permission. But let us start this boy with a white boy's name. It's also important that all of the children carry the name 'McCabe' because our land is recorded under that name and it must remain that way."

Now Clara gently tickled John's chin, delighting in his chuckle. She then walked across the room to a large stack of rabbit skin cloaks, picked up the smallest one, lifted John out of the cradleboard, and wrapped him in the cloak. Holding him high above her head, she laughed as the baby laughed and peeked out at her, his big brown eyes sparkling with his own sense of fun.

"Aren't you the boy, Johnny!" Clara said softly. "And before I know it, you'll be as big as LB! And a handsome boy, too, my Johnny! But now you're going berry picking with me. We'll pick enough for pies for Aunt Eliza, Ben, Cece, Ann Marie, and Uncle Caleb. Come Sunday, we'll all go visit them, and we'll be taking our pies and the rabbit cloaks! Won't we have a grand party, though. That's when we'll give them the rabbit cloaks, and won't they be surprised!" She chuckled to herself, thinking about it, and thinking of the pleasure the gifts gave her and Tall.

Two years ago, Caleb had asked Tall about the cloaks. He'd seen Tall, Clara, Blue Bird, and Little Bear wearing them, and he had remembered O'Shea's story about their warmth. He wanted to buy some for his own family.

"How many squirrels does it take, Tall, to make such a hooded cloak? How are they made?" he'd asked.

"Forty skins for a young child. A hundred or more for a man. After we cut the pelt from the rabbit, we twist it to make a long twist. The fur is on the outside. After we have many of the long, dried twists, the women weave them."

Tall had remembered Caleb's desire for the cloaks, as he'd remembered many things about this man who, with O'Shea, had saved his life. He would obtain the cloaks and give them to him as gifts. He would do this through his favorite cousin, Gray Squirrel, and he would make the arrangements at the next family reunion in September when Tall and Clara took their children and traveled back over the Cascades. There, on the lower mountain slopes, groves of trees bearing piñon nuts grew. It was here where they met Paiutes, Tall's parents, grandparents, brothers, sisters, aunts, uncles, and cousins.

It was a yearly event and a time of celebration. A time when Tall learned news of his family. Children had been born; perhaps an old aunt or uncle had died. Maybe one or two of his younger cousins had a new wife.

This was also a time of the nut gathering. The men would beat the tree branches with willow, lashed to long poles, fifteen to eighteen feet long, while the young boys climbed the trees to knock down the piñon cones. The girls would gather the cones in winnowing baskets, where the unwanted needles and twigs were removed; then they loaded the clean cones into large, conical burden baskets and carried them back to camp, where the older women husked the nuts. Some of the nuts were ground to a paste and used as porridge; some were dried for flavorings and used as an added substance to a winter meal of stewed dried fish heads and entrails.

At the end of the nut-gathering day, the people sat around a fire and ate, sang songs, played games, and listened to the Teller of Tales, often Tall. The stories always included the story of the Paiutes, a time when animals and man talked to each other—a time of great harmony. And the story of Coyote, the beast who, by stealing fire, had saved man from the eternal doom of living in a world of cold and darkness.

Last year at the reunion, Tall had asked Gray Squirrel if he was interested in a trade. Tall would give him two roans if Gray Squirrel would give Tall five rabbit skin cloaks. Gray Squirrel was pleased, and the arrangement was made. Last month, in September, Tall took two roans to the festival, as promised, but was disappointed to find that Gray Squirrel was not there. Gray Squirrel, Tall learned, was off somewhere south, around the gold mines. Tall had laughed when he'd heard this. It sounded like Gray Squirrel. Always looking for adventure, never settling down. But Tall always enjoyed Gray Squirrel's company. He was brave, and funny, and smart, and dependable. Even though he wasn't at this reunion, he had sent a pile of rabbit skin cloaks with another cousin, Big Moon. Gray Squirrel also sent word, through Big Moon, that he planned to visit Tall and Clara sometime this fall.

Now, Clara looked at the pile of hooded cloaks. If there was a chance of a freeze tonight, she would take the cloaks outside and lay them along the fence. A good freeze would kill off fleas that were harbored inside the skins. But when Clara looked at the heavy, gray clouds, a freeze didn't seem likely.

Strapping John back into the cradleboard and securing it to her back, she picked up a pitch-coated water basket and a toting basket. New baskets, given to her as presents from Tall's mother. Today, on the way home, Clara would stop at the spring and fill the water basket. She would use the toting basket for her berries, and with John strapped to her back, she could easily manage to bring both baskets and baby home.

It was cool up on the ridge, and the wind had come up. Clara slid the cradleboard off her back and set it against a tree. She then went to work, picking the berries fast with both hands, stopping every now and then to look at John. She had almost finished stripping the patch clean when the sound of a clanging iron caused her to stop her picking and straighten. It was her calling piece and the jangling sound met one thing. "Come."

Clara quickly picked up the cradleboard, slipped it back on, and grabbed her baskets. Then, hobbling along the trail, she hurried as fast as she could toward home, telling herself there wasn't anything to worry about.

Coming to the crest of the hill, she stopped for a moment to catch her breath, while looking down on her place. She always enjoyed stopping here where she could see her house and her garden. Even on this gray day her zinnias, hollyhocks, and marigolds showed their colors of purple, red, gold, and pink. But today a strange horse was hobbled in front of her place, a horse that looked like one of Tall's. Company! But who? Well, she told herself as she hurried on, she would soon found out.

Walking along the stony path that led through her garden, she heard hoots of laughter as Gray Squirrel burst out the door, followed by Blue Bird, Little Bear, and Tall.

"I have come to visit," Gray Squirrel called, striding out to meet her and taking her baskets. He then peered down at John and laughed. "What a handsome boy! He looks just like me!" They all laughed.

"It's good to see you, Gray Squirrel," Clara said. "Tall moped about like a sulking boy when he found out you weren't with your family last month. And the cloaks are beautiful. We know our friends will like them very much."

Inside the house, Clara took John out of the cradleboard and gave him to Gray Squirrel, who was now seated with Tall at the table. "Since you are both so handsome, Gray Squirrel, you and John will get along just fine!" They all laughed as Gray Squirrel rocked the smiling baby in the crook of one arm.

Clara quickly started up her cooking fire, sweetening her simmering stew with potatoes, turnips, and carrots she picked out of a dirt cellar just outside the back door. If she had time, she would bake up a huckleberry pie. Tall sent the children down to the barn to finish up their chores, promising them that when they returned they could listen to Gray Squirrel's stories, which meant they could stay up later than usual.

As Clara worked in her kitchen, she smiled, hearing

Tall and Gray Squirrel's low talk, and smelling the sweet smell of tobacco smoke. But a frown crossed her face and she joined them for a moment, taking John and holding him as she listened to Gray Squirrel.

"I will tell you," Gray Squirrel said, "that I saw many things between the land where we live and the land of our brothers to the south. I will tell you that the white men are destroying our country; that many of the great stands of the piñon trees have been leveled for fuel. Yes. The white men cut the trees and burn them for their fires. The white man's horses and cattle have grazed and trampled our seed plots and a terrible sickness has killed thousands of our people. Many of our people now run from the white men because they are afraid. Sometimes our people bury their children up to their necks in the sand and place sagebrush over their heads. They dread meeting the white man; they try to hide their children; they hope the terrible disease will stay away from them."

"You may tell us more of this, Gray Squirrel, but another time," Tall said, his voice firm. "Our children are now coming into our house, and I do not want to speak of it in front of them. I would ask that you tell some of your good stories. This, they will like." Gray Squirrel nodded. He knew many stories the children would like to hear, and like Tall, Gray Squirrel was a fine teller of tales.

They sat until late that night, Tall, Clara, Blue Bird, Little Bear, and Gray Squirrel. Occasionally the fire in the big fireplace snapped, and every now and then, the cabin echoed with laughter and exclamations of wonder as Gray Squirrel told story after story of the people he had seen in California.

Then, after everybody had said good night and gone to bed, Clara stayed up for a few moments, watching the dying fire. As she looked into the coals, she was suddenly aware of the northwestern wind—the wind that would sweep the great fall and winter storms inland from the

Pacific. A feeling of great sorrow swept over her and she shuddered. Picking up her lamp, she quickly looked on all of her children, all of them sound asleep; she then blew out her lantern and went to bed.

It rained the next day. Inside the house the children played rousing games of checkers, every now and then stopping to listen to Tall and Gray Squirrel reminisce about their childhood while Clara spent the day baking pies and breads. "Even if it rains tomorrow, Tall, we must ride to the Prides. BB and LB say that Cece told them that's when Caleb is expected home. Eliza's latest letter from him tells her that."

Tall nodded. "We will all go. Gray Squirrel, you too. We will take your good food, Clara, and we will all ride in our wagon. We will also take the cloaks. Yes. We will go, even if it rains."

Clara smiled at Tall, who always knew what was important for her, and rarely disappointed her.

"The man named Caleb," Gray Squirrel said and he frowned. "Is this the man that the story was written about in the newspaper?" Gray Squirrel looked closely at Clara and Tall.

"Yes!" Tall replied. "He is. He and his family are the people we got the cloaks for. They are our good friends."

"How far does this man live from here?" Clara saw worry in Gray Squirrel's eyes. Something was wrong.

"Not far. Three miles. Why do you ask?"

"As I traveled from California back to my country, I came upon three men. Two of them were white men, the worst men I have met in my life. One man had only one eye, but wears no patch on his face. The other man has a wrinkled, shrunken head. He has been burned at some time in his life. The third man was Tomschini. Now, Tomschini did not know me, and I made no effort to let

406

him know who I was. But I would not be surprised, Tall, to learn that Tomschini still considers himself as your brother-in-law."

Tall looked at his children, who were listening, wide-eyed. "LB! BB! There is work you must do at the barn. Go now and take care of your work. Perhaps then we will go riding with Gray Squirrel yet today. Go now." Blue Bird and Little Bear reluctantly got up, put on their jackets, and went outside.

"I do not want them to hear such things, Gray Squirrel. It is not necessary. But now, continue with what you know."

"I believe Tomschini knows that you live, Tall. And he rides with these two men. As I rode north, I rode past places where those men had been. White men's places, burned out. The women raped and murdered. The children, too. I hear that Tomschini will ride hundreds of miles to kill white people. He has no reason. He is mad."

Tall's face was creased in a frown. "Where did you come upon these men?"

"Far from here, Tall. We were coming home from California and we came on a single wikiup. The three were camped there. But I fear Tomschini. He is a terrible man, and I swear to you that he is mad. He is as huge as I remembered him, and his hair is long and dirty and matted. And now he carries a lance strung with the scalps of white people. He did not speak. But the man with one eye said he and the man with the shrunken head are looking for a white man named Caleb Pride. They had a newspaper with them that they showed us. There was a story in the newspaper about the people you traveled with when you came here, Tall. They said the man who calls himself Caleb uses a false name. They say they know a woman told them where Caleb Pride lives. The woman, they said, was drunk when she talked, but they said she used to live in this valley. They said they now know that this man, Caleb, lives in this valley and that a Paiute whom their friend, Tomschini, seeks lives in this valley with a white woman."

Clara stifled a cry. Tall reached across the table and put one of his hands over hers. Tall's voice was quiet when he asked Gray Squirrel what else he might know.

"The man with the shrunken head asked me if I had ever been to this valley and I said no. Then they laughed and said that is where they would go. The party I was traveling with and I rode on, but a day later all three of those men passed us by, heading north, as we were."

Tall nodded, got up from the table, moved toward the hearth, and picked up his rifle. "We will all leave here and ride to Eliza's. Clara, get John ready to go. Gray Squirrel, come with me to the barn. We will bring back the horses, and the children, then we will leave."

"You ride to the woman's house, Tall," Gray Squirrel said. "You will ride fast while I stay here with your family."

"No," Tall said. "We will all stay together. We will all go. Come now, Gray Squirrel. We do not have time to argue."

Tall then moved fast, stopping just long enough to grab the iron bar and bang the triangle over and over, as hard as he could. He must warn Eliza. He must! Again he banged the triangle and then he and Gray Squirrel ran faster than Clara had ever seen Tall run, up the hill that separated the house from the barn and the corral.

Clara quickly strapped John in his cradleboard, set him against one wall, and grabbed her shawl. As she slung her shawl around her shoulders, she looked out the window, where she saw a movement in the trees, just beyond her garden. She stood absolutely still for a moment as she saw the thing she'd never wanted to see again in her life. Ross and Earl stood in her garden with Tomschini. They were all quietly watching her house. Clara sucked in he breath, and prayed that John wouldn't make a sound. Then, picking up her rifle she calculated that the men didn't know who might be in the cabin or anywhere else. But now she had to hide John. If they heard the boy, they would find him in a minute and kill him.

The dirt cellar! She quickly picked up the baby and scuttled out the back door. Wet leaves and blow from last night's wind and rain covered the hole in the ground. Groping, she found the iron ring, lifted the heavy lid, and thrust John inside. She then set the lid back down, propping it with twigs just enough to give her baby air. That was all she could do for John.

Clutching her rifle and skirting the forest, Clara started for the barn. She looked back toward her cabin and she saw Tomschini walking through her garden. Clara ducked back through the fir trees; at the same time she saw Ross and Earl walk boldly up onto the front porch. As Clara turned and again started toward the barn, she saw Tall, Gray Squirrel, Blue Bird, and Little Bear at the crest of the hill. Gunshots split the stillness of the afternoon. Again she looked back toward her cabin and this time she saw Tomschini, stopped in her garden, aiming a rifle toward her children, Tall, and Gray Squirrel. Lifting her rifle, Clara took careful aim and pulled the trigger. She heard the big Indian's cry, at the same time she saw Tall, riding through her garden and an explosion of red zinnias and pink hollyhocks scattered against the sky as Tall fell.

The air was suddenly smokey as flames from the cabin's roof licked up against the dark sky, then she heard her children scream.

God! Oh! God! BB! LB! Oh! God! Gray Squirrel's head floated for a moment, bloody and ragged before her eyes, and Little Bear lay in a pool of blood. John! She must get back to her baby! She scuttled fast, moving through the bushes toward her cabin. Not far from her back door, she felt a sharpness pierce her side, followed by a heavy feeling, a numbing that spread through her as she fell.

She tasted dirt and blood. She tried to move, she tried to cry out. She prayed for death as she saw her beautiful daughter raped and murdered; she watched the fire engulf her fine cabin, and then she saw the men ride away. As she watched the flames, red against the sky, she heard her baby cry inside the ground, and she wondered for a moment if she might see her beloved man and her beloved children in heaven.

Chapter 46

Ben looked at the deer that hung on a peg in the Prides' feed shed, the blood barely dripping out of the carcass onto the floor of clean hay.

"Your papa will be proud of you, Ben," Eliza said as she quickly cut off chunks of meat and dropped them in a large pail. Ben grinned. He knew that, and he felt himself swell with pride.

Four days ago, right after coming home from school, Ben had shot the buck, only a few yards from the Prides' house. He and Cece had lugged it up to the shed, where Eliza had helped hoist it up onto the peg. Ben had then dressed it out as his father had taught him to do, and it was left to bleed and season until today, when Eliza decided it was time to butcher it for her family.

Eliza looked at Ben and smiled. "We'll be having a fine venison roast for Papa's return tomorrow. Meantime tonight, we'll be having venison steaks. I'll salt down the rest later. Your papa loves to eat it that way." She chuckled. "I think it must remind him of the deer meat we all ate when coming across."

Placing her knife back in its sheath, she picked up the pail while Ben picked up the antlers. These he would clean and varnish, and he and his mother would mount

411

them on their living room wall right after supper. Ben grinned, thinking about that. If his papa rode according to his want, he'd be riding into the Prides' yard late tonight or early tomorrow. Oh, Ben was anxious to see his papa! And he was so proud! So proud of his papa, driving all those cattle all the way from Texas to the Malheur.

Later, inside her kitchen, Eliza set her pail of meat on her kitchen table and started to cut the steaks for supper. Looking into her front room, she saw Ann Marie and Ben, sitting at the big table. Ann Marie's head of red curls was bent over a book as she carefully picked out words that Ben and Cece had taught her. Eliza walked into the room, and leaned over and patted Dog, who lay in front of the big fireplace, his gray muzzle resting on his forepaws. She then lit another lamp, letting the wick burn bright as she carried it over to the table.

"You'll be needing more light," she said, placing the lamp on the table between them. She then looked out the window at the heavy, gray skies. It had rained all day. The boughs of the fir trees hung low, dripping steady drops of water into little rivulets that ran through matted brown needles on the soaked ground. A heavy mist hung over the valley, veiling the trees across the ridge where Tall and Clara lived. Gusts of blustering wind, caught under the cabin's low eaves, whistled and then faded away. Eliza shuddered and wished that Cece were here.

Eliza always missed Cece when she stayed at the Shaws. It didn't happen often, but now with Pips just recently home, Cece had asked Eliza if today she could stay after school, take a long lesson from Pips, and practice with him, so that by the time her papa got home, she would have several fine new tunes for him to hear. She would ride home tomorrow; Pips would come too. That had seemed reasonable to Eliza, and she had said yes.

Looking down at the table, Eliza saw Caleb's last letter placed in Fielding's book, *Tom Jones*. She took the letter out, unfolded it, and read it again. The first paragraph bothered her and she frowned. He would be home, he wrote, no later than October 28. But then he wrote he had had a bad dream about a clanging bell, and he had wanted her to know about it.

Clanging bell? There were no bells in this part of the valley. A church bell, yes, way out in town, but there were no bells here for her to hear. After pondering Caleb's message, she shook her head, trying to rid herself of his fret.

Again, Eliza looked out the window, hoping to see a break in the gray sky. She had so hoped that the good weather would hold until he was home, and it had, until today. But now Eliza knew this fall storm was probably the first of many, closing off chances of sunshine and blue skies. These storms also brought snow to the Cascades, and snow in the mountains would be the only thing that could delay Caleb's return.

Now, reading the rest of Caleb's letter, she smiled.

With luck, and if my weary horse can stand it, I might be home before Sunday, Ellie. That's the part I like to think about. So, my darling, I can say to you, look for me, Ellie! I'll be coming on by. If I get to the valley at night, you'll hear a commotion and look up and see me walking in our house, and I'll sweep you up and kiss you, and then I'll sweep up Ben, and Ann Marie, and Cece and I'll hold you all in my arms for a long time.

Eliza smiled. Yes, she thought. And later, after the children are in bed, we will hold each other and love each other long into the night, and I'll tell you then, Caleb, that I want another child.

She would also ask him questions about his trip, the most important was what had he thought about the country around the Malheur Lake? What about the O'Sheas' offer? What did he want to do? She knew without doubt what her own answer would be. She had known ever since the O'Sheas had made their proposal; she needed to hear what Caleb's was.

Suddenly the sound of a jangling triangle pierced the air. Ben stopped his lesson, and held his ink pen in midair. Ann Marie looked at her mother with a question in her big brown eyes. Old Dog raised his head, his ears up and alert.

"What's going on over at Uncle Tall's and Aunt Clara's?" Ben asked, a frown creased his brow.

The sound of the calling piece was always an easy, almost musical sound. This was different. This was a harsh sound that rang out, over and over again.

Ben laughed. "Sounds like LB's beating the tar out of Aunt Clara's calling piece," he said, but he kept his eyes on Eliza.

"I know! Papa's home!" Ann Marie cried. "He's over there at their house and he's so anxious to see us, he's raising a signal." But then Ann Marie's voice died. Tall and Clara didn't live on any road Caleb would take coming home. Caleb would take the main road from town.

Eliza grabbed her shawl. "Wait here. I'm going outside for just a moment. You all stay in and keep Dog."

Wrapping the shawl around her shoulders, she stepped out on the front porch, her eyes fastened on the wooded ridge across the way, barely visible now in the late afternoon mist. Her ears were tuned to the slightest sound as she remembered Caleb's letter about the clanging bell. But it didn't make sense. What could Tall and Clara's calling piece have to do with her? Unless . . . was there something wrong? Could it be a cry for help? Should she take Ben and Ann Marie and ride over to see what might be going on? On this dark evening that seemed unwise. And she didn't hear the sound again. Th

414

only sound she heard now was the gusting wind, moving through the dripping trees. She decided the pounding on the calling piece must have been Clara or Tall calling for LB, who loved to roam the wooded hills alone.

To take her mind off her worry she would read again a letter Caleb had written, describing part of his journey. It was the children's favorite letter; reading it would be a good thing to do.

When she walked back into the house she was keenly aware that both Ben and Ann Marie watched her with anxious eyes as she carefully slid the big bolt into the sleeve of the lock on the front door. She then turned to them and smiled.

"Think about Papa coming home, probably tomorrow," she said.

"Think about Cece riding home tomorrow with Pips, and then think about the grand feast we'll have for Papa and for our friends."

"Roast venison and corn and potatoes! And I get to make him an apple pie!" Ann Marie's eyes were shining again, the veil of trouble gone.

Eliza smiled. "That's right! And Ben, we'll hang those antlers right after supper. Now, how about one more read of Papa's letter. *The* letter! Then we'll have supper." Both children grinned. They liked that idea just fine.

Eliza reached for a book in the bookcase, took out a packet of letters that she quickly leafed through, and pulled out one letter. Then, seated squaw fashion on the black bear rug in front of the fire, Ben on one side of her, Ann Marie on the other, she began to read.

My darling family. I'm now on my way home, and let me tell you something about this trip. Ben, I wish you were with me. You'd be a big help, better than some of the hands

415

Eliza hugged Ben, noting his proud smile.

Cece, you and Mama could cook, and Ann Marie, you could pick wild flowers and make our table pretty. And of course Dog would be with us too!

You would have liked seeing the branding that I saw before we left Bell County. It was done with Mr. O'Shea's brand, a big, curly S. All of the cattle were herded into a long chute where seven men worked, branding about twenty-five at a time. The animals all moaned and bawled and rolled their eyes, but then after they were branded, they jumped right up and forgot all about it!

We had us a whale of a storm two nights ago. We don't have storms at home like this, but Mama will remember the storm that came up on us on our trek west. Out at the marshy lake she likes to talk about. This storm the other night started out with big, fat raindrops falling on all the cattle, who were bedded down, snug and contented as could be! But then the storm struck and we had a terrible wind, more rain and hail as big as plums! We had to let the cattle drift and it was dark as ink! I was in the lead, and Ben, this is when you should have been with me. You could have helped me hold the cattle, who were spooked by the flashes of lightning that lit up the sky. I rode on, not able to see much, but knowing the cattle, were all around me because I could hear their puffing and snorting. Then the storm blew itself out and the next morning we had to ride some to gather up all the scattered animals.

Buffalo! Buffalo! Not as many as Mama and I saw when we came across, but still the same beast! Galloping and bellowing and rolling their big, red eyes! A curious animal, when you stop and think.

Then in Texas, we crossed a river called the

Brazos. It was around there that I saw a sight I'd never seen before. In that part of the country, corn and cotton are the main crops. Like ours is wheat, and orchards of fruit trees. It was there, around the Brazos, that I saw many Negroes, picking cotton. I have to admit, I stopped my horse once or twice and stared. The women pick faster than the men. They use both hands, right and left, right and left, fast, fast, fast, they pick. They pick half a row on one side then they move back and pick the other half. But those folks don't get paid for their work and that's a big part of all the trouble we hear about now. That's the notion of slavery, when one man can own another man. I hear a lot about it here. Much more than at home.

One day found us riding through country where not a whole lot of folks live. Good grass country, waving tall, like our own wheat field, but bigger, and oak and walnut trees growing close to the water. There were also lots of wild turkeys! Fat birds, living off all the nuts, and they waddle around, hardly able to walk! And can you imagine, catching a turkey by your bare hands? No, you all say! But we did! I made a bet with one of my men, a good man, who enjoys a laugh. By the way, he's called a vaquero. He's a Spaniard. Works real well with the cattle. Name is Deemo. I bet this man, Deemo, a plug of tobacco we could catch one of those birds. Deemo bet we couldn't. So, early one morning he and I spotted a good fat bird and started trailing him. Of course the bird saw us and we had to move carefully, keeping him out of the woods. Once he got in the woods, we'd lose him. So, we trotted along, brisk at times, and then the turkey turned around, heading home, I suppose, and all of a sudden his wings just dropped and he couldn't go further. So we rode up, and picked him up while he squawked like all get-out. We didn't give a hoot though and we had a good turkey feast that night, I'll tell you that.

You've all heard Mama and me talk about cooking with "buffalo chips" on our trek out. It isn't any different now out on the plains, and that's one of the cook's jobs. All day, as he rides along with us, he gathers the chips and sticks them in a real dry cowhide stretched under his wagon. That way the "chips" stay dry as a bone. None of us thought about doing that when we came across, did we, Ellie.

Well, my little ones. This trip has been a long one and I'll be mighty glad to get home. But we've made good time. Especially after crossing the Rocky Mountains. Today I feel like I'm getting close to home. We start across the Snake desert tomorrow. Mama and I sure remember that. Then we'll come on down Snake River where we'll feast with Indians on fresh salmon. In just a few more weeks Mr. O'-Shea and I will be on his land with his cattle, out in the Malheur country. Then I'll come home to you all with presents in my pockets, and we'll have our own feast. Hugs and kisses to all of my darlings.

Papa.

Chapter 47

"I want to be just like Papa when I grow up," Ben said softly as Eliza folded the letter and put it back in the book. "Me too," Ann Marie echoed. Eliza laughed. "You both have a pretty good chance of that," she said as she stood up. "Come, now. I'll finish supper. Ben, poke the fire up, and after we eat, we'll find the right place for the antlers."

Eliza returned to the kitchen, picked up her knife, and quickly finished slicing the meat. A noise outside the kitchen window caused her to pause and peer through the glass. It was a black night, with no moon or stars. Gusts of slanty rain beat against the windowpane. A sense of unease swept over her and she quickly walked over to her back door and pulled the heavy bolt across. Attributing her feelings to Caleb's letter about the jangling bell, and then hearing Clara and Tall's calling piece, she sternly told herself nothing could be wrong. Her doors were both bolted; the big rifle was handy in the corner by the hearth, and besides, who would bother her and her family?

Then she heard a horse nicker. Could that possibly mean that Caleb was home? No. That didn't fit. Caleb would make a lot of noise; he'd yell, and shout, "Ellie! I'm coming on by!" Eliza frowned, and still holding the knife in one hand, she walked back into the front room. Dog growled and at the same time Ben cried out.

"Mama, someone's here!"

Eliza's heart pounded as she instinctively slipped the knife into her skirt pocket. Then as she looked out the front window, she saw the face of the man she'd seen in all of her nightmares for the last ten years. A man with only one eye. She knew she and her children were in mortal danger.

A heavy thud hit against the front door, but the door didn't budge. Ben, who had grabbed the rifle, leveled it at the window, but with an explosion of glass, two men, the one-eyed man and the man with the bald, scarred head, landed in Eliza's front room. Ann Marie's high shrill scream of terror followed, and Eliza screamed. "Get out! Get out!" At the same time Dog, leaping at the one-eyed man's throat, was flattened by the man's rifle butt. The man then rammed his gun through Dog's head. At the same time, the big rifle banged and blood spurted from the one-eyed man's arm. Grabbing at his wounded arm, the man lifted his boot and kicked Ben, sending him sprawled on the floor while the clattering rifle was swiftly picked up by the bald-headed man. Eliza put her hand in her pocket, feeling the sharp edge of her knife. She knew she would have one chance to use it. Only one. She then jabbered, desperately trying to bargain for her children's lives.

"You can have all of this!" she said, her breath coming in short pants. "Everything! You can have this house and all of our land, and the horses too. We've got fine horses and you can have the cattle and everything. Please. Please. My God, dear Mother of God, spare my children! Kill me if you must. Kill me, but I beg you to spare my children! Please. Dear Mother of God! Spare my children!"

Suddenly Ann Marie, holding a pair of sewing scissors in one hand, flew at the bald man as Eliza screamed, "Ann! Ann! No!" The man lifted Ann Marie off the floor like a doll, and in one second, the child lay on the floor, her throat cut clean across. Eliza's scream was that of a wild animal as she tried to reach her child.

"Hold her!" the one-eyed man yelled. "I got to bind this arm. Take care of the boy and then we'll tell the little lady who we are."

The bald man pinned Eliza's arm behind her and she was vaguely aware of excruciating pain. Her screams rent the night as she saw Ben murdered and a lock of his fair hair cut then tied to the one-eyed man's belt.

"Ain't no one on earth that's gonna hear you, little lady," the one-eyed man said, holding on to his arm, which bled through one of Eliza's towels and dripped on her braided rug. "Mrs. Pride! Mrs. Caleb Pride! Mrs. Max Pridentz! Our names is Ross 'n' Earl and your mister did us wrong a long time ago, and we've been huntin' for him ever since!"

Shoving Eliza down on the floor, the bald man started to hoist her skirt and Eliza made one last effort to save herself as she wildly slashed the knife at the man's neck and face. She heard his scream as he fell heavily on her and then a sharp blow to her head rocked her into a bloody night where she saw the man with the burned head. Again her skirt was hoisted and she screamed and begged for death.

"For God's sake! Kill me! Kill me! Jesus Christ! Son of God! Oh! God! Kill me! Kill me!" she begged, and in the black, bloody night she heard a burst of gunfire and she saw Caleb and Pips floating above her, until blackness shut them away.

"My name is Eliza Landon and you can have anything you want. My name is Eliza Landon . . ." She spoke in a toneless voice, repeating the words over and over as she rode with a man on a horse. She held on to the man,

421

and when she leaned her head into the man's back, she smelled the acrid smell of smoke, grease, and sweat in his buckskin coat and she gagged again and again. There was something about his smell though. She'd smelled it before—a long time ago—but she didn't know where or who the man was or where he had come from. But it didn't matter. It didn't matter at all.

"My name is Eliza Landon . . ." Why were they riding so fast? And did it always rain in this godforsaken country? God! She hated it here! Wherever here was. Then, why did she stay? She stopped talking and she lifted her face up into the rain, and she didn't know why she stayed here. For a moment she thought about a place somewhere where stars shined like diamonds in the sky and hundreds of bright birds sat on long strappy leaves near a sparkling lake and the birds sang in the sun. That's where she had been happy once, but she had no idea where that place was.

"My name is . . ." She felt a sticky wetness between her legs and she hurt there. God! She hurt! She wondered . . . was it her time? If it was, she'd never hurt like this before. Was she bleeding? If she was, she didn't care because it didn't matter. It didn't matter at all.

Suddenly the man she was riding with screamed. She frowned. She'd never heard a man scream. He screamed to no one that could hear him, except her, and the sound of his torment made her shake.

"Oh God! God! My God!" he screamed. "My children! My Ellie!" he screamed. Then he screamed again and then he was silent as whipped his horse with his quirt urging his horse on faster and faster. Poor horse, Eliza thought, listening to the horse's hooves pounding on the rocky, wet road. She would tell the man to stop. She could feel the animal's slippery flanks between her legs, and she thought of the beast, lathered with sweat, as the man urged it on and on, through the black, wet night. *Ddddlm ddddlmp ddddlmp.* No one Eliza had ever known had treated a horse like this. Perhaps this man was cruel. But if he was, she didn't care. It didn't matter. It didn't matter at all.

Ddddlmmp ddddlmmp ddddllmmp. That almost sounded like a song, and she hummed and sang a ditty in a breathless voice. *"Ddddlmmp ddddlmmmp ddddlmmmp.* My name is Eliza Landon and you can . . ."

She saw the sky turn light gray and a sour smell of smoke drifted through the air. The man abruptly reined in his horse in front of a burned-out cabin and dismounted. A man ran up to join the man who had brought Eliza here. The man said something to Eliza, but Eliza didn't understand him. She told him her name was Eliza Landon and he could have . . .

Behind the men, Eliza saw two dead Indians lying in a garden where rain dripped from pink and red flowers. One of the Indians was huge and he had a big, bloody hole in his neck. The other Indian was very tall, and there was something about him that made Eliza want to cry. Where in God's name was she? Who had lived here? Why had the man brought her to this dreadful place where the thick logs of the burned cabin still glowed red and sizzled and smoked and steamed in the early morning light. Besides, she hurt and she knew she was bleeding and she didn't know if she could walk. But it didn't matter. It didn't matter at all.

She watched the men kneel down by the body of a woman with blond hair, and Eliza heard herself whimper. Then she saw the body of a young girl and a younger boy. Half-breeds. That's what the children were called. Eliza thought about that. What a strange name to call people. But did it matter? No. It didn't matter at all.

The man who had brought her here stood beside the charred walls of this place, and he screamed again. The same as before, and he leaned his head against one of the blackened walls and she saw the man's body shake. She wondered why he was crying, but it didn't matter. It didn't matter at all.

As she watched the man cry, she wondered for a moment who would do such a terrible thing. She hoped the man would stop crying and hurry and come back and take her away. She had no business here.

Somewhere a baby cried. She started to get off the horse. Maybe she should go get the baby. But no. She was tired, and besides, it didn't matter if the baby cried. Did she know these people? No. How would she have known anyone who had been so badly treated? She didn't know them at all.

Something bothered her though. She would tell the man about hearing the baby cry. But when the man came up to her, she discovered she couldn't speak. She couldn't say her name anymore. And she was very tired. She shrugged her shoulders and bowed her head and put her hand to her heart while pointing to where she had heard the baby cry. Then the man turned from her and left. She would wait awhile. It didn't matter how long. It didn't matter at all.

Daylight came through the trees; long, pale strands of light. She saw the man coming from somewhere behind the burned-out cabin. He was carrying a baby. The man then took ahold of her hand and and said something to her. Whatever he said, she couldn't understand, but as she looked at him, she recoiled at the look of his terrible eyes. She had never seen such terrible eyes. He looked mad. Yes. That was it. This man was mad. She wondered for a moment what the man was going to do with her. Then the man gave her the baby and watched her for a moment. That was all right. She would hold the baby even if she didn't want to. She didn't like babies anymore. But she couldn't just drop the baby on the ground, and the man had to guide the horse somewhere, or ride the horse; whatever he was going to do. He couldn't hold the baby. The man then got back on the horse, and together, with her holding the baby, they rode away.

Chapter 48

Spring 1862

Eliza sat in a chair in the big, sunny room and played with her rings. She'd always liked her wedding ring, a plain slender band of gold, and she'd always worn it with the little pearl ring Janie Marie had given her . . . how many years ago? She looked down at her smooth, white hands and laughed. Her hands hadn't looked like this since she was very young. Then she got up from her chair and walked over to the window. The sun was shining. She could see the cherry blossoms on the trees she and Caleb had planted . . . how long ago? The trees he and Nathan had bought in Portland the summer Ann Marie was born.

Where was everybody? Cece, Ben, and Ann Marie should be coming home from school soon. What day was today? She frowned. She didn't know. And was Caleb home from Texas yet? She stood in the middle of the room, trying to remember, but nothing came to her. Then she realized this wasn't her house! This house was built of wood, not logs, and the rugs were blue wool, and not braided like her own rugs. She was standing in a pretty living room, but none of the furniture belonged to her. This furniture looked like it belonged in Lorene's house, polished wood, with red and blue velvet seats on the chairs and the settee. As she walked slowly around the room, she knew that something was wrong. She felt as if she had been gone for a very long time. She wasn't afraid, but she was puzzled. Then, reassurance swept over her as she saw Smithy's drawings on one wall.

She walked over and looked at the familiar drawings of *The Oregon Roll*. Eliza herself, standing beside *The Lone Eagle*, Caleb on his horse, and Dog beside him. Eliza looked around. Where was Dog? Well, she didn't want to think about Dog right now. She looked back at Smithy's drawings. She saw the beautiful painting he'd done of the striped hills, and next to it her favorite drawing. The drawing of the country out by the Malheur Lake with the wonderful canyons, the pleated chasms, and the rimrock. She looked closely at the drawing. Somebody had written *Glory of the Oregon* in a neat hand at the bottom of the drawing. Eliza liked it, but she was puzzled as to who had come up with such a fitting name.

Turning away from the drawings, she started to walk into the kitchen, and at the same time Cece came in, carrying a big basket. But Cece looked different, too. She looked older than ten years. Without saying a word to Eliza, without even looking at her, Cece set her basket on a worktable and took out potatoes, onions, and carrots.

"Cece?" Eliza asked. Her voice was a whisper.

Startled, Cece turned and looked at Eliza. For a moment Cece didn't move as she stood, still holding a potato in one hand. "Mama! Mama!" she asked. She put the potato down and walked toward Eliza. "You know me?" Cece stared at her, her brown eyes wide.

"Of course, I do. But something's wrong. This isn't my house, and you look grown up. What's happened to me, Cece?" Eliza wanted to cry, but seeing the instant expression of dismay on Cece's face, Eliza bit her lips. For some reason it was very important that she not cry. "Where's Ben and Ann Marie? Where's Papa?" she asked.

Cece took Eliza's arm. "Mama, terrible things happened to us, three years ago. But I think Papa should tell you. Come. Papa's outside with John."

"John? Who's John?"

Cece didn't answer as she led Eliza outside where she saw Caleb. Caleb was home, thank God! He was home, out there hoeing in the garden. And there was Ben, right beside him. Oh, thank God! Eliza started to cry out to him, but then she stopped. The little boy with straight black hair wasn't Ben.

Something clicked then in Eliza's mind as she remembered a night when she had prayed to die. She remembered the bloodied, slashed face of a man with a bald head. She remembered a one-eyed man holding up a thick blond forelock. She remembered a little girl, her throat slashed. And she remembered a man ripping her dress and pinning her down, and then the searing pain, and darkness as an explosion of orange light had torn through the room and . . . had it been Caleb's face she had seen? Caleb's face, blackened and filthy, his eyes red-rimmed and his mouth had worked, but no sound had come out. That was all she remembered of that night.

Now, watching Caleb working in her garden, Eliza put her hands to her temples and pressed against her head, controlling herself, knowing that she mustn't cry.

"Oh, Cece. Oh, my God," she cried. Then, picking up her skirt, she raced out toward Caleb. "Cal! Oh! Cal! Cal!" She stopped as he turned and looked at her, again she willed herself not to cry. She must not cry. Not now. Maybe later, but she must not cry now. Caleb stared at her and then he dropped the hoe and slowly walked to her.

"Ellie?" She felt his rough palms on her cheeks as he

cupped her face. She looked in his eyes—eyes as blue as the summer skies.

"You have to help me, Cal. Please! Where have I been?"

"Ellie! You've come back to us! You've come back!"

Eliza nodded, unable to speak, as it came to her that for these past years, she had been living in the dark world of madness. She didn't know for how long, and everything was still twisted and askew, but she knew who she was and she knew the world around her. Now she had to learn what had happened.

Reaching for Cece, Eliza put her arm around her slender waist. Everything about Cece was clear—who she was and why she was here, because she had not been in the house that night. She'd been at the home of those people . . . the Shaws. Yes, at Maude and Nathan's and Pips' place. But other things weren't clear and those were the things she had to learn about.

She looked down and saw the little boy holding on to one of Caleb's legs, not wanting to let go. She saw Caleb reach down and put one hand on the little boy's head. For a moment there wasn't a sound, but somewhere a robin sang.

Eliza then knelt and ran her fingers through the little boy's hair. The boy stared at her with solemn black eyes. Eyes that reminded her of a man she had known a long time ago. An Indian, tall and fine. An Indian named Tall Singer, whose woman had been Clara McCabe.

"Oh, Cal," Eliza said softly. "This boy is the baby, isn't he. This is John. Clara and Tall's boy. What happened . . ."

Caleb put his finger to his lips. "I'll tell you," he said. "At the right time."

John continued to stare up at Eliza. "You talk now," he said.

"Yes, John," Eliza said. "What a fine boy you are!"

"He's a good boy, Mama," Cece said. "He's a good boy. If it hadn't been for you, he'd have died. And if it hadn't been for John, I don't know if Papa could have . . ."

Eliza nodded. "I remember now and I need to know. I need to know where they are. You have to take me there."

Caleb nodded, lifted John up on his shoulders, and beckoned to Cece. "Come," he said. "We'll take Mama up the hill."

As Caleb took Eliza's hand, she felt it, calloused and hard, and she stopped, and she held his hand to her lips for a moment. She then looked at Caleb and Cece.

"I need to know what year this is."

"It's 1862, Mama," Cece said. "I'm fourteen years old."

Eliza nodded. "Fourteen! I've lost over three years!" She then took one of Cece's hands, and silently they all walked up the hill, passing clumps of yellow buttercups and creamy white trillium growing in the tall green grass. They stopped at a place where a magnificent oak tree spread its graceful limbs. There, Eliza saw seven wooden grave markers.

Ben Pride   1849–1859
Ann Marie Pride   1852–1859;
Tall Singer   a Paiute friend   d. 1859
Clara McCabe   Tall Singer's woman   d. 1859
Gray Squirrel   d. 1859
Little Bear   1846–1859
Blue Bird   1847–1859

Eliza looked at each grave for a long time. And then she knelt in the grass with Caleb, Cece, and John by her side.

Chapter 49

After supper that night, after Cece and John were in bed, Eliza and Caleb talked. Caleb's voice was steady as he described to Eliza the dream he'd had while coming home from Texas.

"If a man ever had a vision, Ellie, I did. I had that dream out on the Snake Plains and I tried to put it out of mind. But I couldn't. There was the plain sound of your calling piece being whanged over and over again. And there was the vision of the two men . . . the two . . ."

Eliza saw that his eyes were veiled and his face was drawn. Putting her hand on his arm, she leaned across the table. "Tell me what you can, Cal. No more. There's lots of time to tell me what you don't want to tell me tonight."

Caleb nodded. "I'm all right. The fellow I sent my letter with, the letter telling you about my worry, was traveling fast. He knew about Judge Shaw and Pips and he took it for them to deliver to you. That was all I could do. Then, when Paddy and I got to the Malheur with the cattle, Mary was there with some folks from the Sacramento Valley. They had a fine camp all set up, prepared to stay for the winter, and . . . well, that's another story for another time."

Eliza nodded. Whatever suited him to tell her was

fine. "I was planning on staying with them for a couple of nights. Like we'd talked when we made our plans. But the dream picked at me and I only stayed one night. Coming across that desert and over the Cascades—I tell you Ellie, I rode like the wind. I was able to pay for two fresh mounts, which helped considerably. When I got to the Shaws', I saw that Cece was there, and I felt better, but it was Pips who put ice in my heart when he said that early that day he'd seen three bad-looking fellows ride by and when he described them, well . . . my God, Ellie. I knew. Cece begged to come on home with me, but I made her stay with Maude and Nathan. Pips insisted on coming, though, and I remembered that he rode well and he was a damned good man with a gun. So, Nathan got me a fresh horse and Pips and I . . . we started for home. And then . . . then I got here." His voice dropped to a whisper. "Our children were dead and so was Dog. One of the men was violating you; you'd got the other fellow, clean across his face, and I shot the man on . . . on top . . ." Again Caleb's voice broke, and he turned his head.

"No need, Cal. No need to say more about that," Eliza said.

Caleb looked at her, his eyes full of tears. "You had gone crazy, Ellie. You'd lost your sense. You didn't know me at all, and you kept telling me over and over, that your name was Eliza Landon and I could have everything I wanted, but not to kill the children, and you just plucked and picked at my coat. Then Pips and I figured Tall and Clara were in trouble too. Pips rode on ahead of me. I did what I could for you, Ellie, and then I took you with me. But when we got to Clara and Tall's, it was too late. They'd got there first. Before coming here. The whole family, and a cousin of Tall's Grey Squirrel, they were all murdered. But somebody had killed Tomschini, and from the looks of things, we figured it had to have been Clara. We also figured that between you and Clara, John was saved."

"Me and Clara?" Eliza asked, incredulous. "How in God's name could I have . . ."

Caleb nodded. "I'd forgotten there even was a baby, Ellie. Remember, John was born after I'd left, so I'd never laid eyes on him. I didn't even know his name. But Pips remembered, and while we were searching . . . searching for his body, 'cause we knew he'd have been killed too, well, you heard him cry. You couldn't talk. It was like you'd forgotten how, you couldn't even say your own name anymore, but you showed us by putting your hand on your heart and turning your head toward the sound. So Pips and I searched more and listened for his cry and we found him in the root cellar. No matter how bad off you were in your mind, you heard him cry and you let me know.

"Then you held the baby while I took us out to the Shaws', where we stayed for a year. You were in your own world, Ellie. There were lots of days when all you did was cry, and you didn't know any of us. Not me, and not Cece, and for sure not the Shaws, or Sam, or Clancy or Lorene, or any of the McVeys. They'd come to visit now and then, but you only stared at them like they were strangers. Sometimes you'd smile a little, but mostly you sat and looked at nothing at all. We'd been there about a month when Pips and Nathan and I went back to our place and I took Smithy's drawings, and your mama's china and your papa's books and yours and Cece's and my clothes out of the cabin. Then we burned the place to the ground, cleared the site, and built this place. I asked Lorene to pick out this furniture." He waved his hand, indicating the pretty furniture. Nice things that she thought you'd like, and I bought them, and had them shipped here. During that whole time I had doctors for you. Doctors from here in the valley, and doctors from Portland. Fine doctors, but they all said the same thing. There was nothing they could do. Rest and time, they said.

"Now, about John. I learned right away that his name was John McCabe. Nathan told me that Tall had deliberately named him that because of the land. Cece and I talked about changing it because I was having a hard time with the name 'McCabe' but Cece decided you wouldn't want that. You would want him to keep the name Clara and Tall had given him, so we did. We also decided that when you got all right again, and if you wanted to change his name, we would do that. That decision, along with others that we'll be talking about, will be yours. When you're ready."

Eliza nodded. "You should know, Cal, that I don't put a connection of a name with those men. Besides, their name wasn't McCabe. I'll tell you about that another time. Something I learned from Clara, a long time ago. And I like the name 'John McCabe' just fine. I like you and Cece deciding to keep it because of Clara and Tall. So that decision is made. But tell me, when did we come back here?"

"This house was pretty well finished when I brought you back. I thought that might help you, but it didn't. Nothing mattered to you, Ellie. You didn't care where you were. But I never stopped knowing that someday when the sun was shining and the day was right, the light would come back in your eyes, and you'd come back."

It was two months later when Eliza announced that she would take the Prides' small, single horse-drawn buggy, the one Cece used to drive herself to school, and drive to the Shaws. "I want to visit Maude," she said. "And I want to go alone like I used to to. There's no need for someone to have to go with me, trailing along, acting as if I was a child."

This announcement pleased and worried Caleb who still feared something might trigger Eliza into a setback. "How about a compromise," he suggested. "I've got to see Nathan about buying more trees, come fall. You go on ahead, take the buggy, and I'll follow along. Not right behind, but close enough. I'll tend to my business with Nathan while you and Maude have tea and then we'll ride home together."

Eliza agreed. It was a small thing to argue about, and Eliza's primary purpose was to feel again like her once independent self. She also wanted to visit with Maude.

It was a fair June morning when Eliza started out. She enjoyed spring in the the valley. The soft greens of April and May had turned to a darker hue. The country looked as if it was covered with green velvet. Green velvet hills, green velvet trees. Oh, so pretty, this green valley.

Suddenly she frowned and slowed her horse's gait. There, up ahead, was the hill where the Connors' place should be. Clearly, the place was no longer there. Then the image of a big, dark-haired woman came to her mind. Her name? Lydia. Lydia Wilson. No, Lydia Wills. Lydia Wells. That was it. Eliza wondered what might have happened to the strange soul.

Curious now, Eliza turned off the main road and drove up the weed-choked lane to where the big rambling log house once stood. Now there was nothing but a stump of a rock chimney, surrounded by piles of charred logs and loose rubble. Eliza shook her head. It must have been a terrible fire. She must ask Caleb or, better yet, ask Maude about it this afternoon. But Eliza felt no sorrow for what she had just found out.

Maude had known for over a week that Eliza was coming for tea. Excited and overjoyed at Eliza's recovery, Maude had wanted to invite several valley women, including Lorene, for tea. But on thinking it over, Maude decided that this day would be reserved for only herself and Eliza.

Eliza would be delighted with the boarding school

435

that she and Clancy had established. It was a fine school, located six miles from the Shaws'. This was where Cece attended school, boarding during the week and driving home on weekends. Clancy was a fine principal and mathematics teacher. Pips taught music and art, and Maude taught English and history. The Evanses had built a beautiful new home close to the school, keeping their home in town as well.

Maude smiled as she arranged Lela's cookies on a cookie plate and poured steaming tea into her silver tea-pot. Yes, she and Eliza had a lot to catch up on.

Two hours later Eliza and Maude sat, savoring their long visit. "I must ask you, Maude. How did the Connors' place burn, and what happened to Lydia Wells?"

"Caleb hasn't told you?" Maude sounded surprised.

"No. Should he have?"

"Oh Lordy, Ellie. It's another strange thing. Lydia returned here, you see. About a year after . . . after . . ."

"After what happened to us?"

"Yes. But she was shunned by valley folks. Every-body knew of her odd behavior. Everybody knew that she'd let you down when you needed her. As you know, valley folks don't forget that sort of thing. Well, she'd been here about a month, when one night her place burned and she was found the next day. She'd hung herself."

Eliza arched her brows. "She hung herself? Good Lord, Maude, why?"

Maude shrugged. "Who knows? There was a service of sorts for her, but Nathan and I were the only ones there."

"Cal didn't go?"

"Oh, no. Indeed not. I think if I ever knew Caleb Pride to loathe a person, it was that woman."

Eliza frowned. "But that doesn't sound like Cal. He also forgives and forgets." Eliza then changed the subject.

There were other things to talk about and Eliza would ask Caleb about Lydia. She had a sense that something else lay behind what Maude had told her and she wanted to know what it was.

"I'll be glad when everything's said that must be said." Caleb looked at Eliza as he poured himself another cup of coffee. It was after supper, Cece was reading in the living room, John was in bed, and Eliza and Caleb sat at the kitchen table.

"Is this a painful story, Cal? If so, it, too, can wait."

"It's not painful in the sense of pain. It's a terrible story though. And, of course, it's got to be told. As Maude told you, the woman returned. We didn't pay any mind to her at all, Cece and me. While we were still living at the Shaws', I was riding out here one day, and as I passed her place, she rode out to stop me. She looked bad. Worse than usual, and I could tell by the way she acted and by the awful smell that she'd been drinking. It was a terrible talk, Ellie. She told me how she'd gone to Portland that time, ahead of Nathan and me. She said she only wanted to spend a little time with me alone." Caleb visibly shuddered. "She said she knew that her chances of doing that out here weren't high; that she'd made some attempts, but she . . . well, she knew it wouldn't work. I was so taken aback, well, I hardly knew what to say. She stammered, and she didn't ever look at me, direct. But she said she thought that going to Portland was enough and she only wanted to watch me. I figured then that she was as crazy as anybody I'd ever known. She told Mrs. Logan's boy she was my cousin and she'd wait for me and she went to my room. She waited a little and then left, knowing, Ellie, knowing where I'd be sleeping that night!"

Eliza stared at Caleb, her eyes wide with astonishment. Then she laughed. "Oh Cal, maybe it's not funny,

437

but for some reason, it is. The poor tormented woman was out of her mind for wanting you."

"Hear me out, Ellie." Caleb's tone was sharp, and Eliza held her tongue.

"She went to the tavern, knowing I'd be coming in, and she watched me come there and she waited and she watched me leave. Then she watched my window. That's how crazy she was. And I'll admit I felt sorry for her. I did. I thought that any person with that kind of torment must go through their own special hell every day. Then she said she thought I'd figured out that she was there and she was ashamed and she left Portland before I did. True enough she went on back to California.

"Well, I told her I was sorry for her and I knew you'd feel the same way. But I also told her she'd be better off leaving here, getting out of this valley. She then tried to tell me something else and she asked me to come with her into her place and she grabbed at my arm. I shoved her off and told her I never wanted to see her again. She looked at me, real funny, and then she turned and walked back to her house, I guess. I didn't stay around to find out. But that night her house burned, and she was found strung up on the rafters. She'd hung herself and set fire to the place at the same time."

Eliza shook her head. "I can't imagine such torment. It seems so wild and so unnatural. So unseeming!" Then pouring herself and Caleb another cup of coffee, she smiled and took his hand. "So let it be. I'll tell you, Cal, this valley won't remember her for long. I'd say that closes the story of Miss Lydia Wells."

"Not quite," Caleb said. "Some days after the burning, Cece and I drove into the place. Curious, I guess. I don't know. Just as we all do, when there's been a fire out here. Cece was kicking through the rubble, and she found a pile of paintings. Remember, Ellie, the woman said she was an artist? Well, there was a pile of her work that hadn't burned. And it was as if they'd been put someplace where they wouldn't be burned either. They sure weren't in the house, I could tell that. In that pile there were several paintings. As Cece was looking at them, curious enough, I saw one that made my heart nearly stop. It was a painting of Tomschini, Ross, and Earl. It couldn't have been plainer. She'd done it. I saw her signature. She knew those men and I have to think that she was the one who told them where we all lived. Tall, Clara, you, and me. Now that's the last time I ever want to speak of her again. Please."

Eliza sat in silence for a long time. She wondered for a while why she didn't feel a rage of hatred against Lydia Wells, and she decided then that enough was enough. She looked at Caleb, who was watching her close. "We shouldn't speak about all of this again." she said. "It would do none of us good." She then got up from the table and looked out at the late evening sky.

It was a beautiful summer night with the soft feeling of black velvet spread over the land. Stars winked and a half-moon showed its pale light. It came to Eliza, clearly enough, that all the necessary words about what had happened nearly four years ago had been said. The agony and exquisite anguish would be with both of them always. But now it was time to get on with living. It was time to think of tomorrow, and next week, and next year.

Turning back to Caleb, she walked over to where he still sat. Standing behind him, she put her arms around him. "Cal," she said, her tone soft. "I remember that when I was looking for you to come home from Texas, I was hoping we might have another child." She leaned down and kissed the nape of his neck and one of his ears. "I still feel that way, Cal."

When he stood and faced her, she saw the glint of tears in his eyes. "Eliza Pride. How lucky I am."

Gently, he took her in his arms and kissed her, and

439

Eliza felt her powerful love for him and her passion for him that had not diminished. Together they walked up stairs to their bedroom, where they loved one another far into the night. Later, as Eliza lay beside him, she was certain that his hot seed, welcome by her, was the start of a new life.

It was midmorning on a day in late July. The Prides wheat fields were beginning to look gold and Eliza now considered herself nearly recovered. She'd taught herself how to avoid thoughts of what had happened almost four years ago. If she saw a thing carrying with it a memory—shock of a boy's blond hair, perhaps a little red-haired girl, a gray-muzzled dog, a blond woman, or a fine-looking Indian—she turned her thoughts to the good times they had shared and the good they had all brought into her and Caleb's lives. She had also disciplined herself against thinking about that night; instead she found strength in telling herself every day when she first awoke that life, her life, Caleb's life, Cece's life, and John's, must go on. They must be good lives. They *would* be good lives.

As the days progressed, her memory returned strong and keen, and one thing that came back to her vividly was the O'Sheas' offer. Nothing had been said about that. She remembered that when Caleb had told her about arriving at Mary's camp with Mr. O'Shea he'd stopped short of saying anything more. He'd said it was a story for another time. Since then he hadn't said one more word about it. Maybe he hadn't liked the country out there as much as he'd thought he would. Maybe he had no thought anymore of living there. Maybe her own illness had changed things and Mr. O'Shea and Mary had withdrawn the offer. A number of possibilities came to Eliza's mind, but today she had decided it was time to find out.

She quickly finished kneeding her bread dough and then prepared her loaves for the rising, pausing now and then to listen to Cece, practicing her violin in the front room. Cece was doing so well and Eliza and Caleb were determined to see that she would be well educated.

Peering out her kitchen window, Eliza saw John playing with some small iron soldiers and horses. Presents Caleb had brought back from Texas for Ben. She smiled. John was a fine boy, and as Caleb had said, he reminded her of Tall.

That brought to mind the important thing she had to tell Cal. She was pregnant. She had calculated this morning that the child would be born in March, and she knew Caleb would be as pleased as she.

The sun was high when Caleb came in the back door for noon supper, John tagging directly behind him. Caleb stopped and looked closely at Eliza for a moment. Eliza laughed. "Cal, when are you going to stop doing that?"

"Maybe never," he said, putting his arm around her and kissing the tip of her nose. "Maybe never!"

Cece then joined them, and after everybody had washed up, they all sat down together at the big kitchen table.

"Tell me," Eliza said. "What happened to that notion of Paddy and Mary O'Shea's? To the offer they made? What's happened to them? You haven't said a word about them at all."

Caleb and Cece looked at each other; neither of them said a word. "Whatever it is," she said, looking at both of them, "you must tell me."

"It never worked out," Caleb said. "The first year after they'd settled in their Malheur camp, Mary wanted to take Paddy east to meet her family. So, she and Paddy left the cattle operation under the direction of a couple of good men, and taking Abbey with them, they sailed to Boston, where they spent six months. Coming home, the ship they were on foundered off the Oregon coast, and all of the passengers drowned."

"Oh, Cal." Eliza put her hand on his arm. "I'm sorry. I'm so sorry! You loved Mr. O'Shea, and Cece . . . losing your friend . . . I'm sorry."

Cece nodded. "I didn't know her very well, Mama, but yes, it was sad. But there's more to tell, isn't there, Papa?"

"In time, Cece. In time."

"Well, then tell me," Eliza said, "what happened to their dream of raising cattle out there?"

"I don't know what happened to the stock, Ellie. I've never been back. Pips has been out there a couple of times." Caleb laughed. "Pips loves that country. He says O'Shea's old camp is still there. But the cattle . . . who knows? Lots of them could have been picked up by wagon trains coming through, some taken by Indians, the rest of them gone wild."

"What was your decision, Cal? After the cattle drive, what did you want to do?"

"What you'd have wanted to do. Clear as day, that's what I'd have done."

"And my notion was to go. I never changed on that. I wanted to go that first day when we all talked. I wanted to go all the while you were gone. If the O'Sheas were still here today and made the same offer, I'd still say yes."

Caleb was quiet for a moment. "Then, as Cece says, there's more to say." Eliza looked at him, and then she looked across the table at Cece, who had her hand clapped over her mouth, her eyes sparkling with delight.

"You tell Mama this part, Cece," Caleb said.

"Mr. and Mrs. O'Shea left you and Papa that land, Mama." Cece's voice was breathless with excitement. "All of it! And when you were so sick, Papa said when you got well, and if you still wanted to go out there, he'd go in a minute!"

442

"Cal!" Eliza said, and she laughed, half believing, but not believing, what she was hearing.

Caleb nodded. "Cece has it right, Ellie. I just need to hear from you that's what you really want to do. Really, in your heart, because it's not going to be a whole lot of fun at first."

"Cece?" Eliza asked, turning to the girl who was watching her with sparkling eyes. "How would you feel about this?"

"Papa and I have talked about it. I feel two ways. I don't want to leave here. I don't want to leave school, and I don't want to leave my music lessons with Pips. Another part of me wants to go. Abbey . . . she was going to a boarding school then, but she was going to spend summers out there. So Papa and I decided if you and Papa ever did decide to go, that I'd stay here at boarding school during the school year. Like I do now, but spend my weekends with the Shaws or the Evanses. They have all said yes, and that they'd be pleased. Then, during summers, I'll come out to be with you."

"Is that what you really want to do, Cece?"

"It is. It really is."

"If we do this, Cal," Eliza said, "what would we do to start up our living out there? We'd have to live in a tent! And where would we get our stock?" But even as she asked the questions, Eliza's heart raced at the thought— the real thought of living out there.

Caleb laughed, his eyes full of joy. "It won't be anything like this . . ." He gestured with a wave of his hand. "Not for a long time to come. But if we do this, first off I'll contact Deemo, the fellow who rode with me from Texas, and I'll hire some vaqueros through him. I'll then bring cattle up from California, but I'll not do the drive. You and I and John and Deemo—we'll camp on the old O'Shea campsite. We'll live in tents, just like we did here at first. Only we'll have help right off. We couldn't do it without good hands. And we have the money, Ellie. so the decision is yours."

Eliza looked at John. "How do you feel about leaving here?" she asked the boy. "Would that make you sad?"

"No," he said. "Not if Papa wants to go."

Eliza laughed. "It's agreed then! Let's go!"

That night as Caleb and Eliza lay in their bed, they watched the moon move up behind a stand of tall firs. "Remember, Cal, back on the Snake Plains when we talked about this? Having our bedroom and the fir trees, and the moon and all?"

"Of course, I do." He brushed his lips gently against her temple.

"Hmm. And by the way, who named Smithy's painting *Glory of the Oregon?* I've been wanting to ask you that."

"I did. If Smithy could have talked, I think that's what he would have named it."

Eliza and Caleb talked far into the night about the folks they had loved so much. Eliza's family, and Janie Marie; they talked about Smithy, and the Petersons. They talked about their blessings in having Cece and John, and they talked about the children they'd lost, Ben and Ann Marie. They also talked about Tall and Clara and LB and BB, and Paddy and Mary O'Shea.

"I'll say to you, though, Caleb Pride," Eliza said in a soft voice. "We'd better get on over the mountains before too long because I don't want to be having a baby while making the trek."

Caleb was quiet for a moment and then he took Eliza in his arms. "So!" he said and he laughed. "Just as we had hoped."

"Yes. I'm happy about that, Cal. A baby will do us just fine."

Then, hearing the wind move in the fir trees, Eliza remembered the time she and Caleb had stood at the summit of the Cascades. She'd been holding Cece and she'd said that the sound of the winds were as the winds of sorrow. Tonight the wind didn't carry that sound. Tonight the winds seemed to carry a song of the Oregon. As Eliza slept, she dreamed of the great marshy lake, and the birdsong that filled the air. She dreamed of the vast land, pleated with canyons and chasms, and the shadows of rimrock that stood against the sky. And she dreamed of Snow Mountain, where the rocks echoed the name of a boy named Smithy and his work, *Glory of the Oregon*. Eliza smiled and she slept.

HISTORICAL ROMANCE FROM PINNACLE BOOKS

LOVE'S RAGING TIDE (381, $4.50)
by Patricia Matthews

Melissa stood on the veranda and looked over the sweeping acres of Great Oaks that had been her family's home for two generations, and her eyes burned with anger and humiliation. Today her home would go beneath the auctioneer's hammer and be lost to her forever. Two men eagerly awaited the auction: Simon Crouse and Luke Devereaux. Both would try to have her, but they would have to contend with the anger and pride of girl turned woman . . .

CASTLE OF DREAMS (334, $4.50)
by Flora M. Speer

Meredith would never forget the moment she first saw the baron of Afoncaer, with his armor glistening and blue eyes shining honest and true. Though she knew she should hate this Norman intruder, she could only admire the lean strength of his body, the golden hue of his face. And the innocent Welsh maiden realized that she had lost her heart to one she could only call enemy.

LOVE'S DARING DREAM (372, $4.50)
by Patricia Matthews

Maggie's escape from the poverty of her family's bleak existence gives fire to her dream of happiness in the arms of a true, loving man. But the men she encounters on her tempestuous journey are men of wealth, greed, and lust. To survive in their world she must control her newly awakened desires, as her beautiful body threatens to betray her at every turn.

Available wherever paperbacks are sold, or order direct from the publisher. Send cover price plus 50¢ per copy for mailing and handling to Pinnacle Books, Dept. 17-549 , 475 Park Avenue South, New York, N.Y. 10016. Residents of New York, New Jersey and Pennsylvania must include sales tax. DO NOT SEND CASH.